Every
Bitter Thing
Sweet

Every Bitter Thing Sweet

Roslyn Carrington

KENSINGTON PUBLISHING CORP.

Dafina Books are published by

Kensington Publishing Corp.
850 Third Avenue
New York, NY 10022

Kensington and the K logo Reg. U.S. Pat. & TM Off.
Dafina Books and the Dafina logo are trademarks of Kensington Publishing Corp.

ISBN 0-7394-1911-0

Printed in the United States of America

Every Bitter Thing Sweet is dedicated with love and respect to Trinidad and Tobago's first Olympic Gold medallist, Mr. Hasely Crawford, who captured the gold and my admiration in the 100-meter sprint in Montreal, 1976. His spectacular success in the face of many obstacles taught me that small-island origins do not rule out big-city dreams, and that when we shine, we do so not just for ourselves, but for the land of our birth as well. Hasely, my friend, my colleague, my hero, you make me want to be a hero, too.

A satisfied soul loathes the honeycomb,
But to a hungry soul, every bitter thing is sweet.

—Proverbs 27:7

Odile

God, there were times when she really hated that bird! The way Miss Ling acted, you'd think it was more important than people. Odile glared at the peacock as it sauntered past, tail furled and sweeping the ground, dragging a good four feet behind it. It sensed her dislike and played on it, cocking its arrogant head in her direction, and she could swear that it gave her a mocking wink.

Scowling, she rubbed the spot on her ankle where it had given her a nasty bite. It wasn't her fault she'd stumbled over it. The thing was everywhere. Was she really expected to keep an eye out for it every minute of the day? She had heavy trays of glasses to carry to and from the sink; you couldn't maneuver in and out of the narrow kitchen and scan the ground for the wandering bastard bird at the same time! As far as she was concerned, it shouldn't be in here at all. This was a bar, not a zoo.

"You know he there! You know he there!" Miss Ling scolded, anxiously examining her pet for any signs of damage Odile might have caused it. Odile noticed that her boss hadn't bothered to ask whether or not she was okay, even though the bird had drawn blood. Rather than answer, she bent her head and concentrated on picking up the shards of glass scattered all over the kitchen. She had no doubt the five broken whiskey tumblers would come out of her pay packet next fortnight. She'd been down that road before.

Miss Ling hovered, sharp eyes on the lookout for any missed pieces, just so she could have the pleasure of pointing them out. When she found nothing, she contented herself with a cluck of the tongue and another of her many pronouncements on Odile's shortcomings. "Clumsy! Clumsy, clumsy, all the time."

Odile sighed. After more than fifty years in Trinidad, and having run a successful business in the brutal man's world of gambling dens and watering holes, Miss Ling still pretended that she barely spoke English. Most of her customers succumbed to the facile comfort of racism, dismissing her as a "stupid Chinee," but the arduous year in her employ had been more than enough time for Odile to figure out that Miss Ling was, in local parlance, "playing dead to catch corbeaux alive," preferring to be thought stupid while listening to every conversation that took place under her roof. The strategy had paid off. Turning herself into a caricature had lulled her opposition into a false sense of security. The competition had tried time and again to squeeze her out, beguile her, muscle in on her, or otherwise shut her down, but she thrived. Miss Ling had caches of money secreted away in places that the taxman would never think to look. Everyone knew that her private quarters was a treasure trove of art that she'd had smuggled out of China in a steady stream, and that the dinginess of the bar's facade and interior stopped dead at the door to her personal space.

"I'm wrapping the glass up in newspaper and throwing it away," Odile informed her. Miss Ling was the kind of boss who demanded that her employees account for every thirty-second increment of their time. Odile had found herself uttering words like "Miss Ling, I'm taking three beers and a rum to table five," or worse: "Miss Ling, I'm going to the Ladies'." To which Miss Ling usually responded, "To do what?"

Odile would say, "I have to, uh, pee, Miss Ling."

"Again?"

"Yes, ma'am."

"One minute, no more," the woman always warned her. Odile often wondered if she were really expected to make it up a long flight of rickety stairs and down a corridor lit by a single forty-watt bulb to the lone toilet shared by male and female employees, and make it back downstairs all in one minute, but she always answered humbly, "Yes, ma'am."

And Miss Ling would wander off, muttering to herself in Cantonese, most likely bewailing her ill fortune at having hired incontinents who needed more than one bathroom break on a shift.

The old lady headed for her private office with the peacock stomping close behind her, claws clacking on the tiled kitchen floor. As she opened the door, she turned to face Odile once again. "Why you still here? Why you no back outside? Back! Back!" She shooed her with both hands as if she were a pesky puppy begging scraps at the back door.

"Yes, Miss Ling," Odile responded automatically. She parted the long beaded curtain that separated the kitchen from the rest of the establishment and stepped through it. The smoke on the other side made a second curtain of its own. She squinted. It was Friday, and the start of the month to boot, which meant that not only the weekly paid but the monthly paid workers as well were flush. They thronged the Smiling Dragon Restaurant, Bar, and Recreation Center in spite of the rain, anxious to get rid of as much money as possible before they had to go home and give the rest to their wives.

The "restaurant" part of it amounted to a corner of the room where one could eat fast and cheap. There was only one meal on the menu, every day, with no exceptions: greasy fried rice soaked in soy sauce, limp chow mein, and minute pieces of roast chicken. It had little going for it other than that it was filling, and for a dollar extra it came with a glass of Coke. While almost every other place took advantage of the spending season by proudly taping its Christmas menu on the wall and perhaps decorating with a few sprigs of plastic holly, the Smiling Dragon menu remained unchanged.

The only recreation available, apart from a few games of pool and the illegal gambling that went on all day, every day behind a false wall at the back of the bar, took place in the many tiny bedrooms that riddled the second floor like a rabbit's warren. For this purpose, anywhere from four to eight young girls hung around, cadging drinks off customers and retouching their lipstick as regularly and as ostentatiously as possible.

Sometimes the whores were local—most of them country girls turning up in the capital, Port of Spain, looking for glamour but eventually settling for sleaze once the stars faded from their eyes. Most of the time, though, they were illegals from Venezuela or Colombia. The clients invariably paid more for these, as the thrill of pressing against white flesh was one that few could resist.

Whatever their origins, none were known to last more than six months. Between police raids, immigration busts, and the usual ebb and flow of human activity, girls came and went. This wasn't a problem. They were replaced within days with other hopefuls.

The barmaids, who weren't expected to put in time upstairs (although there was no house rule *against* it, so long as Miss Ling got her cut), lasted a little longer—most likely because the wear and tear on the spirit was less. Even so, Odile, with a year of service, was the grande dame of the bar, with the longest tenure of anyone other than the bouncers.

"Odile!" The voice was loud enough to be heard over the considerable din. She moved in its direction, but progress was slow, as she had to push past throngs of men who thought nothing of indulging in a little frottage as she passed.

One couldn't blame them for trying. Odile, at twenty-one,

had fulfilled every prophecy of beauty held in her at seventeen. She was uncommonly tall, sleek but not thin, with long, powerful muscles that remained athletic even though she had long given up her passion for cricket and running. Her skin glowed like hand-buffed bronze, even in the dim light of the room. Many bemoaned her decision to cut her stunning thick, black hair, which once fell to the middle of her back, to within an inch of her skull, but she liked it that way. It gave her the freedom to get up and go, and it distinguished her from the cheap but elaborate weaves and cold waves of most of the women who wandered into the bar.

The only thing that stole the thunder from her wide-set, intelligent brown eyes was the lushness of her mouth. Even without lipstick, which Odile rarely wore, it always appeared slightly swollen, almost bruised. When men addressed her, they were hard-pressed to choose a point of focus, and their gaze wandered from her eyes to her mouth, to her abundant breasts, which, try as she might, resisted every attempt to keep them docile under the brief white blouse of her uniform.

"Oh-diiile!" The voice was getting impatient now. "Where you, girl?"

"Here!" She was tired and her feet hurt, and her skirt was both too short and too tight to make maneuvering easy, so the journey across the short space took a few moments. She made it to the source of the voice to discover that the client in question was a regular called Rollock, who had taken a shine to her, but who couldn't understand why she was not as forthcoming with her favors as the Colombian girls. "What you want?" she asked gruffly. Rollock wasn't a bad fellow, it was just that sometimes he got on her nerves.

He let a hand slide down over her bottom, to rest just below her truncated hemline, on her upper thigh. "Why you have to be so? I just calling you to say good evening."

She swatted at the hand, but it didn't move. "You just calling me to say good evening, eh? I'm a busy woman, Rollock, so if you calling me, you better have an order." She held up her notebook and pencil for emphasis.

Rollock grinned, showing his gums. "Okay, baby. One of you—to go." He looked around the table at his companions, pleased at his own wit, and seeking confirmation of same from them. The men laughed raucously, slamming their palms down on the table, making the clutter of bottles and glasses leap.

Odile didn't crack a smile. "You drinking or not? Because I have other things to do." This time she grasped his wrist firmly, making sure her nails grazed the skin, and shoved his hand away from its intimate quest.

Rollock was too far gone to feel the scratch. "All right, baby. Bring another nip of rum for we. And some ice."

She held out her open hand. "Twenty. Up front."

He pretended to be insulted. "Up front? But baby, I always here. You don't know me by now?"

Her lips twitched. "I *know* you. That's why I want the money before you get the nip."

With an ostentatious sigh, he peeled off a purple twenty from a roll of bills in his pocket and gave it to her. She tucked it into the pocket of her apron and turned to go. He stopped her. "You know, I thinking about something."

She rolled her eyes. "You? *Think?*"

He was impervious to the slur. "Yeah. I thinking that you should finish with that Chinee man you been friendin' with. Whatever he got, believe me, I got more." He grasped his groin suggestively with both hands. "Don't take my word for it. Check it out and see."

Odile considered responding, decided it wasn't worth it, and returned to the counter. "Nip of white," she said to the other barmaid. The woman on the other side grasped a twenty-ounce flask of white rum from the liquor stock behind her, foraged on a low shelf for an empty flask bottle, and held it up in the dim light, checking for any impurities that might have found their way inside. Finding no roaches or cigarette butts in the old bottle, she cracked the seal on the new one and carefully poured out half the rum, making sure the level of the liquid rose midway up the logo on the label but no further. No sense wasting good rum. The used bottle hadn't been boiled or anything, but they had washed it out fairly well, and besides, the alcohol would kill anything that might have been brewing inside. The system of selling half a bottle was a special service to the clients who might not have the money for a full flask. Neither Odile nor her colleague was particularly distraught over the questions of sanitation that this practice might raise in more fastidious clients. If the customer wasn't ready to spring for a full flask, well, then he would just have to take his risks.

"This for Rollock?" the other woman asked. She pursed her lips in expectation of a positive answer.

Odile nodded, holding out her hand for the nip.

The woman wouldn't release the bottle until she dealt with business. "He pay you yet?"

Odile fished in her apron pocket and passed over the twenty, took the bottle, and began loading up her tray with Rollock's ice and glasses. At the base of her neck, tense nerves throbbed. The tray wasn't heavy, but she had been on her feet for hours without the chance to sneak a breather. It was going to be a long night.

Rory

"Trouble?"

"Yeah." Rory didn't bother to look up. Water streamed down his close-cropped hair, soaking him to the scalp. It clung to his thick, black eyelashes, blurring his vision as he tried to blink it away, found the natural channels of his broad nose, seeped into the corners of his wide mouth, and dribbled off his jaw. The drizzle that greeted him as he left the house this morning had persisted throughout the day without any modulation in force or intensity, and instead had wrapped the entire city of Arima—if not most of the northern part of the island—in its endless, monotonous damp grayness.

The stranger stuck his head familiarly under the upraised hood of the ancient steel blue Datsun and stared at the clutter of engine parts, wires, and hoses that had, for reasons unknown, conspired to stop dead, bringing the rusted, cranky heap to a standstill at one of the city's most congested intersections at five-thirty on a Friday afternoon.

Off to the side, the landmark clock known as the Arima Dial stood as it had for over a hundred years, running a full ten minutes behind this evening, but working, at least. The Dial served as a roundabout of sorts, with cars from all directions being obliged to pass it on their way to wherever.

The breathless rush that characterized December, with Christmas suddenly seeming more imminent than anyone actually expected, intensified the mayhem that always prevailed at the city center. Trinidadians loved to fix up their houses for Christmas, and every street hustler for miles sought to take advantage of the potential windfall. They added to the congestion, shouting out the merits of their wares to anyone within earshot: leather shoes, plastic kitchen items, children's clothing, knockoff designer watches, toiletries that would kick up a rash on the least sensitive of skins, and, enterprisingly, umbrellas. The maddening smell of hot pastries emanated from the nearest bakery, and a bike-borne ice-cream vendor dinged his little bell as he rode past, conceding defeat: in this weather, he might do well just to pack up and go home.

The sidewalk was too high for Rory even to push the car up onto it, using it as a temporary lay-by, and with the street as clogged as it was, there was no way he could even consider pushing it out of the way. Traffic backed up behind, impatient horns blared, and pedestrians took advantage of the unforeseen breach in the usually endless flow of cars to cross both in front of and behind Rory's car, making the situation significantly worse and bringing ripe curses from drivers trying to get past.

The older man who was showing so much interest in his misfortune was dressed like a typical lower-level civil servant, in chocolate brown gabardine pants and a threadbare cream shirt-jac, a hybrid that melded the respectability of a single-breasted jacket with the coolness and comfort of a short-sleeved shirt. The odor of mothballs and bay rum clung to him. He leaned in even closer for a better look, propping both hands on his kneecaps for support and humming busily to himself, heavy black glasses sliding down his rain-slicked face.

Rory wished he wouldn't. The twisted strip of metal that initially served to hold the hood up had rusted away even before he bought himself the wreck three months ago as an eighteenth birthday present, so he was obliged to hold the hood up himself. When one arm tired, he switched to the other. But he'd been stuck in the road for quite some time, with no promise of the cause of the problem revealing itself, so by now both arms ached. He didn't want to be responsible for the stranger's skull if his arm were to give way suddenly. He gritted his teeth and switched arms once again.

The rain didn't make things any easier or any more pleasant. The city, like many of the more built-up parts of the island, was prone to flooding at the slightest hint of rain, and after nearly twelve steady hours of it, much of the roadway was hidden by an ugly, swirling mass of black water. Empty cigarette packages, coconut husks, orange peels, and plastic bottles nudged past his feet. His socks, he knew, would never be white again. His shoes were cheap, and he didn't have to examine them to know that the glue had begun to dissolve and the uppers to separate from the soles. He let his breath out in a gust.

His newfound companion chose that moment to speak again. "Radiator?"

"No," Rory answered shortly.

"Transmission?"

"Transmission's fine."

The man made no move to assist or step away. Probably lonely, Rory thought. Nothing better to do. Amazing what some people would do just for a little human conversation. The man scratched his head, dark and pointed as a dried-up cocoa pod, and squinted intently into the space under the hood.

"Electrical system," Rory volunteered, relenting a little.

The other man smiled knowingly. "Ah, yes."

"Third time this week."

"Yes," he sympathized. He didn't look inclined to offer a solution.

Rory touched a wire lightly. "You could jiggle this for me while I try to start it?"

The man looked surprised. Actually rendering assistance had evidently not been part of the plan. He seemed about to blurt out an excuse and dart off, but then something stopped him: perhaps the exhaustion in the black eyes that were now fixed on him; perhaps the glamor of being able to pretend expertise in something about which he obviously had no clue. While he pondered the matter for a few seconds, a driver, infuriated by the role Rory's inanimate vehicle was playing in the snarl-up, cursed loudly and spat as he passed.

That made up the old man's mind for him. He nodded vigorously. "Go on, boy. Try to get it start. I goin' help."

Grateful, thinking that angels might exist after all, Rory waded through the dank water and stuck an arm in the window on the driver's side, which was halfway down—not by design, but because that was where the glass had been stuck for weeks—and turned the key in the ignition.

Nothing.

"Jiggle it," he shouted.

The answer was muffled, but the annoyance in the tone manifest. "I jiggling! I jiggling! How hard you want me to jiggle it? I do it any harder, it go break off!"

Rory sighed. The muscles between his shoulder blades felt as if they were being torn, fiber by fiber, from their moorings. He was so hungry that he had to struggle to stay steady on his feet. All he wanted, please God, was one tiny miracle—just a little spark of life in a dead engine that would get him up and running, out of this wet place with the darkness gathering fast around him, so that he could make it back to the relative peace of home. Just a spark, Lord.

"You causing traffic."

Rory stiffened, making the pain in his back even worse, head coming into contact with the roof of the car with a thud that resounded within his skull. He didn't need to turn around to identify the source of the comment. The arrogance in the tone was identification enough. Cop.

His chest rose as the air rushed in, and then stopped, stilled by naked fear. Some people were afraid of spiders; some wouldn't go near snakes, or climb high buildings. Rory didn't like cops. *Fool,* he sneered at himself, trying with effort to breathe normally. *Afraid of a cop. Big man like you, scared like a girl.* But he could chide himself all he wanted; the fear was there. It was huge, it was real, and it had been for a very long time.

For four long years he'd been running scared from the specter of his own guilt, having committed a sin so ghastly that the boy he had been then had become a man in an instant. Four years since that cold, wet evening at a river's edge, with rain in his eyes and ears, pretty much as it was tonight, but with his vision clouded with color and humiliation and the fourteen years of emotions that he had piled up behind an imaginary wall in the hope that the wall would hold and keep him safe from feeling. The wall had fallen down.

In those elastic years that stretched out in his memory until they felt much, much longer than that, he was grateful when a night passed in which he didn't lie awake in bed, listening to the sirens speeding along the busy road outside his house, and imagine they were coming for him. Any night that the police dogs didn't hunt him down in his dreams was a blessed night indeed.

But this cop, the one tapping his foot impatiently behind him, didn't know he was wicked. He couldn't see into Rory's soul and read the bitter condemnation written there, like graffiti on a slum wall. *This* one just wanted the traffic moving again. And he said so in so many words.

Slowly, hoping he wasn't visibly trembling, Rory extricated himself from the open window and turned to face the officer. The slender man was a good foot shorter than Rory, gleaming hair stuck to his wet forehead under his black cap, black raincoat hanging off his thin frame like a wet tarpaulin off a rack. The rare, startling hazel eyes widened in surprise as he took in the size of the man he had accosted. Rory's bulk was at odds with his obviously young face; his six-foot-four frame, huge hands, and massive shoulders turned the unlined jaw, which didn't even warrant shaving, into something of a physical oxymoron. The cop looked about to ask if he was old enough to drive, but then seemed to think better of it.

"Officer . . ." Rory began. He swallowed hard. Somewhere in the back of his mind, a pack of dogs bayed, his scent in their nostrils. He didn't know what to say in his own defense.

The policeman recovered from the surprise of Rory's appearance enough to reassert the power of his badge. He bounced on his toes and pointed at the sorry heap of metal. "Move it."

"I'm trying to." Rory managed to keep his tone even. No sense in starting anything. "It won't start."

"Start it," the officer suggested unhelpfully. He caught the gleam in the black eyes and flinched. For a brief moment, it was hard to tell which was more wary of the other, but then Rory bowed his large head slightly and called out to the stranger under the hood. "Try jiggling the other wire; see what happens."

What happened was nothing. Awaiting a response and finding none, Rory sloshed through the water to the front to discover that his new friend hadn't liked policemen any more than he did. He'd thrown up the hood against the windscreen as a shield and had quietly disappeared.

The policeman's thin lips pulled back. "You got two minutes, then you get a ticket. Two more, you get another one. *Comprende?*"

Rory understood. Cursing, he hammered the connections with the heel of his palm and tugged at random wires, no longer caring which wire was connected to which part and for what purpose. For good measure, he punched the battery so hard it rocked in its bracket, made his way back to the ignition switch, and wrenched the key. The old car shuddered, took a long, asthmatic breath, and caught.

Rory was almost shocked enough to shut it off again, but stopped his hand in time. Grateful, he squeezed his bulk into the too-small car seat, and slammed the door. God had a unique sense of timing. He almost smiled.

"You shoulda give him a ticket anyway, officer!" a laughing young woman threw over her shoulder as she passed. She looked like a secretary or store clerk on her way home from a long shift, straightened hair dyed a discreet auburn and pulled back into a roll, high heels matching her stockings. Rory was distracted briefly by the roll of her bottom, printed out against her cheap wet skirt, panty lines undulating as she hustled to get out of the rain; but the cop, thwarted from the pleasure of writing up a ticket, demanded his full attention once again. He stuck a long, bony coffee-colored finger through the window, inches from Rory's face. His astonishing hazel eyes were now a flat, cold yellow.

"Next time," he promised.

Rory saw no need to argue. "Maybe, sir."

"Get out of here."

"Yes, sir."

The cop stood watching as he joined the snarl of cars, buses, and people. Rory didn't let him out of his sight until he rounded the corner, eyes turned up to the rearview mirror, keeping the predator in view. His nerves could not have pulled any more taut without snapping. Any encounter with a cop, no matter how brief, was one encounter too many.

The most frustrating thing about having been stuck there was that he was less than five minutes away from home. Tonight, though, with the car needing to be urged on like a sick, reluctant donkey, with the rain making sludge out of the city grime, and with the usual Friday melee still in full swing, those five stretched into twenty.

Predictably, the car shuddered into morose silence a full fifty yards from the tiny house that he rented near the noisy Arima bus route. He didn't bother to curse or give in to his impulse to punch the steering wheel silly. The car wasn't going any further—not tonight. Without questioning the fate that had determined that every step he took in life should be like walking barefoot on glass, he got out, back into the rain, and pushed the vehicle along the rest of the way, rolling to a stop in front of the bedraggled sweet-lime hedge that served as a fence.

There was no need to worry about getting the car into the yard; there wasn't any yard to get into. The narrow old house stood just two feet back from the sidewalk, so close to the hedge that he never even bothered trying to squeeze between hedge and house, not even to go round to the back. The masonry was old-fashioned, more mud and plaster than cement, and chunks of it crumbled daily into powder, leaving a scattering of flakes, like dandruff, on the ground around the entire perimeter. Once a cheery yellow, it had faded to a color he thought of as perpetual dinge. The sole front window lacked a pane, and he had made do with a sheet of plyboard tacked onto the frame. He wasn't keen on looking out onto this particular street anyway.

As he entered the ungated property, white sweet-lime blossoms and tiny, hard green fruits the size of fat peas crunched under his feet, dispersing their powerful citrusy perfume. Four sloping steps led to a cramped veranda whose wooden floorboards creaked underfoot, being more of a shell housing colonies of wood lice than an actual floor. The lock on the door was big and old, virtually useless. Chunks of rust in the workings made it difficult even to insert the key. He'd been meaning to replace it but hadn't had the time. Besides, there was very little left to steal after the neighborhood crackheads had made off with the few valuables he had possessed. It was not that he didn't have the wherewithal to do the job; it was simply that he couldn't for a moment imagine that anyone would want to get *into* this house. So he let it be.

He nudged the door open and was about to walk through it when something halted him. He took a step back and surveyed the street. It was now fully dark out. The streetlights glowed hazily through the white rain, and the houses were lit up—all except his. Not a glimmer throughout. That could only mean one of two things. Either his father was inside, passed out cold since early afternoon, and thus oblivious to the encroaching darkness, or the power had been cut again.

His money was on the second possibility. After all, why did he think his day would get any better simply because he had made it home? Shutting the door behind him, he made his way across the sitting room without faltering. He'd crossed it in the dark innumerable times before, and there was very little furniture for him to bump into, anyway.

The door to his room was ajar. He walked in and kicked it shut, stepping out of his ruined shoes, peeling off the wet clothes, and letting them all fall into a muddy heap. Naked, he felt around for a towel, and finding none, he settled for a soft cotton T-shirt, the first thing he laid his hands on. Balling it up, he vigorously rubbed himself dry, concentrating on his back and chest, as that was where he felt coldest.

He was just trying to take the chill off his feet when the door was thrown open, the old brass doorknob slamming into the wall, deepening the round impression that it had made over years of such treatment. Rory didn't turn around, even when the light of a candle held aloft fell on his naked body. He tossed the wet T-shirt into a corner and began searching for something dry to put on.

"You get pay?"

He tugged open the drawer of the lopsided mahogany dresser and felt around inside for a pair of undershorts, a clean shirt, and his jeans, and concentrated on getting dressed. Saul Steadman brought the light closer, and Rory knew that he was examining him, watching the black, naked smoothness and the ripple of muscle under his gleaming skin. Resentment and jealousy were in every look his father ever gave him. The man, once huge and powerful, had shrunk into a wrecked echo of his youthful self, thanks to alcohol, sloth, and a spirit of contention. If his father could strangle Rory in his sleep and then drape that magnificent youthful body around himself like a cloak, he would.

The flame of the candle was now near enough to his face to sear it. "It's Friday, boy. You get pay?"

Steadily, Rory placed a hand on his father's arm and moved it slowly away. "Why they cut the lights?"

The older man frowned. "What you mean?"

"Exactly that. I gave you money to pay the bill. If you paid the bill like you told me, why they cut the lights?"

Saul shrugged heavily but avoided his gaze. "I dunno. A mistake, maybe."

He'd lived with his father a little too long to fall for that one. "No. No mistake. You drank the money."

Saul looked puzzled. "What? No, I . . ."

Rory had no wish to listen to this again. It was all his fault anyway. Why did he always allow his father to convince him that this time he would do the right thing and pay the bills and manage the house while Rory was out earning a living for both of them? Why didn't he ask to see the receipts for these things, or better yet, take the time to go see about them himself? Was he really that gullible? He was like a wife who believed her repentant husband every time he came home with a confession of wrongdoing and a promise that it would never happen again.

He squeezed past his father and stalked to the kitchen. "You have to remember, I'm busy *making* the money. I don't have time to pay the bills. The least you could do is handle the business of the house. I can't do everything. And it's not like you're too sick to do anything for yourself. You can still work. You just don't want to." He fished around for a candle and matches.

His father was right behind him. "I *am* too sick to work, boy. My asthma—"

"Your asthma don't stop you from drinking or gambling. And if you quit smoking, maybe you'd be better off."

"Every day, every day, I get up wheezing," he whined. "My breath short, is the drink that help me breathe . . ."

Rory snorted. "Not tonight, okay? I can't pay the bill until

Monday, so we have no lights until then. I'm cold, and tired, and hungry, and the last thing I want to hear about is your *asthma*—"

The punch to his jaw didn't even send his head reeling back. It was like getting clocked with a pillow. But it was enough to cut him off mid-sentence.

"Don't think you too old to get hit, boy. You hear me? Show me some respect in my house. Watch what you say." Saul breathed heavily through his mouth, emotion making his breaths come fast.

Rory could have answered that since *he* was the one who paid the bills—and had been since he was sixteen—he considered it *his* house. Instead, he lit the candle and went over to the stove. Apart from the usual array of dirty dishes and smelly empty pots, there was nothing there. "What," he asked slowly, carefully, "did you cook?"

His father sneered. "Chicken."

The spite behind the jibe hurt him as the blow to his face had not. *Chicken.* His father's idea of a joke. Rory didn't eat chicken—*couldn't* eat chicken. The sound of wings fluttered faintly in his ears. Gracie's ghost.

In what was to him another incarnation, Gracie had followed clucking at his heels wherever he went, or sat in the tamarind tree overlooking the yard in Port of Spain where he grew up, watching him play cricket with the girl next door. More often, she was content to be tucked under his arm like a precious package. His father had hated her, and kept Rory in line as much with his incessant threats to stuff her into a pot as he did with his vicious beatings.

But Gracie was dead—murdered one awful day, part of a series of events in which her brutal death paled next to all that came after. Rory shuddered at the memory and brought up his cool hands to press them against his suddenly hot forehead.

His father cackled. "Give me some money."

"Not tonight."

"Hand it over, boy. You want me to hit you again?"

He didn't bother to point out that the blows had long ceased to be of consequence. He had never, not once, retaliated, or even raised a hand to block a punch. The pathetic flailings of the aging man represented his last shred of masculinity, and Rory let him continue to believe that his physical power was something of import, partly because he no longer feared it, and partly out of kindness. His father was, after all, his father, and all the family he knew.

Trying not to see the greedy, glittering eyes now fixed on his battered wallet, he counted out a few bills and pressed them into Saul's palm.

"That's all?" The weak mouth took on an aggressive curl.

Rory nodded curtly. "That's all. From now on, I handle the bills myself. Understand?"

Black eyes locked with black eyes, and seconds passed. Saul let his gaze drop, and he turned away to shuffle out of the kitchen. "Just remember, you not too old to get hit," he repeated. He blew out the candle and made his way to his room in the dark.

Rory stood alone in the kitchen for a long time, arms folded across his chest for warmth.

Saul

Saul gave the door to his room a vicious kick. Fucking stubborn boy of his didn't realize he was a man and he needed things. Money in particular. He heaved his body down on the edge of the bed and lit a cigarette, keeping the lighter going so he could see to count the money again. He knew he hadn't miscounted in the kitchen, but he wanted to check it over, rub salt into his own wounds. It still came up short of what he needed to live on.

He considered going back outside and landing a few kicks on the boy's hide, but Rory didn't feel anything anymore. It would just be a waste of energy. Besides, he'd been drinking all day: if he tried to raise his leg too high he might keel over backward, and how would that look? Damn laughable. Better to just let him be—for now.

He let the money fall from his fingers, swallowed up in the darkness around his ankles, and took a long, deep drag on the cigarette. He needed that. All that talk about smokes not being good for him, what with his lungs shot to hell and all, that was bullshit. *He* decided what he stuck in his mouth, not his son, and not any of the doctors he was always trying to take him to.

He flopped backward onto the bed. With the rain going nonstop all day, the sheets were damp, sucking wetness out of the air, sticking to his skin. The bed was crawling with nasty fat rain flies, buzzing around and losing their wings all over the place before they crawled into the walls and ate their way through the wood. He could feel them squirming under his sweaty back, feel the wings they shed clinging to him. Little black wings got everywhere, even in his mouth and nose.

He rolled over onto his stomach. He kept the lighter aglow, giving him enough light to hunt out the bugs in his bed. The flint was hot and his thumb burned, but a man didn't let go for something as stupid as pain in the thumb. He brought the flame close to the bed, enjoying the sizzle and pop of a rain fly exploding in the heat. He roasted another, and this one glowed for seconds before going out. The third time he tried it, the flame danced, flickering under the gust of his exhaled breath, or from the wind coming in through the gaping hole of the window, and the sheet, damp as it was, caught.

Hastily, he dropped the lighter and pounded the tiny flame out with his fist. It left a brown, crusty hole the size of a twenty-five-cent coin in the sheet. He spat on it and rubbed it hard to make sure it was truly out. No sense burning the house down, although he had to admit that seeing this piece of shit on fire would be good for laughs. He was sure Rory would like to see *that*.

He stuck his cigarette back in his mouth and sucked on it, enjoying the way the orange glow on his fingers made them seem warm and alive, rather than dull and grayish, as they were looking these days. He couldn't believe how old he felt. Rain actually made his knees hurt. Who'd have thought it: he, Saul, with his legs like tree trunks and chest like a stone wall, with creaky joints on a wet night?

He laughed briefly, harshly, the sound exploding from him. Him, looking like he did, and Rory, taller every day God sent, getting stronger and harder: the image of Saul as he had been some thirty years ago. *Damn* the boy. Giving him attitude in his own house. Coming home and demanding to know what he cooked, like he was a kept woman. Looking at him like he smelled bad. Begrudging his own father money, after all the years he had put food on the table and clothes on his back. Treating him like shit.

Just like his mother.

Saul dropped the cigarette, fumbled on the floor for it, and put it back to his lips. *Grace.* Long time he hadn't thought about the woman. What had brought her into his head? She used to be as condemning as her son was now, watching him out of the corner of her eye while she washed the dishes or made his dinner, not saying anything; but he knew she was trying to figure out how much he had drunk that day and what kind of mood he was going to be in. She had a way about her that could make him feel like nothing, and no matter how hard he tried to teach her to show some respect, she still used to just look at him, quiet, like nothing he said or did got through. She was the kind of woman that demanded a lot of patience from a man.

The day she left came as a total shock. He got up, just as normal, went to work, just as normal. An ordinary day. But then he came home to find the boy sitting on the porch, waiting to be let in—in those days, he didn't have a key yet—and Grace nowhere to be seen. Of course, he ran around the house, cussing, shouting in through the windows, because sometimes the bitch used to fall asleep and forget the time, and his dinner would be late. Eventually he kicked the door down, even though his key was right there in his pocket, and ran in to find dinner on the table under a clean white cloth and places set for two. Nothing in her closet, her shoes gone from under the bed, and all her shampoo and woman-shit gone from the bathroom. Little Rory, with his eyes wide and his mouth open, asking over and over for his mother, until he couldn't stand it anymore and threw his ass outside. He half-remembered making the boy spend the night on the porch.

The funny thing about Grace was that Saul could have sworn he hadn't hit her for ages before she left. Weeks, even.

It wasn't like he was a monster. But still she got up and walked out. Cool as you please. Somebody told him later that she took back her name and went to Canada, but people lied; you could never take their word for anything. Wherever she ran to, he knew she was gone for good, and had left her child behind to boot. For him to mind.

The boy was so young and stupid he actually expected his mother to return. Saul used to come home from work and find him on the porch steps, day after day, for a year or so, bathed and changed out of his school uniform, staring out past the tamarind tree in their old yard. Waiting for his mother. Saul let him wait. No sense spoiling it for him.

After a while he took up with that chicken of his, fooling himself into thinking that as long as it was close by, his missing mother didn't matter. Talking to it like it could understand. He even *named* the bird after her. And nothing Saul said or did could wipe that faraway look from his eyes—the same look his mother used to get when she decided to be difficult. Like the body was there but the mind gone wandering off somewhere. Unreachable. Untouchable. *Damn* the boy.

Odile

The Smiling Dragon crowd showed no sign of thinning until well after three in the morning. Most of the clients had staggered on home, while the few that were left were upstairs paying forty dollars for two hours' "rental" of the rooms, the girls' charges not included. Odile lit up her first cigarette of the night and perched on the edge of a table, shoving aside bottles and glasses to make room for herself.

"Odile." The voice was behind her, faint over the pounding of scratchy old records that sounded even louder in the emptiness of the bar.

Somebody else wanted something from her. She wasn't sure if she had the energy to handle another request for a drink, or another crude proposition. She'd had enough. She plucked the cigarette from her lips, leaped to her feet, and rounded on the man who had called her. "What now?"

She stopped short. It was only Vincent. She bit the curse off before it left her. "Vincent," she said softly.

"Babes." He reached out and tugged her close, face to face, so he could kiss her lightly on the mouth. He smelled of cigarette smoke and the sweat of fatigue. It was the first she had seen of him all night. Vincent oversaw the gambling in the back rooms and seldom came out front except when things were quiet, with just a few halfhearted games of wappie and all-fours going on rather than big-stakes cards. He looked as tired as she felt.

"You want to call it a night?" he asked softly.

She looked around at the few stragglers still nursing their drinks. "We still got people in the bar. I shouldn't leave."

He waved away the suggestion. "Let the other girls handle it. Come upstairs with me."

Still she protested. "But your grandmother . . ."

"Went to bed hours ago. Come on." He shouted a few last-minute instructions to the bouncers from across the room and shepherded her to the stairs.

Too tired to argue, and secretly grateful for his intervention, she popped her lit cigarette into a half-empty beer bottle and followed, linking her fingers loosely with his. She tried to ignore the animal grunts coming from behind the thin plywood walls of the rooms on both sides of the upstairs corridor. She should have become inured to them over time, but never had. They seemed to represent to her the ultimate in loneliness: bodies coming together in an effort to scour away the sensation of isolation. Deep down, she was sure that the exchange of money was secondary for both seller and buyer to the sheer need for human contact.

She hated her own proximity to all this, and the narrowness of the line that separated her from the girls on the other side of the wall. That thin line was drawn by sheer circumstance and fate, not through any moral abstention on her part. What was the difference between her and any of those girls? Had they, at one time, stood where she had and told themselves that they'd never come to that? What had happened to them to make them take that first dreadful step? It was through the grace of God alone, she knew, that she was still able to earn a living on her feet rather than her back.

Releasing her hand, Vincent fished in his pockets for his keys and opened the door to the single room they had shared for eight months. It was no different from any of the others on the floor, and had in fact been originally constructed for the same purpose, but Miss Ling had given it to Vincent several years ago for his own use—even though to this day she still complained about the loss of income the gift represented.

It was barely big enough for one, far less two, but for Odile it represented independence, her first step away from her mother's house and the suffocation she had always found there. She often reassured herself that she had come by her job honestly; it was not a case of sleeping with the boss to win perks. She had genuine affection for Vincent, and he treated her well. And the last thing she got out of her relationship with him was special concessions from his grandmother.

He pointed to the narrow bed, which was covered with musty, old-fashioned chintz. "Sit."

She sat.

Vincent eased himself to his knees before her and pried her shoes off, first the left, then the right, gently, for the swelling of her ankles told him that to yank would be to bring her pain. "Okay now?" he asked softly, kissing the reddened sole of one foot.

"They're dirty."

"They're fine."

"And smelly," she added self-consciously, but the warmth was already spreading up her legs. She reached down and touched his thick, glossy black hair, which spilled to his shoulders when not held back with a rubber band. His skin was pale against hers, and in stark contrast to the hair that fell against it. His face was long and narrow, handsome, the expression on it usually solemn and contemplative. On the rare occasions he broke into a smile, his full lips thinned and curved, pulling taut a white, opaque crescent scar just under his small nose. The scar was a reminder of his failure to duck in time to avoid a flying beer bottle hurled at him from ten paces by a customer who hadn't been happy with the outcome of a card game.

Vincent didn't respond, but got to his feet and removed his clothes, leaving them where they landed. She did the same, glad to be free of their constriction. The hard, uncomfortable underwire of her bra left red lines circling her rib cage, and the stockings made wheals across the tops of her thighs. He ran his thumb along them, whispering commiseration.

She let him put his arms around her, resting her face against his chest, even though he was gamey from the long, tense hours in the back room. She was sure she smelled as bad. Without further words, they kissed, his thin mustache soft against her mouth.

She fell back onto the bed, wanting him, wanting to hold out her arms, but the fatigue in her limbs wouldn't allow her to raise them. Vincent laid himself over her. They were a perfect fit; he was exactly the same height and weight as she. He moved against her, slowly, but she didn't respond with anything more than a soft exhalation.

Propping himself up on his elbows, he looked down into her face. She met his patient, questioning eyes with her guilty ones.

"Tired?" he asked at last.

"Yeah," she confessed.

He pondered for a second and then rolled off. "Okay."

"Don't go," she protested.

He reassured her. "I'm not going anywhere." He slid behind her, nudging her to her side, so she could feel the hardness of his chest and the warmth of his erection against her back.

"Tomorrow night, before we start work," she promised.

He nuzzled her cheek. "Okay."

Vincent

Vincent was surprised to see Odile fall asleep so quickly. She wasn't one for sleeping. Most nights, she tossed and moaned, threw the thin coverlet off, then bent over, picked it up off the floor, and covered herself once again without even opening her eyes. This went on for hours, even after long, exhausting shifts like the one they'd both just been through. When she did fall asleep, he could swear she had nightmares; she would thrash about and whisper unintelligibly in a strained voice, as if she was choking on emotions she couldn't speak of out loud.

Tonight, thank God, she was asleep in minutes, her tense body going limp against his. He ran his hand through her hair, feeling it light and springy against his fingers. He liked her hair as short as it was: it made her seem strong and confident. Boyish, but alluring nonetheless. It wasn't a very good haircut—a little choppy in places—but Odile never liked wasting money on hairdressers. Once a month or so she went to a barely competent young barber who offered fifteen-dollar cuts on the front steps of his mother's pastry shop. And although Vincent thought it suited her, he wished he had known her in the days when she wore it long, just out of curiosity.

From what she told him, she cut it all off herself just days before wandering into the Smiling Dragon looking for a job—shucked her long locks off like shackles. He remembered feeling her walk in that first day—feeling her, not seeing her—as she stepped over the threshold out of the sunlight. He had his back to the door, deep in conversation with a customer, but this woman stepped inside and sent ripples of sensation through him, sight unseen, from clear across the room.

He'd stood at one of the tables and watched her talk to his grandmother, obviously asking for a job, and recognized the glow in Miss Ling's eyes as she sized her up, trying to figure out how well she would do in the upstairs rooms. Usually, the girls didn't come right out and say they were willing to whore, but Miss Ling hired them as barmaids on a wait-and-see basis, knowing full well that in a matter of weeks most of them would take that first fateful trip up those narrow stairs, and then there would be another vacancy for the position of barmaid.

But if his grandmother ever truly thought that this tall, strong-looking woman, whose speech and bearing betrayed more education than one usually found in a place like this, would graduate from beers to fares, she was really getting old. Vincent saw in Odile dignity that wouldn't allow itself to be cowed, to be forced to stoop to lower things. That was what first drew him to her.

She kept to herself and didn't mess much with the other waitresses or the whores. Men, being men, tried their luck with her, and she put up with their freshness without showing them bad-face, while still managing to let them know that if they crossed the line they weren't going to like what happened next. The downside to her coolness and control was that for a long time she treated him much like she did the others: tolerating, but not interested in, his presence. She was as quick to put him in his place as she was with any of the punters. That stung, but it was nice to know she wasn't easy.

He used to catch her off-guard, reading books in her slow periods. Not trashy books with bright, ugly covers, or weekly tabloids full of fad diets and made-up stories about wolf-boys. Real books, the kind they made children read in school and write essays about later. Whenever she caught him staring at her bent over one of those books, she used to flush and hide it in her apron, guilty, as if it was porn. The books she read set her apart from every woman he had ever met.

He learned fast that she wasn't interested in gifts or money and didn't care for fancy food places, either. He began bringing her books he thought she would like. She took them gratefully and was always happy to talk about what she read in them. Sometimes he pretended he knew what she was talking about. Sometimes he just shut up and let her teach him a thing or two. Either way, he knew he'd found the way in.

She put up with his pursuit rather than encouraged it, but didn't resist him, either. When she finally capitulated, it was less because she had begun to love him than because giving in was the path of least resistance. That knowledge hurt, just a little, but he really didn't mind. The rest would come in time.

Pressed against his body, Odile sighed in her sleep. The last thing he wanted was for her to wake, because if she did, she'd stay up until morning. Tired as he was, he got up naked and rummaged around in the dark to find a packet of incense sticks. He drew one out and lit it, sitting cross-legged on the bed with the incense in one hand, waving it slightly to get the scent flowing. This one had ylang-ylang in it. That was supposed to be good for sleep. It didn't do a bad job of covering up the mustiness of the room, either.

He looked around him, not seeing much in the dark, but aware of every inch of the room and every detail of the scant furnishings. To think that this was all he had, all his life amounted to. A hand-me-down brothel room with thin walls and a bed in which women had been used by a thousand men. Loving Odile on that bed made him feel unclean.

In thirty-five years, shouldn't he have amounted to more than this? After all he had put into the business, shouldn't he have gotten more out than this? He was the only one of Miss

Ling's dynasty able to tolerate her foibles and despotic behavior, and, except for his grandmother, he was the highest authority here. He assumed he would inherit when she went, although she had never told him so, and he had never been forward enough to ask.

But he had plans for this place. Once he was in charge, so help him, he would turn it into something more presentable and, hopefully, more profitable, although he had to admit that the girls brought in money—and that would be hard to beat. But as long as his *apo* was alive, nothing, from the menu to the furnishings to the wallpaper, could be changed. He loved her because she was his grandmother, but she was a stubborn old fish and set in her ways, and no matter how hard he tried to reason with her, the Dragon would be run just the way she pleased, which was as cheaply as possible, with as little change as possible.

But that wouldn't last—not as long as he had any say in the matter. However it had to be done, whatever it took, he was hauling the Dragon out of the past where his grandmother had left it mired for decades. He was a patient man, but as they said, the longest rope had an end, and he was quickly coming to it.

Rory

Children should have been in school, and people in their offices, or wherever they worked. Yet the streets of Port of Spain swarmed. Teenagers in school uniform loitered on street corners with their bookbags strapped to their backs or propped carelessly at their feet. People milled about, looking purpose-driven, crossing the car-clogged streets without looking.

Rory stepped from the busy sidewalk into the pharmacy. It was small, but clean and well stocked. The glass front doors were shiny except for the crooked little Christmas trees sprayed on with snow from a can.

"Rudy." The security guard at the entrance, clad in a sky blue mock-military shirt, acknowledged him with a slight inclination of his head. He nonchalantly let his hand rest on the butt of the revolver that protruded from the holster at his waist.

"Rory," he corrected automatically. Months of making deliveries and the man still couldn't remember his name. Not that there was any reason he should; Rory never thought of himself as anything other than nondescript. Anonymity was a sanctuary. It allowed him to slip in and out of the world unnoticed, and when that happened, his faults and weaknesses could be seen by no one but himself.

He passed the turnstile, glad for the chilled air that rushed to welcome him. His was a job that had him out in the sweltering heat every day; air-conditioning was considered a perk. The pharmaceutical company he delivered orders for sent him on a daily round of drugstores throughout the northern part of the island. He didn't have to pitch the products; that was the job of the sales staff. He just came around later after the orders were processed and made sure that they were filled.

That arrangement suited him just fine. He loved being on the road, loved to feel the sun in his face, and enjoyed being mobile—or at least as mobile as his junk heap would allow. As small as it was, the city was endlessly exciting. Everywhere you looked there was a fascinating parade, no matter what the hour. Sometimes, on his lunch break, he would lean against a wall on the sidewalk on Independence Square, Port of Spain's most populous thoroughfare, and eat a cheap, greasy meal from a brown paper bag and watch the people go by. As he watched, he pretended that he was a chameleon, able to assume the coloring of his background at will so that he might observe while remaining unobserved.

His position was the lowest in the organizational hierarchy, but the only other position that offered the same opportunities for travel—that of salesman—panicked him. The salesmen earned more money than he did, and more money was something he would never have complained about, but as things were now, he rarely had to do much talking with the store proprietors, preferring to hand over his package of supplies, get it signed off by the pharmacist, and leave. Sales meant talking, wheedling, cajoling, and Rory just couldn't get his tongue around the words needed to close a sale.

He worked his way through the aisles to the back of the store, holding a large parcel wrapped in brown paper under one arm. Overhead, tinny speakers resonated with the sounds of parang, a high-pitched female voice singing in broken Spanish about José, María, and a baby. The pharmacist, a usually garrulous young woman with glasses much too large for her face, checked the order against his delivery slip and her own copy of the order form, signed off, and handed it back to him. Big red-and-white plastic candy canes bobbed in her earlobes—her concession to the season. With a nod, he turned to go.

"Rory." She halted him.

Oh no, he thought.

"The boss-lady wants to talk to you."

Rory bit his lip. "I have nine other people to see today, Nadine," he began, looking at his watch. It was a poor excuse, he knew; this was only his first stop of the day, and he could easily make the others before the close of business. He wished a better excuse would come to him, but he simply wasn't quick enough on the draw.

Nadine smiled and shrugged. "Well, maybe, but she told me not to let you leave without seeing her. You want me to get into trouble for not telling you?"

He shook his head.

"Besides," she went on kindly, "if it's an extra order, you can just claim the commission on it."

It was no extra order, but the last thing he wanted was for this young woman to know this. Not wanting to bring more attention to himself by protesting any further, he smiled weakly and slipped past the "Employees Only" counter that set the manager's office apart. Once there, he knocked lightly and held his breath, waiting for a response.

It was quick in coming. "Yes?"

"It's Rory."

There was a heartbeat of a pause, then, "So why you still outside?"

Squaring his shoulders, he nudged the door open and crossed the threshold. Zenobia Bedassie sat on the business side of a wide desk that was littered with notebooks, desk calendars, pharmaceutical samples, promotional giveaways, and executive toys. The moment she saw him she leaned back in her heavy leatherette chair, one hand tugging at her chin-length glossy-black hair, the other idly turning a yellow pencil around with long, red-tipped fingers.

She smiled. "How you doing?"

He kept his back to the door. "Fine."

Her smile broadened. She had a large, wide mouth that was made even wider by her vermilion lipstick, which she always took outside her lip line. Like the shape God gave her wasn't good enough. It was a scary mouth, alluring and threatening at the same time. He had some stupid fear that he would fall into it one day.

She set the pencil down carefully in a white ceramic cup she kept for such sundries and then reached out and turned the large framed photo that dominated her desk face-down onto the shiny surface. Rory knew the photo. It was one of her smiling into the camera, her husband standing behind her with his hands on her shoulders, her two teenage daughters on either side of her. Rory's collar got an inch tighter.

"You standing at the door all day?" she asked. He could see her eyeteeth as she smiled.

He took a few more steps into the room.

"Lock it," she pointed at the door.

"Zen," he began, the constriction in his throat making speech near impossible, "I have a lot of deliveries today. Fifteen," he lied, but locked the door anyway and walked over to her desk. Zenobia was a planet whose gravitational pull could not be resisted.

"This won't take long," she dismissed his protest. "You ever take long?" Her mouth twisted almost contemptuously.

"No." He could feel the blood of shame in his face.

"Well, then. What you fighting it for?" She was condescending, speaking as if to a child reluctant to take medicine he knew was good for him.

¡O Virgin María! ¡O Virgin María!. . . In her office, the parang was noisier than it was outside. Rory came around to the other side of her desk and perched at the edge, facing her, delivery book and car keys still clutched in his damp hand.

She pried them from him and laid them down, still smiling, chin tilted up, mouth glossy, straight black hair falling into her eyes. "Why you didn't make that delivery last week? Why you let that nasty Bernard man do it for you?"

"I was . . . sick."

. . . A la medianoche, Fue que la anuncio . . .

"Sick? Of me?"

He shook his head vigorously. "No, just sick. A cold. I got caught in the rain, and . . ."

"Healthy boy like you? You joking. Besides, twenty different kinds of cough syrup on my shelves, you feeling sick and you don't even come by so I could make you feel better?" She was mocking him. She laid a tiny hand on his chest, sliding it from his taut, quivering abdomen upward to his thudding heart, letting her nail lightly scratch the thin fabric over it. "Why you don't let me buy you some shirts? You really want to wear *this* all your life?"

He felt the blood in his face. "I like it."

"Nobody *likes* polyester," she contradicted him, but then waved it away. "You missed me?" She tugged open his leather belt. Her face was close. "You missed this?"

Terror and yearning. He wasn't sure at what point he had stopped breathing, and wasn't taking bets on whether he would ever begin again. It was useless to resist any further. She always brought him to this. She was smaller than he by far, although a good thirty pounds overweight and more than twice his age, but *she* was the strong one. Her power over him came from a different source, rooted in the spot where his own physical need clashed with his fear of women: the mystery of their bodies and the conundrum of their personalities. He feared that which he wanted, and the immensity of his wanting made him more afraid.

He let himself be led. She placed his hand on her breast— it spilled over the top of her expensive red blouse, soft as over-raised dough—and shoved her own greedy hand down the front of his trousers, grabbing for him. He was so hard it hurt, all the way up his spine, his eyes, his temples. There was blood throbbing in his field of vision, thrumming in his ears. He tried not to think of the photo lying face-down just inches from his thigh. She leaned forward slightly, hungry mouth open to take him, when he stopped her.

"Zen," he began.

She looked irritated: gratification delayed. "What?"

He leaned forward, dipping his head low toward her mouth. His voice was pleading. "Let me kiss you. Just once, let me kiss you."

"No."

"Not for long. Just a little one, before we do this . . ."

"It's not for *you* to kiss me. *That's* for my husband." She still had him clutched in her tight fist. "Now, you want this, or not?"

He closed his eyes. One little kiss would have given this at least a little dignity. One kiss would have made him feel he was, for her, a man with a prick attached, rather than the other way around. But somehow, he understood her refusal to make their encounter anything more than a few impersonal moments of distraction. He was just a little black boy from wherever the hell had spawned him. She was a woman who knew what it was like to have money and a pretty home and a name in society. What could he be worth to her?

He wasn't too stupid to know that the very blackness of his skin was part of the thrill for her. Her well-known, traditionalist Indian husband would be enraged by the thought of his businesswoman wife, the mother of his girls and a woman of good lineage, fishing down the pants of an inconsequential coal black delivery boy when she was supposed to be doing the books. Which was precisely why she did it. He could almost see her recounting the scene to her equally well-placed girlfriends at her women's group meetings. He could almost hear them laughing.

Through the speakers above, the music persisted: . . . *A la Virgin María, a la Virgin María . . . Que debe de nacer el divino Dios . . .*

Zenobia was waiting. "Well? I asked you if you wanted it. You could leave, you know. You only have to unlock the door and . . ."

His hand snaked into her thick sleek hair. "No, please . . ."

She smiled in her victory. Her mouth was hot. Pleasure and hunger swamped his self-loathing, taking precedence over every part of him that still had the strength to give reasons why this should not be happening. But these voices were always silenced, every single time, by the need for touch, hers or anyone's. He was willing to borrow another man's wife, even if it had to be on these usurious terms.

In his anxiety, and because of his perpetual state of frustration, their encounter didn't last long. His tremors were immediately followed by the familiar spasm of guilt, the same sensation that came when he brought about his release by his own hand—only much, much worse.

Zenobia sat back, eyes bright, reveling in her victory over his weakness, and tossed him a small packet of paper handkerchiefs to clean himself up with. He did so, embarrassed at being thus exposed before her, now that their brief and tenuous intimacy was over. By the time he had stood to his feet and readjusted his clothing, she had cooled, becoming distant and businesslike, and he was back to being the delivery boy again.

He opened the door without another word.

"Rory."

He stopped, considered not bothering to look around, but then did, purely out of good manners. "Yes?"

Red lipstick smeared her long white teeth. "Tell them back at the office to double the order for bandages next week, and send me a sample of that new antihistamine."

She was mocking him. Putting him back in his place, reminding him that what they had just done was nothing. *He* was nothing. As he watched her leaning back into her big chair, deliberately distant, he felt heat in his feet and his spine and behind his eyes. There it was again. His demon. His personal monster, the one that wanted to round on her, upend the desk in one fluid move, and shake her equilibrium just long enough for her to see him, open her eyes, look into his, and read the rage that lived there. Instead, he threw open the door, walked through it, and left it ajar. "Tell that to Sales," he answered shortly.

He walked to the front and out of the store, pretending not to notice either the pharmacist or the security guard. He was sure that if he looked at their faces he would see their knowledge of what had happened. Embarrassment and anger propelled him out into the street and to his car, which he would have kicked if he was sure it would survive the assault. Women. Damn them. And damn him for needing them. Damn him for being so stupid, big, slow, and clumsy—incapable of thinking in their presence, and unable to understand what they really wanted.

But his fear of them was in fact a fear of himself. He wanted to know them but had no idea how, wanted to touch them but didn't know where to start. He was pathetic in his inexperience, not only in matters sexual, but in simpler things as well. And he was the only person he had to blame for his miseducation, for not knowing how to touch, what to touch, what to say.

It was his fault that at his age his experience was near nil. He had only once summoned the courage to forget his own inadequacies, surmounting his terror of rejection to reach out in love to a girl-woman who now represented the lone glimmer of light in his past. Her name had been Odile.

Zenobia

Tell that to Sales. So the youngster was giving her back-chat for a change. Zenobia didn't know whether to be amused or offended. She settled in her chair and stared at the door to her office, still half open, as he had left it. Rory was turning out to be full of surprises. Usually he was polite and knew his place, no matter how far she pushed him. But this time she'd seen something flash across his face that she never had before. A kind of anger. It was there and gone so fast, she almost doubted she had really seen it. Like a wild animal making a lunge for an open cage door before its trainer yanked on its chain and brought it back under control. A big animal, a scary one, alive inside a man large enough to break her if he wanted without effort or strain. She shivered, mainly out of apprehension, but there was excitement there, too.

"Girl, you pushing it," she tut-tutted to herself, but she knew she wouldn't be stopping any time soon. These little morning games were a great diversion, especially if you played them well. You had to pick a partner—or victim, if you like—that you knew you could beat. Shy ones were good. Young ones even better. She never asked Rory how old he was, but she was sure he wasn't out of his teens. Probably a virgin. You could tell that by the way they flushed and hung their heads, excited but afraid to look at you in case you might figure out their secret. As if it wasn't obvious enough anyway.

This wasn't a game she played often—and never with more than one at the same time. Usually she got bored, but more often than not she panicked that these stupid little boys would have something to hold over her, get smart or get greedy and start talking about how interested her husband would be in what they would have to tell him if they chose to. So she always headed them off at the pass, built them up fast and cut them down early, reminding them just whose word would prevail over whose if they ever got stupid enough to talk. Then she slipped them some cash or gave them a cheap watch or some other piece of nonsense and told them it was all very nice, thank you, but she didn't want to see them again.

But Rory was different. He was bold. As deferent and respectful as he was with her, as much as he treated her like a lady rather than a whore, he always tried to push back the boundaries. He wanted more. He wanted to kiss, to hold her. True, some of them tried that early on, but she was always able to slap them back down the first time. Most were happy to let her call the shots. After all, it wasn't every day you found yourself on the receiving end of a woman's attention, no questions asked, no strings attached. Rory? He kept on trying. Wanted some kind of emotion or significance to the whole mess. It would make her laugh if it weren't so pitiful. Sincerity. Something only the young possessed. She wondered how long it would take for it to wear off him, like the gold leaf off the rim of a teacup. Not long, in this world.

It almost made her like him. That and the fact he was so strong, so tall, so good-looking. Skin like calf's leather: taut, smooth, and fine-grained. He was so damn gorgeous and he didn't even know it. Maybe that was why she had kept him around well past his time—several months past, if she remembered right. She knew in her heart it was time to get rid of him, and all would be well with her world for a while, until six months or a year went by and time began stretching out in front of her again, yawning and empty, and she started looking around for something to fill it with. Maybe she would see him just once more. Maybe twice.

Her head hurt a little, and it seemed to her that the music was getting louder. She had a variety of Christmas music piped into her store all through the season, from parang to classical choirs to scratchy oldies like Johnny Mathis and Bing, because it whipped shoppers into a feeding frenzy. Usually, she loved it because it helped her unload all the sundries that she stocked the pharmacy with at the end of the year: tinsel and wrapping paper, matchbox cars in plastic bubbles, and bug-eyed, balding dolls with cheap cotton dresses and no underwear. As far as she was concerned, Christmas could come around twice a year. But right now, the music seemed a little too loud and a little too cheerful.

Zenobia got to her feet, walked around the desk, and nudged the door shut. It didn't help with the noise, because of the speaker right above her head. She wondered idly if she should have it disconnected. She sat down again and pulled her compact from her drawer to check her makeup. Lipstick all over. Red stains on her chin. She could smell Rory's maleness on herself, deep and musky, but young and fresh and real. She wished she could bask in it, but she was a businesswoman and there was work to do. She set about cleaning herself up with wet towelettes, regretfully erasing every trace of the young boy.

As she put away her makeup, her elbow hit the little framed photo on her desk. It toppled over, like an omen. She straightened it, lining it up with her clock and telephone. The eyes of her two daughters caught her own, and she felt a nibble of shame in the pit of her belly. *If you knew what your mother was up to while you were in school,* she thought. *If you knew, would you understand?* Not at that age, probably. They'd be shocked and disgusted and revolted and embarrassed. She tried to imagine what those two pairs of brown eyes would be like, turned on her in horror.

To be truthful, she hoped desperately they never *would* understand. You couldn't peer in from the outside and fully accept the spectacle of a respectable woman, well-born and well-married, giving shines to delivery boys in a locked office in the middle of the day. This was the kind of thing you understood only if you were in it. And God, she hoped they would never be in it. She would see to that. She would see to it that her girls didn't get just enough of an education to make them fitting wives. She'd see to it that their marriages were of passion rather than practicality, and their men loving rather than suitable. Even though passion always died, it left something in its place: comfort and contentment, if you were lucky. Suitability grew, mutated, corrupted, into duty and restriction and constriction and obligation. Suitable husbands bought you businesses and let you run them for no reason other than the fact that it kept you out of their hair.

She shifted her gaze from her daughters' eyes, which had somehow grown condemning, to her husband's face. His eyes were impossible to hold—although in the photo he was staring straight ahead. She hated the way he had his hands on her shoulders. From anyone else, the gesture would have been reassuring, supportive, even affectionate. From him, they seemed like braces holding her in place. He grinned like a man totally satisfied with himself and all that he had accomplished. Decent wife, good-looking children, a business, a name, and an expensive suit and watch. No, "grin" wasn't how she would describe his rictus. His teeth were bared, partly in victory, partly like a dog standing over its dinner dish, warning off all comers. If *he* knew what she was doing while she was at work, would he understand?

Reaching out, she picked up the phone, stabbing at the numbers with a long-nailed finger. The phone rang forever. What was that bitch doing on the other end of the line? Eventually, her husband's secretary answered.

"Let me speak to my husband." Clipped and precise. No need for pleasantries. They were wasted on the silly cow.

"He's in a meeting," the woman said.

"Get him out of the meeting." Her voice was icy even to her own ears.

Zenobia could hear the pleasure the woman took in her answer. "He says he's not to be disturbed."

"Listen, Coral, Corrine, whatever your fucking name is, get my husband on the line. Now."

Coral/Corrine wasn't deterred. She spoke crisply, the temperature in her voice equaling Zenobia's. "Mrs. Bedassie, I have my orders. He's not to be disturbed. You wouldn't want me to cross my boss, would you?"

"I own half the company. You work for him, you work for me. Put me through."

"Why don't you try him on his direct line? When he sees that it's you on the other end, I'm *sure* he'll pick up." The girl was laughing at her now, Zenobia just knew it. The little dig only served to prove her suspicion. The reason she could never get through to her husband on his direct line was simple: he was spotting her number coming up on the display and letting the phone ring. The only way she could get to him was past the twenty-three-year-old viper at his front desk. And the woman put her through only when it suited her. Lately, it didn't suit her.

Zenobia threw the handset back down into the cradle without another word. She didn't really expect to get him on the line anyway. He didn't like her bothering him while he was at work, he always told her. Why should he be saddled with her calls when there was money to be made? For a while she had wondered if the problem was that he was screwing the secretary, but after thinking about it for a while she realized that would have been too easy. And so not like him. Bedassie wasn't having much sex these days—not with his wife, and most likely not with anyone else. The only thing that got his dick hard anymore was making money. Not even having it or spending it excited him. It was all about the hunt, the pursuit, and the capture.

She twisted her lips. He wanted to hunt? No problem. Let him. Because while he was busy stalking his prey in the corporate world, she was doing a little hunting herself. And that suited her just fine.

Odile

"She won't be around forever." Vincent comforted himself out loud. "When she's gone, I get the business, and we can start over. Gut the whole place, strip the walls, burn the old furniture, get rid of the whores. Make something of the place, like my father always talked about."

Odile let him dream. Miss Ling wasn't going anywhere, not for a long time. The old woman was healthy, strong, and well preserved, pickled from the inside out by the herbs and mulled rice wine she consumed in huge quantities. Nobody, not even her grandson, knew her age. Some said eighty; others were willing to go as high as ninety; most believed that not even Miss Ling had any idea. So fascinating to the Dragon's clients was the subject of her age that a pool had been running for several years, with all bets being kept in a small green-backed notebook that was always in the possession of one or the other of the bouncers. It was almost certain that nobody would ever collect. She had arrived from China a mature woman, with few substantiating documents, and those she did have were forgeries. The money bet, for all intents and purposes, was money lost. In any case, Odile was sure that the old biddy and her damned bird would outlive them all, out of sheer spite.

But she let Vincent talk, concentrating on getting dressed. Whenever she visited her mother, she took extra care with her clothes, although she had the feeling that nothing she did with her appearance would satisfy Myra, whose lips always took on a disapproving pull when she saw her. It was an unending source of chagrin to her that her mother did not condone her living accommodations, her place of employment, or her choice of man—this coming from a woman who once shamelessly flaunted her own sensuality, sauntering around town with a much younger man, belly swelling with his child while carrying on with someone else. . . .

Odile shrugged off the thought. That was then. Myra had now settled down to motherhood a second time around, eighteen years after giving birth to her. She'd learned to dress a little more discreetly, had put on maybe eight or ten pounds, and now somehow thought it incumbent upon her to cast aspersions on how Odile was living *her* life. Funny, Odile thought, what a little domesticity could do to you.

She shut her little black purse, slung it over her shoulder, and checked in the mirror to make sure her plain shirt and slim skirt were straight. She looked like a Jehovah's Witness on the way out to sell magazines door to door. It was nowhere near Odile's normal mode of dress, but this evening it suited her mission. She pursed her lips as she fussed with her hem.

Vincent watched her from the bed. "What you worried about? You looking fine."

She smiled at the compliment but didn't take his word for it. It was all well and good for him to talk: he didn't know her mother. She slicked back her damp hair close to her head, considered perfume but decided against it, and figured that this was as good as it would get today.

"I gone," she told him. "I'll be back in time for shift change."

He made no move to get up and see her out.

Her low-heeled shoes felt strange on the bar floor that she was used to navigating in dangerous stilettos. At the counter, the peacock stood with its head buried in one of the wooden bowls. It was munching on its favourite snack: deep-fried *channa*, heavily salted and peppered to keep the patrons thirsty. Its tail, as usual, was well tucked in—it only unfurled for Miss Ling.

Although it disgusted her, Odile had become used to seeing the animal eating off the counters and tables. The bar staff knew better than to point out the health drawbacks of such permissiveness. The last person in the restaurant to complain about the bird eating what it wanted, where it wanted, had been summarily fired by an irate Miss Ling—and that had been Vincent's father.

"You gone, girlie," Patrick observed as she stepped to the front door. The bouncer was an ex-wrestler, known back in the seventies for his ability to crack skulls with his own. The super-heavyweight had never amounted to much, although it wasn't for lack of trying. His greatest triumph had been representing his country in Cuba decades ago at an amateur regional meet. Nothing he achieved after had ever come close. Now he had run to fat—a huge amount of fat—but he cut an intimidating figure and he served his purpose in the bar. He tried to hold the door open for her, but with his enormous gut, which flowed over his belt in one round, solid protrusion, it was hard for him to stand in the doorway and allow her to squeeze through at the same time. The other bouncer, Teeth, came to his rescue.

"Tell your Ma hello for me," Teeth told her as she stepped outside, his huge grin revealing a two-inch gap between his upper and lower jaws. The story he preferred to circulate was that he'd lost his teeth in a valiant attempt to save one of Miss Ling's working girls from being raped in the alley behind the bar. Just a few of his friends knew the truth: that he had in fact lost all seven of them falling face-first off the back of an open-tray truck, having tried to hitch a ride, unknown to the driver, one night when he was too drunk to make it home under his own steam.

Odile didn't stay around for any other messages Teeth might

wish to send. He was one of Myra's faithful customers at her little sandwich stand on the other side of the city and, like most of her male clientele, was quite sweet on her. It irritated Odile that her mother still attracted so much attention from men. It had bothered her when she was a teenager, struggling to be noticed but forever living in the shadow of her mother's beauty; and it bothered her now, as an adult, that her mother's allure refused to fade in spite of her more moderate behavior. Was she to spend her entire life being known to all and sundry as "Myra's daughter," who was nice to look at but who lacked that certain something that came naturally to her mother?

The sunlight outside hurt her eyes. She spent so many of the daylight hours sleeping, and so many of the dark ones awake and on her feet, that she was slowly mutating into a creature of the night, shrinking from light, like a bat or an owl. She certainly hated being out in the city, with its dust, traffic, and endlessly chattering people—a thousand conversations taking place around her, smashing into her brain like the crash of cymbals. What did all these people have to talk about?

The smell was another reason she would sooner stay indoors. The Smiling Dragon stood on South Quay, near the wharf. Nearby, almost abutting the solitary, disused lighthouse at the very entrance to the city, was an expanse of black water. Each low tide it receded, revealing mudflats and the rotted hulls of fishing boats that had become mired and were abandoned years ago. Large crabs scurried over heaps of garbage scattered about the squatters' shanties that rose out of the mud. Further along the wharf, the commercial ships were moored, from lowly fishing and cargo vessels to awesome multistoried cruise ships bringing eager tourists loaded with foreign currency. The overwhelming combination of seaweed, decay, rotting fish, bilgewater, and dumped boat oil gave off a stench that swamped the whole of South Quay whenever the wind changed direction. Odile was sure the smell would eventually penetrate her pores and become a permanent part of her being.

She turned her back on the bar and headed north. On the way she stopped off at a street vendor's lopsided wooden table and bought a pink plastic harmonica shaped like a banana, and further up, a pound of grapes. They were quite expensive, an indulgence that practical Myra would never have countenanced. But it was *her* money, and if Odile wanted to spend it on *her* baby brother, she was entitled.

As she walked away from the promenade, the tenor of the city changed abruptly, becoming more modern, with brightly lit store facades on either side, trendy clothes taking up space in the display windows, and people swarming in and out of jewelry stores and upscale boutiques clutching shopping bags and chattering. The stores competed aggressively for the favor of the Christmas shoppers, with loudspeakers in every doorway breaking noise laws, rattling the glass with the force of the parang that spewed from them. The heady Latin beat, thickened and enriched with the calypso rhythms that flowed through it like country chocolate, stirred something deep inside her.

It was a long time since she had celebrated Christmas: Myra had never been partial to it, except to profit from the fact that in December people got their bonuses and had a little extra to spend. In her own attempt to cash in on that largesse, her mother added salty *pastelles* wrapped in banana leaves and rum-soaked black cake to her menu at the sandwich counter. As for celebration at home, though, they'd usually settled for sticking a tamarind branch into a pot of dirt in the living room and decorating it with silver tinsel and a single strand of red lights.

But Christmas was something nobody could be indifferent to. As she skillfully avoided clamoring vendors waving linens and plastic flowers at her—"Brighten up the house for the season, darlin'"—she smiled and inhaled the scents of fruit heaped upon upturned plyboard crates on the sidewalk, mingled with the acrid-smelling illegal fireworks being sold boldly out in the open.

Woodford Square, to the north, was the only green spot in that part of downtown Port of Spain. Despite its proximity to the expensive shops, the Hall of Justice and the Red House in which Parliament sat, it remained the meeting place of the common man.

Vagrants, most made homeless by alcohol, crack, and a social system that didn't give a damn, sat dejectedly at the entrance, begging for coins. Some chose to cool off and rid themselves of street grime by unabashedly bathing in the large old-fashioned fountain at the Square's center, hanging their clothes over the carved mermaids that sat on the edge with their tails curled. Others picked through garbage, competing with the pigeons and dogs for scraps.

Clusters of passersby gathered to listen to the maniacs and geniuses who visited the Square every day to loudly expound on every subject from politics to the coming Apocalypse. The heat, the haze, and the humming of many voices made sweat roll down the small of her back.

Odile squeezed past a vendor of herbal medicines who had laid out his wares on the sidewalk at the southern end of the square. She avoided his frankly admiring gaze. A hand-lettered sign in blue crayon on old white cardboard advertised *bois bandé*, a stimulant guaranteed to bring an erection so persistent that those daring enough to sample it sometimes had to seek medical rescue from their condition. Next to the sign were little piles of rank-smelling herbs, tightly rolled pieces of brown paper with God-knew-what inside, and old ketchup bottles filled with murky monkey-apple juice.

The long folds of the vendor's African gown flapped in the wind as he stepped back to let her by, and she caught the cloying smell of oils on his waist-length, tangled dreadlocks.

"Niceness . . ." he hissed, stringing out his sibilants. His voice was low and intimate, the voice a man reserved for the woman lying next to him. It made her feel queasy, as if he

had actually touched her. She quickened her step. Again, another reason to hate the city: it left her feeling naked and exposed. After all the years of longing to be noticed in the way
her mother was, it had finally happened, and now she felt
both intruded-upon and unworthy, as if the men who let
their admiration show were actually looking for Myra and
had mistaken Odile for her.

It was time to get out of there. She climbed into one of the
route taxis that patiently waited outside the square to be
filled, and was immediately wedged in by a corpulent woman
in a blinding yellow dress who sweated heavily and fanned
herself with a folded-up newspaper. But Odile didn't mind.
She didn't care how she got out of here; she just wanted to
go.

The groaning old taxi rounded the savannah and was
about to turn into St. Ann's when she stopped the driver. "I'll
get out here," she told him, handing him three wrinkled red
dollar bills.

"It's not St. Ann's you going?" The driver looked puzzled.
A statuette of St. Christopher, patron saint of drivers, dangled from the mirror above his head.

She shrugged. "Yeah, but I prefer to walk in."

He shrugged. What did he care? He had already been paid.
He let her out just past the gate of the President's House,
under the heavy-lidded gaze of bored uniformed soldiers who
were happy for the distraction provided by the arrival of a
beautiful woman. Odile tried to ignore them, glad that their
position prevented them from giving voice to their obviously
prurient thoughts, and began to walk past the botanical gar-
dens and into the St. Ann's Valley.

The valley was immediately cooler, either because of the
shelter of the nearby hills, the influence of the river that ran
through it, or her own nostalgia. Whichever it was, she always found something soothing about it, and whenever she
returned to her childhood home, she chose to walk.

It took a full forty-five minutes to make it to her old yard.

She kept to the main road, passing the better neighborhoods where the old established families lived in white-latticed ginger-bread houses and pulled their curtains closed against the inconvenience of urban sprawl, until she reached a quiet street where working people paid an honest rent for a simple, honest home.

She opened the latch on the gate to her mother's yard, noticing as she did so that it moved smoothly, without so much as a squeak. Most likely the work of her mother's man, Jacob, who was handy with tools and unhappy unless he was fixing something. She ran her thumb along the new latch. Neatly done, just like everything Jacob did. He was a man like that.

He'd turned up in their yard about four years ago, round about the time things had started getting rough between her and her mother. He was a country man, from way out in Sangre Grande. His silent humility and unpretentious demeanor belied the fact that he was a living legend, a stickfighter known for his mastery of a bloodsport that used sticks, not swords. A backyard hero whose skill at cracking skulls made his name one that children—and women—whispered as he passed by. But his youth was well behind him, and a crippling leg injury had turned his stick from a weapon into a crutch.

That hadn't stopped Myra from seeking him out, even as she carried another man's child in her belly. She let Jacob be her protector. He let Myra be his solace. Between them, they made up a little patchwork family, hemming Odile haphazardly into the weave of their fabric. Now he did leatherwork in the tiny room at the back of the yard by day and spent his nights in the bedroom that he and Myra called their own.

The yard was just big enough to hold a long building segmented into three apartments. The first was inhabited by a young couple, David and Jillian, and their new baby. On the small balcony, their old brown dog lay with his muzzle on his crossed forepaws. He lifted his head at her approach, recognised her, then lost interest and returned to his snooze. There was a time when he spent his days barking by the gate or down at the river behind the yard, but age was creeping up on him, and the sunny porch held his interest more than the thrill of wandering.

The next apartment looked as if the inhabitant was unwilling or unable to keep it in good repair. Odile knew Jacob well enough to figure that the only reason he hadn't set his hand to it was that the strange, reclusive woman who lived there must have refused his offer of help. The only sign of life there was a series of large, colorful panties, which the owner inexplicably insisted on hanging on a makeshift line right on the porch, rather than around the back as the others did.

That used to be Rory's home—his and his father's. Every evening when she came home from school she would find him there, pretending to be playing cricket in the company of the little chicken he used to keep, but, she knew, really waiting for her. He was a funny-looking thing, head, hands, and feet way out of proportion with the rest of him like an oversized puppy, skin a victim of his own hormones. Shy, and a little childish for his age.

Odile twisted her lips ruefully. Rory had always been the only person who had never wanted anything from her but her time, who wished everything good for her, whether it spilled over to himself or not. At the lowest point of her life, he had been there. She'd been seventeen, pregnant, and too terrified to talk to anyone about it, and though he hadn't known enough about life to guess at her condition, he'd sensed that she was in pain, and that had been all he needed to know. Throughout this terrible time, he remained quietly at her side, happy just to be alone with her, ready to catch her if she fell.

But he had been just about fourteen or fifteen then—a child, and a naive one at that, deprived by the awful circumstances in which he lived of the ability to read his own emotions, let alone control them. What had happened between them down by the river had been as much her fault as his.

Poor Rory. He'd set out to find her in the maddening rain the night her own personal distress forced her into flight. All she'd wanted to do was get away from her mother's worried, disappointed looks, and even from her own body, which was swelling and taking on an unfamiliar and terrifying shape. Where no one else could find her, Rory had, braving the swollen river rather than staying back to tend to Gracie's body. Looking for her instead of staying in the yard to take on that bastard Slim, her mother's ugly yellow-headed lover, who had seen nothing in the little bird but a chance to vent his anger. Mad at Myra and the world because she didn't want or need his reckless, abusive behavior anymore, and because she told him he didn't have to take care of the baby he'd put in her belly if he didn't want to, Slim had broken Gracie's neck and tossed her aside like she was nothing.

And she, Odile, making Rory's grief worse than it should have been. Throwing her pregnancy in his face and then laughing at his sweet fourteen-year-old fantasy that he could step in and be a man for her, make it right.

Make it right? Nothing could have been right again. With every inch that her waistline grew, she'd lost a bit of her future. Nothing to face but the same life of drudgery that had befallen her mother seventeen years before, when Odile herself had been born. The repetition of history.

So, she'd laughed at his love. Glad to be cruel. Happy to hurt someone more than the world was hurting her. And he'd reacted. Pushed beyond endurance, gathering up all the years of pain, shoveling them up like shards of broken glass and throwing them back at her.

He had fallen upon her like a bursting dam. To this day, her only memory of that experience was one of blurred fists. Baby gone. Washed away between her ankles into the surging red water. But somehow, when she thought of him, bitterness was not the first emotion to come to her. Instead, there was a sensation of sadness, and of things undone that couldn't be done now, and words unsaid that there would never be a chance to say.

She hesitated before her mother's porch. Once, her busy mother's lack of time and energy had left it dingy. Now it shone brilliant white, with emerald trim along the risers of the stairs, the windows, the porch and gate, and the bright new zinc-sheeted roof. Lining the few stairs that climbed to the balcony were plants, set in real clay pots painted green and white, rather than empty powdered milk tins like the ones that graced Jillian's little corner of the yard. Again, Jacob's doing. The crippled stick fighter who once lived as a hermit in the tiny room at the back of the yard turned his hands daily to projects that would make Myra happy.

The front door flew open and a ball of energy hurled itself outside. "Odile!"

A rare, genuine smile of pleasure bloomed on her lips, and she dropped to her haunches, arms open to catch the little boy who threw himself into them. Lil' Sebastian was heavy, too large for three and too energetic for any age. A grubby cotton vest left him naked from the waist down. Myra only dressed him fully when they had to leave the yard, but lately she had been murmuring that he was a big boy now, and maybe she should start making him cover himself up.

He had his father's unfortunate coloring; dull-yellow skin and jute-colored hair that was already getting too tough to manage, but as much as she hated the fact that Slim's odious presence haunted the boy like a ghost, she loved him with the sheer, pure, clean love that she held for no one else.

"What you bring for me?" With unerring accuracy, the boy went for the bag on her shoulder, knowing that Odile's arrival always meant a special treat. She didn't bother to tease him by pretending there was nothing there, but let him forage. He rooted around like a terrier, tossing aside keys, compact, tissues, and gum, until he withdrew the harmonica and grapes. He held one in each hand, looking indecisive, aware that he could not indulge in both at the same time, but not sure where to start first.

The wooden floor of the veranda creaked. Odile looked up, her smile slightly less broad. Myra's hair, once left to fly wild in the breeze, was French-braided down both sides of her head and tucked under at the back. Her face and apron were smeared with flour, and dough stuck to her fingers. She was smiling.

"Odile."

Odile set Lil' Sebastian down and got to her feet. "Ma." Unconsciously, she smoothed down the front of her skirt and touched her hair.

Myra's eyes flicked over her daughter, and she wiped her hands nervously with a towel. The little boy looked from one to the other, then ran to his mother to show her his spoils. If Myra disapproved of the expense of the grape purchase, she said nothing, just shooed him inside, patting him lightly on his bare behind.

The two women faced each other, Myra in the shade of the porch, Odile still in the sun. "You coming inside?" Myra finally asked.

Odile gathered up her spilled belongings before following her mother into the house.

Saul

Saul wasn't much of a Dragon man. The beers weren't always cold enough, and they had the gall to charge fifty cents more than anyone else on the street. But right now he had overdue tabs in half the other bars he liked to go to, and word was that a few of them had collectors looking for him, so for the time being, the old Chinee lady's little hole in the wall would have to do.

He begged a cigarette off one of the better-dressed patrons and took a seat near the door. He was a man of habit, and experience had taught him that the habit of staying as close as you could to the door when you drank, especially in a place like this, was a good one. That way you could scope out the whole crowd and be close enough to the exit to save your own ass if any shit went down inside. Funny how few people knew that.

He took a sip of his drink and rocked back in his chair. It was still early afternoon, but there was a good-sized crowd in there already—hard-core drinkers like himself rather than casual limers, who usually came out after dark. A few of the *jammettes* were already working. Those bitches had no shame; they couldn't even wait for cover of night to do their thing. Not that he could blame them. Money was money, and you took it when and where you got it.

He watched a sweet little brown-skinned beauty in tight

jeans lead a scrawny young man toward a door at the rear of the bar. She didn't look old enough to be out of school, but something about the way she held herself told him she had already learned all she needed to. Saul knew where that door led; he had been through it a few times, although not recently. There were rooms up there, where you could get girls to do you almost anything, if you paid them right. The memory of his own little trips upstairs, added to the image of himself in the place of the skinny man, going up there again with that sweet-looking young thing, made him squirm in his chair. He reached surreptitiously under the table to adjust himself in his pants. Ah, if only there was money enough . . .

As the girl in the jeans passed through the door, another came out, much taller than the first, and darker, too. She had her hair cut very short. Saul didn't go for that much; women ought to look like women. But even from way over here he could see she was beautiful. She didn't look like she had any lipstick on, but her mouth was fat and ripe. She was dressed like she was on her way to church, but maybe that was her thing—her special game with her clients. Some of them liked you dressed like a slut, and some of them liked you dressed up like their little sister. He grinned. Each man had a right to choose his own poison. He himself didn't care much what they had on when they came to him, so long as they took it off, real fast.

His eyes stayed with the tall whore all the way across the floor, until she was quite close to him. Both of the idiot bouncers jumped up and ran for the door to open it for her: the fat one first, and then the smaller one. Assholes. What did women have arms for, if it wasn't to open doors their own damn selves?

But he stared unashamedly at the woman as she talked to the bouncers in the open doorway. She really was something. Then she turned her head a little and smiled, and Saul's hand stuck halfway to his mouth with his drink clenched in it. He was sure he knew her. Another bar, maybe? That was possible; these girls got around. And if he did know her from another bar, did he fuck her or did she just bring him a drink? Probably just a drink. He didn't think he could have done a sweet piece of ass like that and then forgotten about it. He wasn't *that* far gone.

His arm continued its journey to his mouth, and he took a deep, long gulp, eyes still fixed on the girl over the rim of his glass. Then, clang-clang, pieces fell into place. He knew who she was. The last time he had seen her, she was still in school uniform, with braided hair almost down to her tailbone. Used to have a throwing arm on her at cricket. And a walk that made her hips move from side to side—man, it was like music.

She was the little girl that lived next door, back in St. Ann's. Had that mother who used to cook up a storm in the kitchen and screw up a storm in the bedroom with a little yellow Rasta man. And the grandfather who used to sit on the concrete outside the gate and drool like a freak. Rory used to be sweet on her. As a matter of fact, he got so chained up by her that one night he lost his mind and hit her. That was why they had to run away from the valley in the first place, because he wasn't hanging around waiting for no trouble on that matter. If trouble wanted to find him, well, it would have to come looking.

Saul watched as she finished talking to the two men, his eyes moving from the face that had gotten a little older but otherwise hadn't changed much, to the ass that had filled out enough to be prominent even under that old-maid dress she had decided to put on. Just because his son once had a thing for the woman once didn't mean he couldn't enjoy a little gape himself. His eyes lingered until she was out of sight, and then he finished his drink in one swig.

The cigarette glowed at the end of his fingers. Think about it. Snooty Myra Cole couldn't give him a glance all the time he knew her, even though they lived next door, for Chrissakes. Full of attitude, she was barrack yard royalty, and now

her daughter was down on South Quay, turning tricks upstairs a bar. It was too funny. He grinned. Wouldn't Rory be
surprised.

He laughed openly. Yes, wouldn't Rory love to hear about
what his little schoolgirl goddess was up to now! It almost
made him anxious to get home, just so he could have the
pleasure of telling him.

Saul put the butt out and looked around the bar for somebody else to bum a smoke from. All the while his brain was
churning, trying to fit one last piece in the puzzle before the
picture was complete. What was the girl's name? It was one
of those stupid frigging names, not a real name. It was the
kind people had no right calling their children, because for
the rest of their lives they had to put up with people spelling
it wrong, saying it wrong, and forgetting it. He scratched his
head and thought hard, delving through the debris of the
years.

And then there it was. Odile. That was her name, wasn't
it?

Rory

Eli Walker spat in the sink. "You do my heart sad, boy." The locker room smelled of sweat and socks, and the floor was damp from the men who stepped naked and barefoot from the showers and went about the business of drying off and getting dressed. There was no free soap at the sinks, no toilet paper in the stalls, no hand towels on racks next to the cracked mirrors; you brought whatever you needed with you. Outside, there were no fancy weight machines, no juice bar, no women in pastels doing aerobics to loud American music. Just steel, sweat, rickety bikes, and vinyl benches, a place where men met and talked shit and beat each other up in any one of the three wrestling and boxing rings on the upper floor.

Rory extended a hand to Eli and let the old man remove the laces from his black twelve-ounce boxing gloves and then carefully unwrap the lengths of white bandages he used to protect his hands from the relentless pounding during his training. He'd just done a two-hour circuit of the weights, followed by half an hour on the sandbags and another half sparring with a giant called Mako, the only person able to hold his own against Rory in a training bout.

Every muscle ached deliciously, in that way they had when he forced them beyond endurance and discovered that his en-

.durance limit was further than he thought. His pulse was only just slowing, his limbs were heavy, and sweat glistened against his black skin like a mist of stars in the night sky. Rory was feeling good, and he had been hoping Eli wouldn't bring the same old topic up again to spoil things for him tonight.

"Eli," he began again, patiently, although they had both covered this same ground time and again. "I told you. I like to box, but only for exercise. That's all. I don't want to fight anybody. Fighting in a ring, with people watching, that just don't . . ."

Eli cut in, distressed, waving the white binding tapes in his arthritic hands. "What you mean, boy? You mad? You born to fight. Look at you. You think the Father put you here, in the body of a lion, for you to make a living carry packages all over town? You a fighter . . ."

Rory shook out his hands, feeling the blood tingle back into them, and stood up. "I do the sandbags for strength, and I fight Mako for speed, and to exercise my wits. I come here to relax and keep fit. Why you can't accept that? I don't need to compete. I get all I want right here."

That wasn't exactly true. Boxing was more to him than a good way to break a sweat. There was a thrill to it, a soaring, giddying delight that filled him, coursing through his limbs as he punched and danced and feinted. Ah, the solid feel of the canvas and the thrill of glory when he brought his opponent down. The battle made his spirit glide and his energy surge through him like liquid fire. But serious boxing? For money? Oh, no. He couldn't. He began pacing the length of the small room, hands clenching and unclenching in agitation.

Eli stayed seated, tilting his head back to keep focused on Rory's face. Rory tried to avoid the disappointed look. He understood the old man's pain. Eli was a man with an unerring eye for talent. Fathers who dreamed of seeing their boys in the boxing ring brought them to Eli for evaluation and left either crushed or exultant with his appraisal. In more than forty years of coaching, he had developed a reputation for pushing the talented ones he spotted toward excellence, using a combination of paternal kindness and dogged persistence.

This time, though, his badgering had got him nowhere. For over a year, Rory had seen him try every means at his disposal to seduce, cajole or bully him into a "real" competition; and for over a year Rory had listened, patiently and respectfully, and then declined.

Eli tried again. "What you mean, 'keep fit?' 'Keep fit' is for fat women at the YMCA! Think, boy! What they paying you where you working? And how much more you think they will pay you five years or ten years from now? That is all you want for yourself? You know how many men wish they had a body like you, hands like you, reflexes like you? You know how many men wish they could watch the other man in a fight and know where the next blow coming from? God give you talent, boy, and plenty of it. What you hiding it for?"

Rory undid his shoes, stripped off his shorts, stepped unself-consciously into the shower, and let the water run over him. He loved Eli—had nothing but respect for the wise coaching he had always offered—but on this matter, he would not bend. "*God* don't give nobody talent to fight. That ain't no gift, it's a curse, and it come from the Devil, not the Lord."

Eli went to the shower door and stood near, not caring that the water splashed the front of his shirt. "No, boy. That's where you wrong. Your strength is a gift, your brains is a gift, and the only thing you going to hell for is if you waste your whole life and don't use it. I ain't asking you to give up your job and go professional. I just talking about the amateur league. I been to every game in this country in forty years, boy, and I have to tell you, somebody like you only come along once in every ten. The rest of them ain't want nothing with you; they only have to see you step into a ring and they know they judgement day come.

"Think about the money. One fight and you could win more than they paying you at that damn job. And you could travel. Ain't you say you never leave the country yet? Boy, you take up with the league, you could go all the way up the islands, maybe America. You fight in America, they pay you prize money in U.S. dollars, boy! You understand what I telling you?"

Eli's white-rimmed pupils dilated. Rory was embarrassed by his praise. He was a discovery, the old man always told him, *his* discovery, probably his last before his time came, his final bid for glory . . . and he wasn't fighting. It was Eli's personal tragedy, but there was nothing to be done for it.

Rory soaped himself slowly, carefully, listening as much to Eli as he was to the pounding in his chest. His heart beat faster than it had in the ring with Mako. He didn't want to hear what the old man had to say. He remained silent.

Defeated, Eli backed away from the shower, shoulders drooping. He shook his head ruefully. "You hurt my heart, son. You born to fight—"

"No!"

Eli jumped, startled by the roar that burst from the young man with such explosive force. He spun around to face him. Rory's face was contorted with something that wasn't rage, but was even more frightening.

Rory stood close, a foot taller than Eli, fire blazing through him. "I was *not* born to fight, you understand? Not that. That ain't my destiny. I don't want it, and I don't need it. I wasn't born with no blood-mark on my forehead. The fight won't have me. It can call me; it can call me all it wants, but I ain't going to answer. You hear?"

Eli stared into his face, mouth agape, shocked at the raw

power on display, and frightened, too. He was used to Rory's obedience, his quiet, respectful fulfillment of Eli's every instruction. He punched the way Eli told him to punch and held back when Eli said he should. But something in Rory was awake now, something he had never seen, and it was awesome. Beyond anger, beyond fear, there was something he didn't want to identify. Eyes down, without another word, Eli walked out of the room.

Rory dropped onto a bench, head in his hands, ashamed at having turned on his mentor. But Eli was too sharp; his eyes had seen what Rory struggled every day of his life to hide. The blood-mark. He'd denied it with the fervor of Peter rejecting Christ, but he knew that it was his. His father had made sure of that.

Since he was a boy, every day that his father had hit him was a day in which the mark deepened upon his soul. Every night he spent on the porch back in St. Ann's, plugging his ears with his fingers, while his father vented his temper and his alcohol on his mother inside, he shut a little piece of himself away, behind a wall that no one could penetrate.

The sins of the father. They were for real. Waiting for them to blossom out from inside him and produce poison fruit as they had once before, the evening he had hit Odile, was like being locked in a dark cave with a tunnel at one end. Somewhere down the tunnel—and nobody ever knew just how deep the tunnel went—there lived a monster. The kind of monster that, if you stayed real quiet, you could hear it breathe, and if you squinted into the darkness, you could see the red glint of its eyes as it waited and watched. And you knew that one day you'd be pushed too far and wake up to realize that the monster was you.

Eli wanted him to box in a ring, in front of people, with the cheering of the crowd all around him and the smell of another man's blood on his fists. Blood in his nostrils like a drug, maddening him. He couldn't let it happen. What if he started pounding away, loving the feel of flesh hitting flesh, enjoying the dominance and the knowledge of his own power, and found that he couldn't stop?

Sad, and sick at the way he had treated Eli, he rose, dressed, and headed for home.

Odile and Myra

"I told you before. I tell you every time I come here: selling drinks in a bar don't make me a whore." Odile knit her brows and concentrated on the heap of dried coconut chunks that she was grating into her mother's large enamel bowl. The rough metal grater was made up of a sheet of aluminum punctured across the face with nails. It was efficient, but not fast, and the slightest distraction could mean grated knuckles. When she had the money, she was going to buy Myra an electric blender.

No matter what she did, no matter how carefully she dressed, it always came back to this. At some point during their conversation, Myra would say something disapproving, either with her mouth or her large expressive eyes, and Odile would wind up defending herself. It had become almost a ritual for the two women, like a well-choreographed dance in which the music never faded.

Myra folded her arms and watched Odile, waiting on the coconut she needed to mix into the bread batter in her bowl. She could have done the grating much faster than Odile could, because of her years of practice, but Odile liked to help when she visited, so Myra always let her.

"I didn't say you're a whore. I said . . ."

"You *think* I am!" Odile retorted. "I see it in your eyes every time you look at me. I see your nostrils flare, like you're trying to sniff me out, see if you can pick up the scent of those men—"

"What I said," Myra cut across her, "is that that place isn't the place for you anyway. Whether you selling yourself or not, people will always see you the same way. You think those men see any difference between a waitress and a *jammette*? Is all the same to them, and believe me, money is money, they just as soon give it to you as any one of them other girls. And those girls, Odile, those girls will drag you down. . . ."

"You act like something wrong with them! You talk about them and turn your nose up like they smell bad. But you don't know them. All they want to do is make a dollar and survive, just like anybody else. They no different from me."

Myra slammed her hands down on the table between them, making everything leap, and a small bottle of vanilla tipped over, spreading a brown stain across the patched white tablecloth and filling the air with its perfume. Myra tried to rescue it but was too late, and cursing, she arced it across the room, where it clattered into the sink but did not break. The abruptness and violence of the gesture made Odile stop grating in mid-stroke and stare at her mother, jaw slack. This wasn't like Myra. Her mother didn't like showing her emotions; she felt it made her weak. But the anger and anxiety in her voice were disconcertingly real.

"That's the problem, girl! You different! You not like them! You can't see that? Those girls, they have no hope, and for them what they do is better than anything they have to face home. Them girls see a life like that as a way out, they think one day some sailor going to walk off the Port of Spain dock from some big ship and take them away with him. So they stick with it and take man after man, and sometimes they get what they want and find somebody to take care of them, but most of the time they stay in the business until it either kill them or they manage to walk away.

"But not you, Odile. You, with all your education and all

your brains! You had a place in university waiting for you and you turn your back on it. You had a chance to get out of here, to move up, like I always wanted for you, and instead you move *down?*"

Vanilla burned in Odile's nose. Shreds of coconut covered the finger she pointed accusingly at her mother. "You see, that's the problem. You talking about what *you* want for me. It was always that. Not what I want for me, but what you want."

"I'm your mother, I have a *right* to want something for you. I have a right not to want to see you stuck the same place I get stuck, feeding people for a living, day in, day out, with the years coming and going and nothing changing. Not that I minded doing it. Every morning I had to get up and fry bakes until the oil splash up and burn my arms, and bone fish and chop onions and knead dough, and then cart all that into town to sell and come back and start all over again, but I didn't mind. When your grandfather was alive, I take care of him even when I was so tired I thought my back was opening up, so you could have the time to study. Because I knew you were smarter than me and there was no way you with all your brains was ever going to wind up like me. And now you let your life just slip away, and act like your education is a shameful thing.

"You wanted to be a doctor or a lawyer, something special. And you used to work hard for it. Then one day you get up and walk out and find yourself in a nasty bar on South Quay, holed up with some old Chinee man . . ."

"Vincent is not old." She didn't even want to talk about the other part, that Myra didn't like the idea that he was Chinese, rather than what Myra called "normal." Slowly, deliberately, she picked up a hand towel and began to wipe the coconut off her hands.

Myra seemed to have forgotten that she had coconut bread to bake, and in her agitation had begun poking around on the stove, looking under lids and stirring pots that didn't need stirring. "Don't try to change the—"

Odile's voice was louder than she meant it to be. "I am not trying to change the subject. I just don't want to hear it any more. If I have to hear it again, maybe next time I won't bother to come—"

A whimper at her feet cut her short. She looked down. Lil' Sebastian had toddled unnoticed into the room and was standing with one hand clutching her skirt, the other clenched around his little pink harmonica. His mouth and vest were purple with grape juice, and his eyes were wide and white. The raised voices had brought him, and the fact that his two favorite people were obviously not happy didn't make *him* happy.

She stooped to soothe him, trying to force the stress out of her ragged voice. "Sweetie, come . . ." She pulled him to her, planting light kisses on his sticky cheek. "Come." She took him into her arms, feeling the harmonica pressed between their bodies, jabbing her breast.

Funny, the way God worked. Just as she was about to utter the words that rose to her lips frighteningly often, to promise to leave and never come back—and once she did that, would she ever have the courage to back down and admit she wasn't really serious?—the very reason that she always returned home every week was there.

Myra patted her hair, leaving traces of flour in it, and began mixing the grated coconut into her dough. She didn't look up. "You will spoil that boy like fish," she murmured.

Odile kissed Sebastian's smooth forehead. "Picking him up don't mean spoiling him," she countered.

"I'm just saying . . ." her eyes ran over her daughter's face, and she stopped.

Odile was glad her mother let it drop. The fact that they were mother and daughter aside, they were both women, and shared something only women understood. Sebastian was, for both of them, more than just son and brother. Myra's father, whose mind had failed him long before his body had, had been a burden upon the household for many years, wandering off as he always did, spending his days in the streets outside, the object of mockery for schoolchildren and the cause of frustration for every motorist who suffered his well-meaning attempts to "conduct traffic." But he had been a part of their family, and they had loved him. He'd slipped away quietly one night, just weeks after Myra brought her baby home from the hospital, as if graciously making space for him. They named the baby Sebastian, a legacy from a man who had left his imprint on all their lives.

For Odile, Lil' Sebastian filled her arms as her own baby never had. The fear, loathing, terror, and remorse at her own pregnancy may have been rendered moot by her miscarriage, but her loss by the river was a real one. Since that evening, something inside her had split in two. Her release from the sentence of teenage motherhood had come at a price: she would forever suffer the pain of not knowing what might have been, and a longing that could be fulfilled either by a ghost or a living child. Odile chose the living child, even though it was not her own.

Instinctively, her arms tightened around the squirming infant. She eyed her mother across the room, daring her to challenge her for the boy's attention. Both women were fiercely competitive, and Sebastian was usually the object of their subtle vying. Odile was sure that her mother's protestations about the many gifts she bought the boy were less motivated by a reluctance to spoil him than they were by a fear that Odile could hold sway over his affections. She hated her mother's jealousy, but hated herself all the more because the urge to compete for the love of the child, to have him come to her more willingly than to the woman who had borne him, was too real.

Lil' Sebastian decided that enough was enough, and that Odile's grip was getting much too tight for his liking, so with an irritable squeal, he wriggled free and ran from the kitchen, bare bottom winking. Myra could disguise neither her relief at seeing him go nor her shame at feeling that relief. She sucked in her lower lip and gnawed on it.

She steadied herself and returned to their conversation as if it had never been marked by her outburst. "All I'm saying is that you're smart and pretty," she paused. She didn't often compliment her daughter, especially not on her looks. She went on. "You could have any man you want. You could find someone who could give you anything, help you build a better life."

Odile's eyes narrowed. "You see? That's all you think men are for. That's what they've always been for you. A means to an end. Every man you ever had, even Slim, and now Jacob, was to help you get something—"

"Not true!"

"Or help you *be* something. Slim made you the neighborhood sweetman's girlfriend. He got you pretty things and took you dancing. People looked at you, and you liked it. And then he didn't want you when your belly got big for him—"

"*I* didn't want *him*," Myra corrected. "His child wasn't good enough for him, so he wasn't good enough for me."

Odile went on regardless. "Now Jacob's making you a respectable housewife. Look at yourself! From hot and wild to straight and narrow. You change to suit the man you're with. Everything that you become, you become because a man makes you so."

Myra objected hotly. "That's not fair!"

"Not fair, but true. Jacob's a good man, but all you see yourself to be, you see yourself to be because of him or through him. You sat around all your life and waited to be rescued. You waited for a knight, and you got a stickfighter, and you're happy with that. Now you think that qualifies you to expect the same for me? *I* decide who I am. I don't need to wait for a man to define it for me!"

Myra shoved the bread into the oven and slammed the door shut, rocking the pots of food on top of the stove. "And what *are* you? What did you decide you are?"

Odile wanted a cigarette, and she wanted it now, but her mother didn't know she smoked. Now was not the time for her to discover this. "When I find out, I'll tell you. But I won't find out at the hands of a man. Not like you did. If it takes me ten years to do it, fine. And if I spend those ten years working in the bar, or doing anything else you make up your mind isn't good enough for me, tough. Whatever it takes, it takes. But it won't be on a man's terms. I don't need to see myself through a man's eyes to decide what I am." She tugged at the strings of her apron, folded it up meticulously, and laid it over the back of a chair. "I'll leave that for *you* to do."

She hated the look of pain on her mother's face, but it had to be said. For years, Myra had thought her a virgin, an untouchable, even when she was spreading her legs for schoolboys in a furtive bid to prove to her mother that she was a woman, too. Now, Myra's perception of her had swayed like a pendulum to the far side. Now she saw her as a whore, or well on her way to becoming one. In either case, Myra found no way to define her other than in terms of whether she had a man or not, and whether she was sleeping with one, or many, or none at all. If that was the only frame of reference that Myra knew, fine. But it wasn't hers.

Myra spoke. "Listen to me. Let me tell you something. You're young, and maybe you'll find this out for yourself. But I'll tell you anyway. This man-woman business, that's a funny thing. I let men do things for me, but that's all you see. You don't see the things I do for them. And things I give them. Pride. Hope. Love. Having a man, that's not a one-sided thing. It cuts both ways. It's not just take; it's *give* and take. I hope you learn that, because if you don't, I'll feel sorry for you." She rushed to the sink and began gulping down water straight from the tap, trying to wash away the taste of her words.

Odile didn't know how to answer. She didn't want her mother to be right. She thought about Vincent: she didn't take anything from him—not that she knew of—and she wasn't aware that he took anything from her. They were just keeping each other company. Her mother was talking rubbish.

She murmured something about having to go back to the bar and hurried from the kitchen, slamming into a man's broad chest in the doorway. She looked up to catch dark, impassive eyes on her.

"Jacob." She acknowledged him, hoping he hadn't been there long, although she had no doubt that Myra would relate the conversation to him in detail anyway.

He half-bowed, courtly as always. "Odile." The stick-fighter turned leather-man stepped aside, limping slightly. His old leg injury bothered him during the rainy season, and he usually had to rely more on the thick mahogany staff he carried in one hand. The *bois* had been his companion and weapon throughout his fighting youth. Now, for him, it was an old friend and a means of support.

Odile passed through the doorway, trying not to brush against him. She hadn't liked the man during his relentless courtship of her mother, and even though that dislike had long dissipated, and though she acknowledged that he was good for her mother, she never knew what to say around him. She'd grown up in a house without a father, with a grandfather whose illness had made him the child and her the parent. A "father" in the home was something she couldn't quite come to terms with. She had never admitted it to Myra, but Jacob's moving in had been more than a minor influence in her decision to move out.

Jacob smiled at her. "You not eating with us before you go?"

He was inviting her to stay for a meal in what used to be *her* home. She shook her head. "I . . . um . . . have to get back," she lied. It was hours before there would be anything going on in the bar for her to get back to.

He gave no indication as to how much he had heard of what she had said to her mother. His eyes flickered above her head to catch Myra's, and for a moment Odile felt a spark of jealousy as a silent conversation, the kind that only existed between two people linked by spirit, took place. Some kind of understanding passed between them, and Jacob dipped his head in acknowledgment. He reached out to lay a hand on Odile's shoulder, then seemed to think better of it and took his staff between both hands and looked down at it intently.

"We'll see you next week?" he asked, sounding hopeful.

She nodded mutely, looking from him to Myra.

"When you coming, let me know, so I can be here. We'll eat together then."

She fled the house without stopping to tell Lil' Sebastian goodbye.

The sky was darker than it had been when she went into the house, and it had nothing to do with the setting of the sun. Clouds like black lead hung low over the treetops, and the smell of impending rain was as metallic as a dull knife. The threat of rain made the inside of her skull swell, air filling her nose and pressing up against her brain. The damp had settled in her bones months ago, when the rains had begun to escalate, and now was invading her soul.

The weather was perplexing. When she was a child, she remembered dry Christmases after the rain tapered off in November, leaving the valley lush, green, and fresh. Now the world seemed to be spinning all wrong, and the sky seemed to have forgotten where one season ended and the other was supposed to begin.

As soon as she was out of the line of vision of the house, she stopped, fished her cigarettes from her bag, and lit up gratefully, sucking hard, hungry for the warmth and the calm it brought with it.

Heroes. Why did her mother think she needed one? The bar was rough, the hours long, and the pay very bad. But it was her time and her money, and if she decided one night to kick off those torturous high heels and walk away from the Smiling Dragon, she was free and able to do so. If she decided to stay, she was free to do that as well. She just didn't need a man to help her *be* anything. It was *her* life and *her* terms.

A taxi driver slowed down behind her, spotting a potential fare, and tooted the horn lightly. Odile ignored him. She had walked into the valley; she would walk back out again. If the rain came, as it seemed likely to do quite soon, well, then she'd just get wet. She flicked the cigarette butt into the gutter and lit up another.

Rory and Saul

The car sensed Rory's distress and was kind enough to take him home from the gym without trouble, which was just as well, as there was no doubt that if it had so much as balked tonight he would have abandoned it where it stopped, walked the rest of the way, and let the sanitation people take care of the problem.

The moment he drew near his house, the first irrational thought he had was that it was on fire. Light blazed from it, pouring through the open door and out through the windows on the sides. Even the outside lights were on, lights that Rory himself ritually turned on every night, last thing before retiring.

He slammed the door of the Datsun and fiddled with the lock for a few moments before running through the gateway and into the house. The blaring music inside was so loud he couldn't even hear his own footsteps on the bare wooden floor. First things first: he located the source of the racket. It was his radio, the small one he had bought just weeks ago to replace the one that had been stolen the last time the neighborhood crack-heads had paid them a visit. It was up to maximum volume, set to the noisiest station on the air. Rory put an end to the garish, crashing dub music by yanking the cord out of the wall, and then there was the silence of death in the house.

Now for Saul. He had to be around somewhere. Rory didn't have to look far; his father was sprawled out under the dining table, his bare feet, soles black with dirt, poking out from underneath. He grasped his ankles and dragged him out with a single rough tug, and as he did so, Saul's head bumped along the floor in a way he would certainly have cussed him out for, if he hadn't been passed out.

He stank from the rum that he exuded through every pore. He had on old work pants—or at least the pants he used to wear back in the days when he was still inclined to work—and a cheap sleeveless cotton undershirt.

Rory let go of his father's ankles and sat back on his haunches, looking at him, stomach curdling. The heat and anger and dread that had propelled him home had gone, leaving nothing but a chill that started in the center of him and spread outward. Saul's face was slack, skin falling back, mouth open. The once-vigorous black thicket of hair on his head was now a dull grayish mat, and there was much, much less of it.

He was a man who snored badly, ceasing to breathe for such long periods of time that Rory was often afraid that he'd just forget how and never wake up again. Then his system would receive some sort of biological jump-start, and he would take a huge, rattling breath, sparking into life like Rory's reluctant car, and the threat of suffocation would be vanquished one more time. When this happened, Rory would fall prey to another fear, one that plagued him as severely as the first did; and that was that his father would *not* cease to breathe in the middle of the night, but instead, when he woke up, Saul would still be there, like a malevolent spirit.

Rory lifted him into his arms, not exactly without effort, because Saul was still a big man; but it was getting easier every time, even though he was dead weight. His heavy limbs were becoming less dense, and the fearsome muscle had run to fat. He deposited him on the bed, trying to support him with one arm while he shoved aside the messy heap of dirty clothes, bottles, and bits of stale food. He laid him out and wrested the undershirt over his head and let it join the heap on the floor. That was about as much as he could do for him tonight.

He stood at the foot of the bed, arms folded, and stared down at his father. This was the man he had feared so much throughout his boyhood. Later, the fear had turned to contempt when he realized that his father's blows and threats were no match for his own solid strength and ability to distance himself from physical pain. Now the fear was back.

There was little that Saul could do to Rory to hurt him anymore. The blows meant nothing, and the threats meant nothing. What he feared of his father now had been placed within Rory as far back as the moment of his conception: Saul's own genes. In Saul, he saw sadness—the impotence brought on by a futile, stagnant life. He saw discontent, ugliness, violence, and decay. And it was his greatest fear that when he looked at him, he was seeing the phantom of his future self.

Goat don't make sheep. It was Nature's fundamental rule. Wasn't it true that what you were, and what you would eventually become, was planted inside you long before your birth? Was this creature splayed on the bed a foreshadowing of all that life held for him?

The rain had started up again, with the wind agitating the galvanized roofing and no doubt sending water sheeting in through the eastern windows, which his father, for reasons known only to his *babash*-soaked brain, had opened. If he didn't tear himself away from his dark thoughts and close them, he would be sleeping in a wet bed tonight. He turned.

"What happen at the gym tonight? You let the sandbag win this time?"

Rory spun around. Saul was awake, still prostrate but fully alert, eyes glittering demon black with malice and drink.

"What happen, boy? You come home because you tired hitting bags and punching air instead of fighting men? Big horse like you, and you ain't even got the guts to put on your gloves and fight . . ."

He didn't have to listen to this, not twice in one evening. Without answering, he walked out.

Saul was spoiling for a battle, and his son's reluctance to indulge him infuriated him. "Coward!" he shouted after him. "You make me shame! When you going to be a man, eh? I never raise you to be this way. I never raise you to be no pussy."

Rory realized Saul had followed him down the short corridor as far as his bedroom. He answered without facing him. "You," he told his father, "barely raised me at all." His anger turned to ice in his throat.

"What?"

"You think I'm a disappointment to you? What about *you* being a disappointment to *me?*" He shut one of the bedroom windows, struggling against the gusts of wind to tug it in and drenching his front as he did so.

"What you talking about?" Alcohol made Saul's voice loud and hoarse. "I keep a roof over you all your years and feed you every day. What more you wanted?"

"Lodging ain't all. Food ain't all. You think feeding me make you a father? Think again."

"What you wanted me to do? Hug you and kiss you, take you down to the savannah and fly kites? That don't make a boy grow into a man. You have to learn to be tough. . . ."

"I didn't want you to hug me or even touch me, and you can bet I didn't want you to play no cricket with me. But I had a mother, and you made her go away."

"I . . . ?" he pounded his chest with an incredulous fist.

"You. My mother left because she couldn't live with *you!*"

Saul waved his arms over his head. "That had nothing to do with me. She was good until she make you. . . ."

"Oh no, don't blame me. You blamed me all my life, but now, enough. She left because you hit her when the food was late and hit her when you came in drunk and hit her because you just felt like it. That's why she left. Because you can't keep your hands at your sides."

Saul was quiet, but there was no remorse on his face. A slow, sly smile crept across it, and the demon gleam deepened. "You don't do so bad yourself, *son.*" His tongue flicked out like a lizard's, wetting his lips. "The number you pull on that little girl from next door, down by the river. Remember?" He leaned in close to Rory's ear, rank with stale sweat and liquor, and whispered. "I musta taught you *something . . .*"

Rory wanted to evade him, but the windows were at his back. Short of forging his way through his father, there was nowhere for him to go. "That was once," he told him. "And that was the last time. Never again."

"You think so?"

"I know so."

"You think the next time someone push you like she push you, and get your blood hot, and you hear the spirit speak to you, and tell you to lash out, and lash out hard, you think you will be able to turn your back and walk away?"

His jaw was clenched so hard it hurt. "Yes."

Saul shrugged, slowly and elaborately. "Well, what you want me to say? We will see." He let up the pressure, backing away, and Rory could breathe once again. "But I hope you know I not the only one to leave my mark on a woman's life. You think that little girl you beat will ever be the same?"

He wasn't going to let his father do this to him. He knew Odile: she was strong and bright and a survivor. He hadn't ruined her life. He was sure she wouldn't have let him. "She was smart. She had an education. She did her A Levels and she was going to go to university. She'll do better than you or I ever will in life."

Saul snorted and left the room, his parting shot trailing behind him. "If you say so."

That wasn't an answer. He ran after him, getting there just in time for Saul to slam the bedroom door shut in his face.

"What you mean?" He hammered on the door. He'd knock it down if he had to. "What you mean by that? If you know something, tell me."

When the door opened, his father was smirking. Whatever his newest weapon was, it was too sharp to resist using. Quietly, Rory suffered the agony of waiting a little longer, just as his father wanted.

Then Saul raised his eyebrows; elaborate innocence. "You mean, you don't know your girl whoring down by some bar in town?"

The anger was gone. In its place was a hollow, a hole with nothing in it. "Liar."

Saul didn't speak.

"You *lie!*" A vein at his temple squirmed like a fat worm against his skin. He put his hand on the lintel for support.

Saul shrugged.

"Which one? Which bar?"

"I dunno."

"What you mean, you don't know?" He grabbed his father's arm and shook him. He had to get the information before the hole inside him swallowed him up. "Which one?"

"What you asking me? The whole of Independence Square full of bars, and I been in every one of them. You think I would remember?"

Truth or lie, he wasn't getting anything more from his father. But then again, there was nothing his father could tell him or keep from him that he couldn't find out for himself. He was tired, wet, and hungry, but began a frantic search for his keys.

His father watched him, keeping his silence until he found them. "Where you going?" he taunted.

"Out."

"Out where?"

"Just out."

"Looking for her?"

Saul's pleasure at the pain he was causing was sweet on his

face. Rory hesitated. "Yes," he ground out finally, and stepped out into the downpour. He was popping open the lock on the car door when his father ran out to him.

"Boy," he called.

The water was running rivers down his face. It blurred his vision until all he could see of his father was a grin. He didn't speak, but was waiting.

Saul took careful aim, and fired. "She's an expensive-looking piece. You sure you got enough money?"

The bouncer was getting irritated. He bit a matchstick in two and began to crush the sulfur-tipped half between his teeth. He used the other half to punctuate his words, pointing it an inch from Rory's unflinching face.

"Listen, Dread, it have nobody named Odile here. I don't know who you talking 'bout. But between you and me, man to man..." He bent nearer, like a conspirator. "It have plenty other skirts in here. Why not just pay your money and let me find another one for you? It ain't healthy to get hooked up on one girl, you know, especially not a young fella like you."

Close up, the man was rancid with old smoke and old beer. Rory tried not to grimace. He was tired, and each time he got dry enough, he had to go back out into the rain, to move on to the next bar. Half the night was gone. Information wasn't something that came easy in places like this, especially when you were huge like him, and young like him, and combing sailor bars looking for a girl. Not just any girl, a specific girl.

He tried again. One last-ditch effort before he slunk off into the bleakness outside. "She's about this tall," he held up his hand to shoulder height, "with long black hair, very curly, down her back. Maybe she got it in cane-row. Pretty girl." His mouth trembled with the memory of her face. "Very pretty." He was afraid to exhale again before the man spoke, in case he dispersed any magic that might possibly be in the air and working on his side.

"Soldier," the shorter man began again. The fine edge in his voice made the congenial form of address a lie, "let me explain something to you. It have nobody here by that name. . . ."

"By another name, with the same description?" he interrupted hopefully.

The man went on as if he hadn't heard him. ". . . So the way I see it, you have a choice. You could take a seat and buy yourself a drink and forget about this woman, whatever she do you. You could buy a drink for one of the fine young ladies on the premises. If you give her enough change, she will let you call her Odile all night long. Or you could start to walk. Because this is a business, and I am a businessman. I have a job to do, and that job don't include playing twenty questions with you all night. You get me?"

The bouncer stepped back and put his arms akimbo, still smiling, like somebody was yanking his lips into a curve with fishhooks on string.

Rory scratched his scalp. His throat was parched. He'd spent three hours in five bars, looking around and asking questions, but hadn't gotten around to ordering a single drink. He rarely touched alcohol—couldn't stand the smell or taste of it—but right now, his anguish and confusion were no less than they had been when he had rushed out of his house: anything wet enough to slake his thirst would be welcome.

But he shook his head, mumbled his thanks, walked back into the dismal blackness. His spirits dragged along more slowly than his feet. Maybe he should branch out a little. Try another part of town. But then again, if he was looking for a bar, this was the neighborhood to be in; there was an endless array to choose from. Independence Square was well known for its watering holes, and for the loyalty of their customers.

Even the persistent, spirit-drenching rain would not leave the bars empty tonight. The type of patron who would steadfastly ignore the reproving presence of the huge Roman Catholic Cathedral looming in the darkness nearby was the type of patron who knew he wouldn't melt in the rain. The streets in the vicinity were as crowded as they would be on any other night.

The problem was that he had no way of knowing how long his quest would last. The bars were notoriously protective of their girls; Lord knew there had been enough nasty incidents in the past involving jealous lovers, disgruntled clients, or even cops on a mission, to keep everyone on alert whenever a stranger walked into a bar asking after a specific girl. He had no way of knowing if the bouncer was telling the truth, or whether Odile was not at this very moment hidden away in some dark passage behind a wall, or upstairs, or in a cellar. . . .

His head hurt. He used to be able to sense her near him. Why couldn't he now? As a boy, he would lie in his uncomfortable bed, pressed up against the thin wall that separated Odile's home from his, and her bed from his. He used to screw his eyes up tight and think about her on the other side of the wall, lay his palm flat against it, and make believe that he was actually touching her. When the house was especially quiet, he was sure he could hear her breathe. But modesty always prevented him from actually visualizing her in the bed, or imagining what she would be wearing in bed, if anything at all. He had been too shy to allow his own mind to fill in the blanks. That would have been blasphemy. She'd been his angel: untouchable, intensely physical yet somehow ethereal.

How could his angel have fallen so far? He remembered their sweetest day down on the river, perched safe and dry upon the flat stone where they had spent so much time together. She'd shared her body with him once there, and he had approached her with an attitude of worship, humbly, bringing her flowers afterward, fresh-picked at the river's edge. It had been his first time, and in his stupidity he had presumed it to have been hers. If he'd known anything at the time about women—even now he marveled at his own ignorance—he'd have recognized her sweet plumpness for what it was: some other boy's baby in her belly.

So, the angel had been tarnished even then. Could her wings have been so severely singed by the fires of carnality that she had plunged to earth, plummeting downward in a streak of flame, to crash into a place like this? On a night like tonight? It couldn't be.

But his father had told him so, and if there was anyone with information about who was doing what in which bar, it was he. Saul had had at least one round of drinks in every bar along the wide corridor that stretched from the heart of the city all the way east to Arima. And Rory had no doubt that much of the money he faithfully handed over to his father every Friday also wound up in the red-nailed hands of many of the bar girls who . . .

The thought stopped him in his tracks. How had Saul known that Odile was a prostitute? Was this something he had observed from afar? When he discovered her, recognized her in the darkened bar, however it had happened, what had he done? Had he approached her, sent money over for her, had her sent up to some dark room where he could meet her later? He wouldn't, would he?

Would *she*? Saul was capable of anything. Rory had no doubt that his father would think, say, or do whatever took his fancy. But what about Odile? She had hated Saul as a girl, avoided him at all costs. Many a time when he and she squatted under the huge tamarind tree that dominated their yard, winded from a game of cricket, she had asked him, demanded to know, why he didn't just get up one day and start walking, find his mother, get a job, do anything to get away from the man who made his every day hell. She'd never been afraid to let Saul know she didn't like him; staring him down from across the yard with her nose wrinkled up like she could smell him from all the way over there.

Saul used to curse her, call her a skinny bitch, tell her to get her high ass back into her mother's house before he came over there and taught her that little girls weren't supposed to look big men in the eye. But Odile was stalwart; he never fazed her. The bold stare would always go on unwavering.

So she'd hated him, almost as much as Rory himself had. Did that hatred still stand, or had what she had become so changed her, inured her to trivial distinctions such as "like," "love," and "hate," that she could lay herself down with anybody if they paid her well enough?

He felt bile in his throat and he leaned over the water-clogged gutter, mouth open, waiting for the vomit to heave up from his empty stomach. It never came. His belly was clenched in a tight, vicious fist. His nostrils dilated, and his air was cut off, but the heaving spasms brought nothing more than a pungent bitterness at the back of his mouth. Water from the eaves of the storefront behind him beat into the back of his head.

When the nausea passed, he steadied himself. He wasn't able to send the churning emotions up out of his belly and into the street. They lurched in him, making it hard to breathe, bringing bright colors pounding behind his eyelids. He tried to shake his head to clear his vision.

It was a lie. Saul was a liar, proved it with every word that proceeded from his mouth. Why wouldn't he lie about this? His father would do anything to cause him pain. He was at home now, liquor wearing off, grinning to himself, smug that he had succeeded in goading his enemy-son out into the black, wet night.

Fool.

Rory reeled around a corner, heading south in the direction of the wharf. By rights, he should be heading home and having it out with that liar who lay in wait for him there, but his spirit urged him on, whispering in his ear: *One more. One more bar, just to prove him a liar. Walk into the next one you see, and five minutes later, you can walk out again, no harm done. Then you can go home, let the old man laugh at you, and go to bed.*

Shivering, throat already sore from the chill, he plodded through the puddles, tugging his huge denim jacket even closer around him, until he came to a stop at the threshold of the Smiling Dragon Restaurant, Bar, and Recreation Center. The loud music playing inside spilled out onto the sidewalk: resonant, asynchronous, thumping. He let it draw him in.

Odile

"You're tired. Go to bed."

"I haven't finished my shift yet."

Vincent nudged Odile backward against the kitchen sink, laying one hand on her waist. The moisture that dripped off the counter as the glasses drained soaked into the back of her skirt, leaving a dark, wet line there, square across her bottom. He was half playful, half serious, all insistent. "I know you haven't finished your shift yet, but I'm telling you you don't have to finish it. I'm the boss, I can do that."

She flicked him lightly across the face with a damp dishtowel, pushing up hard against him in an effort to get her bottom away from the wet counter. Vincent had a habit of pressing her into corners, trapping her as she passed on her way into or out of the bar area, or along the corridors, just because he happened to want to hold her at the time. On the surface, it was affectionate, impulsive, and Odile didn't mind being touched, even in public. But he always seemed to have the urge to hold her when she was at her busiest, as if he was loath to see her attention fully directed to anything or any person other than himself. So whenever he tried to get her in his grip like that, her first instinct was to struggle free.

"You the boss, eh? How come you only the boss when your grandmother's asleep?" She realized her mistake as soon as she had spoken. Vincent stiffened, his fine bone-china skin flushing a mottled pink, long-lashed eyes becoming slits. She didn't need to feel his heart beating under her hand to know it was racing.

"That won't last forever," he retorted. He waved his arm to encompass the dilapidated kitchen with its stained linoleum and patched plumbing. "*This* won't last forever. *This* going to change. And it's going to changer sooner than you think."

He was back again, with that talk about taking over. Every few months he grew agitated and waxed warm about his plans for the Dragon. And then he would approach Miss Ling, making each time the first time, as if he hadn't done it before and been shot down in flames. And every time she repelled him, he was inexplicably surprised, and his enthusiasm would remain dampened and his demeanor accepting, almost cowed—until the next upsurgence of fire and hope. That irritated her, and her answer was more sharp than playful. "What? You going to hold a pillow over your grandma's face in her sleep? Because that's the only way anything's going to be changing around here."

Vincent flinched, flush deepening, lips parting, breath coming out in rushed puffs. Odile watched him closely. That wasn't guilt, was it? She knew that at night when he mulled over the events of the evening, reliving every small humiliation Miss Ling had heaped upon him and his manhood during the day, he would close his eyes and wish her away, will her away, but surely . . .

"It doesn't have to be that way," he told her tightly. He didn't bother to deny or affirm. "I'm going to *talk* to her."

A cynical smile began to form on her lips, but before it was in full, bitter bloom, he grabbed at her arm. "Look, I have it figured out. The whores upstairs, they have to go. The gambling room, that too. The kitchen, we strip it out, put in new sinks, ovens, dishwashers . . ."

He had gone over that ground a dozen times with her. A dozen dozen. She didn't need to listen to it all again, at least not now. There were men outside, waiting on service, and they weren't a patient lot. She pondered the wisdom of breaking free to go outside to do her work, as opposed to letting him dream aloud one more time. Her eyes must have taken on a distant look, because his grip tightened.

"No, Odile, listen—"

"You talk and talk, Vincent . . ."

"Not this time. This isn't talk. This time, I'm going to make her see—"

"Miss Ling doesn't see anything other than what she wants to see. You can't reason with her, and the only truth is her truth." Odile shrugged off his hand and smoothed down the short skirt of her uniform. "I have to go outside. The bar's full, and I have orders outstanding. I have to go."

She felt bad about being so abrupt, and almost relented. "Later," she offered. "Tonight, when we go to bed. We can talk then."

Vincent slipped past her and blocked her path to the door. "Not later. Now."

She sighed but didn't try to evade him any further.

"Okay, Odile, you're right; she doesn't listen. Not to anybody. My father tried, and she threw him out for his trouble. But that was a long time ago, and she's older now, and maybe more willing to listen to reason. And it's my turn to make her see." His eyes glittered, shiny, sapodilla-seed black. "You'd think with all she went through in China, and all she had to face to get away and find herself here, she'd want to watch her business grow. But she's just given up. She came so far, and now she's letting it all rot. But I'm not going to let it happen." His voice quavered.

Odile understood his anguish. She knew little of Miss Ling's history, other than the fact that she had been part of a mass exodus out of China fifty years ago, after her first husband had been killed—how and by whom, Vincent had never told her. The long and winding route she had taken over three years of hiding, bartering and begging for food, lodging, and transport, crossing half the world before finding her way to such a tiny island as this, to fall into the welcoming arms of an even tinier Chinese community, was a secret she never shared. But her husband, and seven of her eleven children, had never made it to safety. So maybe one could understand her inflexibility, Odile thought. Change had brought nothing good to Miss Ling. In his burning quest for modernization, Vincent could only see the future, while Miss Ling could only see her own past. Amazing how Vincent could be so blind to this.

"Maybe she's too tired to change things now," she suggested. "Maybe she just wants things to go on as they are for the time she has left."

He was determined. "Change will come for you when it's ready, whether you like it or not," he asserted. "You can't fight it or turn your back on it. It just comes."

Odile lifted her shoulders. "Maybe, Vincent. Maybe you're right. But I have to get back to work. Like I said, we'll talk tonight, okay?" She wedged a tray laden with clean glasses against her hip, waiting for him to let her through.

He couldn't disguise the disappointment on his face. "I'd have thought you'd be more interested, Odile. I'm not just talking about change for me and for the bar. I'm talking about change for you. You want to be what you are all your life?"

"What?" She hadn't heard what she thought she'd heard.

"You want to tend bars forever? I fix this place up, you stand to benefit, too. You could do so much more, and be so much more. We got a good thing going, and if you stick with me, who knows? With my help—"

"With *your* help?" she echoed, incredulous.

He missed the warning note in her voice and went on, oblivious. "Yeah. I can teach you how to manage this place; we can work together. Think how far you could go—"

First her mother, and now him. Both insisting that what she was should be defined by a man's perception. Her grip tightened on the tray of glasses, making them rattle. This was the man who stretched out next to her at night, who woke up pressed against her in the morning and gently stroked the sleep from her eyes. Did he really know her so little?

"What I am," she said slowly, "is whatever I decide to be right now. What I become is whatever I choose. Not what you make me—"

"You misunderstand—"

"—and not what anybody else says I am, hear?" She shouldered aside the strings of beads hanging in the kitchen doorway without waiting for an answer and stepped back into the smoke and darkness on the other side. Her face was warm with the anger that had risen so fast in her breast she was afraid it would choke her. The hands that held the tray of glasses shook slightly, making them tinkle like the brass wind chimes laden with good-luck messages that hung just inside the door to Miss Ling's private quarters. In her agitated state, her heightened awareness allowed her to hear their high-pitched clinking in spite of the racket in the bar.

She shoved the tray onto the counter. Several of the glasses fell over, and Savi, the frenzied girl behind the counter, stopped what she was doing long enough to raise a razored-out, penciled-in eyebrow.

Plump, underage, and resentful of everything and everybody, Savi had run away from the southern cane-farming village of Monkey Town, where an arranged Hindu marriage to a fifty-three-year-old cane cutter awaited her. She had turned up at the bar with nothing more than the clothes that pulled taut on her round body, half a dozen hand-beaten gold bangles jangling on one arm, and the determination never to return to a town where cane ash tinted everything gray and the disused train tracks on which the cane carts once ran led nowhere anymore. In an uncharacteristic fit of compassion, Miss Ling had set her to work downstairs in the bar, rather than upstairs in the rooms.

"I was beginning to think you wasn't coming back outta there," Savi said. Her silver-painted lips were a thin line. "I woulda' thought, if you had to fool around with the boss man, you woulda' do it when you off duty, at least, so the rest of us wouldn't have to take up your slack." She took the glasses off the tray two by two and slammed them face-down onto the counter, aligning them with the few that were rapidly being depleted. If Odile had not succeeded in breaking any glasses on her angry way out of the kitchen, Savi was sure to rectify that problem.

"Nobody has to take up my slack, Savi," Odile assured her crisply, but feeling bad because she really had left her to face the thirsty hordes alone. She held out a hand. "Pass me the orders, and I'll fill them."

"Well, to begin with," Savi popped the caps off two Carib beers and sent them sliding across the countertop to a waiting customer, dripping foam as they went, "your good friend over there wants to see you. He been kicking up noise fifteen minutes now."

She was puzzled. "Who?"

"You know who. Rollock and his boys. He say he don't want no drinks from nobody but you." Savi scratched a long fingernail along the diamond *narphoor,* what the Hindus called a nose-flower, that was perched upon her left nostril. "I figure, if he willing to let his throat go dry while you busy taking man in the kitchen, well, he could feel free."

Odile rushed to her own defense, but cut herself off short. "I wasn't . . . don't bother. What did Rollock want?"

"After all this time, you don't know what he want?"

Savi had a point. Odile armed herself with a nip of white rum and a one-liter styrofoam container of ice and squeezed through the crowd to Rollock's habitual table. She was greeted with enthusiastic cries from the four men.

"Beautiful, come let me bless my eyes on you. . . ."

"But girl, you don't know better than to keep big, big men waiting?"

"Odile, but you rare like chicken teeth around here. I swear you walk off the job or something. . . ."

She couldn't hold back a smile. As annoying as they could be, as fresh as they often got with her, their liking for her was genuine, or as close to genuine as this bunch of ne'er-do-wells could muster. She removed the cover and set the nip down in the middle of the table, then poured ice into the men's glasses.

"Y'all having anything to eat tonight, or you just planning to sit here and drink?" she asked, knowing the answer already.

"We just planning to sit here and drink," Rollock informed her with a broad grin. He filled his glass, dipped his finger into it, and licked it off with an exaggerated sigh of pleasure. "Take a drink with your boy, Odile. Pull up a chair."

"They got lots of girls in here looking to take a drink with you fellas. I got people to serve."

"But we don't want the other girls. We want to take a drink with *you*." He let his hand encircle her wrist, long fingers easily holding her hand prisoner. "Come, girlie. Have a heart. It's my birthday."

Odile wasn't buying it. "It was your birthday last month, too. You getting old real fast."

"Well, have one with us for Christmas, then."

"Weeks away."

"If we start now, we could get in a lot of practice."

Laughter shook her body, and some of the tension from her encounter with Vincent oozed out of her. Rollock could be funny when he wanted to. But she had work to do, and if she took any longer at his table, she would have Savi to deal with when she got back to the counter. "Look, fellas, let me make my rounds, and I'll swing by later and take that drink with you, okay?"

Instead of releasing her, Rollock slid his other arm around her wide hips, left hand cupping her bottom possessively, gold band glinting on the fourth finger. "Oy, girl," he pleaded playfully. "Don't go yet. You don't know how you torture me. I come all the way up here from San Fernando just to see you. You know how far San'do is from here? And besides, it have plenty bars down south for a man to drink. But I take my time and drive all the way up here just to see you, and this is how you treating me, girl?" He grinned from her to the other men around him, then turned his eyes back to her. "What, you don't know how I feel about you? I love you like cooked food, child. I love you like salt!"

His companions laughed raucously, enjoying the spectacle, supporting their friend's pleadings by banging their glasses noisily on the tabletop.

Tell that to your wife, she was about to joke back, but before the words could become sound, something exploded. For a fast frantic second she looked up, sure that lightning had hit the bar, as the crack she heard was so real and so near. Rollock's table went skating into the wall, sending glasses, rum bottle, and ice smashing to the floor. The four men sat transfixed, as bewildered as she.

"Hands off." A huge man thrust himself into their midst, jacket dripping with water, one arm raised and pointed at Rollock.

Rollock gaped, and the hand that he had slid up Odile's thigh seemed fused there, so shocked was he.

Odile's head whipped around, wide eyes taking in the enraged face of the stranger who had burst in on them. Who could he be, and what could he want, taking objection to the way another patron touched her?

The face was contorted, slick with rain, so black that it was darker than the shadows behind it. White teeth gritted, gleaming in the center of the face, biting off the words. "I . . . said . . . let . . . her . . . go." He took another step closer, and something inside Odile's ribs squeezed hard, in remembered fear and pain.

The face. Young-old, soft-hard . . .

Men around them got to their feet, a chorus of chairs grating on the bar floor, curious, yet defensive of the woman in their midst.

The height. Taller now, half a head taller than the tallest man in the room . . .

Rollock finally discovered nerves in his arm, and slowly took it away from Odile's skin, fingers twitching, still shocked, but resentment and annoyance was rising there, too. He got up, lanky, much shorter than the intruder, but a man who could hold his own in a brawl. He glanced down at the overturned table, where his twenty dollars' worth of rum was now puddled on the floor, and then lifted his eyes to the stranger, sizing him up, looking for a weak spot.

The chest. Broad before, but now stretching on forever, looking as if it took up more space than it should, agitated, heaving . . .

"Rory." It hurt to say his name.

The black eyes were on her, glittering, a mixture of fear, shock, and, almost . . . wonder. "You remembered." The savage growl was replaced by a faint, almost shy whisper. The teeth glinted again, not in a menacing grimace, but halfway toward a smile.

Remembered? Did he think she would forget? The eyes that used to follow her into the yard every evening, soft and admiring, the same eyes that glowed whenever she smiled at him, looked away whenever she caught them staring, and turned to black glass when the demon that slept within him was awakened.

Rollock recovered his composure, and with it, his bravado. He sidled up next to her, bristling, ready to protect. "Odile, you know this joker?" He looked Rory up and down, contempt obliterating puzzlement.

The man-Rory who had replaced the boy-Rory that she had known turned his eyes upon hers, pleading for her to acknowledge him. But the body was tightly coiled and on guard. One huge hand clasped the other one, thick fingers circling the wrist, the effort being exerted in keeping it down showing in the bulging muscles along the arm. Odile felt the hair on her scalp prickle. That one hand, striving to raise itself, to form itself into a fist, against his instructions, and the other doing its damnedest to keep it down. She was in the presence of a mighty struggle, and she didn't dare speak.

Rory's voice became pleading. "Odile?" He waited for her to say yes.

She never had the chance to. Of one accord, the crowd drew back as another human explosion, as large as the one Rory had brought with him, threw him to the ground. He fell forward, taken by surprise, with all three hundred and twenty pounds of Patrick on his back. The other bouncer, Teeth, was dancing around to the front, poised to kick Rory in the face if he attempted to throw Patrick off and get up.

What to do? The men, her friends, were protecting her, but there hadn't been enough time to figure out what Rory wanted, or whether he meant her any harm. She clutched at Teeth's shirt sleeve, but he was so focused on the prostrate figure that he didn't even feel her.

"Teeth, Patrick, don't—"

Patrick slid one arm around Rory's neck in a half nelson, immobilizing him. The fat, normally jovial ex-wrestler, whose pervading calm usually bordered on nonchalance, was tense, rigid, and menacing. He increased the pressure on Rory's spine, just to let him know that he was serious, and said loudly, for all to hear, "Listen to me, pardner. I going to let you up now, hear? And after I let you up, you and me, we walking to the door. I don't know what you got with the lady, but whatever it is, let it go. Okay?"

Odile watched the figure on the floor. The dark head moved in a nod, and Patrick eased up on him, still cautious, allowing him to get slowly to his feet. Rory was barely halfway up off the floor when he seemed to expand, suddenly, like a sound wave, chest heaving, arms flung wide, head snapping back to collide with Patrick's mouth, sending him reeling backward. Patrick was a fighting man, yes, and a strong one, too, but he was also an easy thirty years older than Rory and hadn't seen the inside of a gym in a decade. He landed with a thud, rolls of fat slapping the hard concrete. Teeth responded too slowly, drawing back his foot to aim a kick at Rory as he rose, but with one swift hand wrapped around his ankle, Rory twisted and sent him sprawling.

Before Odile could react, Rory lunged at her, a madman, tugging at her arm. "You can't be here," he puffed, more overcome by emotion than winded from his encounter with Patrick and Teeth. "Come, Odile. Come on, let's go. This isn't the place for you."

That was it. She had been vacillating between fear of and concern for her old friend, and he had helped her to decide which emotion would dominate. Neither. She tore herself free of his grip and stuck her face close to his. "You mad?"

By now, the bouncers had recovered their balance and were standing, one on either side, poised to attack again— this time in tandem—but the fact that Odile seemed prepared to talk to him made them refrain. Rollock, too, had had enough, and was only waiting on a signal from her to join Patrick and Teeth. Three sharks surrounding an orca.

Rory stared at her, not comprehending the question. He tried again. "Odile, what you doing here? In a place like this? What happened?"

"Nothing happened," she grated. *Apart from you,* she wanted to add. "I grew up. I got a job. You got a problem with that?"

"What your Ma going to say? She know you doing this?"

"Doing what?"

He waved his arm to encompass the crowd of curious on-lookers, who were still too fascinated by the scene playing out before them to go back to their drinking. "Here." He paused painfully. "You know, with . . . men."

She put her fingers to her forehead, frustrated, but unsure whether to laugh or not. Her mother, Vincent, and this apparition from her past. One thought she was unambitious. The other two thought she was a whore. Her eyes flicked briefly around her, searching out Vincent's face in the crowd, not seeing him. He had probably gone back behind the far wall, in the gambling room, and wouldn't hear the commotion from there. In spite of herself, disappointment prickled at her. She needed him. Couldn't he sense it?

But so what? Hadn't she had enough rescue attempts for the day? Why did everyone think she needed saving? They were all on a mission to rescue her from herself, including the man trembling before her, full of righteous indignation and delusions of knighthood.

She stepped back. She didn't bother to disabuse him of the idea that she was whoring for a living. "Rory, listen. Whatever you think about me, and whatever reason you suddenly decide, after all these years, to save me from myself, forget it. I ain't no little girl no more, and you ain't no little boy. You big enough to understand, so I'm not going to repeat this. Go away. Hear? Leave me alone."

The shock took a few seconds to register in his face, eyes growing even wider, mouth distorted in a rictus of dismay. Whatever he had anticipated, however he had expected her to treat him, it had not been like this. He drew a breath, tried to speak, and then tried again. "Odile, your Ma don't want this for you—"

"I don't care what my Ma want for me!" she shouted. She turned to the gaping crowd. "Y'all don't have nothing better to look at?"

Shamefacedly, many of them dispersed, but a few bold ones still lingered, determined to see the little drama to its end.

Rory continued. "*I* don't want this for you—"

"And who the hell," she countered, cold with rage, "are you?"

"Your—" he paused and swallowed, realizing what a fool he was making of himself—"your *friend*."

She watched him, and then her eyes darted to the men at his side, who had already read from her face and her voice that she didn't wish to hold this conversation anymore. Patrick wiped his face with the back of his hand, blood trickling from his nose after the blow from Rory's head as he had freed himself from his grasp. Odile knew he wanted nothing more than to avenge himself. And she realized, with detached wonder, that she didn't care if he did.

She stepped away even further, out of his reach, but he didn't try to hold her back. "Friends, Rory? That was then. That was in St. Ann's. You and I got out of the valley a long time ago. Maybe we should both get the valley out of us."

He frowned, puzzled. Then something seemed to strike him for the first time. His gaze shifted upward to the top of her head. "Your hair. What happened to it?" He scratched his own close-cropped scalp. "It was so long. It's all gone. It was so . . ." He inhaled, sadness in his eyes, like he was looking at a ruined painting or a littered beach. "So beautiful."

"You can't go back, Rory." She turned and slipped away through the cluttered tables and upturned chairs, pausing only once to glance back. The hum of the crowd turned to a roar as the two bouncers and Rollock exacted retribution upon Rory before making him leave. They were on him, all three at once, arms raised, fists connecting. She hesitated, considering ordering them off. But Rory was a natural fighter; he could handle himself.

Then she saw something on the young man's face that shocked her. Each falling fist was met with little more than a wince, as if he had willed himself not even to know he was there within the body that was being pummeled. He didn't even raise an arm to ward off the blows, but struggled to keep his balance, fists clenched at his sides as though bound there by wires.

When the three men realized they were not even raising a defensive response from him, they redoubled their efforts, but Rory barely flinched. Irate and frustrated, they gave up on their assault and decided to remove him from their sight. With hands on his jacket, they dragged him, the huge weight of him, across the floor, through the snarl of tables, past the booing onlookers who would have much preferred to see a more spirited resistance from Rory, and out to the doorway. Teeth struggled against the wind, forcing the door open, the gap in his front teeth black and broad with amusement as they tossed the passive figure out into the rain.

The prickles on the back of Odile's neck did not subside. Something in her jangled like warning bells, bringing back visions on fast-moving film. The insanity of her and Rory down by the river all those years ago, screaming at each other, her hurling contempt at him for being stupid enough to think that just because he loved her she would love him back, came to her in a flood. He had responded to the brutality of her words with the strength of his hands, each one using the weapon they were best with. But the memory of that didn't frighten her. Seeing Rory fighting mad didn't frighten her.

Seeing him impassive, blows bouncing off a body that felt nothing because his spirit had risen up out of him and left the scene, fists twitching with the desire to respond while some other force held the coil of powerful muscle in abeyance, well, that was very, very scary indeed.

Rory and Zenobia

R ory let Zenobia feed on him once again, and when she was satiated she slumped back into her big, creaky overstuffed vinyl chair and watched him as he adjusted his clothing, struggling to catch his breath. With his release had come the familiar backwash of guilt, embarrassment, self-consciousness, and resentment. He felt the heat in his face and was glad he was too dark to blush visibly.

He let his eyes wander around the room, taking in the clutter of samples and the trappings of her business, and tried to forget how weak she made him, how defenseless he was in his need. Overhead, Christmas carols poured scratchily out of the speakers, in English this time, obnoxiously foisting joy, peace, and happiness on them both.

Zenobia folded her arms, tiny hand looping over tiny hand, the pressure of both causing her heavy breasts to be pushed up against the deep-maroon velour of her dress. A small sprig of plastic poinsettia hung slightly askew on her right bosom. Her blood-dark lipstick was smudged across her chin, and he longed to lean over and stroke it away with his thumb, but he was afraid of being rebuffed. Her dark eyes were on him, curious.

"What happened to you? Somebody rob you in the street?"

Self-consciously, his hand moved to the swollen purplish

bruise on the side of his face. He was lucky the blow hadn't landed half an inch higher, or his eye would have swollen shut, effectively preventing him from driving. Not only would that have meant a loss of income, but it would have forced him to stay home for at least a few days, and that would have been intolerable. As it was, Saul's raucous laughter when he returned home the night before, bruised and bleeding from the beating put on him by the three men in Odile's bar, was bad enough.

"Looks like I raised you to be a pussy after all," his father commented gleefully before Rory had had time to lock himself into his room. When he had left for work earlier this morning, his father was still amused. Stay home and nurse his wounds? He'd rather pass out from the pain in the street.

Zenobia was persistent. "Come on, Rory. Tell me. You owe somebody money? A loan shark beat you up?"

He shook his head. The effects of dizzying sexual exhilaration and the subsequent crash were abating, and it was time to think about leaving. When she was through, her greed for him was usually replaced by impatience to see him go. He checked that his belt was straight and looked around for his car keys.

"I . . ." he stopped, as always, unable to find something appropriate to say. In his fantasies, which were fueled more by imagination than experience, acts of the flesh were preceded and succeeded by tender whispers, lovers' words. But with Zenobia, nothing he thought he should say would sound right. "Thanks," he said finally, and inched toward the door.

"Stay."

That froze him where he stood. "What?"

She showed her uneven, sharp teeth. "Don't go. You can't go until you tell me who beat you up. I have to know. How could it happen? Big man like you! Strong man like you! Couldn't be you let just a man hit you and not do anything about it!"

He thought about Saul, and remained silent.

Zenobia pressed harder. "It had to be a whole gang, huh? With guns?"

He shook his head, staring at his boots. "No, not a whole gang. Three of them. And they didn't have no guns."

"Three men? What you do to make three men beat you so bad? You get a few blows in, too, right? You get at least one of them before they take you down, yeah?" Her eyes were glinting, eager for a story. "What you do to make three men beat you?" she asked again.

He looked into her face, reading the anticipation there. Anticipation and more. Bored working wife eager for excitement: for her, his pain should simply unfold like a screenplay, with just the right mix of sex and action. In him, she saw danger, or the potential for danger, just distant enough that she could flirt with it and return unscathed to her safe little existence. She was a vampire, as thirsty now for his dirty little secrets as she had been for his sex mere minutes ago.

Rory let his left hand trail across his chest, barely aware that he was touching the tender ribs and swollen muscle under his shirt. He took a slow, controlled breath: to inhale any faster would mean dull, muted pain, like a blow from a sledgehammer muffled by a pillow. "No, Zen."

The look on her face told him she was not used to hearing the word. The smile tautened, but did not falter. "No?"

"I don't want to talk about it. Nothing happened. Nothing you want to hear about. Okay?" It was hard enough, lying awake all night, with humiliation provoking him like a monkey. Shame. What a fool he had been, rushing in like that, trying to save a girl who didn't want to be saved. Who chose to stay in that . . . place . . . with all those men. He fought to keep the pictures from coming again to his mind, Odile and the men. He didn't want to wonder which of them she'd been with, how many others, and how much they'd paid. Didn't want to let his mind run along those tracks. Now he was being asked to talk about it? Oh, no.

Zenobia acted as though he had not denied her. Her eyes, rimmed with thick, uneven lines of black *kajal,* narrowed, shrewd and knowing. "It was a woman."

His sore ribs tightened. He closed his eyes briefly to shut out the vision of Odile turning, slowly turning, walking away just as the first blow, dealt by the fat man who had tried to hold him down, landed in his gut. The force had been enough to send a shock wave rippling through him, despite the hardness of his belly. Then the other two men had started on him. This he understood: vengeance was part of the natural law of the universe. But as the punches grew more and more vicious, propelled by their frustration at his refusal to respond in kind, all he saw was Odile, her receding back wending its way through the excited crowd. His beleaguered flesh, insensitive to pain, knew little of the attack. All he could see and feel and remember was that one moment in which Odile had stopped and turned her head.

There was something written there, separate and apart from the shock of seeing him after all this time. He couldn't identify it, wished he could, wished he understood more about what took place in the minds and hearts of women, but in this, he was without a clue. It wasn't the arrogance with which she used to stride past him when they were children, when she knew she was beautiful and that he was nothing. It wasn't the flattered tolerance with which she had met his childish words of adoration. It was horror, mixed with something ugly and nameless.

Zenobia watched the emotions flicker across his face with the fascination of someone engrossed in a staged drama. When Rory didn't answer, she spoke again. "Come on, Rory. Tell me. Tell me about this woman. Does she know about me?"

He stared at her, dragged from his musings by her ludicrous self-importance. For Zenobia, anything and everything that happened around her was *about* her. Rory almost smiled.

She waited, head tilted back, swathes of hair framing her

small face and curling under her chin, mouth open. A hummingbird no longer probing for nectar but waiting for it to be fed to her.

He gave up the battle and began to speak. Maybe it was good that he had someone who was interested in what he had to say. That didn't happen often. "I went to see a woman last night—"

"Where?" she interrupted.

"South Quay. In a bar. One of the Chinese bars, near the wharf . . ." He tailed off when her smirk broadened; then her amusement voiced itself in sharp, contemptuous laughter.

"Rory, baby. You don't know better than to go after girls on South Quay? They will only bring you trouble. Handsome boy like you, you could get a better girl from a better neighborhood. You don't know that?"

He racked his brain for a response.

Zenobia pressed him. "So, this girl. She one of them bar girls?"

He nodded.

"Stripper?"

His chest hurt. "I don't know."

"But she takes money from men, yeah?"

"Yes." He tried to look away but was a prisoner of her glittering eyes. He tried not to give way to the same speculation that had tormented him all night: whether his father had been one of those men. His Adam's apple was physically lodged in his throat, and he was almost afraid it would cut off his air for good.

"You pay her, too? To let you do things to her?"

Rory jerked backward, hands up before him in denial. "No! No, never." To contemplate such a thing was desecration of a sacred place inside him, that place where he cherished the memory of their day by the river, stretched out on that big rock. . . .

Zenobia sighed and rolled her eyes, calling down patience

from the heavens, as one did with a particularly trying child. "So what you doing with this little *jammette,* then, boy?"

"I knew her. Growing up. And I heard she was in that place. So I went."

"You went to rescue her? Take her away from all that?" Put into her words, his intentions sounded banal, silly.

"And she didn't let you show her the error of her ways?"

"So it seems," he answered dryly.

Zenobia got to her feet and stepped nearer, closing the distance he had tried to put between them. She nudged his chin gently with two fingers—reaching up to do so, for she was over a foot and a half shorter than he, and peered at his bruises in fascination. "And her pimps beat you up?"

His broad shoulders rose and fell. "Pimps, bouncers, boyfriends, I don't know."

"And you didn't try to defend yourself?"

"No."

She looked disappointed, as if something in her needed him to have made a heroic stand, and he had failed her.

Rory put his hand on her arm—a bold move for him, since she never let him touch her other than the times when she guided him to her breast with her own hand. He didn't care. There was something he needed to know, and she was the only person honest enough to answer. "Zen?"

"Hmmm?" Her eyeliner drew her eyes into cat's eyes, both knowing and searching.

"You think I'm a fool?"

Her amused look returned. "A fool? For what? For running to a little black hole on South Quay and trying to save some little damned soul that doesn't want to be saved?"

"You don't think she wants me to? Deep inside?"

A pointed glance from her was all it took to make him release his grip. She stepped back, widening the space again, and sending the temperature in the room plummeting. She sighed, fidgeted, and glanced at the clock on the wall.

He knew the signal well. Zenobia's attention span could not be captured for very long, and it had reached its outer limit. *Not yet!* He wanted to shout at her, and drag her near again. He had so many questions. He persisted, desperately. "If it was you, you'd want me to come and get you out of there. Right?"

Her chin lifted, lips taking on their habitual self-indulgent pout. "Rory, you don't have other stops to make today?"

Then it occurred to him that she was not impatient, but angry. She liked the focus to be on her, enjoyed the fact that she was his only source of sexual release. She liked the power it gave her. To see him enthralled enough by a woman to take a beating for her, well, that didn't sit too nicely. But he persisted. He needed to talk. He had to get an answer. "Zen, please!"

Zenobia returned to her desk and sat, soft fat rippling under her blouse. Her fingers drummed on the desktop.

He had to know. He asked again. "You think I'm a fool? For wanting to get her out?"

"I think . . ." She paused, making him wait, enjoying his desperation. ". . . that you better put something on that bruise. I have samples here . . ." She tilted her head down, cutting off his gaze, and rummaged about in a drawer.

"Zen . . ."

She held out a small green-and-white tube of ointment, her face schooled into a look of fraudulent concern. "Three times a day," she told him. "It's on the label. It won't stain your clothes."

His glance shifted from the proffered tube in her hand to her face, but he made no move to take her gift. There'd be no getting answers from her today. He'd satisfied her curiosity, and now he was dismissed. Murmuring something that he himself couldn't hear, he made to go.

"Rory?" She called after him, softly.

He stopped, half hopeful, but his understanding and acceptance of the way his life worked—that nothing he needed or wanted ever came to pass—told him that there was no profit in turning around to face her again. "Yes?"

"You'll be back again, yeah?"

He didn't even need to think about it. "Yes." He closed the door with a soft click.

Zenobia

Girls fed, homework done, bedtime for both of them, and still no sign of her husband. That didn't surprise her. His "meetings" came more and more regularly, and ended later and later. Some of them real, certainly, but most of them just drinks with other men like him who had wives they didn't feel like going home to, either. Sometimes she could swear he just drove around and around, from one end of the highway to the next and back again, or in and out of side streets, taking the long and winding way home, all to delay the inevitable moment when he pulled into the garage and locked up the car and came inside and discovered that once again he had nothing to say to her. Why not? She did the same herself. It was so humiliating, being avoided for no reason other than lack of conversation. Another woman would have been better.

So after the girls had eaten and she had played with her food, she sat in the drawing room on the huge white leather couch, the one the children weren't allowed to touch, and waited for the sound of the car. And still, although hours and hours had passed, she couldn't stop thinking about Rory.

Face cut up for no reason. For a bar girl. And he didn't even put up a fight. Men were such fools; they let women make them soft. Gallantry was just stupidity spelled another way. And him asking her questions about the girl. Asking *her* for advice. Could you believe it? After what she'd done for him just moments before?

She needed a drink but was too lazy to get up and make one. Maybe she should just cut to the chase and pop a Valium. Maybe a drink *and* a Valium. That ought to do it.

That stupid, stupid, beautiful boy. When was the last time anyone wanted to save her from anything? When was the last time anyone took a punch for her? Bedassie certainly wouldn't. In Rory's place he'd just tell her to clean herself up and stop embarrassing him. That made her laugh. Which would her husband hate more? Finding her in a bar like Rory did this woman, or finding out about what went on in her office once a week? Either way, it would be worth all the trouble that came after, just to see his face.

The old people had a saying: the moon ran till daylight caught up with it. But she was smarter than that. She wasn't about to get caught. Not by Bedassie—he was too complacent to put two and two together. Not by her own lapses in control. If she could find herself sitting at home late at night, mooning about over a teenager who meant nothing to her— who *should* mean nothing to her—then it was time for him to go. She was a grown woman. He was still half a heartbeat out of childhood. He was a toy. He was a game. And now the game was over.

Well, soon.

Odile and Vincent and Miss Ling

"I don't belong, Vincent," Odile protested, but she kept on getting dressed all the same. She chose one of her more demure dresses: plain, A-line, in pale lemon. It fell modestly to the knee and didn't hug her too tightly at any given point. It was the kind of dress she usually wore when she went to visit her mother. She couldn't fathom why she was bothering to act the ingenue, not while she was on her way to have Sunday lunch with Miss Ling, because it was on Miss Ling's insistence that she spent her nights in high heels, miniskirts, and white blouses tight enough to leave red wheals encircling her torso each time she removed them. But she was going—unwillingly,—not in her capacity as a waitress at the Smiling Dragon, but as the girlfriend of the matriarch's grandson; and as such, the normal gestures of respect seemed to be the only obvious option.

The idea of penetrating Miss Ling's inner sanctum, of venturing behind the heavy gold brocade curtains that obscured the door at the far side of the kitchen and entering a realm rumored to be breathtakingly opulent and worth more than the rest of the establishment as a whole, was intimidating. But all she had to go on were rumors. No member of staff had ever been invited into Miss Ling's private space, with the exception of an elderly domestic who came and left at precisely the same time every day, never having taken a day off in over ten years, and who never so much as acknowledged the existence of the other employees. This determination on Miss Ling's part to ensure that her privacy remained inviolate was the source of Odile's concern.

"Don't be silly," Vincent said dismissively. "What you mean you don't belong? You belong because you're my woman. I'm her grandson, and I'm going to visit. On *her* invitation."

"She invited *you* to lunch," she protested, "not me."

He shrugged. "So you'll be my guest. It's time she acknowledged that you're more than a waitress around here. Forget about the Dragon—"

"Forget? How you want me to forget? I'm on shift here tonight." She turned her back to let him tug her zipper closed. When he was done, he pressed against her, hands coming around to slide under her breasts, pulling her to him. He was as tall as she, and with his chest against her back and his hips against her bottom, they fit together like a matched set. His proximity soothed her concern somewhat, but she persisted. "How you want me to forget she's my boss? You think I don't know she doesn't like the idea of you and me? Don't tell me she doesn't think you can do better. Find some nice little Chinese girl, import one if you have to . . ."

"What *I* want is what counts," he asserted, releasing her. He leaned against the chest of drawers in their cramped room, folding his arms and watching her finish dressing.

Odile didn't disagree with him, at least not out loud. Maybe he knew a side of his grandmother that she wasn't privy to, a kind one that recognized family as being separate from business. But her spirit remained heavy. This was no ordinary visit; Vincent was going to approach his grandmother once again to pitch his proposed improvements to the Dragon, and Odile wasn't optimistic about the outcome. She wasn't sure how her presence at the intimate family discussion would help. Vincent insisted that he needed her close, so that he could draw on her strength, but she had a sneaking suspicion that he believed the presence of a woman would help calm his grandmother and show her that he was serious about his personal life, that he could be stable and reliable. Odile couldn't shake the feeling that she was the last person Miss Ling wanted her grandson to be serious about.

She gave her lips a reluctant swipe with the only lipstick she possessed; for her, cosmetics were something that other women wore. They cost money and were a waste of time. Nothing irritated her more than walking into a bathroom to see women jostling at the mirror for space to retouch their makeup. What was the point of putting on something that wore right off? A freshly scrubbed face and clean hair were her only concession to beauty care; in that she was like her mother.

On the other hand, she loved perfumes. She was about to spray herself lightly with a tiny crystal bottle that Vincent had given her when he held up a cautioning hand.

"Not too much, now, remember my grandmother—"

"Doesn't like to be around anyone smelling better than she does," Odile finished dryly, and let the bottle clank back onto the dresser without using it.

He looked reproachful. "Don't be like that. She's an old lady and she likes her perfumes."

"I'm not being like anything," she retorted. She contemplated taking her handbag, to add to the image of propriety, but that would have been a little ludicrous since she was only going as far as the floor below. "Let's go."

Wisely, he didn't push it any further and followed her out of the room, past the maze of little bedrooms used by Miss Ling's bar girls for the purpose of their business. Half the rooms were actually full on this, the third Sunday of Advent, when decent people should be streaming out of church with this morning's lesson still in their hearts. As she always did, she pretended she could not hear the chorus of grunts and high-pitched stage moans emanating from the wafer-thin walls.

She was grateful that he held her hand as they went down the stairs.

Even on a Sunday, in broad daylight, the bar was open and doing good business. Odile scanned the crowd, as she had these past few days, searching for the faces of any customers who might have witnessed her embarrassment on the night that Rory had stormed in. It was bad enough that the story of his appearance—and eventual dispatch by Patrick and the other two men—had reached Vincent in the back room within a matter of minutes, setting off an avalanche of questions that she still couldn't bring herself to answer; but the curious stares of the witnesses were hard to take. Speculation flew fast and furious around the bar that the mysterious man who had stormed in out of the rain had been a wronged lover, a younger brother who disapproved of her career choice, a man to whom she owed money, or a disgruntled pimp. The fact that she hadn't intervened to stop the beating fueled the gossip like an exploding pitch-oil tank over a lit stove.

The eyes of the curious only exacerbated her own confusion. What in the name of God could have sent Rory charging in here, after not having seen her or sought her out in four years? However he had found her, whoever had told him she was there, he somehow seemed to think she was one of the prostitutes. Although she hadn't attempted to disabuse him of his mistake, the implied accusation stung.

Not as much as his presumption had, though. Her lips twisted with the memory. The boy—well, not a boy anymore, but obviously still as stupid—had come roaring in like a bull, full of horror and indignation, ready to rescue her. *Rescue her,* as though she didn't have a mind of her own with which to make her own choices, or feet of her own on which to walk away. The little boy who had adored her when they were children had become convinced that she'd fallen like a star from the heavens, and was determined to pick her up and reinstate her in his own private constellation so that all would be well with his world.

She thought of Jacob, her mother's lover, with his old-time morality and chivalry, and how much her mother had given in to his own brand of rescue, and shook her head. She and her mother were a generation apart; what worked for Myra would not work for her. Any man who decided on her behalf that he knew what was in her best interest deserved her contempt.

"Odile?" Vincent sounded concerned.

"What?"

"I asked you a question." They were standing near the bar, and she hadn't even realized she had made it down the stairs and into the main room.

She shook her head to clear it. "Sorry. I was, um . . ."

The pale, curved scar above his lip flattened, becoming even whiter as his jaw tensed. His heavy-lidded eyes were on her, shrewd, piercing, and the glossy black brows tugged closer together in the middle. She'd slipped away mentally once or twice since the beating incident with Rory, and each time he witnessed it he had demanded that she share her thoughts with him. Each time she had refused. Remorsefully she tried to focus on him. "What'd you ask me?"

He was intuitive enough to know that her reveries were about the stranger who had burst into the bar, but nothing he said could induce her to speak about it. "Nothing. It isn't important." He waved it away.

She slid her hand around his neck, feeling the silk of his neat black ponytail against the backs of her fingers. "No, tell me."

Vincent sighed heavily. She could feel the expelled breath on her face. "I wish . . ." he looked uncertain as to whether he should continue, and Odile chose wisely not to speak until he went on. "I wish you told me things. Shared things with me. So many things go on inside of you, and you never let me see. You let me inside your body, but you never let me into your mind. You leave me outside, like an uninvited guest in the rain. Staring up at the curtains in the window and wondering."

He was interrupted by a snort of disgust and a muttered curse in Hindi. Both Odile and Vincent spun quickly around, unaware that they had an audience. Short, plump, young Savi was on duty behind the bar, unironed apron hanging untidily off her blockish body. With the characteristic cynicism and bitterness of her age group, she was unshakable in her conviction that Odile's relationship with Vincent won her special favors on the job. She resisted no opportunity to needle Odile about her perceived employment strategy: personal advancement by pussy.

"Y'all have a good lunch," Savi smirked. Her mouth was painted an ugly magenta and lined with the same black pencil that turned her eyebrows into thick, solid lines on her forehead. She took up a heavy plastic bag of party ice in her square hands and threw it against the floor to break up the cubes that had stuck together.

It seemed to Odile that she slammed it down with unnecessary relish. She stepped away from Vincent and put her hands on her hips. "Savi, you have a problem?"

Savi wouldn't meet her eye but concentrated on tearing open the ice bag and pouring the shattered contents into a grimy Styrofoam cooler. "Who, me? No. I ain't got no problem. I'm just the one that always got to work on a Sunday, that's all."

"I'm working today, too," Odile bristled. She vowed over and over not to let the sullen teenager get to her, and almost every day she failed. "I just have the morning off."

"Yeah, you got the morning off." Savi turned her back on them both, inexplicably interested in jabbing at the narrow floor area behind the counter with a broom. "How you manage to get the morning off, that's the question. If I did what you did, I'da been spending Sunday mornings having lunch with the boss-lady, too. But my mother never teach me to get around on my back. . . ."

Odile was about to dart around the counter to confront her face to face when Vincent's hand closed around her upper arm, holding her at bay.

"Savi, that's enough." His usually soft voice was loud and hard in anger. "I don't want to hear any more of this from you, understand? Odile's business is not your business. If I so much as hear you say anything more . . ."

"What?" Savi gave up all pretense of attending to the mucky floor and threw the broom down with a jerk of her arm. "What you going to do, Vincent?" The *narphoor* twitched on her left nostril.

"Don't forget: I'm the manager here. Watch your mouth with me, little girl, or you will find yourself out of here and back on the road to Monkey Town where you came from."

"You?" She was pushing her luck now, and she knew it. Savi sidled sideways out of Vincent's reach like a cornered crab, gnawing lipstick off her lower lip, wary eyes on him, but still willing to put up a fight. "You planning to send me away? What make you think you can? Your grandma like me, and if she say I stay, I stay. You think you the manager here? For truth? Let me tell you, boy. Let me tell you something all of us in here know, including your girlfriend." She threw a malicious glance past him at Odile. "You only the manager here when your grandmother not in the room. You not a boss, you a decoy. You only here to satisfy the customers who don't feel like taking instructions from no old woman. That's all you worth. And if you wasn't here . . ." she paused for effect, enjoying the sight of the blood draining from Vincent's already pale face. The few early-bird customers scattered around the bar perked up, all eyes on the trio.

"If you wasn't here," Savi went on, "it would take your

grandmother just two, three days to hire another *casa* to hold the money in the back room, and that would be good enough for her. You think the blood between the two of you so thick? You just as easily replaceable as me. That damn bird she got inside there got more authority than you."

Now it was Odile's turn to restrain *him*. She tugged at his arm, feeling the biceps rise under her fingers as his body tensed. "Vincent, come," she whispered desperately as Savi struck again and again at his Achilles' heel. Vincent took his role as *casa*, chief of the gambling den, very seriously. He prided himself on his judgement calls and on his ability to control the fractious punters who frequented the establishment. The self-same customers nearby watched intently, waiting for him to reassert his manhood.

Odile forced him to tear his eyes away from Savi's sneering face. "That's a lie, Vincent. You know it. Everybody recognizes your authority here. She's just trying to needle you. Come. Let's go on. Miss Ling's waiting on us."

Vincent turned his face, still handsome in spite of the emotion that mottled it, from Savi, who was gloating like a toad in her corner, to Odile, whose eyes were filled with worry. He inhaled sharply and loudly through his nose, then glanced around at the expectant faces at the tables on the far side of the counter, and a flood of hot blood sweeping up under his skin overwhelmed the chalky pallor of his face. He seemed to be thinking furiously, torn between keeping the peace by retaining control of his temper, and avenging his public embarrassment. He let Odile grasp his fingers in hers, and finally, swallowing hard, he turned to accompany her into the kitchen.

Savi wasn't about to give up that easily. She was enjoying the attention of the patrons, glad for the rare opportunity to showboat before them. "And you, Miss Thing, you think you better than them girls upstairs? Think again. They just take their cash up front."

The beaded curtains that separated the kitchen from the

bar area closed behind them, and although it was not thick enough to shut out the chorus of murmurs that rose up behind them, punctuated by Savi's high-pitched, nasal laughter, it offered them both a semblance of sanctuary.

Once there, each sought anxiously to comfort the other. "What she said about you isn't true," they said at the same time, and half smiled, partly because they had spoken simultaneously and partly because neither fully believed the other.

Vincent shrugged and wiped his moustache with the back of his hand, a gesture that always betrayed his nervousness. They were standing at the curtains that shrouded the door to Miss Ling's quarters. The curtains looked ancient, threadbare in places, and were covered with a film of dust that told Odile they hadn't been taken down and laundered since the day they were originally hung there. The generous gold workings had faded to a dullish green, and the original cream background was a grimy brown. Wind chimes hung soundlessly in front of them.

"Let's just try to forget . . ." he began.

"Okay."

Vincent drew aside one curtain and rapped on the door. They waited quietly, each eyeing the other for signs of distress. Odile hoped desperately that Savi's attack hadn't undermined Vincent's confidence to the point that he was unable to plead his case to his grandmother.

Long moments passed, and Vincent knocked again, louder this time. Before he could finish, the door flew open, and Miss Ling was there. Instinctively Odile stepped back a little, obscuring herself behind Vincent. She wasn't sure she could go through with this; whenever the old lady was around, Odile found it hard to breathe normally. Savi's words echoed in her head. Did Miss Ling see her as her grandson's private whore, too?

"*Apo.*" Vincent addressed her respectfully in Cantonese and bowed deeply. "Grandmama."

"Tak-Wing." Miss Ling greeted her grandson using his Chinese name. She inclined her head, murmured something indistinguishable, and then stepped back to allow them in.

"Good morning, Miss Ling," Odile said softly, unsure as to whether she should bow as well, but certain that it would be silly to do so, because in all her time at the Smiling Dragon, she never had. "Thank you for inviting me," she added politely, although she knew very well that the invitation had actually been Vincent's. She wished she had brought flowers.

Miss Ling watched her thoughtfully for a few seconds, tiny, rheumy eyes almost obscured by the wrinkled folds of skin around them. Her face betrayed no sign of pleasure or disdain at Odile's presence here; in fact, she seemed not to care one way or the other.

She was dressed in worn black silk pajamas embroidered with bright red, gold, and green birds, whose impossibly long tails curved down the front and around to the back. It was held together with six or eight gold handmade buttons shaped like joints of bamboo, which Odile knew from past observation were detachable and which Miss Ling would transfer from outfit to outfit as it pleased her. Her small, callused feet, which by some miracle had escaped the torture of binding in her youth, were thrust into black embroidered slippers. She smelled heavily of her favorite toilet water: oleander and lavender.

Miss Ling let them follow her deeper into the sitting room and motioned for them to sit on the lone couch at the far end of it. The springs squeaked as they sat. Without another word, she walked through the open doorway into the mysterious recesses beyond, leaving them alone. In the doorway her peacock stood, head tilted to one side, glaring at them with one eye, feathers bristling with resentment at their having penetrated its private space. Odile glared back but then looked away, sighing. It wasn't worth it. She had never won a staring contest with the wretch.

"You okay?" Vincent asked her, squeezing her elbow comfortingly.

She nodded wordlessly. Savi's obnoxious behavior and her disquiet at having to be sociable with her difficult employer began to recede in her mind. Now that she had breached the frontier, her anxiety was replaced by intrigue. She had always been curious about the treasures hidden behind the door in the kitchen, and now she was here. Odile let her eyes explore the room.

It was larger than one would have thought from the outside, and somehow managed to be sparse yet cluttered at the same time. Apart from the couch on which they sat, there was one old brown armchair, its stuffing poking out through cracks in the arms and back, and a short, narrow coffee table with a small television and a number of brass ashtrays filled with pipe ash. A well-used clay pipe lay on its side next to a box of matches. A flat brass plate held tiny cones of incense, which Odile guessed Miss Ling used to cover up the smell when she smoked.

Stacks of dusty Chinese newspapers, tied up in bundles with coarse packing twine, covered most of the available space on the floor. A rectangular almanac hung on a wall. Printed on cheap paper, it pictured a smiling, moon-faced Oriental chocolate-box beauty holding a bunch of plastic flowers lovingly against her cheek. Her skin was liberally whitened with powder, and her cheeks were circles of cherry-blossom pink. The calendar was the kind generously given away by businesses in Port of Spain at Christmastime and was boldly printed with the name "LEUNG TANG'S DRIED GOODS LIMITED," and under it, "STEPHEN R. LEUNG TANG, PROPRIETOR. SUPPLIERS OF GENERAL MERCHANDISE AND IMPORTED DRIED GOODS." It was two years out of date.

Because of its location in the center of the building, the room had no windows. It was cooled by a lopsided electric fan in one corner, which had all but lost the power of oscillation: while it turned smoothly to the left, its arc to the right was halted by the loud grinding of metal gears. As a result of the lack of fresh air, the entire room had a musty odor that rose from the floor and hung there heavily.

A narrow wooden mantel ran around all four walls of the room, interrupted only by the door leading outside and the one that separated them from the rest of Miss Ling's quarters. It was lined with a variety of oddments: matchboxes, mayonnaise jars with rusted tops, candles, cheap porcelain ornaments, plastic cups filled with pens and pencils, three clocks that each carried a different time (none of which was correct), piles of razor blades in and out of their little paper envelopes, numerous balls of string, heaps of rubber bands melting and gumming together in the heat, aspirin, arthritis balm, and soft drink bottles filled with dark liquid. Odile recognized a few of the bottles as being herbal medicines Miss Ling used from time to time to treat the prostitutes experiencing minor female ailments and sexual complaints. Everything, everywhere, was covered with a light film of dust.

Every inch of wall space was covered with small, ugly paintings on glass. There were pastoral scenes, animals, flowers and plants, and a few of people: some working in the fields, building, reaping, or tending to animals; others in long and elegant elaborate robes. All were depicted in garish colors that clashed in a wild assault on the eyes. They didn't look valuable. Odile furrowed her brow.

Vincent's eyes were on her, amused. "Looking for the art stash she's supposed to have in here?"

She flushed, abashed.

"Ah, now you see how rumors can fly out of hand."

"There isn't any?"

He shook his head wryly. "Just what you see. The only treasure she owns is the Dragon itself, and even then, she doesn't seem to know how much it could be worth, if only . . ." He sighed as if his heart hurt.

"And the dust? What happened to the cleaning lady who comes here every day?"

"Chloris. She's half crippled from arthritis and should have retired ten years ago. I suspect my grandmother keeps her on for the company. Lord knows it's not for the cleaning. I think they sit around here all day and sip tea and watch the soaps."

Strange to think of the prickly old lady holed up in here with her servant, who was almost as old as she, sitting together on this lumpy, uncomfortable furniture, keeping each other company. Odile was ashamed to say it, but it had never occurred to her that Miss Ling needed any company other than her ill-tempered peacock.

She let her eyes keep roaming, still fascinated by the darkened room. Against the wall opposite them was a wooden curio cabinet crammed with brass and wooden boxes, small jade statuettes, little china dinner bells painted with flowers, a blue-and-white porcelain tea-service, rows of dusty drinking glasses that probably never got used, colored bottles holding mysterious liquids, and crumbling photo albums. On the top of the cabinet was an altar of sorts, with multicolored candles made rough by the wax drippings that hardened on their outsides, and sticks of incense that, even unlit, still managed to infuse the stale air with the smell of anise and sandalwood.

"Come." Vincent stood and held out his hand.

She didn't take it, but he didn't seem offended. She walked with him over to the cabinet, dying for a closer look, curious in spite of herself.

"These," he pointed to faded black-and-white photos at the center of the altar, "are my ancestors. This is my grandfather, Minh-Wei." It was a head-and-shoulders shot of a

Chinese man in a Western suit and tie, smiling broadly at the camera, short black hair slicked damply back from his forehead. The photo showed water damage, and had been burned in one corner. The ancient technology had not prevented it from fading, and now the handsome young face, startlingly like Vincent's, hovered between dimensions like a ghost's.

"He was killed in World War Two, by the Japanese, before my grandmother could make it out of China."

"Japanese?" Odile was surprised. "In China?"

Vincent stared at her for a while, making her cringe at her own ignorance of world history. "The Japanese massacred huge numbers of Chinese during the war," he explained. "That's why so many of us fled to the West."

He indicated another photograph showing a tiny, beautiful woman holding a baby and flanked by a number of children whose ages ranged from about three to their late teens. "That's my *apo*, my grandmother," he told her, "with some of my aunts and uncles. The baby in her arms," he touched the photograph lightly, "is my father."

He gently took the photo up and held it in both hands. "These two, the two youngest after my father, starved to death in camps. My father survived only because he was still on the breast. This little one, her name was Faye-Kam, she was eight at the time. . . ." Vincent bit his lip. "She was beheaded by the Japanese for stealing rice cakes and fruit to feed the little ones. The day she was killed was the day my grandmother made up her mind to escape, no matter what it took. She made it out via Hong Kong a year later. And these four," he counted them off slowly, "died on the way here. Typhus and cholera. My grandmother was smuggled into Trinidad by boat, after hiding and running for three years, with only four children left."

Odile only knew snippets of the story, but now, to hear even these few words about such brutality, and to see the photographs of the ones who had lived it, made it seem all the more real. She thought of Miss Ling and her perpetual coldness and cruelty. Did knowing what made a person the way they were make it any easier for you to forgive them?

Vincent went on, showing her different people in turn. "The color photographs are all of my aunts and uncles grown up, my father and mother, my cousins. That's my mother and me. I was three."

"In the sailor suit?" She smiled her first genuinely amused smile for the day.

He looked embarrassed. "Yeah, my mother's choice, not my own . . ." A noise behind them made them both spin around.

Miss Ling was standing there, with her peacock at her side, hands folded in front of her. Odile felt inexplicably guilty, as if she had been caught snooping. She felt Vincent's hand touch the small of her back lightly, and was grateful for his reassurance.

"Tak-Wing, Odile, come and eat," Miss Ling said. "Everything is on the table waiting for you." The thick Chinese accent and mutilated caricature of English she used every day was nowhere in evidence.

Odile's eyes widened, half in surprise, half in triumph. Her speculation was correct: Miss Ling's clumsiness with the language and fumbling to express herself outside in the bar *was* an act, the better to lull her competitors into mistaking her lack of eloquence for stupidity. It was a strategy that had probably ensured her survival during those many hard years, when it would have been disastrous for a woman to seem too intelligent or too self-sufficient, especially in the man's world in which she chose to make a living. For the second time in a few minutes, Odile smiled, a new admiration for this complex woman forming in her.

A large, heavy wooden table dominated the next room. It looked surprisingly valuable, well made, and sturdy, its wood darkened by age and repeated polishings. It was covered with a length of clear plastic, upon which were a number of serving dishes and settings for three.

They washed their hands at a small porcelain washbasin in the same room, with a sliver of well-used green soap that perched upon the hard-caked remnants of all the soap bars that had passed before it. Odile sat where Miss Ling pointed, almost tripping over the peacock as she did so. The bird seemed anxious to get the meal started, and strode along the perimeter of the table, letting its body brush against the table legs like a cat.

Odile folded her arms in her lap, waiting. She was unsure of what to do. Would she be expected to eat with chopsticks? What if she couldn't figure out how? Suppose she dropped food on the floor? Her nervousness returned.

But there was heavy cutlery neatly wrapped in paper napkins next to each glass, and the meal proceeded as it would in any Creole household. Miss Ling began filling their plates with sweet-scented clumps of sticky jasmine rice, steamed vegetables that retained their intense color, and large portions of what looked like boiled duck. She brushed away Vincent's protestations that the food was far too much for them.

"Eat, *Di-di*," she shushed him, and then made matters worse by adding a heap of strong-scented brown meat to each of their plates. "You're getting too thin."

"I'm not getting thin, Grandmama!" Vincent protested, but didn't force the point any further. He surveyed the mountains of food on his plate with the determination of a marathoner at the starting line.

They began to eat. Odile eyed the mysterious brown meat with caution. Duck she could identify, but what was that?

"It's called *moi huang*," Miss Ling told her helpfully. She was already making inroads into her own meal. For a woman of her age, she had quite a hearty appetite. "Ground pork, with rotten fish."

"Why do they call it that?" Odile asked faintly. The pungent smell of the dish began to take on a familiarity she wasn't sure was exactly pleasant.

"Because that's what it is. Rotten fish." Miss Ling looked almost amused.

Odile knew she blanched.

"She's just teasing," Vincent covered her hand with his, tilting his head toward her and smiling. "It's not exactly rotten. It's just hung up and dried for a long time. My grandmother dries it herself, in her own kitchen. Don't worry, it's delicious."

She decided to take his word for it and discreetly concentrated on the duck. She was only a few bites into her lunch when, with a noise like a braying jackass, and with a flutter of wings, the peacock was on the table. The bird strode confidently across, its long, drooping tail dragging in the dishes in the center, before stopping at her plate to peck leisurely at her rice.

Miss Ling's face was expressionless, as if this were an everyday occurrence. She made no move to stop it. For several seconds, the peacock rooted around in Odile's plate with its beak, until Vincent stopped it with a clap of the hands. Slowly, it tilted its head and glared at Vincent for having interrupted it, then continued nonchalantly on its way to the other end, seeking refuge in its mistress. Cooing softly in her own language, Miss Ling fed it pieces of meat with her small fingers.

Odile fixed her gaze on her meal, deciding that her best recourse would be to pretend that she was eating rather than offend her hostess by shoving her plate away, although that was what she wanted to do more than anything. She drew trails in her food with her fork, glad that Miss Ling was too absorbed with her pet to notice that she had stopped eating.

Satisfied, the bird hopped off the table, and with a final peeved glance at Vincent, settled on a chair and fell into a snooze. It was only then that Vincent and Miss Ling began to chat.

Hungry, but unable to bring herself to eat, Odile tried to divert her attention from her growling belly by listening to but not participating in the general conversation. She marveled at the gentleness and affection the two showed each other, and at her own new awareness of Miss Ling's hidden humanity. There was a lull, and when Vincent cleared his throat and took a deep draught of water, Odile stiffened.

"Grandmama," Vincent began, almost hesitantly.

"Yes?" Miss Ling sighed heavily. She, too, knew what was coming, and didn't seem happy about it. She stood and began clearing away the serving dishes. Vincent tried to stop her. "Please, I'll do it for you later. Just sit and listen to me."

Miss Ling ignored him, loading up her arms with dirty dishes and disappearing through the door. "I can hear you from here, you know."

Vincent bit his lip and shook his head, waiting for her to reappear. She made two more trips, the first to remove their plates, including Odile's uneaten *moi huang* and rice, and the second to set down a teapot from which curled the most delightful sweet smell. Jasmine, Odile was sure.

When she was seated again, Vincent spoke. "Did you read the papers I gave you?"

Miss Ling held her grandson's eyes steadily with hers. "Yes, I did."

"And?"

"And what, Vincent?" She took a long sip of her tea. Once again, Odile witnessed a transformation. The almost pleasant, astonishingly normal old lady who had replaced the blustering caricature was in turn being forced into the background by a cool, astute businesswoman. The dining table, plastic tablecloth and all, might just as well have been a boardroom table, and Vincent a nervous consultant presenting his idea.

Vincent tried not to let his exasperation show. "And what do you think of what I wrote? My plans for the Dragon? My plans to change out the kitchens, and strip out all that old wallpaper—"

"There's nothing wrong with the wallpaper," Miss Ling interrupted. "There's nothing wrong with the kitchens. What do we need dishwashers for when we can pay someone to wash the dishes? What do we need a new kitchen for when our customers don't come here to eat?"

"There *is* something wrong with a lot of things in here!" Vincent protested. "And if we changed out the kitchens, and served better food in here maybe people *would* come here to eat!"

"Why, Vincent? This place is always full. The rooms upstairs are always full. Why you want to change that?"

"Because we can get a better kind of client if we had a better place. You know how I feel about the girls. You know how I feel about the back room. If we fixed things up and got a gambling license, we could do everything up front, out in the open."

"When you go out in the open, when you get a license, you pay fees. And taxes. You want to give the government your money now?"

"But we lose almost the same amount of money paying out bribes just so we don't get raided! Why don't we just do it the right way and be done with it? Besides, we could get rid of the kind of scum we have to be nice to every night in here . . ."

Miss Ling's hairless brows rose sharply. "This is what you say about the men who pay your wages? And what's wrong with the back room? It is good enough for me. It was good enough for your father. Now, all of a sudden, you get so big that it isn't good enough for you?"

Odile's eyes darted to Vincent's face. His father's dismissal by Miss Ling was a sore spot with him. In ten years, the man had not set foot in the Smiling Dragon, and had never attempted to see his mother again. He was just one of the many relatives Miss Ling had managed to alienate with her stubbornness.

"It *wasn't* good enough for my father," Vincent reminded her. "He tried to do the same things I did, but you wouldn't let him. He wanted to make things better for all of us, and you pushed him out the door like he was nothing—not your son." Needing to work off his agitation, he leaped up and began pacing the length of the table, tapping the back of each chair as he did so. The peacock shifted in its snooze, ruffling its ragged feathers, but didn't bother to open its eyes.

"What's wrong with the men is that they walk in here with violence inside them. It doesn't take much for them to open up and let it fly. My plan will let us turn this into a club for gentlemen, men with breeding. We could make it a place of honor . . ."

Vincent's agitation was contagious. Miss Ling got to her tiny feet and began to pace along the other side of the table, movements reflecting Vincent's as though in a mirror. They looked like two restless tigers eyeing each other for a weak spot. Odile sat, caught in the middle, wishing she were anywhere but there, but at the same time fascinated by the pulsing energy that both connected them and set them apart, and the similarity between them that she had never really noticed before.

"Honor?" Miss Ling snapped. "What you know of honor, little boy? What you know about that, eh? You seen the things I have? You drink from the cup I did? No. You born here, in a country that never knew a war. On a little dot that nobody even willing to fight over. You grew up never facing hunger a day in your life, never had a weapon pointed in your face. Never made a hard choice. Everything you have, you have because I gave it to you. The air in your lungs, you have it because of me and everything I gave so your ungrateful wretch of a father could taste life. And you want to talk to me about honor?"

Vincent read the passion in her face and hastened to soften the injury he had caused. "*Apo,* please . . ."

"No dishonor in what we do, Vincent. We don't steal from nobody, and we don't kill nobody."

Vincent still wasn't giving up. "Yes, *Apo,* there *is* dishonor in what we do! We dishonor the girls every time we take a cut in what they earn, every time we let a man who ought to know better take them up those stairs—"

"All we do is rent the rooms. We can't control what they do once they get there." She nodded vehemently, looking as if she were trying to convince herself.

"Bullshit!" Vincent roared, and Miss Ling flinched. Odile stared at him. She had never heard him curse in front of his grandmother. She wanted to stop him, now, before it was too late. But Vincent seemed unable to call a halt to the passion that was pouring out of him. His hand fell lightly on the crown of Odile's head, and to her surprise, she heard him say, "We don't just dishonor the girls upstairs with what we do. We dishonor women, period. You think I'm not ashamed for Odile when I see her waiting tables on the floor, having to deal every night with men who are just waiting for her to fall like the others? Because most of them started where she did, out on the floor, toting ice and selling beers. And most of them never dreamed that they would wind up one night in a room without a window, under a man, giving themselves up for money. Those men out there, they know all you have to do is wait, and one day, if they're lucky, beer won't be the only thing you can buy off the waitresses. All it takes is time."

Odile cringed, closing her eyes, almost hating him for drawing attention to her like that. Definitely hating him for giving voice to her own deepest fear. Here? In front of another woman? Oh, no.

"You think when I lie in bed next to Odile and listen to what's happening on the other side of the wall, I don't feel dirty and sick? For her and for me?"

Stop, stop, stop, Odile begged him silently. She couldn't look at her employer, but her eyes couldn't stay fixed on any other object, either. The metal fan in the room whirred noisily, even above the sound of Vincent's voice, but all it pushed in her direction was hot air.

The Cantonese words that were spat from Miss Ling's mouth were like fist-sized stones being thrown hard against plate glass. Vincent rocked back, eyes round and staring at her face. Odile was glad she couldn't follow what they were saying. Vincent responded, voice equally harsh and grating, syllables ugly and distorted to her ear. Whatever he said was enough to send his grandmother charging at him, arms windmilling.

Odile didn't need to understand Cantonese to know what that meant. Miss Ling wanted them out. Now. Shaking, humiliated, wishing she had never agreed to join Vincent on this benighted visit, she rose and searched wildly for her handbag for several moments before she remembered she hadn't brought one.

Vincent had already left the room, abandoning her in his wrath, and was stalking through the sitting room toward the door. Odile groped for something to say to allow her to leave with at least a shred of dignity. "Thank you for having me," she began, but the old woman brushed past her, strings of vituperation still pouring from her, not wanting Vincent to miss a word of it.

Miserably, she took off after them, managing just in time to slip through the door that separated the rooms from the kitchen outside, before Miss Ling slammed it shut and forcefully drove the bolt into place.

"Vincent," she called after him, but he had all but forgotten her presence. Without looking back, he burst through the beaded curtains and into the bar. A string of beads popped, pouring onto the tiled floor like hard rain on a tin roof.

Odile let him go. The last thing he wanted right now was her help—if she had the faintest idea what she could do to help him. Drained, she slumped forward, supporting her hands on her knees, chest hurting as if she had been running. She discovered that she was panting.

Vincent

He shouldn't have left her there, all alone with his *apo*. She and Odile didn't get along, mainly because they were both strong women who didn't like to give an inch. Shame on him for running away like that, scared of Grandmama and her razor words. Not man enough to run the business? Weak, like his father?

So wrong. Grandmama was so, so wrong. His eyes hurt, lashes were wet, and a million wild ants were scurrying through his scalp. He didn't stop running until he was out of the Dragon, across the road, and all the way down to Sea Lots. It was early still, and sweltering outside, so the little half-circle of mudbank on the edge of the dank, dead water, which the city planners called a 'park,' was empty of the idlers and lovers who would come out later.

He sat on one of the white benches, feeling its hard, flaking paint and jagged surface scratching at the backs of his arms. The whitewashed lighthouse jutted out behind him like a giant erection, yet was so insubstantial that it didn't even cast a shadow. People in and around the makeshift hovels of plyboard, galvanized roofing, and old planks barely glanced his way. Even they had their Sunday tasks to perform. Some busied themselves washing clothes in buckets and laying them out on clumps of bushes to dry; others cooked outdoors on open fires, scurrying back inside with pots of boiling rice to feed their children. Men huddled together in dejected clusters, smoking cigarettes and the occasional spliff, faces wilting. For them, Sunday was just another day in which they had no work. Vincent recognized a few of them. Whenever they managed to hustle a dollar, many of them would turn up in the back room of the Dragon, hopeful that they could turn it into more. Most of the time, they were mistaken.

He looked down at his feet. His dress shoes were already covered with the unbelievably black muck that clung to everything here: a mixture of boat oil and mud, decaying mangrove, and rotting fish. But even the stink that rose off the stagnant water wasn't enough to chase the smell of his grandmama's perfumed oils from his nostrils. The clamor of the squatters was not enough to drown the echo of her insults from his ears.

His manhood had shrunk in there, curled up inside his belly like a shy fern. He laughed aloud, bitterly, at the vision of himself trying to make love to Odile tonight, and found himself coming up a few inches and a pair of balls short. *Apo* had a way of doing that to a man.

By rights, he should walk away. Leave his grandmother to run the business into the ground, and start another on his own. Maybe even across the street—give her a little competition. That'd be funny. After all, he wasn't a boy. He was a grown man, thirty-five, not sixteen. There was nothing to stop him from bursting out of there and starting over from scratch.

But the Dragon was a family business, and the operative word there was *family*. Ownership had skipped his father's generation, but it wouldn't skip his. Making the Dragon work was up to him, or no one at all.

He wondered briefly if he should go to his father and ask for advice. Probably wouldn't help. Peng Tan had washed his hands of both the Dragon and his mother years before, and wouldn't care if the Dragon burned to the ground.

Abruptly, Vincent got up. Think. Time to think like a man. One whose genitals were quite intact, thank you very much, Grandmama. Odile had been right; he had tried the same old tack too many times. It was time for him to open his eyes and realize that if you couldn't get in through the front door, you broke a goddam window and crawled in through there.

Think. Form a plan. There were ways to force her hand. Ways to make her see. Odile had joked about putting a pillow over her face as she slept. She probably had no idea that there were nights when he woke up sweating, shocked at where his mind had taken him in the vulnerability of sleep. But a pillow wasn't necessary. It didn't need to come to that. To his own surprise, he dismissed the idea more out of a question of expediency than of morality.

There was a way—an easy one, and one that couldn't help but work. Logic told him it had to. He stopped his pacing and looked down at a small, smooth stone that lay between his feet. A good plan should be like a perfect stone: smooth, even, and solid. He turned the stone over with the tip of his shoe, searching for flaws in it. Looking for cracks, bumps, obstacles.

The bar was always full. How could he do what he needed to when there were people all around? Even on slow days the bar was full. Vincent turned his back on the Gulf and faced the city. Fast cars spewed exhaust in his face. He was close enough to the highway to feel the rush of wind as they passed. These days the Christmas shopping frenzy didn't even let up on a Sunday like it used to. The merchants kept the money machine churning right down to the day before Christmas. After that, there would be peace.

Ah, that was it. His window. A tiny one, but he could slip through it all the same. The Dragon closed only one day of the year: Christmas Eve. Not a good day for bars. Even punters had families, and wives who made them clean up and dragged them off to church for midnight mass or kept them home to hang up curtains and help with the ham and put the final coat of paint or varnish down so that when the children woke up on Christmas Day, everything would be clean and bright and feel like a holiday. On that night the bar would be closed, with Patrick and Teeth off attending to their own affairs. Even the bar girls would have their agendas—late-night parties where they could either have some fun if they had boyfriends or make a little extra change if they didn't. Some might stay behind to catch up on their sleep, though, but that wasn't as big a problem as it seemed. The place mightn't be completely empty, but it would be empty enough.

He needed to find a way to get rid of Odile, just for the evening. But even if he couldn't, well, he was a smart man. He could think of a way to get the job done, even if she was around. He just had to figure out all the details.

Vincent sat down on the park bench again and propped his chin on his hands. Details were easy. He had an eye for them. All he needed to do was walk it through in his mind once, twice, a dozen times, trying to figure out what could go wrong, and make sure it didn't. It wouldn't be hard to do. All it took . . . was balls.

Rory

"They didn't fit," Rory growled, disgusted. "Much too small for my hands. I just can't perform when I'm not comfortable."

Eli looked at him with his sad, gray-rimmed eyes. "They're the best I could do, boy. You got big hands; you just don't find spare gloves lying around and expect them to fit you perfectly."

"I know." He allowed Eli to tug off the gloves, which were so old and dry-rotted from lying around in a cupboard in the locker room that they were cracking across the knuckles. The old man unwound the tapes from his hands. He flexed and extended his fingers to get the blood circulating to the tips once again. After two hours of forced confinement, his hands were numb and his palms damp and sweaty. All around them men exercised, sparred, worked out with the barbells, or attacked the sandbags. In the ring that he had recently vacated, two teenage welterweights slugged away at each other. Their form wasn't all that good, but considering his own performance there this afternoon, he didn't have any right to criticize. He sat on a low, roughly made wooden bench and leaned back against the gym wall.

Eli joined him. "You sure your gloves gone for good, boy?" he asked optimistically. "Maybe you lost them."

Rory wasn't about to let Eli get his hopes up. "I'm sure

they're gone. I'm not careless with my things. I know where I put all my belongings. I didn't lose them; they got stolen. Them and my belt."

"Right out of your house?"

"Yes," Rory said bitterly.

"But how they could come in just so and take your things? The house wasn't empty. Your father . . ."

Rory cut him off. "I don't rely on my father to protect anything belonging to me. He was probably stone drunk and left the door open again. Or one of the windows. And the crackheads just walked in, took what they wanted, and walked back out."

"They take anything else?"

He laughed harshly. "Anything else? No, Eli, they didn't take anything else. But that's because they took it all already. I have no TV, practically no furniture, no clock on the wall. It's all been taken away in dribbles and bits. Right under his damn drunken nose." He snorted disgustedly. "Can't even trust him to do that much."

Before Eli could speak again, a large shadow fell over both men. It was cast by Mako, Rory's sparring partner, the only man in the gym larger and stronger than Rory. Mako came over to the bench and sat down. It creaked under his weight. He was light-skinned, near white, with almost colorless eyes and smooth hair, but born and raised behind the bridge—he considered himself a ghetto boy. His face was a mass of pulped flesh and healed-over scars after a career in illegal backyard rings where anything went as long as you could get up and walk away with your prize money at the end of the last round. He stuck his big reddened hand out past Eli, and Rory shook it.

"Not your day today, youngster," Mako sympathized.

Rory shook his head. "Cramps in the hands," he said dismissively. "Damn gloves." He'd lost a blistering ten-round training fight to Mako mere moments ago, and the loss stung. Mako might have been blessed with the greater strength and the longer reach, but Rory had the speed and the agility. The two were well matched and loved to pit themselves against each other, even though the outcome was usually in Rory's favor. It wasn't losing that Rory minded; it was losing for a stupid reason.

Mako nodded. "Yeah. I heard. You sure you didn't lose them nowhere? You look in the locker room?"

Rory wasn't in the mood to repeat himself. He sighed heavily. "They didn't get lost, Mako. They got stolen."

Mako let it slide. "And you sure it's just the gloves got you fighting like that?"

"What?"

"You sure you ain't got nothing on your mind, too? You let me land some punches you woulda' seen coming a mile away, if you was in your right mind. But half the fight you was daydreaming. Looking the other way. I never thought you woulda' done so bad. You fight like a girl this afternoon, soldier."

His relationship with Mako was long enough and cordial enough that he didn't even bristle at the slur. Before he could come up with an excuse, or a means of diverting the attention from himself, Eli piped up.

"He right, boy. Them gloves is one thing, but what was going on in your head is a next. I wasn't going to say nothing, but since it all out in the open now, I have to agree with Mako. You having problems?"

"What problems?" Rory responded acidly. "Other than my belongings growing legs and waltzing out of my house?"

Eli only waited.

Rory sighed. He had to restrain himself from touching the bruises on his face for the tenth time today. He knew he hadn't entirely fobbed off their earlier questions about his injuries with his garbled story about "a little sidestreet brawl, no big deal." Both men were curious, and to be fair, as his friends, they deserved to know. The trouble was, he just didn't want to get into it.

Mako decided to push him just a little further. "Listen, boy. All of we is men in here, so let me talk straight. That look on your face could only mean one thing: you got some little youngins on your mind. All of we been through that fire, and let me tell you, no woman ain't worth that. Don't never let a woman get under your skin so deep that when she ain't around, you still got no control over your life. When you with a woman, tell her anything she want to hear and do whatever it take to keep her happy, but when she ain't around, forget she exist. That's my advice to you."

Rory concentrated on the welterweights in the ring, spotting their mistakes and trying to think of how he would have done better. The two men at his side waited for a response. None came.

"Rory," Eli began after it became obvious that he wasn't prepared to speak. "We your friends. And from the looks of it, you ain't got a whole lot more in stock. So you don't think you could tell us if something going on with you? We both older than you: whatever it is, me or Mako probably been there before. We could help."

He wished they could. But where could he begin to explain? What could he say about Odile? How after knowing her all the years of his life and not having seen her for four, he could set eyes on her face and be fourteen again, tongue-tied, feet clumsy, brain slow? How the guilt of what he'd done to her stalked him, and the pain of her laughing at his boyish love still cut at him like blades, pain as fresh as the day it was first inflicted? About the nights they sat out together in the yard under the sprawling tamarind tree, looking up at the stars, her mere presence making him so happy that he prayed to God that if it be His will that he die young, let it be then, under the dark, open sky, next to her, perfectly satisfied? No, it was not a question of where he should begin talking, but of whether he could find the strength to stop once he did begin.

He shook his head, wishing the two pairs of concerned

eyes would turn away from his face. He got up, unable to glance at them, and mumbled something about having to go.

Eli looked at him, sad but resigned. "You done here for the day?"

"Yeah. I'm done for the day." It didn't make any sense pressing on. His spirit wasn't in it.

"Where you going?" Mako wanted to know.

Rory thought about it, chewing on his lip and scratching his head. Where he wanted to go next would bring him nothing but grief. But his destination drew him. Call it folly. Call it a homing instinct. Whatever it was, it was building up in him a disquiet that could only be quelled by answering the summons. He didn't think he had a choice.

"Going to get me a new weight-belt made," he answered, already walking off. "By the best leather man in town."

He was too consumed by his determination to do what needed to be done and get it over with to take the time to shower and change. The sweat on his skin was drying, the dark patches on his sleeveless vest becoming lighter. He exited the gym and walked directly into the sunlight, ignoring his car. He was too keyed up to drive, and besides, the Christmas traffic was so heavy that he would cross town faster on foot anyway.

He was going to St. Ann's, back to the place he had fled as a boy, back to the little room at the rear of the yard that always smelled of leather and tannins. He would meet Jacob again, and Odile's mother. What would they say to him? What would he say to them? He didn't want to think too hard about that, in case his courage failed him. He would deal with that confrontation when he got there. But first, he had to make a detour.

Saul

Saul didn't get shit for the gloves and belt. Thirty stinking dollars. For everything. What the fuck was a pawnshop good for if you couldn't make an honest dollar off them every once in a while? The 'honest' part made him laugh out loud. Well, if not honest, at least hard-earned. It wasn't easy swiping things from right under Rory's nose. He was so damn finicky about where he kept his possessions, and was always trying to hide them from the sprangers.

Sprangers. Stealing from him. That was funny.

But at least he kept his things in good condition. Most of the time that got him a good price. *Most* of the time. And no matter how hard the boy tried to keep an eye on his things, he couldn't be there in the daytime. So he left house and home in his father's gentle care. And was stupid enough to be surprised when he came home and found this or that missing, and cursed every crack-head on the block, and swore that if he ever found any of them actually in his house and touching his shit he'd wipe the floor with their ass. What a damn blind, trusting fool.

This morning he listened from his bed while Rory turned the house upside down looking for his belt and gloves, and pretended to be asleep when he came in to ask if Saul had seen them. It wasn't easy, lying there like a *manicou*, perfectly still with his eyes squeezed shut, because there was this big grin just dying to bust out of his face and three hard lumps of leather hidden between him and the mattress. When the boy finally left, still cursing and fretting like a woman, he was so amused he had to fire a drink. Living with Rory was a scream. What did he expect? That he could give him a few pathetic dollars every week and not think he would have to make up the shortfall? He was a big man. He had a life to lead. Damned if he let some little pup tell him how much he could spend and on what.

He hawked up a gob and spat it on the ground outside the pawnshop. Shoulda spat it up in the man's face back in there, if he'da thought of it then. Well, too bad. Missed his chance. Thirty dollars. Damn. He could drink that out in an afternoon.

At least, he was sure as shit gonna try.

Rory and Jacob

Even in the heat of the afternoon, and on a Sunday at that, the Smiling Dragon was not short of customers. Rory stood across the street with his hands in the pockets of his track pants, waiting patiently. He had been waiting there for over an hour, watching men walk in erect, and others stagger out less so. To distract himself, he played mind games, counting red cars, then blue ones, then bicycles. His nostrils had become accustomed to the stench of the clogged drain over which he stood, and to the clouds of fumes expelled by the unending traffic that crawled by.

He flinched visibly when a police car nosed past him, hoping to God that nothing about him would cause them to look in his direction. He recognized his paranoia for what it was, but understanding it didn't make it any easier to bear. He stepped gingerly back so that the lamppost partially obscured him from view, and pretended to examine large posters advertising New Year's Eve parties. The police car steadfastly ignored him, turning east toward the highway, so he returned to his observation post.

At one point he was sure he spotted one of the bouncers who had put that cut-ass on him the last time he was here, the fat one with the body of an aging fighter. Had some moves on him, that one. But the fat man had never looked across the street in his direction. He held his conversation with the departing client, slapped him cordially on the back, and then withdrew into the bar.

The door swung open again, and Rory looked up expectantly. Five or six short Orientals with flat, brown faces and thick black hair stumbled out, grinning and chattering, each one trying heroically to keep the other from falling face-first into the gutter. They wheeled around for a moment, turning this way and that, trying to get their bearings, before deciding that the direction of the harbor was the one for them. Probably came from the Vietnamese seafood processing plant down at Sea Lots, Rory decided. Either there or from one of the many trawlers moored out in the bay. He wondered vaguely about the legality of their landed status, and watched interestedly until they rounded the corner.

A prickle ran over his skin, like a sweet, light breeze coming up unexpectedly on a muggy day. He whipped around, all his senses awake now. The sudden and intense sensation could only come from one source.

Odile.

He looked frantically at the bar door. There was no one there. He slapped his forehead. How could he have allowed himself to be distracted? He scanned the faces in the street, frantic, but none of them was hers. Then he spotted it: a flash of butter yellow, a length of leg, rounding the corner in the direction of the city's heart. He knew it was her. He took off in an easy lope, darting between the cars to the other side of the road and around the bend, almost colliding with her at a fruit stand.

Startled by his sudden proximity, she stepped aside to allow him to pass, clutching her purse to her body, but did not look around.

So close to her, and still she didn't know him. He, on the other hand, had sensed her from across the street. He wasn't offended. She had always been in her own cocoon, and he had always been obliged to insinuate himself past her barriers just to be noticed.

"Odile." His mouth was close to her ear.

She spun around so fast, she almost lost her balance. She knew at once who he was; he could tell from the shock in her eyes as she faced him. "Rory, what . . . ?"

He touched her lightly on her arm to convince her that he meant no harm, but then took it away, afraid that this violation of her space would send her running.

"Did you follow me?" she asked accusingly, lush brows wrinkling.

He shook his head vehemently. "No. Not really. I needed to see you, so I waited outside the bar. I figured you'd have to come out eventually."

She was incredulous. "And what if I didn't?"

"Then I'd wait some more," he said simply.

"What if it started to rain again?"

"Then I'd get wet."

She stared at him, probably trying to decide whether to stay put or run. Her eyes flicked upward to take in the still-obvious bruises on his face, and she had the grace to flush guiltily. Then, dismissing him as a threat, she turned her back on him and faced the Rastafarian fruit vendor behind the makeshift, gaudily painted stand on the sidewalk. No larger than a desk, it listed under the weight of heaps of oranges, bananas, and costly imported apples and pears, still in their gray cardboard packing nests. A row of one-gallon mayonnaise jars held an assortment of treats: individually wrapped peppermints, slices of peppery mango dyed a brilliant red, Chinese licorice prunes, many-colored lollipops, and loose cigarettes that sold for seventy-five cents.

"A pound of grapes, please," Odile told him, angling her body to shut Rory out.

Her deliberate rudeness amused him. "Two," he corrected over her shoulder.

She turned, cut her eyes at him, and repeated her order. "*One* pound."

The Rastafarian glanced from one to the other, not sure of

what to do next. Rory dug in his pocket, fished out a crumpled twenty, and leaned past her to hand it to the man. "Two pounds." The man took it without question and began snipping at the large bunches that hung by pieces of twine from a blue plastic clothesline strung across the top. He concentrated on ignoring Odile's glare as he weighed out the grapes and packed them into a plastic bag. It was, after all, in his best interest to fill the larger order. Let the man and the woman sort it out themselves.

Rory took the bag of grapes and handed them over to Odile, praying she wouldn't reject them. The splurge meant he would have to do without lunch money for the next few days, but giving her a gift, small as it was, was worth it.

She glanced from the bag to his face and back again before gingerly taking it. She tried to force it into her handbag, but it wouldn't fit, so she held it limply at her side. She seemed to be wondering if he had effectively bought a few minutes of her conversation, as a man does when he sends a drink over to a lady in a bar. Eventually, unwilling to debate the matter much longer, she thanked him and walked away.

He was beside her in a few quick strides. "Odile . . . "

"What?" She didn't stop walking.

"I just wanted to talk to you for a while."

"Why?"

That stumped him. What could he answer to that? He thought fast. "I need your help," he told her finally.

She asked no further questions but didn't tell him to let her be, either. That was a good sign. He persevered. "Jacob, your mother's . . . uh . . . the leather-man. Does he still take in jobs?"

She looked at him as if he were mad. "Of course. He didn't win the lottery and retire. Why?"

They crossed the road at Independence Square and began heading north across the red-tiled promenade. The broad paved strip cut clear across the city, stretching as far as the cruise ship docking area on the more presentable side of the port. It was lined with trees on both sides and dotted with benches and tables, where you could sit and catch your breath before reentering the frenzied crowds, or read a book, or play chess on the little checkerboard marble tabletops. In all directions, shoppers scurried, lovers strolled, and old men rummaged through garbage cans looking for a bite.

"I need something made," he said in answer to her question. "And I want him to make it for me."

"Because Jacob's the only leather-man in town?"

"No," he shook his head. "Because he's the best."

She shrugged, making it patently obvious that she couldn't care less about the quality of Jacob's work. "So go by him and get whatever it is you want made. What's that got to do with me?"

"I want you to come with me to St. Ann's. To see him."

She stood stock-still, incredulous. "You mad? What you need me for?"

He fidgeted. Now he wished he hadn't come, because the reason he couldn't face that yard or its inhabitants alone was the same reason he had never sought her out or tried to speak to her before. And now, to speak of the way they had parted was unavoidable. "Because I need your company. I don't know if I can go there by myself. I haven't been back into the yard since I left, and I can't face it on my own. I can't face Jacob on my own. I wouldn't know what to say. . . . " He couldn't go on. But nothing needed to be clarified. She understood.

She looked as uncomfortable as he did, waving away his unspoken words. She was as reluctant to hear what he had to say as he was to say it. Something in her sagged.

He tugged at her arm, trying to get her to go with him to one of the benches. What he needed to tell her couldn't be said on their feet in a thoroughfare, with all these people rushing past. "Come. Sit down."

She wrenched her arm away. "No! Why?"

"Because I need to say something."

"Say it here." She folded her arms mulishly, resisting his coaxing. That was another thing he remembered about her: she could be stubborn.

He pleaded again. "Odile, please. Just give me five minutes. Please sit."

She shook her head vehemently. In the old days, when she had her long black braids, they would have swung from side to side across her face. Now the angle of her back and her thrusting jaw conveyed the same message of determined resistance. "No. Just say what you have to say. Do it now or forget it."

He sighed. Where to start? "I want you to know how sorry I am. For what happened down by the river. For what I did to you."

She stared at him, mouth tightly closed. He wondered if she was going to pretend she didn't follow what he was talking about. But then she shrugged slightly. "I hurt you, too, you know. The things I said."

Could she really know how deeply her ridicule of him, his ignorance, and his juvenile devotion had hurt? He'd thought that pain was his own secret. But the pain she inflicted on him with her words was nothing compared to what he had caused with his hands and his temper. He wasn't letting himself off that easily. He wasn't letting her back away from his confession that easily. The thing he had hidden in his belly all this time had crawled up into his mouth, and he was spitting it out, like it or not. "But your baby . . . Because of me, you lost it." That made him a killer, didn't it? A murderer at fourteen.

Another shrug, a lying one. "I didn't want it, remember? I used to wish it would disappear. I prayed every day it would die, and then one night it did." Her eyes were black with emotion that the rest of her face struggled not to show. That was the Odile he remembered—always trying to prove how strong she was, always pretending that nothing could hurt her.

"That's not the point," he persisted. How could he get through to her? "The point is that I—"

"You, you, you, Rory!" She punctuated her vehement words with her free hand, pointing in his face. "Why is it all about you? What *you* did. You enjoy blaming yourself every day? You like eating guilt with your dinner? Is this fun for you?"

"No, it isn't fun for me!" He tried to keep his voice down, but his passion wouldn't let him. People were stopping and staring, and he hated that. He was a man who thrived on anonymity. He practiced being a chameleon, blending in and disappearing in full view, and now here he was, making a show of himself. He wished again he could convince her to find some quiet corner with him, but he knew it wasn't worth trying. "It's not fun for me," he repeated, lowering his head nearer to hers so he didn't have to shout. "It's torture. Every night in my sleep, dogs are after me. Every morning I wake up and wonder if this is the day I go to jail. . . ."

"That's ridiculous! Nobody ever went to the police. None of us wanted to see you get into trouble. . . ."

"It doesn't matter. I sense the cops after me all the same. They walk past me and I sweat. I see a cop car in my mirror and my hands shake on the wheel. I see them and know that if they look hard enough they'll pick up some kind of glow or light coming off me, or a sound, like an alarm. To set me apart from the rest of the crowd. A wanted man. But the police, they the least of my worries. After all, there's worse to come: even if they don't get me, hell will."

"You believe in hell?" She barked a short, dismissive laugh. She pursed her lips at him the way she always used to do, in the way that said *stupid little boy*.

"Believe in it?" It amazed him that she could laugh at his anguish. "Yes, I believe in it. Sometimes I smell the smoke and the sulfur and hear the voices of the damned. And I know that one day my own voice . . ."

Odile took a few steps away from him, as if she were

about to flee, and then returned, took a few more in the opposite direction, and then came to a halt in front of him
again. Whatever battle she was fighting inside, she wanted to
desert it and run. She was taking in huge gulps of air, swallowing them, like they were needed to fuel what she was
about to say next. "I'm going to help you sleep better, Rory.
I'm going to tell you something that will stop those dogs in
the night."

He eyed her, wary but eager, a drowning man waiting for a
line to be thrown out to him. If anyone could stop those
dogs, it was she. "What?"

Now it was her turn to glance around for eavesdroppers
and then speak into his ear. Her cheek brushed against his
chin as she leaned in near. "Maybe you didn't do wrong by
me that day. Maybe you did me a favor."

No. No. That is obscene. Murder is no favor.

She went on, unprompted, still close. "Maybe you just did
for me what I never had the guts to do for myself. What my
mother wanted to take me to a doctor for. Maybe you gave
me what I wanted, so that there would never be any blood on
my hands. You bore the guilt, and I got set free."

"You can't mean that!" He backed away from the acid she
was pouring into his ear. Could a mother really be glad her
child was no more?

"Why not? I was seventeen, and I had exams coming up.
I was supposed to go to university. And then along comes
that . . ." Revulsion made her briefly ugly. "That . . . *thing* . . .
and everything changed. Everywhere I went, I had to hide my
belly. And then my mother turns up pregnant by that shit-
hound she was running around with. Two babies on the way,
and not enough food for both of them. And then there was
only one: hers. Mine slipped away and then there was nothing where it used to be. I could do whatever I wanted again,
and nobody ever had to know what happened. You don't
think I'm better off now?"

All he had wanted was her forgiveness, which would at

least help him shut his eyes to sleep. And now he was hearing that what he saw as her loss, she saw as her freedom. Words that monstrous shouldn't fall from that mouth. What she was saying was indecent. Besides, what he had seen of her in the bar made a liar of her. He had to make her face that lie. "So you're better off?"

"Yes, I am." She looked as if she believed it.

"Where is it, then?"

She squinted, not reading him. "Where is what?"

"Where is that education the baby was preventing you from getting? Where's the degree? Where is all the success I set you free to achieve?"

She glared at him, not liking where the conversation had turned. "Don't, Rory."

He persisted. "What'd that freedom get you? What you done with it? You lost a baby, and that sets you free to work in a bar, in a nasty South Quay bar, doing I don't know what—" He couldn't continue. The image of her and a parade of faceless, nameless men with bills crumpled in their fists had haunted him for days. An abomination in his eyes. They stung, and his vision blurred.

Odile looked as if he had slapped her in the face. Her head reeled from an unseen blow and then righted itself as the arm holding the bag of grapes shot up, like a puppet's tied to a string, and came down, slamming it onto the concrete tiles, splitting the bag and sending the pulp flying at their feet. "I am *not* a whore, Rory!" she shouted. "I sell *drinks* to those men—not myself!"

Nearby, a woman with a large pink doll wrapped in plastic tucked under her arm snickered, shamelessly stopping to ogle. They both barely noticed her.

Rory felt the air in his head expand as relief flooded in. He had no way of knowing if what she said was true, but he wanted it to be so. It *had* to be so. He was prepared to believe it whether it sounded true or not. "You mean that?" Faith would live or die upon her answer.

"Yes, I mean that. Why you all so quick to jump to conclusions? Between you and my mother, I don't know . . ."

Myra, think the same thing? Not possible. Myra thought her daughter was without blemish, as he once had. How things changed. "Miss Cole thinks you . . ."

"I don't give a shit what my mother thinks." She looked down at the smashed grapes, avoiding his eyes. "I know what I do and don't do, and that's all that matters."

"But my father says he saw you . . ."

She looked at him, contempt naked now. "Your *father* says? He says so, and that makes it the truth? Oh, his word must be worth so much . . ."

She was right. Saul lied about so many things. But only to suit his own purposes. What good would it have done him to make things up about Odile? The simple pleasure of hurting him might be worth a lot to Saul, but still, cruelty like that was beyond human, beyond even Saul. . . .

Before his thoughts could wander any further down that path, she pushed harder. "And you mean you still have something to do with that bastard? After what he did to you? After all that talk about leaving him as soon as you were old enough? What, you not old enough yet? Why you still listening to him? You mean to say you had more balls when you were a little boy that you got now?"

He was embarrassed at his weakness, ashamed at having wrongfully—oh, he hoped!—accused her, and furious at his father for parading his vicious lie as the truth. But she had the wrong idea about the way things were with him and Saul, and he needed her to know that. "*He* lives with *me*. Not the other way around."

She smiled on one side of her face. "He lives with you. A man who kept you in a trap so cruel you used to talk about chewing off your own paw just to get away. Now you have the chance to walk, and you don't?"

"He's still my father." Rory wished she would understand. "He needs me. If I put him out, what would he do? He's sick and old . . ." If he needed to explain his reasons any further, then she'd never get it. He waited.

But Saul wasn't at the front of her mind. She was still stinging from his unkind cut, still lashing out. "And you have the gall to talk to *me* about my freedom? At least *I'm* where I want to be."

Rory felt very tired. He wondered whether he should abandon his crazy idea of going to St. Ann's, and instead just return home, put his pillow over his head, and go to sleep for the rest of the day. But Odile wasn't prepared to let him.

"You want forgiveness, Rory? Fine, if it will make you feel better. Here, here, take it. Take all you can carry." She leaned forward, making wild scooping gestures with her hands, throwing armloads of air at him. "There, is that enough for you?" She waved one over her head with a flourish, magic wand invisible. "You're forgiven." Her breath rushed out between her bared teeth. She shuddered like a winded animal.

They faced each other, both silent, emotionally spent. He wished there were something right to say, some kind of balm that would smooth it all over. Was she making a mockery of his guilt—thus condemning him to it—or did she really mean what she said about him having freed her? And did perceiving her loss as freedom make her callous, or just weaker than he had always thought?

He wished he could say more, ask more questions, but by the set of her jaw he knew better than to broach the subject again. Finally, he wrenched their exchange back to the point at which it had begun. "So will you come with me to see Jacob?"

A laugh popped out of her unawares. "You never let things go, eh?"

"No."

She looked as if she didn't care. "I'm heading there anyway, to see my mother. I see her every weekend, when I'm not working. You can come along if you like."

The offhanded invitation elated him, but he tried to hide

it. Oh, so many emotions surging through him in such a short space of time! And he, a man who once could barely name them, much less feel them. He tried not to look too pleased, for fear that she would rescind her promise. "My car . . ."

She bent over and picked up the damaged grapes, turning the burst bag over in her hand, looking to see if any of them could be salvaged. "*I'm* going by taxi. You could drive there on your own, or you could come in the taxi with me. Your choice." She walked over to a blackened garbage bin and tossed the package in.

Rory didn't argue. Odile began stepping briskly toward Woodford Square, where the St. Ann's taxis waited, making it obvious that he could keep up or fall behind—it was his choice.

With the grapes gone, he wanted to offer her something more. "You ate lunch yet?"

Inexplicably, this seemed to amuse her. "You could say that."

"Yes or no?"

"A bit of both."

This woman was born to frustrate him. "What does that mean?" he asked. "Either you ate or you didn't."

"I got *served* lunch. I didn't exactly eat it."

"What did you get served?"

"Rotten fish."

Now he knew she was making fun of him. He played along all the same. If it was her idea of a joke, well, then he'd keep her company while she laughed, even if he was the brunt of it. "And who served this to you, this rotten fish?"

Odile glanced at him, something like mischief making her face glow. "An old witch. A wicked old, old witch. She cast a spell on this man I . . ." She stopped, thinking hard.

"This man you . . . ?" he prompted. No wonder they painted jealousy green. It was the color of bile.

" . . . know," she finished, but she didn't look satisfied. She passed her hand over her short hair, then pressed it lightly to her throat.

He let his steps keep time with hers, trying to read the angles of her profile, but the clues on her shuttered face were written in a strange language. He probed further, knowing that his attempt was clumsy. "Just 'know'? Nothing more?"

"Knowing is a place to start," she said.

He wondered if this man she "knew" sat any better with him than the unnumbered men she swore she didn't, at least not for money. Was a single nameless man, one on one against him in the ring, a better risk than the sea of blurred faces outside it? His hands twitched: a competitor's instinct. But there was no ring and there was no competition. This man, whoever he was, was enough to put her at a loss for words. That told him more than he cared to know.

But like a big dog with a toothache, he prodded at the sore spot. "And you plan on saving him from this witch? With your own magic?"

Her lashes fluttered as she looked up at him. As a boy he was always full of questions, and she'd been the only one he could take them to. Hindsight told him he'd been annoying then. Astuteness told him he was annoying now. That didn't bother him. It occurred to him that he was enjoying the game.

She wasn't. She rolled an answer around on the tip of her tongue, tasted it, and grimaced. Bitter, perhaps. Like his bile.

"Well?" he insisted.

"Never mind," she said.

Walking into St. Ann's again after so much time was like slipping through a crack in the wall that separated him from his past. That he could work every day so close to this small suburb and never have occasion to enter, either through the demands of his business or from sheer curiosity, was almost eerie. He had simply blinded himself to its existence as best he could. If it ceased to exist, it couldn't torment him.

He walked silently alongside Odile—as always, she insisted on getting out of the taxi at the foot of the hill and walking the rest of the way. He let his head swivel from side to side, taking in the landmarks that had, over time, etched themselves onto his young soul: Queen's Hall with its domed amphitheater, where as a boy he used to run down to loiter on the other side of the road and watch the fancy people arrive for the opera; the tiny private art galleries tucked away in old British colonial houses; and the nightclubs where people flocked looking for happiness, at least for a few alcohol-lubricated hours. Farther up, the valley made its dual personality felt, as the character of the neighborhood subtly changed, and all the glitter of the social hot spots and the sedateness of the more established homes gave way to a complacent shabbiness.

The air was familiarly damp, and would have been even if it had not rained all morning. The valley had always been a place of water. He tried not to think of the river. Wet fallen leaves from the huge samaans and flamboyants made the sidewalk slick under their feet, and he kept his body taut, ready to catch her should she slip. He knew this was ridiculous. Odile never slipped. She never fell.

She had been quiet for so long that he struggled between breaking the silence—thus risking another conflagration—and leaving her with her thoughts. His own need to touch her, even verbally, finally won out. "Think we'll have a rainy Christmas?" Brilliant thing to say. He grimaced.

She didn't glance at him. "Maybe."

"It should never rain on Christmas Day," he persisted. "Not supposed to. The sun should always shine for Christmas." The little boy in him believed that.

This time her lips curved a little. "I guess. I don't really care. Christmas ain't nothing big for me."

He tried not to be shocked. Even he, who had no family to speak of, who hadn't received a Christmas present since the year before his mother walked out on him and Saul, believed in Christmas. Every year on Christmas Eve he put on his only tie and went out to midnight mass at whatever church took his fancy, and the next morning he tried his best to be civil to his father. He served ham with piccalilli and hot beef *pastelles* and eggs and toast, and indulged in apples for breakfast. And while Saul left the house to swill down hundred-proof puncheon rum with his cronies before returning home blind drunk, he would sit on his porch and listen to Christmas carols and parang on the radio and watch the children on his street parade up and down, showing off their new bikes, carts, and skateboards. One year, he had even had a small Christmas tree, but that was stolen off the porch in no time: tree, lights, ornaments, star, and all. But in spite of the loneliness of the season, it was one he looked forward to and revered. How could Odile not like Christmas?

"You mean you don't spend the day with your mother?"

"'Course."

"And doesn't she make you nice things to eat? And fruit cake? And you get presents?"

"Yeah." Her disinterested gaze was far off.

He was aghast. She had so much and didn't care. Didn't she know how much she had? But there was no more time for further conversation. They neared the gate of the yard, and at its threshold, he stopped.

He almost expected to see old Sebastian, Odile's grandfather, wheeling past them with his little green pram filled with toys, stones, papers, anything that caught his eye. Mind gone years before the body had. At the ultimate stage of his delirium, Sebastian had appointed himself the guardian of the sidewalk and would hunker out on the curb, day in and day out, attempting to guide pedestrians across the road. He'd become an object of mockery for passing schoolchildren, who made a game out of taunting him, but Sebastian had never seemed hurt by their cruelty. Maybe he was past feeling pain then. Rory had heard that the old man died a while after he left the valley. It was a pity. Sebastian had been kind.

He noticed that the sagging, creaking old gate had been fixed, and knew instinctively that such a service could only have come from Jacob. He didn't move to go past it.

Odile had walked through, expecting him to trail behind her, but when he didn't, she stopped and turned around. "What?" she asked, impatient.

He stood on the outside, looking in at David and Jillian's neat little home, then at the old, ugly segment that had been his, and at the brightly painted one that was Myra's, full of flowering plants and an air of contentment. Jacob's little room at the back couldn't be seen from here.

Odile folded her arms and looked at him, lower lip protruding slightly, waiting.

Rory struggled not to place his hand over his heart; it was forcing its way out through his chest, painfully so. He glanced from Odile, all bristles and energy, ignorant or uncaring of his dilemma, to the yard speckled with shadows. Couldn't she see that it was full of ghosts? The tamarind tree that had given him shade every day of his life was gone, sawed away at the base—Jacob again, he knew—after most of it had crashed into Odile's house that night of the rain. But even so, its pale shadow was there, leaning in to embrace the homes. No longer able to scatter its tiny confetti leaves over everything, but the mud in the yard seemed still to bear its green-and-gold traces.

On the balcony that used to be his but now belonged to someone else, Gracie stood, claws wrapped around the railing, eyes peeking out from under her wing. Every day that he had seen her there, his lungs had expelled their relief. Her presence had meant that for one more day, his father had not made good on his threat to turn her into stew. Poor Gracie. His devotion to her might have been a standing neighborhood joke, but she had been the only constant in his young life, and the only female he understood. So what if she was just a bedraggled white chicken? Friendship was hard to come by. When you found it, the species in which it resided just didn't matter. When you lost it, it hurt just as bad. Like the tamarind tree, Gracie had been cut down the night of the rain. How could one night, one single night, have brought with it such devastation? Why was it that even years after that wretched night, nothing in his life ever felt, tasted, or sounded the same?

For him, it felt as if the rain that had started then had never stopped. He carried the dampness around in his bones. He looked up at the sheet-metal sky, seeking the sun, knowing it would be hidden from his view, but looking anyway.

Odile burst in on his thoughts. "I'm going in." She made no move to go.

Rory barely heard her, as another apparition skidded up to the sidewalk in his noisy, fancy, red, gold, and green road monster, leaving the engine running and the scratchy dub music belching from its faulty radio. Slim forced his way past them, translucent, his twine-colored hair spiky, failing to achieve the dreadlocks to which they aspired, jacket in Rasta colors swinging on his skinny frame, gold weighing down his arms and thin neck. How the young Rory had admired him! Yearned to be like him: energetic, selfish, sexual. Casting about for any man to fill the hollow his father who wasn't a father left in him.

Rory looked around, almost expecting to see his own younger ghost, gawky in his growth phase, face strewn with acne, directly in Slim's path, eyes eager for recognition. Slim had never so much as acknowledged him.

"Rory?" For the first time, there was concern in her voice. She touched him on the elbow, and he hoped she would never take her hand away.

He struggled against the lure of the ghosts and returned to the present. Giving in to their draw embarrassed him. "Sorry," he told her.

She seemed to understand. "Nothing here can hurt you anymore, you know," she told him with surprising compassion. Her hand was still on his arm. "Take it from me. I know. They're all in your head. They won't hurt you unless you let them."

"Who're all in my head?" She couldn't possibly know what he was seeing in the yard. Could she?

She got up slightly on her toes to whisper in his ear, although no one was actually around to hear her. The collar of her butter-colored dress brushed against his arm. "The ghosts."

She saw them too! Such a rare thing, the feeling of not being alone.

She tugged at his hand, coaxing him through the gate into territory that used to be his. "If you pretend not to notice them, they can't notice you. Shut your mind against them, and they'll go away."

He followed her to Myra's little porch, struggling to take her advice, shoving the mudslide of memories out of his field of vision. The last to fade was Gracie.

At the foot of the steps, his courage failed him once again. This time, Odile didn't lose patience. "Don't worry. I'm here."

"Okay," he said gratefully.

She stood next to him and called out, "Ma!"

Almost immediately, Myra's head poked past the white lace curtains in the doorway, and then her whole body emerged. She was balancing a small child on her hip. Slim's child: his every feature was stamped on the face in miniature.

Odile released his hand with haste, but didn't step away from his side. "Look who I brought," she said almost playfully, but there was a catch in her voice.

The recognition on Myra's face was instantaneous. The last time she'd seen him, he had been bringing her daughter unconscious in his arms back from the riverbank. Rory cringed inside, not even daring to hope that her welcome would be a warm one. He would have settled for cool cordiality over open condemnation. But Myra's face registered only delight. She took several steps forward, holding a hand out in greeting. And before he could shake it, she touched his cheek, almost trying to assure herself that he was real and not an illusion. The little boy on her hip gawked at him with Slim's light-colored eyes.

"Rory, my boy . . ." Myra's voice was filled with wonder.

"Miss Cole, ma'am," he mumbled, embarrassed and pleased. Her proximity made him wish he had taken the time to shower at the gym this morning.

"You look so . . ." Myra struggled for words. "You've *grown!*"

He grinned sheepishly, trying to take her in without staring. His obsession with Odile had never blinded him to Myra's own charms. She had always been the queen of the yard: tall, beautiful, commanding with her own elegance. Even now, at perhaps forty or so, Myra looked good, but something about her had changed. She was no less beautiful, but hers had once been a restless beauty. The way she walked, the way she talked, had seemed designed to draw attention to herself, as if she thought that her existence was defined by the way she appeared in the eyes of the men around her. Now, her beauty sat well on her. She was settled, placid, and at ease, exchanging sensationalism for grace. It was obvious that the old leather-man who had become her lover had also become a ground wire through whom she channeled her restless spirit away from herself.

After several moments of silence, Odile piped up, unwilling to stay outside any longer. "You letting us inside?"

Myra slapped her forehead. "Of course, of course. Come in, boy. I have cake." She beckoned to him with her free arm. "Come in."

Rory found that his feet could not budge. Even the discovery that Myra bore him no malice after all that had happened was not enough to allow him to enter her home. He felt shy and clumsy and awkward. He shook his head, struggling to speak. "Miss Myra—Miss Cole, thank you. But I . . . uh . . . I can't. I came to see Jacob." He remembered his manners and corrected himself. "*Mister* Jacob. About work."

Mercifully, she neither looked put out nor insisted. "He's in his workshop. Behind us. You remember?"

He remembered. Too abashed to turn his back on her, he backed away, glancing at Odile. Her eyes were on him. She, too, didn't seem about to insist that he join them. Odile had never been one for making fraudulent social noises. "Let me know when you ready to go," she told him. "We'll walk back together."

She went into the house with her mother. Until he disappeared from view, the eyes of the little boy on Myra's hip never left his.

Around the rear of the house, set away from the road, Jacob's little room stood in half shadows. It looked exactly the same as he remembered it: unpainted, constricting, silent. The sign offering leather work at "reasonable rates" still hung by its solitary nail. The porch in front was dominated by a worktable, behind which Jacob sat, head bent, working on something that he held in both hands.

He lifted his head at the sound of Rory's footsteps, black eyes sharp and alert. His fighter's instincts never allowed him to be approached unawares. Rory hesitated, again unsure of his welcome, but Jacob's face reflected as little surprise as if he had simply walked into his own yard, home from school.

"Son," he acknowledged him.

The two men eyed each other. This time, Rory was unwavering in his examination. Like Myra, Jacob had changed too, but unlike everything else around him, he looked younger rather than older, more vital, more relaxed. He was smooth-shaven, having evidently stopped allowing his stubble to grow for days at a time. The shirt he was wearing was old but clean and hand-pressed, with its crisp sleeves rolled up to the elbow. The hard, normally closed face was more open, not as bitter and defensive. There was less of an air of sullen brooding about him than one of quiet tranquility and concentration. Myra was as good for him as he was for her.

"Mr. Jacob." Emboldened by the absence of aggression in the older man, Rory stepped onto the porch.

Jacob laid down the tool in his hand and got to his feet. Rory noticed he didn't seem to need his staff to do so. He stood quietly as the older man ran his eyes slowly over him, taking in everything, assessing. Then after several painful moments, and without speaking, Jacob offered his huge hand in welcome. Rory took it, amazed to notice that his own hand was as large, his skin as matte black, his grip as powerful as Jacob's. Inexplicably, this discovery filled him with pride. He stood shoulder to shoulder with Jacob, head to head, eye to eye, pleased that they were now equally matched in size and stature. He wondered briefly if God would be kind enough to allow him to age with dignity, into the man who could well be a future reflection of himself, relieving him of the prospect of aging into the decayed wreck of a man he had left drinking at home.

"How you keeping?" Jacob asked him.

"Good."

"Your father? You still see him?"

"He lives with me." He waited for the same disbelief that Odile had showed him earlier. It didn't come.

"Good." Jacob looked approving. "And how is he?"

Rory's smile narrowed. "Well, you know . . ."

Jacob needed no further explanation, and didn't pursue the matter. His eyes moved from the breadth of Rory's chest to his battered face. He asked, "You a fighter now? Wrestling? Boxing?"

Ah, Rory thought. That was the old stickfighter speaking. More than once he had seen Jacob silently watching him from a distance, following him with his eyes as he played cricket in the yard or went about his chores. Only now did he realize that Jacob had seen in him something that Rory himself had not: a fighter's potential. He regretted that unlike Jacob, he had not recognized in himself his father's demon seed. If he had, he would have taken steps—what steps, he had no idea—to exorcise that bellicose spirit long before it had exploded outward. But even though he hated what he was, and hated even more seeing the recognition of it in the eyes of others, he took no offense at Jacob's question. "Boxing," he replied.

Jacob's eyes fell to Rory's huge hands, and he nodded. "Competition? Professional?"

"Just practice. At the gym. No real fights. I couldn't . . . I'd be too afraid . . ." He somehow suspected he didn't need to explain any further.

He was right. Jacob's eyes took on a faraway look. "The heat in the blood," he murmured. Rory stayed quiet, looking on as the man in front of him was suddenly there but not quite, transported backward to his own glory days when his weapon was his mahogany *bois,* and his arena the silent forests of the east.

He watched the memories flicker over Jacob's face, wishing he could share in them. What secrets this man must hold! What battles he must have fought, and how his people must have held him in awe for his prowess. When Rory had lived in the yard, Jacob had seemed to him to be an object of contempt, a wreck of a man with a limp and a past nobody cared about. Now he felt ashamed of his own youthful disdain of the mysterious man who had worked in silence in his little room at the back, hiding the light of his majestic past under a bushel. He regretted never having taken the time to stop and ask questions. Think of all the things Jacob could have taught him, if only he had given him the chance.

The memory-glow on Jacob's face dimmed, and he was back in the present. Before Rory could mull further, Jacob spoke. "Son, listen to me. I'm telling you this because that thing I see in you lives in me, too. And if after all my years in the *gayelle* I can pass on one thing I've learned, let me pass it on to you. Some men learn to fight, but other men, well, they born to fight. You and me both, we born to fight. But that fighting spirit is like a demon. It's like fire: you have to master it, because if you let it master you, you lose everything."

Rory's soul leaped. At last! Someone who understood! Someone who saw into the world of warrior spirits the way he did, and recognized them for what they were. He wasn't alone in his visions, after all. He didn't dare speak and risk breaking Jacob's train of thought, so he let him continue uninterrupted.

"These spirits, they no different from men. They sleep and eat and get happy or vexed, just like you and me. When they sleep, it's like a pressure off your soul. When they sleep, they let you out of their grip, and for a while you lose the urge to smell blood, and you think you in control again. And you feel good because you know that, win or lose, you can fight a man with honor and not feel something inside you urging you to force him to the ground and start hitting. You can step in a ring and know all you'll be thinking about is method and rhythm and pace, and the rules of the game. Yes?"

Rory nodded, slowly, overwhelmed by his accuracy.

Jacob went on, voice low. "And after a while, days or weeks, you start to feel like maybe that spirit let you go and went on to torment someone else. And then you in the ring one day and this thing in you wakes up and stretches, and you get giddy because the man in front of you blurs in your vision and the only thing to bring him back into focus is to destroy. And you have to step away, step away fast, because you know if you don't rip those gloves off your hands and get out of the ring, you and he will both be tasting his blood. Right?"

"Yes."

"That's when you realize he never left. And that he's awake and hungry and waiting to get fed. And we, we so foolish, we feed it just what it wants. You know what you feeding him?"

"Tell me." He held his breath.

"Rage, son. Anger and bitterness and hurt." Jacob shook his head. "You, you're so young, but you been feeding that spirit a long time. When you were here, I used to watch you out in the yard, with that father of yours, how he would come at you, and come at you, and you never once fought back—"

"He was my father," Rory interrupted.

"I know," Jacob said wryly. "But I used to watch you, see your face, and I knew even then that every blow he landed, you drew it inside of you to feed that spirit. Every time you looked at him and thought of hitting back, your demon got stronger and stronger. Now you think that spirit bigger than you, yes?"

Much bigger, Rory thought. Bigger, and darker and heavier than anything he could describe. "How can I get it to leave?"

"You can't."

Anguish. "How do I kill it, then?"

Jacob exhaled noisily, and turned around, searching the ground for his staff. He picked it up and held it in his hands, feeling the heft of it, eyes moving up and down its length. Rory leaned in, almost expecting to see the answer etched there on the dark shaft.

"It never dies, Rory," Jacob said finally. "Yours won't, and mine hasn't. Sometimes I roll over in bed at night and I am sure I hear him shift in the back of my mind, like a prowler in the room, looking for something. Quiet sounds, whispers, just to remind me he's still there."

This was not what he wanted to hear. What did Jacob mean, it never dies? "So, I'm cursed, then? For life?"

Jacob didn't take his eyes away from his *bois*. "*Curse* is a serious word."

"It's a serious problem."

Jacob brought the tip of the staff against Rory's chest, over his heart, like a lance whose point was poised to pierce. Like many weapons of its kind, it was "mounted"—imbued with supernatural strength by the incantations of a country obeah-woman for accuracy, potency, and assured victory. He could feel its power surging at him, connecting him with the old stickfighter, forming a circuit. His skin prickled.

"All of us," Jacob said, "every one of us, has something—something dark, pulling us one way or the other. For some people, it's too much food, or too much rum, or too much church. Too much of anything could never be good. Some people lie, some steal, and some go to their graves without doing an honest day's work. For us, you and me, it's that heat in our blood, that burning."

"And how we supposed to put it out?"

Jacob took the tip of the staff away from Rory's chest and let the end rest on the ground, holding it like a shepherd's crook. "What you think? We're fighters. We fight it."

"How?"

"Face the rage. Look at it and see it for what it is. Don't swallow it whole and pretend it isn't there. You have to learn to force it out of you, dig it out of your belly rather than let it sit there and burn."

Rory shook his head, disappointed. Maybe Jacob didn't understand after all. "If I force it out, I'll hurt somebody."

"No, if it rushes out because you can't control it, *then* you'll hurt somebody. That's the difference between water running down a canal and water bursting out of a dam."

That couldn't be so. Anger was a wild animal that had to be caged, not let loose to roam in the streets. Jacob was wrong. Maybe they were less alike than he had thought, or maybe the similarities he saw between them were born of wanting, not of truth. "You not making any sense."

Jacob closed his eyes and stood quietly for a while. When he opened them, they were sad. "Son, I'm sorry. I can't explain it any other way. You go home and think about it. Think hard. You're the only person who can figure out what to do. Just remember that spirit. Remember what he eats. And then don't give him any."

Rory watched as Jacob went back behind his workbench and sat, laying the dark staff flat down on the ground at his feet, keeping it from rolling away by resting one foot lightly upon it. He couldn't believe he was leaving him like this, with so many questions hanging in the air. But it was obvious that there was no more to say on that issue. Despondent, he waited for Jacob to speak again.

"So, what you came for, boy? Not to talk about fighting."

"No, I came about work," he mumbled. "A job for you."

"What work?"

Rory patted his waist. "A weight belt."

Jacob looked surprised. "You don't have one?"

He had to tell the story yet another time for the day. It wasn't any easier to spit up this time around. "I had one. A good one. It got stolen from my house."

"Sprangers?" Jacob didn't look surprised. It was the same story all over: addicts would snatch anything that wasn't nailed down, and then return with a claw-headed hammer to rip up everything that was.

"Yes. Crack, maybe."

Jacob didn't answer but began rummaging around on his table. It was strewn with sharp metal tools, little plastic margarine tubs filled with tacks, nails, and clips, an awl, and a new addition: a small hand-operated sewing machine. From amid the clutter, he retrieved a frayed measuring tape and then beckoned to Rory to come nearer so that he could measure his waist.

He obeyed respectfully, reluctantly allowing the conversation to turn to business. But as Jacob's light fingers moved over his waist, measuring once, then twice, then writing numbers down with a stub of pencil, he looked out past the dark, bent head into the yard. He'd found answers aplenty to questions he'd almost been born with, but those answers had come with even more questions—the sting in the tail. But one thing that was confirmed for him now: the demon he had believed to be a creation of his own imagination was real and alive and hungry for his personal pain; and whatever it took, however *long* it took, he would find a way to make it starve.

Odile and Rory

Odile sat on the rough, flat stump of the tamarind tree outside her mother's house, facing Jacob's little workshop. From here she could see Rory and the stickfighter talking, heads together over the table, choosing a strip of leather from a few large pieces laid open on it.

In her lap she held a foil-wrapped wedge of Myra's black fruitcake, the more expensive kind, thick with almonds and drenched with brandy, that she reserved for home use rather than for sale. The cake was for Rory.

He was all her mother could talk about this afternoon: how well he had grown, how polite and decent he seemed to have turned out to be, and what a damn shame it was that he was still living with that nasty old Saul. Odile had been glad that for a change the conversation had shifted away from her, and even more relieved that Myra bore him no ill will.

Odile was surprised to discover that she herself was far less upset with him over what he had done to her than she was by their encounter in the bar earlier this week. Although the swellings on his face embarrassed her—she could, after all have stopped Rollock, Patrick, and Teeth before they had gone too far—she still felt justified in being angry with him for charging in like a hero from a bad Western. Life wasn't that clean and neat and ordered. And even if she were guilty of the crime as he believed she was, what did he think? That she would tear her apron off and throw it to the floor, repent of her sins, and follow him out the door? He always had that annoying streak of idealism in him, sometimes seeing flecks of light where every sane person saw only shadow. Maybe just for that he deserved a punch or two. All the same, she had pretended ignorance when her mother had wondered aloud how he had managed to come by such an adornment of bruises.

But as much as his reappearance in her life irked her, she was secretly glad to see him again. They had been friends, had known each other all their lives, and none of her teenage arrogance and mistreatment of the little boy next door had ever daunted him from offering his affection. She could beat him at cricket, but he would be there the next day, waiting for her with bat and ball in hand. She could dunk him in the river until he nearly drowned, but he would be at the gate the next Saturday, in his ragged shorts and with his coarse towel, waiting to accompany her on her next swim. Whatever the adolescent power play she had decided to engage him in, he had taken it in his stride and come out smiling.

Odile watched him with Jacob. That little boy had loved her. Simply. Selflessly. He had been the only person she knew who had never wanted anything in exchange. Just as well, because she had never had anything to give back, tied up as she always was in herself and her own problems. But that had never mattered to him.

She found herself anxious for them to be back on the road again, not because she was ready to leave, but because the road would paradoxically give them the privacy they wouldn't have in the yard. She wanted to ask him questions about himself: what he did for a living; and why, and if he still loved cricket; and what he had used to fill the empty space Gracie had left behind. Anything that would give her a clue about the mystery he had grown into.

Her impatience was about to bubble over when both men stood up and shook hands, their business concluded. She stiffened a little, strangely nervous. Jacob did not merely see Rory to the edge of the porch, but chose to walk him across the yard to the place where she sat. He didn't bring his staff with him.

She watched the two men walk side by side across the space that separated Jacob's workshop from the rest of the yard, noting with surprise that they were now of equal height and bulk. She had realized before that Rory had grown quite a bit, but it was only when placed in the context of Jacob's own size that it became evident to what extent he had. The days in which she could lord her physical advantage over him were long gone.

As they approached, Jacob was the first to speak. "Odile, how you doing?" These days Jacob had taken to looking her in the eye. He was no longer intimidated by the knowledge that she didn't approve much of him or his relationship with her mother, either because he had come to give less of a damn, or because her own disapproval had diminished over time.

She hopped off the tree stump and self-consciously dusted off the back of her skirt. "Jacob."

Rory stood there quietly.

"You finished?" Odile asked him unnecessarily.

He glanced at Jacob and pondered for a few moments before answering. She had the idea he didn't think he was through with him at all. "Yes. All finished. You really going to walk me back?" He sounded unsure whether to believe her or not, half prepared to hear her tell him she was only joking.

She tried to act as if it were of no importance. "Yeah. Why not?"

Rory looked delighted, as if she'd promised him the last dance at the ball. She remembered the piece of cake her mother had sent, and held it out to him.

Surprise showed on his face. "For me?"

"Uh-huh."

He took it but didn't even open the foil to see what was inside. "What is it?"

"Cake."

His smile grew even broader, half warming her, half irritating. Did nobody ever give him anything? "You'll thank your mother for me?"

She waved it away. "It's no big thing. She has tins of cake all over the kitchen. She bakes for a living, you know."

That didn't diminish his pleasure. He held the packet in his big hand, hefted it, then shifted it to the other hand and did the same. Odile didn't like the way Jacob glanced from Rory to her and back again, almost smiling, seeming to see something that she herself couldn't. "Let's go," she told Rory.

The men touched hands briefly again, and Rory promised to return in a few days for his belt. "You tell Miss Myra I said goodbye, okay?" he said to Jacob.

Jacob promised that he would.

As they left the yard, she watched Rory covertly to observe whether he showed any signs of seeing the ghosts of the past that had besieged him on his way in. Nothing about him told her that he did. His vision, instead of facing outward, seemed turned in on himself, and he navigated more by memory than by sight. She let him meditate in peace.

It was late afternoon, and she was due back at the Smiling Dragon in an hour, but after her disastrous luncheon with Vincent and Miss Ling, she was reluctant to return. The bar seemed recently to have become the seat of so much turmoil: Vincent and his grandmother, the rude little waitress who always seemed determined to get her goat, and of course, lately, she and Vincent. Him pushing her way beyond the nonchalant comfort of the association they had agreed—or at least, that she thought they had agreed—existed. Each seeking company and very little more—no fair, no foul on either side if one decided it was no longer what they wanted. Now Vincent was dreaming dreams of top-dollar casinos and glamor and pomp, with her playing hostess, wearing a silver gown and a painted smile. She wasn't sure if that was her destiny, but she knew she didn't have the energy to try to figure it out. Even the disorientation Rory's presence caused was preferable to that. She joined him in his pensive silence.

They came to the spot that had once been their means of access to the river. Where an untended grassy lot had been bisected by a track leading all the way down to the bank, a small school had been built. In the short space of time since its opening, the rambunctious children had managed to batter it into a state of disrepair, leaving the playground a shambles and the fence sagging.

Odile stopped. Instantly, Rory's steps, which, she had not noticed until now, had been in perfect sync with hers, stopped as well. He didn't ask any questions but merely looked at her.

She laid her hand on a broken-down spot along the chicken-wire fencing, thinking hard. Was she crazy? She hadn't been to the river in an age. If Rory's ghosts inhabited the yard they had left, well, hers roamed the riverbank. She was almost sure she heard their muffled summons.

Rory never asked a question, never tried to dissuade her. That convinced her that he heard them, too. He looked at the foil-wrapped piece of cake in his hand, wondering what to do with it, and eventually slipped it into the deep pocket of his sweatpants. He threw his long legs over the fence with ease and, once on the other side, offered his arms to help her over.

She was an athletic woman, long-limbed and strong, and well able to climb over unaided. But it would seem rude to refuse, so she accepted his help, marveling that his hands neither lingered nor strayed, and that as soon as she was safe on the other side he stepped away. Other men, she knew, would not have lost the opportunity to touch her as they would have liked. His face showed no sign that this had ever entered his mind.

He took her hand as they crossed the schoolyard, unselfconsciously, almost unaware that he was even doing so. She didn't take it away. The bones of her hand felt so fine in his. Childlike, he set the swings on the playground in motion as he passed them, enjoying the sight of them swaying high overhead.

At the other end of the yard, he helped her over again and then clambered to the other side after her. From here, they could smell the water that flowed just yards beyond the dense patch of razor grass towering over both their heads. The old path took up again some distance from the fence. From its well-beaten appearance, it was obvious that the children of the neighborhood were not daunted in their pursuit of entertainment by the presence of the school. It certainly had stopped no one from making use of the river at that point.

He took her hand again. This time she was glad for it. The path was muddy from the rain this morning, and her shoes were not made for such terrain. With each step, the mud released her foot reluctantly with a sucking sound.

"You want me to carry you?" he asked when she stopped to fix a buckle that popped out at her ankle. He held out both his arms.

She drew the line at that. "No. I can do this." She had to clench her toes against the soles of the sandals to keep her grip on them. The buckle refused to hold the strap fast, but she didn't let him know that.

"Okay." He didn't look put out and didn't insist.

Now she could see it, their river, coursing past. The unending rainy season had caused it to swell, and turned its clear water brown, but it had also washed it free of the debris that careless people usually tossed onto the banks. Although the water was opaque and the color of tea, there were no scattered bottles, food boxes, or the other usual detritus either bobbing on its surface or strewn on the side.

She was strangely emotionless as she walked. The last time either of them had been here, they had been here together. She remembered she had been cruel to him, mocking his love, too selfish to see his pain. In hindsight, she regretted hurting him more than she did the fact that she had pushed him over the edge until he hurt her. But returning was a test of how much she had healed. Like picking at scabs. And she was surprised and glad to see that the scabs had begun falling off on their own, with only the palest of scars underneath. There was regret here, yes, and much pain.

But ghosts? None that she could see.

They followed the river silently along its course for several minutes until they arrived at the spot for which they had, by unspoken agreement, initially set out. Their rock.

It was quite large and stood on the far side of a wide pool in which they, like the children who came after them, had spent many a hot day immersed. When it rained, the river became so deep at that point that children could easily leap off the rock without risking their necks. It was smooth, domed, and broad. In the dark months of her shameful and terrifying pregnancy, it had been her sanctuary from school, her mother, and prying eyes. Later, toward the end, it had become Rory's sanctuary, too.

This time, he didn't bother asking. He bent over, deftly rolling up the legs of his pants as high as they would go, and then scooped her up, holding her high and against him. She gasped in surprise, but before she could struggle he was striding through water that posed no resistance. Rolling up his pants legs was a waste of time: the water soaked him to the chest, and the tail of her skirt dipped into it, coming up clammy against her bottom. He deposited her onto the top of the rock and clambered up next to her, not even out of breath. He grinned. "You okay?"

"Fine." She settled with her legs stretched out before her, heels together, primly tugging down her skirt as far as it would cover her. She waited for him to say something.

He just seemed happy to be next to her, crossing his ankles and bringing his heels up under him. Water ran out of his

clothes and streaked down the rock. He didn't look perturbed. He let his hands fall onto his thighs and looked
around him.

"At least this is still the same," he remarked after a while.
"Everything else keeps changing, but this . . ." He didn't finish.

"You think things change too fast?" she asked him.

"Yeah. Much too fast."

"What do you wish never changed?"

He thought about that for a while. "I don't know. Nothing
special. Just that sometimes things seem to be running away
from me. Sometimes I just need something to hang onto
when everything around is spinning. You know?"

She knew. After a moment's pause, she asked a question
that had been on her mind. "You ever got another chicken?"

"No. I couldn't."

"Gracie was nice." She wished that didn't sound so inade-
quate.

"Yes, she was," he agreed vehemently.

She was afraid to let the silence fall around them once
more. "And what about things you wish would change but
don't?"

She heard him laugh. It was a deep laugh, and she didn't
know why she was surprised at the vitality in it. Perhaps it
was that for the first time his customary hangdog expression
was replaced by near-serenity. The river often had that effect.

"What I wish would change? Where you want me to
start?" He didn't offer anything more.

She stared at the mud on her shoes, sure they would never
be clean again. She waited.

"Odile," Rory began.

The subtle shift in the tone of his voice made her tense.
"What?"

"I want you to give me something. Something you owe
me."

"I? Owe you? What I could possibly owe you?" She had

no way of knowing what he was coming with next, but she knew that she wouldn't like it. It was so easy for them to just sit there and talk about the river and poor old Gracie. That didn't require much thought. Wherever he was planning to take the conversation now, though, would very likely be somewhere she didn't wish to go.

"You owe me an answer to the question I asked you earlier. In town. If I gave you freedom, like you said, what have you done with it? Why are you working in a bar, surrounded by all these damn dirty men, who don't know to sleep when the night come?"

"I'm not . . ." she began agitatedly. She got to her feet in haste. She wasn't sitting here with him, not if this was all he wanted to talk about. Why couldn't he leave the whole matter dead and buried where it deserved to be?

He seized her hand and pulled her back down again. Her bottom hit the stone with a plop. "I know you're not a . . . a prostitute." He grimaced, the very thought an affront to his sense of decency. "But you wanted to be a doctor, Odile. Or a lawyer. Something big. Something worthwhile. Instead, you sell cigarettes and rum. This is what you do with your freedom?"

Why did he want to force her to reach inside and put all this shame into words? She looked at him, taking in his bright eyes and dilated nostrils. He was so earnest, as if part of him still believed that every question had a straight answer; but at the same time cautious, knowing that the answer wasn't always an easy one to grasp. So hard to pin down, shifting between manhood and boyishness like someone with one foot in the river and the other on the bank.

She took a gulp of air. "I work at the Dragon," she began hesitantly, realizing that this was the first time she had ever given voice to her ugly thoughts, "because it's a good place to hide."

"From what?" he persisted.

Her answer surprised even herself. "From my guilt."

"But you didn't do anything. What are you guilty of?"

"Not any guilt I have now. The guilt I would have if I did succeed. If I'd gone on and got an education, it would be because I wasn't held back by my baby. Everything I stood to lose because of the baby, I stood to regain when it died. But to take it all back, my education, my plans, would have been . . ." She cast about for an explanation but was unable to articulate it.

He understood. ". . . bought at the price of its blood," he finished for her.

She nodded mutely.

"So you prefer to have nothing at all."

"Yes."

She expected him to hold her then; any other man would have. Offer his shoulder as a place to hide her face in case she needed to cry. Instead, he stretched out flat on his back, staring up into the sky, past the tall bamboo that obscured their light. He took up most of the space on the rock. It was beginning to drizzle again; tiny droplets sprinkled his face and began to dance on the surface of the water. The bamboo rustled softly, creaking as the long shafts rubbed against each other, raising up high-pitched sounds like chirping crickets or tiny frogs. "You can't think that," he told her. He made no move to get out of the rain.

"I do." The chill she was feeling had nothing to do with the wind that was picking up. It came from inside.

"But you shouldn't. You can't scuttle your whole life as some kind of punishment to yourself. Look at it from the other side."

Her body felt heavy and tired, and she wanted to lie next to him and rest; but she refused to give in to the need. "What other side?"

Only his eyes shifted, holding hers. "If you do nothing with your life, and if you don't achieve any of the things you always wanted to, then it means that baby died in vain."

She stared at him, her own perspective on her life thrown

out of kilter. Not once had that thought entered her mind, but now that he had placed it there, it seemed so obvious that she couldn't imagine how she could have missed it before. It was like passing by a rainbow and noticing an eighth color, and realizing that it had been there all along, only you had simply never noticed before. "I hadn't thought of that," she finally managed to say.

"Think about it now," he said softly.

"I will," she whispered.

"Let me help you think about it some more." He wasn't asking, not in the shy way he had whenever she was around. He was telling, asserting himself into her space. She knew he was talking past this moment, right here, on the rock.

"Rory, don't forget . . ." She was about to say, *Don't forget I've got someone,* but found that she couldn't. Vincent seemed so separate from her, so far away now. A person and yet not a person—more like a big warm pair of arms she could drape around herself like a blanket and then close her eyes to shut out the light. He was safe, and like the Dragon, he was a place to hide.

Rory was far from safe. In just one afternoon he had dragged her out into the open to face her secrets and her guilt, and he was not prepared to withdraw from such a battle. His offer of "help" was nothing more than a threat to force her to look harder at herself than she cared to. He was still on a crusade, still on a rescue mission. "I don't need your help," she told him gruffly.

"You'll get it anyway," he vowed.

She didn't try to argue but watched him as he rolled over onto his belly and hoisted himself up on all fours, edging around until he was kneeling in front of her. The drizzle hadn't intensified but continued as a light mist.

"What are you doing?" she asked sharply.

He clasped her muddy ankles in his hands, pressing them against each other, and bowed forward, silent, genuflecting. His eyes were downcast, not holding hers anymore, yet not timid. The breadth of his back was curved, tense, and in the silence of the river, he seemed to be praying.

She remembered the time they had made love on that same rock—or at least, the time she had let him make love to her. She had been too immersed in her own wretchedness to have allowed her mind to share that experience with him. She just lay there and let him discover her body on his own. It had been his first time.

The desire that incited her to repeat the act—this time as a participant rather than as a virtual onlooker—was proof that she had gone insane. One day she was having this man beaten for his effrontery, the next she was wanting to be joined to him with a hunger that was shockingly sharp. Not a connection of bodies, she decided. It was a connection of minds that she needed. Maybe if she took him into her now, she would understand what he had become. Then she could overlay all that she knew of him from before with all that she would then learn, and have a better picture of the whole.

But she had a man, waiting for her back at the bar. If Vincent satisfied her, kept her company, and sated her curiosity with his own answers, then where did this desire come from?

He tilted his face toward hers. "And what about this man you . . . *know?*"

"It's complicated," she told him.

"So is this."

"Yes." This didn't feel like cheating. Wasn't it supposed to? Vincent was a change for her. Beautiful, sweet, but not a saga-boy with fancy clothes and all the right moves—the kind of man she had once collected as the currency by which she measured her womanhood. With him, she had made the shift from being defined by men to being self-defined in the company *of* a man. Surely that demanded some sort of loyalty. But it didn't surprise her when she made no effort to get up and move away.

"You remember what we did here?" Rory asked.

His coy reference didn't embarrass her. "Afterward, you picked a water lily for me. You rubbed it on my cheek, and all the yellow pollen dust came off."

"You know why?"

The memory of the gesture charmed her, even now. "To see if I liked butter."

He dropped his gaze. The rock under them suddenly captivated his attention. "No."

"No?" She remembered taking the lily home with her afterward. She slipped her hand up to her cheek, somehow expecting traces of the gold dust to be still scattered there.

He concentrated on not looking at her. "To see if you liked *me*. I was afraid to come right out and ask."

How cruel she must have been to him. "And what did you learn?"

He shrugged. "I learned that flowers don't tell fortunes," he said.

"I'm sorry."

He neither accepted nor rejected her apology. She wasn't even sure she knew what she was being sorry for.

"Did you . . ." He chewed his lower lip. He tried again. "When you let me . . . into you, did you . . . feel anything?"

She remembered her mind had been floating somewhere out on the river, or off in the bamboo, hearing every creak so close to her that she thought her hair was full of singing insects. She remembered his awed touch, his delight and fear as he had peeled away each layer of her clothing to reveal sacred territory that was foreign to his hands and eyes. What had she felt? In the midst of her own personal pain, he had come to her, and she had let him. He had been so young and ignorant that the mound of her belly had never even given him a hint as to the tiny unformed heart that had beat beneath it. He had stretched out above her as on an altar, too stunned to believe his own good fortune. And withdrew from her body shaking and joyful, as if God had bestowed upon him a wonderful gift.

"I felt safe," she finally told him. "I felt . . ." she stopped. This wasn't a word she used, not even in the casual way it was bandied about in idle conversation. But it was the only one that described what he had given her in exchange for her body that afternoon. "I felt loved," she managed.

Something bloomed on his face. "You knew."

"Yes."

"Every time I thought about it, I wondered. I used to ask myself whether you were there at all, or if I was really alone. If I had made it up in my head."

"You didn't make it up."

"I'm glad."

"And you're not alone now, either." The recriminations would come later. "I'll stay grounded here with you this time, if you like. No floating away. I promise." She held her arms out to him, urging him to come into them. But instead of doing so, he released her ankles and took her wrists, turning her palms upward, and stared at them, searching. He studied the brown lines that crisscrossed them as if he was reading a road map.

His silence unnerved her. His refusal to accept the offer of her arms disturbed her even more. She tried to make a joke. "If you think flowers don't tell the future, then I don't think palm reading will, either."

He placed her palms against his face, covering his eyes. She wanted to leave them there, for his sake, but he was still so quiet. She resisted his grip. When her hands came away, they were damp, but the moisture was warmer than raindrops.

Rory, crying? Nobody had ever wept for her before. His lips moved, but there was no sound. She strained to hear what he was saying.

"I waited and waited." His words were finally audible. "But I never knew what I was waiting for. Now this . . ."

"What do you mean, waited? Waited on what?" He couldn't be saying what she thought he was. Surely, he had not been holding himself back since that time on the rock, holding out for her? "Rory, you telling me you haven't been with another woman since me?"

He looked a little abashed. "No. Not exactly. Not the way we were."

"And you're what, seventeen?"

"Eighteen."

At that age, she had all but lost count of her lovers. "Why not?"

"I don't know. I couldn't. It's . . ." Under his dark skin, blood rushed to the surface. "It's never been about anyone but you," he finished finally. He waited tautly, expecting mocking laughter or a rebuff.

She could bring herself to inflict neither upon him. She was flattered, but amazed, too. When she pressed her cheek against the purple bruise under his eye, he didn't even flinch. He submitted meekly, glad to let her lead. The inside of his lip was raw against her tongue—courtesy of one of the Smiling Dragon bouncers, no doubt—and, sure that she was hurting him, she pulled away. His hand against the back of her head stopped her.

"It's okay, Odile. Please."

Again, the lines between past and present blurred, and in spite of his size, Rory was a boy again: clumsy, totally unsure of himself. She felt like a mother ministering to a child. But no mother ever did what she was doing, in quite that way. She nudged him backward against the rock, hitching his wet shirt up out of the waist of his pants. She pressed her hands against the flesh that she had bared by this action, amazed at how black his skin was—more like the absence of light than like the presence of anything else. His chest was warm and hairless under her fingers, and responded to their pressure by somehow pressing back against them. Equal and opposite reaction.

She looked down at him, and he closed his eyes and waited. "Touch me," she instructed him.

His eyes flew open. "Can I?"

This time, she did laugh, but not unkindly. "Yes, Rory. You can do anything you like."

His hands came up to pluck at the buttons on the front of her dress. They were too tiny for him to grasp easily with his large fingers, but she didn't offer to help. He managed to free three of them, then a fourth. The white satin bra was the type that opened in the front, and the little round clasp popped open at his first attempt. Then her breasts were bare to his gaze. He stared so long that she became embarrassed and was unable to suppress a nervous giggle.

"Sorry, I . . ." He let his thumb stroke one nipple, feeling its thickness. He raised up a little so that he could bury his face against her skin. She felt his confidence rise in him as he slid his lips up along her throat and chin, not breaking contact until he took her mouth, one hand back behind her head again, cushioned by her wet hair. With the other hand, he nudged her skirt up over her hips, fingers spanning the cheeks of her bottom, feeling the cotton that covered it and trying his best to get rid of it. His breath was coming in anxious puffs.

Between them they managed to slide her panties down to her ankles, but her shoes were in the way. They got those off and laid them on the rock, and then the panties followed. She moved to wriggle out of her dress, but he stayed her.

"You'll get it muddy if you put it down," he warned.

She didn't care. "I'm already muddy. Besides, it'll wash. Or throw away."

"No. Please, leave it on. It's so pretty, Odile. Against your skin."

She left it on. She threw one knee on each side of his hips, reaching under the skirt that now spread over him like a huge blossom. She tugged at the top of his pants, pulling it down a way, and as she did so, her mother's cake fell out of his pocket. She nudged it out of reach, hoping it wouldn't be too waterlogged to eat later. She reached under her skirt again and held him in the circle of her fingers. He was trembling.

As she drew him into her, she whispered words of comfort to still the momentary paroxysm of panic that ran through him. It seemed that if at that moment she had given him the chance, he would have leaped up and ran. But by her whispers he was soothed.

He was content to let her move against him, unable to do any more than steady her with his hands. The tears flowed freely out of the corners of his eyes and down his temples into his hair. She caught a tear on her fingertip and brought it to her lips.

They moved together, hushed, afraid that any noise would disturb the spirits of the river. By degrees, she noticed her control of their coupling slipping from her to him as he learned her rhythm. Where she had begun as the leader, she became the led, as he discovered what he wanted from her and took it. She knew his strength and was amazed that such power could be reined in, in order to pleasure rather than hurt. He gentled her mouth open and whispered secrets into it, then pulled his head back and let her press her lips closed, so the secrets would be hers and hers alone.

Rory

Rory didn't want to go home yet. Although home meant a shower and a dry set of clothes, possibly even something to eat, it also meant a return to reality, banality, and Saul. Wet as he was and hungry as he was, he'd rather keep on the wings that Odile had given him tonight and glide just above the surface of the ground than shrug them off and walk again like an ordinary man.

After he had walked Odile to her bar, he loitered outside for hours, trying to push his hunger pangs to the back of his mind, watching people come and leave, marveling at how differently he now perceived its clients since Odile had managed to convince him that her duties were restricted to behind the counter. The people who walked in or lurched out were no different from those he had observed from that same post earlier that day, but they no longer seemed threatening, potential defilers of Odile's dignity. His hackles lay unprovoked.

Odile. She had surprised him on the rock. He'd never sought to question or lament destiny's decree that what had happened out on the river was impossible. He'd simply accepted this as fact. But tonight she'd made a fool of destiny. Fate, once fixed, solid, and determinate, was now fluid, allowing itself to be molded to the shape of his most fevered fantasies. He wondered if this change of states would be permanent, or if a day from now, or a week or a month, that same fickle fate would choose to gel and solidify, bricking him in again. Leaving him alone again.

Was that something he was prepared to allow, or would he wriggle and squirm and struggle against any imprisonment now that he had felt and tasted what it was like to be free? Which was it to be: let his head roll back with the punches, or hold his fists before his face and fight? He wasn't even sure there was anything to fight for. Odile was perfectly capable of waking in the morning and deciding that tonight had never happened. If she willed it to be so, and believed it so in her heart, she could wipe her own memory clean, and nothing he said or did would make her admit to it.

But it *had* happened. He had fitted his body to hers, true flesh to true flesh, not the flesh of his fantasies. The love he felt for her was neither augmented nor diminished by the sex they had had; it was finite, and had been from its conception. He was sure he had been born loving her, but there was no breathless romance to that love. Nothing warm, nothing pink, not the kind of love they wrote songs or stories about. It was clear, hard, real. He carried her around in his skin. That was all.

When his feet began to cramp, Rory gave up his vigil at the roadside, having been too close to the source of all that power for too long. He needed to put some distance between himself and her. He tried to remember where he had parked his car, but this afternoon seemed such a long time ago that it took a fair amount of pacing and head-scratching to bring its exact location to his mind. He crossed town without even noticing the distance.

The engine was cold. As he waited for it to stir sluggishly, he glanced around the car. For the first time, he was embarrassed by its shabby interior: seats whose plush covers buckled and clumped together, large pills forming like dustballs gathering under a settee; springs that stuck him in the back and legs; cracking plastic on the dash . . . He tried to look at it through Odile's eyes. She had grown up as poor as he, but she had an eye for fine things. If he drew up at the door of the Smiling Dragon one afternoon and asked her to get in, would she?

If only he knew more about women. If only he knew the right things to say or do, so that even if he failed to impress, they didn't leave thinking him a total fool. How to treat a woman, what to do and say: yet more things his father hadn't taught him. If only there were a teacher capable of imparting that knowledge . . .

The thought hit him so abruptly that his foot was jolted off the clutch just as he was about to pull off. The engine hacked, the muffler farted, and the car stalled. He *did* have a teacher. One who would be a little reluctant, but who had the knowledge all the same. He glanced at the clock on the dusty dash, but that had stopped, so he checked the time on his watch. It was late, but not terribly so.

He needed to find a phone booth. The questions he had to ask couldn't wait till morning. He didn't feel like putting himself through the pain of restarting the car just to reverse into the parking spot he was attempting to leave, so he slammed it into neutral, let down the handbrake, got out, and pushed it back against the sidewalk. He kicked the door shut, not bothering to lock it, and left in search of a phone.

The first two were card phones, and Rory didn't have a card. The next one was a coin phone, but some amateur DJ or electronics buff had neatly sliced away the handset for use as a makeshift microphone. He had to walk all the way back into the heart of the shopping district, back to Frederick Street with its glamorous stores and wide pavements, to find another. This time he was lucky: the one he came across was not only working and taking coins, but it also held a fairly serviceable phone book, hanging by a metal rod from the base of the phone. He flipped through for the number he wanted, dialed, and waited.

Someone on the other end picked up. A man's voice answered, irritated, impatient. "Yes?"

His resolve slipped. He hesitated, wondering if hanging up and running away would be too childish. He swallowed and opened his mouth to speak, but before he could, the voice came again, louder this time.

"What is it?"

This was ridiculous. He was a man, dammit. He spoke clearly and carefully, shoving his nervousness aside. "May I speak to Mrs. Bedassie, please?"

The man paused, then asked, "Who is this?"

"You don't know me, sir, but, your wife and I have . . . business in common."

"This about the pharmacy?"

He lied easily. "Yes."

There was a loud clunk as Bedassie tossed the receiver onto a hard surface. In the distance, Rory heard muffled conversation. He fingered another coin as he waited, running his thumb along its milled edge, holding it ready in case the phone beeped in his ear, hungry for more money. After a long moment, there was a woman's voice on the line, puzzled, but curious. "Hello?"

"Zen," he said softly.

He heard her breath being drawn sharply in. "Is that you?" she asked after a while.

"Yes."

"You *mad?*" she hissed, voice barely discernible. "Who said you could call me here?"

"Don't hang up," he pleaded.

"I'm going to—" she began.

"Don't. Zen, I need—"

The lack of volume in her voice didn't stop the anger in it from being communicated. "I don't care what you need. How dare you—" Then there came the sound of voices muted by her hand over the mouthpiece. When she spoke again, her voice was at normal volume. "Boy, you crazy? What you trying to do to me?"

"Where's your husband?"

"I'm in another room now."

"Good. I need to talk to you." He stopped. Now that he had her, what exactly was he going to ask? There was so much he needed to know, and no place to start. Then it occurred to him that, given all that had passed between him and Zenobia, maybe she wasn't the best person to choose. Did a man ask a woman he had known intimately for advice about another woman?

"Talk, then." Her voice was surprisingly soft. There was something in it that he hadn't heard there before. She sounded flattered, almost coquettish.

This wasn't right. He *was* crazy. What could he do, ramble on about this woman he loved but couldn't have, whom he carried around close to his chest like a crucifix on a chain? Questions would be pointless anyway. Whatever Odile's reasons for reaching for him today probably wouldn't exist tomorrow. She may have let him near her, but nothing in what she said or did told him that she ever would again. Sometimes stars came almost close enough to the earth to kiss it lightly, and then they were on their way, rushing on along whatever path nature had ordained for them. All the knowledge Zenobia or anyone else could give him wouldn't change that.

When he didn't speak, she went on. "Tell that cat to give you your tongue back. What's the matter, you missing me?"

"No, I—"

Disbelief. *"No?"*

He knew what Zen was thinking, and what she was thinking was wrong. He hadn't called out of passion for her, but there was no delicate way to tell her that. This was a mistake. *Turn back time,* he prayed. *Let me walk backward away from the phone. Unmake this call.* He was sweating. "What I mean is—"

"Rory," Zenobia said firmly, but not harshly. "First things first. Don't ever call me here again. My life with my family is mine, private. You don't belong in it. You don't belong anywhere *near* it. Hear?"

"Yes, ma'am."

"Second, I know what you want from me." Her laugh was high-pitched, like a teenage girl's. "But what you're already getting is all you're going to get. I'm tired telling you, this is not a love thing. This ain't no affair. You get what you want, I get what I want, and that's enough for both of us. So don't start getting any ideas. Hear?"

"I wasn't going to ask for—" he began to protest, but there was no use in trying.

Then her coquetry was back, her moods shifting like sand. "But that don't mean we have to stop what we're doing. It just means we have to be careful. No use starting trouble." She paused and then blurted, "Come tomorrow. Come see me." It was a command, not a request.

He wasn't sure he wanted to see her so soon. Her presumption both embarrassed and irritated him. "I haven't got you on my route tomorrow." She wasn't the only one who could be firm.

"Make an excuse. Come on your lunch hour." Then, as an additional enticement, she added, in the manner of one dangling a tempting sweetmeat before a reluctant lover, "I'll let you touch me, you know . . . there. You know you always wanted to do that."

She was right. Each time they met, he begged to touch her, just lightly. Each time, she had bluntly refused. In spite of himself, he tried to imagine what would lie at the apex of those fat thighs, and what it would feel like under his fingers. He was shocked to discover himself painfully erect. Something was building up pressure between his ears. He was amazed that in spite of all that had passed between himself and Odile just hours ago, this greedy selfish woman still excited him. But she was like an addictive black hole, and the mere idea of slipping himself into that hole, even though he knew that doing so would mean that he would be destroyed, left him aching with longing. That longing was immediately counterbalanced by a sense of revulsion—not at her, but at his own response to her. Did his love for Odile leave enough space in him to accommodate lust for a woman who used him for nothing but her own amusement? Apparently it did. That disgusted him.

"You coming, then?" The coquetry had given way to traces of impatience.

"I can't," he managed. "I'm busy. I have too many stops to make—"

"Next day."

"Zen, I'm . . . busy all week. December is a hectic month. . . ."

"Friday then, after work."

He tried to think of an excuse, but none came to him fast enough. Even if he had, he would have torn it to shreds himself before even attempting to pass it by her.

Zenobia sweetened the pot further, her pressure far from subtle. "I'm having a staff Christmas party Friday. With lots of grog, and wild meat. Agouti and wild hog. Curried duck. And me." She waited.

The draw of that black hole was powerful. He shot out an arm to steady himself on the rigging of the phone booth in the hopes that if the suction got too much for him he would be able to hang on tightly enough to prevent himself from being engulfed. He had an image of her, with her teeth bared, smeared not with lipstick but with blood, mouth opening wider, until her face was all mouth, and everything within range of the powerful suction got drawn in—everything around him including passing cars and traffic lights and the grillwork in front of the shuttered stores, until all that remained was him, hanging on to the pole for his life.

Through force of will he pushed the image aside, and then the howling wind around him was quiet. The gaping mouth was gone, leaving him with a new understanding. He could live with his awkwardness with women, he realized. Maybe that was something he'd outgrow eventually. He could live with his self-disgust at the curiosity and lust she instilled in him. That, too, he would probably outgrow. What he couldn't bear for another moment was her conviction that his will could be bent to her desire. It had been true once; she could tell him to come see her, and he would go. She could refuse him the courtesy of a kiss, and he would not insist, for fear of losing the obscenities she offered him in their stead. Hunger made him weak. Loneliness made him even weaker. Tonight, he felt no less hungry and no less lonely than he did on any other night, but tonight he had learned they were both better than shame.

"I'll come Friday," he said, "but we have to talk."

"You dying to see me, and all you want to do is talk? We could think of better things to do with our time, eh, boy?" Again, the little-girl laugh. Her "I won again" laugh.

She was wrong, but this was no time to tell her. Next Friday he'd go to her party, but not for the reasons she was so sure of. He'd show up with a spine for a change, and prove to her and to himself that he was not a toy she could use to help her pass the time, like the little chrome figures she fiddled with endlessly on her desk. Her game, or at least his part in it, would be over. He was sure it wouldn't be a problem for her; he wasn't conceited enough to think he would be hard to replace. Maybe he did understand something about women, after all.

"Friday," he repeated, and hung up.

Zenobia

After Rory hung up, Zenobia held on to the phone, waiting to hear a click that would tell her if her husband was putting down the extension in the living room. After a while, the howling in her ear let her know that the line was dead. Bedassie hadn't been listening. She realized that what she felt at this discovery was pique rather than relief. She threw the handset to the floor, not caring that the howl on the other end was getting louder, begging her to put it back into the cradle. She didn't feel like taking any other calls tonight anyway; so it didn't matter that the line was now tied up. Maybe if it got tired, the howling would stop.

She returned to the living room. What could he be doing, that he didn't even show the slightest interest in the fact that a strange man was calling the house for his wife at this hour? She tracked him down by the smell of those long, nasty brown things he smoked that couldn't make up their minds whether they were cigarettes or cigars. His head was bent over the paper, and the smoke curled around and around.

She stood in the doorway and looked at him. He was reading without his glasses, even though his eyesight was getting so bad lately that it took him twice as long to make it through the paper. The man was vain. Wouldn't be seen dead with bifocals on even in his own house. Even an hour or so before he was ready to go to bed, his hair was neatly slicked down and parted on the left side—he had been parting on the left since he was five, he once told her—and patted into place, and his feet were clad in clean white socks and leather loafers. The kind with little pinholes *and* tassels. She coughed lightly, but he didn't look up.

Zenobia folded her arms. "Damn rude boy, calling me at home this hour of the night," she commented loudly.

Bedassie turned the page.

"Like his mother never told him the night ain't fit to do business."

It occurred to him that she was expecting him to say something. He looked up at her, trying to shift his focus from the page to her face. "Colleague?"

"Supplier." She slipped her hand through her hair and then corrected herself. "Supplier's lackey, actually. Nobody important."

"What did he want at this hour, then? Something wrong?" Bedassie let the top fold of the paper flop over, revealing his whole head. That was a step in the right direction.

Zenobia couldn't stop the smile that split her face. *What he wants is to do me on my desk,* she wanted to tell him. See how he liked *that.* But she said, "No emergency. I don't know what got into him." She let her hand slip from her black, soft hair down to her cheek, and then her fingers followed the shape of her lips. She was sure there were still traces of that rough animal-boy's smell there. Out of malice, she added, "I think he kind of likes me." She waited for a reaction.

Her husband twisted his mouth contemptuously. "Don't be stupid. What makes you think that? You think some supplier's boy got nothing better to do than to spend time watching you that way?"

Her fingers fell away from her lips, the sensuality gone. The scent of Rory gone. "What?"

"You just got too much imagination, that's all. Why you think this boy got anything more on his mind other than to come in and do what he's there for and leave? Those boys meet a dozen young girls on every route. You probably old enough to be his mother. Come on, Zenobia. Be realistic." Then her husband laughed.

He *laughed*. She couldn't believe it. She saw his eyes run over her body, stopping here and there at the points where, all right, her curves were a little too generous. Under his inspection the fat around her waist felt warm and thick, like softening lard. Her hand flew up to her face again, this time to touch the beginnings of a double chin that she had noticed recently but had been trying to ignore.

She watched as her husband drew the paper back up before his chuckling face, shutting her out like a minor but amusing irritant. She was not aware she had crossed the space between them until she was tearing the paper from his hands, ripping it down the center and throwing the pieces in his mocking face. She scratched at the eyes that were unprotected by glasses, snatching at the perfectly combed hair, making a mess of it, ruining that damned left-side part. He pushed her hands away with almost no effort—he wasn't a small man.

"Pipe down!" he shouted at her, the way he did when their daughters were bad. "Woman! Stop! You crazy? That it? You gone mad?"

"I'm telling you this boy likes me, Teddy! He . . . he looks at me. You don't know the way he looks at me!"

He stood up, smoothing his hair with his hands, staring at her in puzzlement. "And a cat can look at a king. You come at me for *that?*" He bent over, carefully collected the pieces of his ruined paper, and placed them on the coffee table. "Look, let's go to bed. It's late enough as it is."

No, he wasn't turning away and leaving her there, feeling fat and ugly like this. He wasn't going to bed convinced that his silly wife was so ugly and undesirable that not even a little messenger boy would want her. She was fixing that right now. She grabbed his arm. He was too stunned to shake her off a second time. "You don't understand. He . . ." She paused, knowing that what she was about to say might very well damn her, too, but she had begun and there was no stopping now. "He touched me."

That got his attention. He stared at her. "Touched you? Where?"

She laid her hand on the top of her breast. The soft tissue under the loose housedress rippled. "Here."

She held his eyes steady as he struggled to process the information. She could feel her pulse under her fingers, even through all that fat, or maybe the pulse was in the tips of her fingers themselves. She waited for emotion to play across his face, searching with bated excitement for jealousy, anger, outrage . . . something. His mouth was a hard line, and his eyes obscure even in this bright light. He opened his mouth to speak, and her own mouth opened in silent echo.

"Don't let it happen again," he told her. He turned and walked out of the room.

God, it was hot in here! The lazy wicker fan overhead just wasn't spinning fast enough. She stripped off her housedress and kicked it across the floor. It was a hideous color, anyway. Far from flattering. Her skin still felt itchy, so her underwear joined the housedress, and then, only slightly cooler now, she strode to the large bay windows and threw them open, feeling the night air hit her. She climbed onto the windowsill and stuck her hand out to see if it was still drizzling. It was, a little, and the air was damp and deliciously chilly. She knew she had to be careful and keep her balance. It was a long way down. The neighbors on the other side had a clear view of her, but fuck them if they wanted to look. She was still in her house, and damn if this didn't feel good.

With both feet planted firmly on the windowsill and both arms outstretched, she closed her eyes and let the wind play over her body. She could hear the insects in the garden, singing along with the frogs. The moon, half hidden behind its halo of color, blew her wet kisses. She was a moon goddess: round like the moon, full like it, and just as beautiful. If her husband couldn't see that, then to hell with him. The moon knew. That was good enough for her.

After a long while, she got down off the windowsill and fixed herself a drink, straight up, no ice. She wished it were Friday already. She wondered if she wouldn't be able to drum up some sort of excuse with Rory's employers to get him over to the pharmacy tomorrow, in spite of his saying he was busy. He wouldn't be busy if he knew what she had in store for him next time he saw her. But in the past few weeks she'd been phoning in enough fake orders to keep her in surplus for a variety of drugs for a long time to come.

So it had all been for nothing. Saving her kisses for her husband, pretending that what she did to those boys wasn't really wrong as long as she stayed in control and remembered she was a married woman. Saving *more* than her kisses, for a man who didn't care either way.

She helped herself to another drink, and then a third sloshed quickly in the wake of the second. If she had to wait until Friday, well, then Friday it would be. But any way you looked at it, Rory was in for a pleasant surprise.

A few drinks later, she still had the good sense to shut the windows and hunt around for her clothes. She didn't put them back on, but at least they wouldn't be lying all over the place when her daughters woke up in the morning. She plumped herself down on the couch with the bottle in her hand. Might as will finish it up. She sucked it straight from the open neck: glasses didn't count when you were alone. Her tummy was almost broad enough for her to balance the bottle on it. That set her off in peals of giggles.

Damn, she felt old.

Odile

When Odile arrived at the Smiling Dragon, she was more than an hour late for her shift, and darkness had long closed in. The rain persisted at the same steady beat, neither deepening nor showing any intention of stopping. Rory had offered to accompany her inside, but she refused. This was her problem. She didn't need help dealing with it. He urged her then to tell him when he could see her again, but she murmured something indistinct and left him just outside the door. She hoped he had the good sense not to push things by trying to come in. Luck was with her; although he didn't walk away just yet, he made no move to step inside. She didn't bother to answer the questions written on the face of Teeth, who was positioned at the entrance, having a smoke.

Savi didn't need to speak when Odile relieved her at the counter; her malevolent glare was eloquent enough. She tore off her apron, tossed it to the ground, and abandoned her post in the middle of taking an order, which Odile filled hastily and apologetically, all the while glancing around for Vincent.

The bar was filling up. Men had awoken from their Sunday afternoon naps to children screaming around the house and wives demanding attention, pointing out windows that needed repairing, or Christmas painting that needed to be done, and had sought refuge in the Dragon. Even a few of the early drinkers that Odile had left in the bar that morning were still there, struggling to remain steady in their chairs. She had no doubt that Vincent's hands would be full in the betting room behind them.

She wasn't sure if there was anything she could say to him right now, nothing that made sense, at least. But she wanted to see him. There was no way of knowing if he would be able just to look at her and know what had happened with Rory, but the possibility that he could had set her on edge. It would be preferable to meet him now and test the waters rather than to wait until they turned in for the night. Either way, he would or wouldn't have the ability to read the guilt on her face, but if she faced him now, the painful suspense would be diminished.

Mechanically she served drinks, trying not to think of how uncomfortable the mud in her shoes made her, wishing she'd had the good sense to change out of her damp clothes before letting Savi leave. She knew it was a false hope to try convincing herself that her apron hid the liberal smears of mud on her ruined dress.

It was quite some time before there was enough of a lull for her to whisper to the other waitress on her shift that she needed to sneak away for a few minutes. She knocked at the door to the back room, poorly disguised as part of the wooden paneling, waited for her identity to be determined via one of the many pinholes and cracks in it, and then entered when it was eased open from the inside. If it were indeed possible, the smoke within the cramped room was thicker than it was outside. It hung from the ceiling like a dense lilac curtain, obscuring the light from the sparse low-wattage bulbs that dotted the walls. The ventilation in the room was poor at best, and thus the smoke and sweat of ages had embedded themselves into every surface, layer upon layer, creating a unique and identifiable stink.

There had been an obvious effort to cram as many tables

and chairs as possible into the available space. These tables were not being used for leisurely games of dominoes and hearts as were the ones outside. They were reserved for serious gambling. At some, tight huddles played the simple game of wappie, in which the players laid bets on who would turn over the highest card. A child's game, actually, but the game most likely to give rise to violence. Many a stabbing had taken place over a wappie game, when some player took it into his head that he could be swift enough to slip a palmed card into the fray without being spotted. Often, he was dead wrong.

Elsewhere, the more skilled game of all-fours went on to a range of reactions, from excited babble to hushed silences from onlookers and bettors alike. Two sets of partners eyed each other across each table, communicating which card they wanted the other to play through elaborate, ritualistic hand signals. Next to the piles of money lay orderly rows of matchsticks laid out in fours, the preferred way to keep score. Fourteen points by either side meant the game was over.

Odile squinted through the smoke, trying to find her way while resisting the temptation to peek at the games going on. Players around her immediately tensed, bringing their hands close to their chests. The gambling room was a phallocracy; forget the old talk about women bringing luck. It was a place where men came to be with other men, and where the women were tolerated only if they came armed with trays of drinks.

She made it through the obscurity to the back of the room, where Vincent would be taking charge of the house games, primarily poker. She had to jostle her way to the table as men grunted and reluctantly let her through. Vincent wasn't there.

Patrick was behind one of the poker tables, his characteristic brightly patterned shirt opened to the waist to reveal his rounded, sweaty belly and an assortment of gold chains. His balding head was perspiring as liberally as the rest of him, and he was in the process of wiping his scalp dry with a large folded handkerchief when Odile edged up next to him and shouted through the din. "Where's Vincent?"

Patrick looked startled at her approach. "What?" he shouted back.

"Vincent!" she yelled.

He shook his head. "He didn't come in tonight, not yet. I holding the *casa* till he turn up."

She should have been surprised but wasn't. Vincent never missed work. He was punctual and meticulous to a fault, and in all the time she had known him, he had never so much as taken a sick day. But after his fight with his grandmother this morning, she was sure he'd gone off to brood somewhere. "You know where he went?"

Patrick shrugged eloquently. "Sweets, what you want me to tell you? I ain't seen him. I don't know where he gone. So I stuck here playing *casa* and bouncer both at the same time. So if you find him, do me a favor, okay? Tell him to find his ass over here pronto."

She nodded and left. The air on the other side of the door, though poor, was welcome. It was a good time to hurry upstairs and get out of her muddy dress while she still had the chance. No sense pushing fire.

The stairway was even darker than usual, for the lone bulb had blown. Odile was obliged to feel her way gingerly by trailing a hand along one of the walls—an action she did not relish, considering that the walls had never, to her knowledge, been scrubbed.

As she made it to the landing, the loud sounds of an argument dominated the brassy crash of the music downstairs. Odile tensed, recognizing one of the voices as belonging to Miss Ling. The possibility that her opponent might be Vincent—she couldn't deal with yet another argument tonight—became nil when the other voice turned out to be female, too.

Two women came into view. A diminutive Colombian

prostitute, as celebrated by the Smiling Dragon's visitors for the rounded perfection of her high, white breasts as she was for her oral talents, was being dragged by the hair by Miss Ling, who was even shorter than she. The girl was in tears, but these didn't seem to be tears of pain at the way she was being handled. She was pleading incoherently in Spanish in a startlingly high-pitched voice.

"You want to go?" Miss Ling quarreled as they went, "Go now. But you go, you don't come back."

"Señora," the girl pleaded, "just for Christmas. Just ten days. I have to see my daughter. Ten days and I come back, *sí?*"

"Stupid girl! You think you can cross the border and back and nobody see you? You do it once to get here, you think you can do it again and again?" Miss Ling let go of her handful of hair, and the girl slumped against the wall behind her, covering her face with her small fingers.

Miss Ling went on, hands punctuating the air. "You stupid young people. You don't listen to the old ones. What good it is for me to get this old, when you don't listen to me? Why I waste my life learning when you don't want me to give you what I learn?"

"I have to see my baby," the girl insisted. "Then I come back. I promise."

Miss Ling laughed harshly. "What, you think you ghost? You think you take some fish boat in the night, cross and cross back, like magic, and everything okay? One year, save your money one more year, then when you go, you take presents for your baby, and you stay there. . . ."

Before the girl could answer, Miss Ling spun around, noticing Odile for the first time, and barked, "Why you no downstairs?" She seemed to have completely forgotten that she had let her charade of incompetence with the English language drop in Odile's presence earlier. She was back into character, and playing it to the hilt.

"I . . ." Odile paused, staring at the reddening face of the

Colombian girl, who was dressed so skimpily that she was bound to be chilly, even in this close, airless place. She realized with sudden clarity that, although the poor girl was unable to see it through her distress, Miss Ling was trying to be kind—at least offering kindness as she perceived it. For all her harshness, she was trying to help.

"You what?" Miss Ling grated. "You want me to pay you to take break now?"

Odile shook her head vehemently. "I was just coming upstairs to change my clothes."

Miss Ling's rheumy eyes dropped to Odile's dress, which had begun to dry only from the heat of her own body, moved slowly down toward her feet and back again. "You . . . fell?" There was a measure of irony in her voice.

Mortified, not trusting herself to speak, Odile squeezed past and ran for the cover of her room, throwing the door open and slamming it shut behind her, to find Vincent lying on his back in bed. He was staring up at the low ceiling, ankles crossed, fingers laced behind his head, still wearing the clothes he had donned for lunch earlier, right down to the shoes.

Odile pulled up fast, stopping her momentum from catapulting her forward onto him. He didn't look around at the sound of her intrusion. She approached, slowly. "Vincent?"

No answer.

"You all right?"

He blinked, surprised by the question, and then grunted. "No."

Odile didn't need to press any further to know he would not be breaking his self-imposed silence soon. She sat on the edge of the bed, laying one hand on his arm. His skin was cool to the touch, transparent, almost bloodless. He wouldn't look at her.

This close to him, sitting on the bed that they shared, she could smell him, inhale the odor that would always characterize him as long as he lived in her memory: smoke, dust, and sweat. The Dragon's taint. He hadn't even been down into the betting room today, and yet that scent was evident, a part of him.

His proximity brought to mind her recklessness with Rory just a few hours earlier. She veered between guilt and shame and a tingling, residual excitement. With Vincent, she always knew where she was; they were on equal footing, and both knew when they came together what they wanted from each other and what each was willing to give. With Rory, dominance and vulnerability had changed hands, back and forth. His innocence was new to her, reminding her of her own, long lost. In him had been need, both simple and complex: curiosity, want, desire, and huge, awesome emotion. That one encounter with Rory had made what she had with Vincent seem almost . . . practical.

Even so, her sense of decency rebelled against the idea of her remaining seated and touching him, with Rory's dried sweat still clinging to her skin. She got up, found a towel, rummaged around for a change of clothes, and was about to leave when Vincent turned his head. "Where you going?"

"For a shower." She didn't elaborate.

He didn't seem to find that strange. He turned away again, leaving her a little nettled that in his fugue he hadn't even noticed the mud on her dress and her shoes. The jealous questions she had anticipated hadn't come. She was almost disappointed.

She shut the door and padded down the corridor to the small bath and toilet she and Vincent shared with the residents of and visitors to that floor. It was, unlike most of the other rooms, quite clean, but that was only because Odile herself cleaned it thoroughly twice a week. She refused to countenance using a bathroom that wasn't sanitary, even if it meant that she was in fact cleaning up after numerous transients.

She stripped off the yellow dress, and as she did so, caked mud crumbled and flaked off the fabric. She tossed it onto the closed toilet seat and stepped under the stream of cold water, letting it pour all over her, easing her soapy hand between her thighs to remove all traces of her infidelity. Although it was night and her thick, curly hair took forever to dry, she bent her neck under the stream. She'd forgotten her shampoo, but plain water could wash away any number of ills.

The chill of the water brought her skin back to life again, making it tingle. She ran her tongue along her lips experimentally, wondering if she could still taste Rory or whether it was only her imagination. His taste had been unlike that of any other man she had experienced, and somehow she was sure that it had nothing to do with his personal chemistry, but rather with the fact that everything he was had flavored their encounter.

It shocked her to realize that the men she'd had throughout her careless teens, and those few who had come later, had each demanded that she pretend to be something: siren, little girl, witch, bitch. But Rory had never made her feel the need to prove herself to him, and that, for her, was a first. It was such a new sensation that she had no idea how she was going to deal with it, whether she wanted to deal with it, or if she had the courage to go through it again. Now, what kind of devil had thought it fit to throw this complication into her life?

She heard the sound of a key in the bathroom lock, and the bolts slid back. Startled, she spun around, looking wildly and futilely for somewhere to duck for cover. Before she could announce to the intruder that the bathroom was occupied, and would he please get the hell out, Vincent entered, locking the door after him.

He wasn't in the habit of barging in on her, being a stickler for privacy himself. She gave him a puzzled frown. "Something wrong?"

He didn't answer, but stepped fully clothed into the shower with her. Before she could protest, he was jerking her against him, her wet body leaving rapidly darkening imprints on his shirt. In his kiss there was only a plea for compliance. His hands fumbled with his clothing, struggling to free his already erect penis from his wet pants, and lifting her onto him without ceremony or preparation.

She allowed him to slake his hunger in her body, struggling for balance on the wet tiles, experiencing sharp, surprising pleasure in spite of her lack of readiness. But she took her cue from his silence, and said not a word. None of her customary endearments crossed her lips. And while the body penetrating hers was quite familiar, almost reassuring, his silence was alien, frightening. Vincent may have been present in every tangible, physical sense, but his mind was far away, in a place she didn't dare try to trespass. And something inside her knew that this boded no good for anyone.

Rory and Saul

The house looked suspiciously normal. It wasn't in darkness, nor were the lights blazing in every room. Could he dare take that to mean that his father was sober? He parked and went through the gateway, inhaling deeply as he passed to draw in the perfume of the sweet-lime hedge at the front. That hedge, with its thick, pervasive scent, was the only thing about his house that made it feel like a home. As he had with that rattletrap he called a car, he wondered what Odile would have thought of it. Not much, probably.

Saul was on the dilapidated porch, stripped to the waist, arms folded and propped against the chest-high, flaking wall that ran around it. A half-consumed beer rested at his elbow. Rory was about to walk straight past him and into the seclusion of his own room when something stopped him. Perhaps his evening with Odile had made him mellow, or perhaps it was his father's humped back and the dejected curve of his neck, but he never made it to the front door.

"Hey," he said to Saul, surprising them both.

Saul didn't move but watched him warily, expecting a confrontation. There was nothing on Rory's face that implied that one was in the offing, so he answered. "Uh-huh."

Rory wondered what he was supposed to say next. He watched his father bring the beer to his lips, noting the way the skin under his arms hung in folds, swinging loose with the movement. The hair on his head and chest seemed totally white now. Up to just recently, there had been some black left in it. Had the final transition happened overnight? His mind ran on Jacob: probably as old as Saul, maybe older, but still tall, handsome, powerful. Maybe your thoughts really did show in your face and body over time. That was something his mother used to tell him. If that were the case, Saul had probably never had a pleasant thought in his life. Revulsion rolled in upon pity.

"You cooked?" Rory asked, to fill the silence.

Saul shrugged. "Just corned beef and cabbage. But you could find a beer in the fridge."

Rory frowned slightly. "Where you got money to buy beer?"

Saul turned his head for the first time to look at him, seemed to be considering a response, but then didn't answer. Rory didn't bother to repeat the question. He went into the kitchen, and bypassing the mishmash of meat and limp cabbage congealing in the uncovered iron pot, he pulled out a beer and held it in his hand, reading the label as if it would make up his mind for him whether he should drink it or not. Deciding that one drink wouldn't bring him total ruination, he cracked off the cap with his teeth and spat it on the counter. Saul had finished his own by the time he got back outside.

Rory held his out, offering him a sip, but Saul shook his head. His eyes were focused on the house across the road. Its residents certainly believed in Christmas. Fairy lights in pastel colors winked around the windows, porch, and facade, outlining the structure's entire front, so that in the darkness it looked like a child's cartoon house, cut out and crayoned in. Along the eaves, incongruous glittering icicles dangled, and on the roof, a pink-cheeked Santa stood with his legs confidently apart, warm in his red fur coat and high black boots.

He followed the direction of Saul's gaze but said nothing, folding his own elbows and propping himself up on the wall in imitation of his father's posture, hoping that the wall was at least sturdy enough to support their combined weight. The beer was bitter in his mouth.

Saul spoke. "Your mother used to like Christmas."

Rory had to clutch the bottle he was holding to prevent it from falling from his fingers. He didn't dare to look at his father, or to answer, or ask any one of the million questions that surged to the forefront of his mind, for fear of somehow cutting off whatever force was propelling him to talk. He waited.

"She used to make me climb that damn tamarind tree in the yard back in St Ann's and hang lights on it. I fucking fell out of it one time. And she used to change her curtains and paint the house from November. And hang balloons. She had a Santa just like that one."

Rory remembered the lights. He remembered the Santa. He tried to get a picture of his mother's face, but that wasn't so clear. "You know how women like this Christmas thing." He couldn't think of anything else to say.

"Yeah."

"Don't seem much worth it, if it's just us men here. Decorations, I mean."

Saul grunted. "Plus I can boil rice and cook a little meat, but I ain't able with Christmas cake and sorrel. So I might as well not bother to try."

Rory remembered the cake in his pocket. He shoved his hand in and pulled it out. It was a little squashed, but the foil had kept it reasonably dry. He shoved it along the top of the wall to him. "Got that from Miss Myra today. You could have it, if you like." He didn't expect his father to express surprise at the source of the gift, or ask how he had managed to come by it. He was not disappointed. He watched as Saul prodded the foil package gingerly, brought it to his nose and sniffed it, set it aside without thanking him, and returned to staring at the house across the way.

Rory coughed slightly, and then dredged up the courage to ask, "You miss my mother?"

Saul didn't blink. "What *miss* supposed to mean? She gone."

He knew the answer to his next question was a foregone conclusion, but he asked it anyhow. "You think she'll ever come back?"

Saul tore his eyes away from the house to look Rory in the eye for what seemed like the first time in years. Then his glance fell longingly to the beer in his son's hand. Rory held it out to him again, and it took an effort for Saul to hold his hand up in a gesture of refusal.

"Boy," he said slowly, "Two things it's time you understand. One, you talking ten years. That's a long time. Two," he took a breath and continued, "women like her don't come back to men like me." He picked up his empty bottle and tossed it in an arc up into the night sky, watching it until it shattered on the sidewalk on the other side of the street, and then shuffled off the porch, down the slick, wet stairs, and out into the drizzle. Rory followed him with his eyes until he turned the corner out of sight.

Odile

Odile drew herself up onto her hands and knees on the
bed, watching Vincent sleep. It was near dawn, and she
hadn't fallen asleep herself yet. After making love in the
shower, they had returned to their respective posts, without
any conversation passing between them. And although he
had accompanied her back upstairs at the end of their shift,
he neither addressed her nor answered her anxious questions
about what he was thinking.

She leaned forward, bringing her face close to his, trying to
read something off him. His shut eyes were rimmed with
dark, featherlike lashes that touched his cheek. The thick
black lines of his brows dipped down in a V shape to meet at
the center. A sign of a tenacious personality. It surprised her
to notice that several silver hairs shone at his temples like
spun metal. Vincent's hair had always been the color of jet.
Did a heavy heart really cause the black to drain from one's
hair?

She eased off the bed, picked up her hairbrush from the
narrow dresser, and returned, hoping that the undulation in
the mattress that she caused as she clambered back on again
wouldn't wake him. The elastic band that held his ponytail
back had slipped a little; it was an easy task to remove it
completely and place it over her wrist so as not to lose it. She
held a lock of his hair in her hands, feeling how soft it was. It

cascaded through her fingers like water. Usually he didn't let it grow past his shoulders, but lately he had been neglecting to have it trimmed.

Slowly she brushed it, fanning it out onto his pillow. As she did so, she thought of Rory. Not a very nice thing to do, she supposed, thinking of one man while perched on another one's bed, but that was just the way it was. It was sweet of him, holding out for her as he had. Childish, yes, a little dumb, maybe, but sweet nonetheless. Rory had a way of putting his faith in things, or people, or ideas, and when he did so, he became blind to anything else. She knew he loved her in much the same way that he had loved that pathetic little white chicken: naturally, unquestioningly, almost complacently, accepting something that had been thrust upon him, without asking why.

That just wasn't good enough, though. He was no longer a boy—that she readily admitted—so her long-standing contemptuous dismissal of him as the little pest next door didn't hold any water. But attaining the age of majority alone didn't make you a man. Nor did it make you the kind of man she wanted. Rory longed for home, hearth, and devotion—all the things his father had stolen from him the day he drove his mother away. He wanted solidity; she was anything but.

Besides, although they shared a common origin, they did not share a common destiny. Rory wasn't the type of man who rose, soared, or shone. He wasn't a kite or a meteor; he was a tree, and as deep as his roots might run, and as solid as they would make him, they would condemn him to a life of stasis. That wasn't what she wanted. She had places to go.

Vincent's eyes fluttered, and he shifted restlessly. She was sure that he would wake, but he sighed under the strokes of her brush and settled down again. What about him, then? If Rory was stasis, did Vincent represent anything better? He was getting nowhere with the bar, not as long as Miss Ling was alive. Even if he did succeed in making all the changes he dreamed of, he somehow expected that Odile would remain at his side, glad for the chance to be coached and cultivated into whatever he saw fit. Did she really want to hitch her destiny to this man's wagon?

Rory's admonition about her new freedom and the way she had been wasting it came back to her. He was right. If her freedom had been a gift, what had she done with it?

Vincent shifted again, his eyelids fluttered, and this time, he did wake. He struggled to focus on her face in the predawn light, trying to determine exactly what she was doing leaning over him. When he felt her touch in his hair, he let his hand fall lightly onto hers. He smiled weakly. "You slept?"

"No."

"Why not?"

She shrugged. "Too tired, maybe. You feeling better?"

His smile died. He didn't need to answer. "I'm not going to wait, you know."

She gave him a puzzled frown, even though she had her suspicions about what he had decided not to wait on.

He continued. "I know a way to make her change her mind. I'm not asking anymore. I'm not begging anymore. I know how to make it happen. You wait." His mouth trembled.

She didn't like the sound of that. There was a darkness in his voice, a gathering of clouds. "What are you going to do?"

He gave her a look that chilled her. "Just wait. You'll see."

Still clutching her brush, she laid her other palm flat on his bare chest, just over his heart. Even though he had barely shaken off his deep sleep, it was racing. Everything inside her told her that whatever his plan, she would do well to find out what it was and, if she could, defuse it. Vincent was a man of equanimity and calm, his every thought rational, his every gesture measured. The light flickering in his eyes was one she had never seen before. That made him dangerous. "Tell me," she coaxed.

He shook his head against the pillow. "Can't."

"Why not?"

"It's a surprise."

Vincent wasn't one for surprises. Miss Ling wasn't one for them, either. She was sure that Vincent's surprise would make neither of them very happy. "Please." She tried to keep the panic out of her voice.

Vincent encircled her wrist, forcing her hand to remain in its position over his heart. "I can't. But trust me. Can you trust me?"

She eyed him uncertainly. All she could hope was that his plan wouldn't harm the old lady. This was a day and age when people hastened along the process of inheritance with the aid of arsenic in an elderly relative's coffee, or ground glass or cement powder in their food. But Vincent was not a violent man, and he loved his grandmother, in spite of how difficult she was. Odile dismissed any idea of foul play, but even with that possibility ruled out, there was still much room for concern.

He seemed ignorant of her reservations. He went on, fully awake now, and almost loquacious after such an extended silence. "Remember this, Odile: everything I do, I do for you and me, okay? I told you, we going to be in this business together. We can make something of ourselves if we try. And one day we will look back at how we were stuck in this little room with nothing to bank but our plans, and laugh."

Odile glanced around them, taking in the airless confines of the drab walls, decrepit furniture, and dearth of pleasant amenities. She understood his need to escape. Vincent had been born in a room on the ground floor of the bar, grown up in Miss Ling's quarters, and as a boy had left the Dragon every morning to cross the city on foot to go to school. It was all he had ever known, and she knew from her own experience just how stifling that could be. For him, manhood would mean escape from the dust and mold, just as for her womanhood meant fleeing the safety of her gentle green valley. Vincent wasn't waiting for his destiny to see what form it would take; he was determined to cast it himself.

She wished him well; from the depth of her, she did. But he wasn't talking about *him;* he was talking about *them*. That was the block upon which she stumbled. As much as she hated to admit it, he had been her source of salvation. The knight's armor that she held in so much disdain glinted faintly beyond his mild and undemanding surface. He had given her the time and space to discover for herself a sexual ethos that didn't mandate that she prove anything to anyone. For that, she supposed, she loved him.

But his talk of partnership—his *we*—scared her. She thought again of Rory and what he had said to her about her own future. Was that future really to be found within the walls of a sailor bar on the dingy side of Port of Spain? Or was it something that she had not yet discovered or created?

Disappointed that her response was not immediate, Vincent spoke up, an edge of anxiety in his voice. "Odile?"

She swallowed hard, her throat sticky and tight. "I'm sorry. I was just . . . thinking."

"About?"

She tried to shift the focus of the conversation. "About all those changes you plan to make. It's a lot of work, Vincent."

He didn't allow her to distract him. "It won't be too much work because we're going to do it together. Right? Because you'll work at it with me." He waited.

She looked away, not wanting to see the plea on his face. The sun was coming up fast, and it was almost as light as it ever got in the dingy little room. She wished she could answer with certainty, but certainty wasn't in great supply right now. She gently withdrew her hand from the hold he had on it, taking it off his chest, and laid down the brush that she held in the other. She cupped both together in front of her, staring down into them. If those hands held a ball of damp clay, and that clay were her future, how would she shape it?

Vincent sat up and pulled them apart, sending her imaginary ball of clay, still formless, plopping onto the cotton bed-
spread. He took one hand in his, holding it more securely
than he needed to, palm upward, and ran his fingers along
the pattern of brown lines on it, much as Rory had done the
evening before. "Right, Odile?" he insisted. His voice begged
for reassurance that the hesitation he was sensing in her wasn't
real.

She tried to look encouraging. Vincent was a good man.
He didn't deserve to have the gift of his esteem thrown back
at him like a rag. She wished she felt his certainty, because
that was what he deserved. It pained her that she couldn't
give him more. "Right." She hoped she sounded convincing.

He tried to believe her. His lips curved upward and his
body relaxed slightly. They were kneeling on the bed face to
face, knee to knee. He leaned forward against her, heavy
enough for her to have to tense her body so as not to be
pushed backward over the edge, trying to reach her mouth.
She allowed the kiss but was troubled by the uncharacteristic
insistence in it. She knew that he wanted tangible proof to
back up her weak words, and for him, that proof would require the physical sealing of a tenuous verbal contract. But
she needed both time and space to think—space not only for
her mind but for her body as well. When he moved to slip her
flimsy nightgown up over her head, she stopped him.

"Why not?" He had progressed from sleeping lassitude to
taut aggression.

She couldn't find a reason that would sound right. Yester-
day, she had held two men in and against her body, each of
them giving her something different, and each taking something different away. Even at her most reckless schoolgirl
stage, this was something she would never have countene-
nanced. Today she needed to set herself apart a little, to see
herself as an individual: separate, intact, not conjoined with
another. How to explain? She shook her head, smoothing her

nightgown modestly down around her. "It's nothing. Just not now, okay?"

"*Why* not now?"

"No reason. I just . . ." She threw her hands up in frustration.

He moved for her nightgown again. "But I need you."

In spite of her guilt, she was becoming annoyed, defensive of the sovereignty of her body. "Just because you need me doesn't mean—"

He leaped off the bed, as naked as he had climbed into it the night before. A flush of embarrassment and anger covered him from head to foot. "Why you keep doing this?"

She was genuinely confused. "Doing what?"

"Pushing me away. And I'm not just talking about . . ." He gesticulated wildly at the rumpled bed, " . . . about that. I'm talking about all of you. Your thoughts. Your secrets. I ask, you refuse. I advance, you retreat. Why?"

She was intimidated by the height advantage that being on his feet gave him, so she rose, too, and faced him. "That's not true. I'm here with you. I'm here *for* you—"

"But you never give without holding something back. You never let me near you without telling me I can come so close and no further. You set limits on everything you do and feel and say—"

"Limits are the only things that make sense sometimes!" She wasn't aware she was shouting until someone on the other side of the wall hammered against it with a fist. She ignored it. The amount and type of noise she had had to endure from those rooms over the past year entitled her to make a little of her own. "What more could you want?"

He turned his back on her without answering, rummaging wildly through the chest of drawers for something to wear. Finding nothing suitable, he retrieved last night's clothes from the floor and dragged them on. Odile watched him dress and head for the door, wanting to do or say something to stop his hurt, but at the same time anxious for him to leave just so that she would have time alone. The need for sanctuary won out. She made no placatory gesture.

He turned to her one last time. His voice was almost calm. "You know, before I met you, I never knew that one person could be so hot and so cold all at the same time." He left without giving her the chance to respond.

Rory

It was quite late when Rory stepped through the door of the pharmacy. He had struggled all day with the decision of whether he would go or not, and even after eroding his resolve with every good reason to stay away, he found himself here. Zenobia had the wrong idea about why he wanted to see her. What he'd needed when he called was help, advice, someone to unravel for him the mystery that was a woman. What she thought he needed was something else entirely. Now he realized that his compulsion to allow this woman to use him was a weakness, a cancer of the character that had to be excised; and today he would do the job, whatever the temptation she chose to throw at him. It didn't make him happy, but he was sinking fast and his legs were entangled in seaweed. It was cut himself free or drown.

Just inside the door, a security guard stopped him, warily taking in Rory's size and slipping a cautious hand to the metal butt of the revolver in the holster at his hip. He wasn't one of the regulars; Rory didn't recognize him. "You can't read or what?" There was unprovoked aggression in his voice.

Before Rory could answer, the man tapped the sign on the glass door. "We closed early today. For a party."

"I know, I'm invited."

The guard looked him up and down, derisively dismissing his best shirt and pants. "This party is for staff and suppliers. Important clients." He didn't have to finish by saying that Rory didn't look like either.

A puff of perfume made Rory turn his head. Two women entered the store behind him, laughing as they shut the door against the wind, chattering between themselves. One wore a large glittery pin on her breast that said "Joy to the world." The other wore a holly-wreath brooch that held together a white silky poinsettia-dotted scarf that looked as if it had taken hours to drape. Their bright dresses and high-heeled pumps made them look festive—and him look even shabbier by comparison. He slid his hand over the other wrist in an attempt to hide his frayed cuff and cheap watch.

The guard looked at him sourly, disbelieving. "What's your name?"

Rory told him.

"I don't see you on no list."

"You don't have a list," Rory pointed out. Bristling, he glanced at the unhooked holster. The gesture was aggressive. He didn't like aggressive. He threw the women an apologetic look for holding things up, but they ignored him, fluffing their hair and making last-minute lipstick checks on their reflections in the plate-glass window. "Listen," he tried to reason with the unreasonable guard. "Mrs. Bedassie invited me. It was a late invitation, so maybe I'm not on her list. But she did invite me. Call her if you like and ask her. But I'm not going away. Okay?"

The man stared at him, stonewalling for several moments, and then looked past Rory at the women, who had stopped twittering and begun to look restive. He stepped aside, still looking disdainful. "Go ahead. But don't let me hear nothing about the boss-lady complaining about you. They down the back, in the canteen."

Rory didn't thank him but stepped aside to allow the

ladies to go on ahead, following them along the aisles of toothbrushes and mouthwashes, past baby products and maternity care, and through the small waist-high door that he himself had used many times on his way to Zenobia's office. This time, instead of going toward the stairs, he skirted the clerks' desks and rounded the corner to the storage rooms, staff lockers, and canteen. Even before the door to the canteen swung open, the music assailed his ears.

At first he thought that the thundering parang with its heady drums, maracas, guitars, and quatros came from records piped over the large rented speakers placed at the four corners of the room. Once he was fully inside, though, he realized that the music was live. A group of eight or ten paranderos in tight black pants and fuchsia flowered shirts whirled around, pausing from time to time to surround one of the guests for a personal serenade. Light-colored straw hats couldn't keep the sweat from pouring down their earnest faces, and their white teeth flashed against their glistening dark skin as they belted out the old classics in bastardized Spanish.

Enthralled by the music, people danced at the center, feet tripping to the beat, women's skirts swirling around their thighs. Those who weren't dancing clapped and snapped their fingers, keeping time with pretend castanets or banging teaspoons or forks against rum bottles half-filled with water. Judging from the flamboyance of the dancers and the stridency of the whoops of approval and encouragement coming from the crowd, the bar had been open for some time.

Rory tried his chameleon trick, moving with his back to the wall and willing himself invisible. He watched the two women in bright dresses who had come in with him melt into the throng and disappear, and that left him truly alone. He couldn't see Zenobia anywhere.

The density of the crowd at the far end of the room told him that the food and drink were most likely located there.

He walked over, trying not to make eye contact with anyone, lest they either try to draw him into the dance or, like the security guard, question his right to be there.

He waited patiently for his turn at the bar, and then, once there, couldn't imagine what he would want to drink. Zenobia, true to form as a woman of excess, had loaded the counters and shelves with every imaginable poison. Several brands of aged scotch, kegs of red rum, bottles of puncheon, vodka, and gin were lined off in rows. On the floor, steel oil barrels cut in half let Carib beers chill in ice, while large bowls filled with nauseatingly pink rum punch sat in a corner of the table cluttered with small crystal punch glasses, attracting the ladies, who tried to scoop out floating bits of canned imported fruit cocktail without appearing to do so. Clear rum bottles, whose labels had been soaked off, held enough home-distilled *babash* to make a police raid well worth the effort.

One of the bartenders clicked his fingers in front of Rory's face, trying to get his attention. "You drinking?" the man asked. "Because if you ain't, it got plenty people behind you who want to."

Rory stopped gaping and composed himself. He had never even tasted half the substances on the other side of the counter. He settled for a beer, having managed to down one with his father just days ago. He was sure that if he tried, he'd learn to stomach them. The bartender handed him a Carib so cold that tiny chips of ice clogged the neck of the bottle.

"There you go. Beastly cold," the bartender told him, and, surprisingly, smiled.

Stumped by the unexpected smile, Rory managed to return one of his own, and then made for the safety of the periphery of the room again. A slender woman, whose long smooth hair and caramel skin identified her as a genuine *panyol*, began crooning a solo, Spanish words oozing from her, the normally harsh syllables rounded out by her melody. The boisterous crowd came as close to quiet as they probably would get for the night. Rory sipped his beer, grimaced, then held it to his chest and listened.

"Rory!" someone shouted from afar. He looked around but couldn't see the source of the call. His name sounded again, and this time he was able to determine the direction from which it came. He was easily one of the tallest men there, and it was only this advantage that allowed him to see the small hand that stretched to wave at him above the shoulders of the others. Long, red nails and glittering bracelet. Zenobia.

Before he could approach her, she shoved her way through to him, diminutive and determined. As she threw her arms up around his neck and yanked him down to kiss his cheek in welcome, he could smell the *babash* on her breath. The bush rum would explain her lack of discretion in shouting out his name in a roomful of people who knew her, and greeting him as she would an old friend rather than the distributor's grunt who dropped supplies off once or twice a week. He brought the beer up to the side of his face. She had never kissed him before, not even so briefly, not even on the cheek.

Before he could wonder at it, she pointed at his beer. "That's all you drinking?"

He shifted the bottle to the other hand almost guiltily, like a man caught red-handed. Drinking soft. Like a woman.

"I have plenty stronger, you know," she told him, smiling hugely.

He looked down at her, thinking that much of the stronger stuff was already in her system. He patted the bottle protectively. "Good enough for me."

She didn't argue. "You eat anything yet? Because I got plenty."

"Not yet," he began, but before he could finish, she plucked at his sleeve.

"Let's go. I'm hungry."

He resisted, holding her back, leaning forward to speak softly enough that he couldn't be overheard but loudly enough for her to hear him over the party noises. "Zen, you sure you want people to see you talking to me here? You know . . ."

She laughed gaily. "You joking. It's Christmastime. They drunk, I drunk. Who you think going to remember anything?" Her eyes glittered. He had the suspicion she was upping the stakes a little; having him sent to her office by her own staff wasn't exciting enough for her anymore. Now, she wanted people to see them, wonder briefly, and then dismiss the thought. She was a decent, wealthy woman of standing; he was a delivery boy. *Of course* she was just being hospitable.

Even so, when she slid her hand onto his forearm, he held back. "Where's your husband, Zen?"

"Oh, him," she waved away the idea of the man. "He couldn't be bothered to come. This is a business party—my business, not his. Nobody important enough for him to meet. He's probably out somewhere else, at somebody else's party; fatter fish to fry. You know what I mean?"

Rory knew. This time, he let himself be dragged to the far end. The tables were enveloped by such an overpowering combination of food smells that the moment they hit him, he gagged. He tried to recall where he had last seen so much food, but couldn't. Large platters and bowls crowded every available surface. As guests parted to let their hostess through, he tried to identify the meats by appearance and scent.

The largest platter was easy: a good-sized young wild boar lay on its side, eyes glazed, fangs bared in a death grimace, most of its flank hacked away, stuffing spilling out of its abdominal cavity, raisins and capers in abundance. Bowls of stewed *lappe,* stained red with *roucou* seeds, and curried agouti stood on either side. Guests helped themselves to piles of red crab simmered with coconut milk and ground provisions like dasheen and eddoes, green bananas, and ripe plantains. They elbowed each other to get at the meats, tearing pieces of flesh off the hog, cracking crabs' legs, exclaiming over the quantity and variety of the fare, jostling like *corbeaux* at the La Basse dump.

Zenobia proudly lifted a heavy platter to his nose. "Manicou. You have no idea how much a pound I paid for this. When you eat by me, you eat good." She was right. There was no doubt thousands of dollars' worth of wild game here, hauled in fresh from the forest, most likely the day before.

Under his nose, the possum's rankness made him recoil in spite of its heavy seasonings: *chadon beni,* garlic, and French thyme. He had been hungry when he came in, but he wasn't sure if he still was. He wasn't much of a meat man, and when he did eat it, he ate it sparingly. The preponderance of flesh made him giddy.

Zenobia was waiting, still holding the heavy platter. "So, what you want to have?"

He backed away from the table, through the crowd, trying to put some distance between himself and the smell. Hastily, she dropped the dish onto the table with a thump and hurried after him.

"What?" she asked, partly anxious, partly irritated. "You not hungry?"

"Not right now, but definitely later," he lied. He wasn't sure he would be hungry again for a long time. The little half-Spanish singer had finished her solo and the band was striking up a more raucous melody, the polar opposite of her devotional to the Madonna and Child. This song was about debauchery and excess, Christmas drunkenness, and indulgence. The other side of the parang coin. Guests clapped even more loudly that they had the first time, singing along to the more ribald hook lines and laughing out loud.

Too many people. Usually, he could hide in a crowd, mask himself with them, and pretend he wasn't there. This time, the sounds and smells and perfume hemmed him in rather than offering escape. Zenobia trailed behind him as he withdrew.

At the edge of the room, she poked him in the ribs, slightly annoyed. "Don't tell me you sick or anything."

"I'm not sick." He scratched his head. This was a mistake. He wasn't a party man and never would be. The noise was too much. The music was too much. And all these people . . . Maybe there was a graceful way to leave without offending her.

She read his thoughts, and hastened to intervene. "You not going anywhere."

"Zen, I—"

She grabbed his wrist, nails digging in, and dragged him with surprising force to the bar. As before, guests parted to allow her passage. The bartender who had served Rory before immediately found a glass, swished it in a large bucket of water, and poured Zenobia a shot of bush rum.

She looked at it on the counter without bothering to pick it up, lifting an overplucked brow. "That the best you can do?"

"Pardon?" The bartender clasped his hands in front of him, waiting politely, in the manner of one used to complaints about service from the rich and the spoilt.

"Double it up, boy. This is a big woman you dealing with, not a child." She shoved the glass at him, folded her arms, and looked mulish.

The man doubled the order silently, not even daring to suggest that maybe she had already had enough for the night. Then he turned to Rory. "Anything for you, sir?"

Rory was a little taken aback, not used to being addressed as *sir*. He looked down at the bottle in his hand, a little surprised to discover it half empty. He didn't remember drinking from it. He declined politely; another drink would mean that for the sake of good manners he would have to linger at least long enough to finish it, and he knew he had reached his limit as far as this party was concerned.

Zenobia gulped the rum as she would have a glass of water, leaving a stain of red around the rim, handed the glass back to the bartender without so much as a "thank you," and addressed Rory. "Okay, let's go."

"Where?" Something was already telling him where, though. Excitement mingled with dread.

Her lips curved. "You know where."

He protested. "Zen, the room's full of people."

"So?"

"Your guests. You're supposed to . . . I don't know . . . entertain them or something."

"They got food, they got grog, they got music. What more they want?" She was already headed for the exit.

He tried again, catching up with her easily. "But they will see us leave, and wonder where . . . or what . . ."

Zenobia turned to look at him, eyes clear, excitement shining from them. The bush rum on her breath reminded him of his father. She spoke carefully, enunciating each syllable the way people do when their tongues have been made thick by drink. "Fuck them." She sailed before him to her office.

She locked the door behind them and held up the keys, jingling them like chimes. "Alone now." She tossed them on the table.

"Yes." He watched her carefully, thinking that maybe the best time to free himself from her was not now. She had coaxed him inside under the illusion that they were about to sink even deeper into the hole they had already dug for themselves; she had a roomful of guests downstairs; and she was not too steady on her feet. It was a recipe for trouble. Maybe he could back out gracefully, promise to come see her again soon, right after Christmas. Tell her then.

She caught his glance toward the door and pouted, sliding one arm up and around his neck. "What you looking at the door for? It got nothing there for you. Look at me. Look hard, and tell me what you see."

The back of his neck prickled where she touched him, but with foreboding rather than sensuality.

"What you see?" she pressed.

He looked, trying to peer past the arrogance and selfishness and insularity that he had always seen in her, and saw strange emotions that he had never thought her subject to. Fear. Unhappiness. Loneliness. The energy and bravado she radiated were gone.

She was waiting for an answer. "Well?" Her lower lip protruded.

Rory took a deep breath. His mission was not to cause hurt. "I see—" he began.

She cut him off. "Am I attractive?"

"Of course." An honest answer.

"Beautiful?" Her eyes were pleading.

To him, she was. "Yes."

She looked at the same time grateful and disbelieving. "Don't shit me, Rory," she scoffed, but there was pleading in her voice for him to insist that he wasn't. "What a nice, healthy, good-looking young man like you doing telling me stupidness like that? I could be your mother."

Her fingernails scraped convulsively at the back of his neck. He wanted to put his hand up and drag hers away, but compassion stayed him. "Zen," he told her earnestly. "You *are* beautiful. And I don't think you're old." He thought of Odile, easily half Zenobia's age, but twice as mature. "And you have so much to teach—"

She smiled ruefully. "So it's teacher, then. Not mother."

"I never saw you as a mother." He felt his face grow hot. If he had, he would never have been able to allow her to do the things she had done to him. The memory of being engulfed in the painful pleasure she brought him made him swallow hard.

His words brought her little comfort. She began to say

something, hesitated briefly, and then found the courage to ask the question. "You think I'm too fat?"

Anguish or relief was riding on his answer. "Not fat," he told her kindly. "Soft. Warm. Your body suits you. It's . . ." He threw his hands up. What more could he say? He had never been allowed to touch that overripe body; she had denied him at every turn. Now she needed him to tell her it was okay? This time, he did take her hand from the base of his neck, gently, and tried to step away; but as one hand came down the other flew up, locking around his neck with a grip he never knew she had. "I have to tell you something," she whispered.

He resisted her pull. "Tell me."

"It's a secret. Come closer."

Against his better judgement, but motivated by compassion and a fear of upsetting her in her fragility, he leaned forward, bringing his ear near. Her warm breath smelled of rum gone sour.

"I promised you something tonight, didn't I?"

"You did."

"I promised you . . . more." The look she gave him was meant to be seductive, but the fear that clung to her turned it into something else.

He tensed as she rose on her toes. In all the months of their liaison, he had yearned for permission to kiss her, begged her for the privilege each time she had pleasured him, and each time, she had refused. The tingle of curiosity at first contact took him by surprise, and in spite of his reservations, the long wait for the kiss—the few months seemed much more than that—made him succumb rather than resist. She let out a small sound of triumph.

But the cloying scent of her perfume, commingled with the taste of rum and desperation, assaulted his senses. Hard little teeth ground against his lower lip, and then, the invasion. Her tongue was thick in his mouth. He gagged and jumped back, his strength prevailing over her insistence. "Stop, Zen. Enough." He was panting as hard as she.

"But this is what you want. What you been asking for all the time." In her chagrin, she sounded more like the Zenobia he knew; less unsure, more impatient. She tilted her face upward, far back, and locked her eyes onto his. "You begged to kiss me all along. You begged for it. Kiss me now." She grabbed his hand and tried to stuff it clumsily down between her breasts. "You wanted to touch me. Now touch."

Something happened, he thought. *Somebody pushed her too hard, and she slipped over the edge. And she wants me to break her fall.* He wrenched his hand away from its enforced nest; her flesh felt too soft and too warm, like a bed that you fell into and became lost in its spongy belly. He put distance between them.

"Stop, Zen. This stops here." He tried to keep his voice level and calm, but the pity that had delayed his initial intent was surpassed by his need to escape.

"What you mean, 'stop'?" She didn't follow him across the room but stood with her hands limp at her sides, looking desolate and abandoned.

"Exactly that." He was surprised at the feeling of empowerment that came with being firm with her for a change. "It's finished. I'm not doing this any more."

She deliberately misunderstood. "But they can't hear us in here. The music. You forget?"

"I don't care if they hear or don't hear. That don't matter any more. And I don't mean I'm not doing this here and now, I mean not ever. It's finished."

If he could have taken away the pain that crossed her face then, he would have. Her shock was cartoonish: mouth wide open, moving but silent, black-rimmed eyes turned to O's, hair electrified. But there was no severance without hurt.

She finally found her words. "What you saying to me?"

"I said it already." He was bewildered by her reaction.

This woman had used him as shamelessly as she did her own workers, offering the meager wage of sexual release as compensation for his compliance with her will, and the guilt and silence she delighted in enforcing upon him. He was a gamepiece in an elaborate game of moves and counter-moves that she played with her life. So why did she look so sad, so stunned? Had none of her young toys never refused to play on when she decided to change the rules?

"You turning me *down?*" She had to cough the words up past some obstruction that made her voice both raspy and high. It scared him, a voice like that.

He sought to soothe while still standing his ground. "It's not like that. It's just—"

"Like what, then? All these months, you been begging me to let you taste my mouth." One hand pressed into her pubis, through the bright red satin of her dress. "To touch me here. You want me to remind you how many times I had to slap your hand away from this?"

He shook his head. He didn't need reminding.

"And now I tell you your time for it come, that we could do what you been wanting, and you say no? What happened?" Some little spark jogged her memory, in spite of the drink in her system and the sting of rejection. When she laughed, she became ugly. "What, Rory, don't tell me it's that *wabine* in the bar you told me about. The one some man kicked your ass over, fucked up your face. Don't tell me this is over some bar girl you let go to your head!"

She was wrong. Odile had nothing to do with this. This was his choice. This thing with Zen wasn't right, and it was time to get out. He denied the charge passionately. "It's got nothing to do with her. It's about you and me. I don't want this anymore. I won't let you use me anymore."

A sharp, high laugh whipped out of her. "Use you? What, you trying to say it was a sacrifice, letting me kneel down in front of you all this time? Because let me tell you, you didn't look like you hated it."

"I didn't hate it—"

"Because you kept on coming back. For more. You know you did."

Decency made him admit this was true. "Yes, but—"

"So how you say I used you? I forced you?"

"No."

"Look at the size of me, and look at the size of you." She closed the space between them until she was near enough to punctuate her speech with angry jabs at his chest. "How I could force a big man like you?"

Her prodding was so ineffectual that he didn't even bother to try to stop her. He peered at her face, trying to read whether she were as obtuse as she was pretending to be. Surely she knew that power lay in many places other than size or strength, and that the balance had always been in her favor. Hadn't that always been the source of the pleasure that she took from him? Her end of the deal was never to be pleasured by him in return, but to revel in his dependency and weakness that always came at that precise moment when he was riveted by the intense heat of her mouth as she worked on him, the moment of agony when everything stood quiet and trembling on the edge of madness, darkness and release. At that moment, her power over him was absolute, and that knowledge gave her a greater thrill than anything he could have done for her with his mouth or prick.

Rory looked anxiously around. His back was against the far wall of her office; the door seemed very far away.

She didn't wait for an answer to her question. Maybe she already had it. She grasped his belt, small, fast hands finding the buckle and popping it open before he even discerned what she was doing. Eager fingers reached for him. Instead of blossoming under her touch, he recoiled. His glance around the room was more frantic now. He had to get away, and the only way out was through her.

Shoving her aside would be easy, but the violence of the gesture made his stomach curdle. Nothing in heaven or hell would make him hit a woman again. He put the force of a blow into his voice. "Stop!" The bellow boomed through the room. Music or no, someone would hear, but he didn't care.

The thunderclap stilled her. She stared at him in shock. For the second time, he threw her hands away from him, fiddling at his buckle to do it up, but she came at him with shrieks and sharp nails, like a wet alley cat, scratching at his arms and his face.

"You're nothing! Nothing!" Her finger caught him in the corner of his eye, tearing at the tissue-thin skin. "You just a little nothing boy I did a favor. I take pity on you and teach you how to feel like a man, *you* have the gall to say no to *me?*" She drew her head back sharply and spat at him, a gob of saliva hitting him full on the mouth. He wiped it away with his sleeve and in one abrupt movement, reached for the keys on her desk. All he had to do was unlock the door and leave, never look back.

She recognized his intent, and being nearer to the desk, beat him to it. Wild, mad laughter erupted from her as she snatched up the jangling bunch and shoved them down the front of her blouse, wedging them in the tight space between her fat breasts.

"Give them to me."

"Come get them."

"That's not funny."

"I'm not joking," she grinned.

"Zenobia, open the door, or I break it down. That's your choice. I'm not coming for those keys."

She didn't have to needle him any further to know he was serious. With a loud obscenity, she drew the keys from her bosom. As she did so, the red satin of her dress sheared soundlessly, tearing downward and splitting apart, stopping at her belly.

Rory averted his eyes from her exposed breast, hastily taking the proffered keys and struggling to open the door. Thus exposed, she surely couldn't follow. There'd be time to set things straight with her later; she'd be sober again eventually, and rational. But not today. Today, the only thing he wanted was to be free and far from this horror.

What happened next was like a landslide. All he could hear was a muffled rumbling, and all he could feel was the shock. Zenobia running past him, one breast spilling out of her torn dress, hands coming up to claw at her own neck, nails scraping flesh and leaving long red trails. Red and white plastic beads spilling from her burst necklace and raining onto the floor. Red high heels stabbing at the tiles. And her screams like a siren, drawing attention.

Then the doors leading to the party burst open, and the hellhounds of his nightmares rushed forth in human form, baying at his heels. The wall of people hit him, and he was down, falling hard. Hands tearing at him, forcing him against the floor, angry voices calling him rapist and mauler and a stream of other ugly things. And above all the clamor, Zenobia's tearful accusations.

His denials went unheard, muffled by the weight of the outrage piled upon him. He went limp, letting the heap of indignant guests above him relax their grip—a fighter's ploy—then, like a prisoner breaking free of his chains, he rose up again, chest expanding with a great guttural roar, arms flung wide, shoving them aside. He was on his feet, separate from the mob, and running. He just had to make it to the door, into the blackness outside. But the crowd, enraged at losing its victim, was close behind, snarling and snapping, fueled by adrenaline and rum. With each stride he wrenched himself from clutching hands. The door was just there, his hand upon it, his full weight shoving it open to escape.

Then a click. A soft one, but one that filled his brain with more pure sound than the curses of the mob that pursued him. Gunmetal at the base of his skull, and the voice of the security guard, resonant with vindication and malice: "I know you was gonna be trouble."

He felt his hands being stretched outward in the doorway, two men struggling to pull on each arm, tearing at the ligaments in his shoulders and back, celebrating his pain. Something hard slammed into the base of his spine and his nerveless legs buckled. He was on his knees, face down to the sidewalk, rain sheeting against his scalp, and that cold, hard metal still not moving away.

He had no idea how much time passed, but then the banshee screech of a police siren, and flashing blue lights diffused by the rain, brought his greatest terror home. Men in uniform pouring out of the car, his hands being dragged behind him, silver clacking onto his wrists, pinning them together. And still, kneeling in the rain.

Then a tall, dark-haired man, his expensive shoes swift along the pavement, climbing over Rory's kneeling figure in the doorway like he was scattered garbage. Zenobia's voice growing even higher and more frantic, heavy with drama, as if her counterfeit terror were becoming real.

The momentum of a kick wheeled him around to face his accuser. Zenobia stood huddled against the tall man, whom he recognized from the photo on her desk. Someone had tried to hold the front of her dress together with big diaper pins taken from a shelf in her store. Her glossy hair was a tangle, her makeup a smear of color, black streaking down from her eyes, over rouged cheeks to the rolls of fat under her chin.

"You see, Teddy? You see? I told you he was touching me! You laughed. I told you. You laughing now?"

Black hate from the man at her side—and more, too. Contempt and outrage that this nothing, this little black boy, could crawl out from whatever hole that spawned him and dare to touch a decent man's wife. Rory saw an image reflected in this man's eyes, and what he saw was not himself.

Not what or who he aspired to be. He saw only coal black skin and niggery hair and a cheap shirt that this man's wife liked to laugh at, because it shouted to everyone that he was poor and low-class and a nobody.

Bedassie was wrong, he decided. What he was could not be defined by this wealthy man whose wife was so bored and lonely that she filled the gaps in her life by dallying with messenger boys. He was more than a cheap shirt with ragged collar and faded fabric that was less than half cotton. More than the dirt yard in St. Ann's that had nurtured him. More than— *better* than—the monster he had become to Odile that night by the river so long ago. And he needed to tell them that.

They had to know. Not for him, because for the first time in his life, he understood. But for them. They had to know that they couldn't stand there in their expensive shoes and look at him as nothing.

From the shelter of her husband's arms, Zenobia caught his eye, a secret smile on her lips that only he saw. His rejection of her repaid—with interest. Her sanctity and purity reestablished. How she must be laughing inside! He felt an involuntary spasm lurch through his muscles. They flexed, ready to send him leaping up against the threat of the gun and the milling cops and break away. His strength must count for *something*. He could take one or two of them unawares if he tried—even if, like Samson, his liberation brought about his own demise, this time under a hail of bullets rather than the collapse of temple walls. But before the constriction of his handcuffs stopped him, rational thought did.

Too long had he struggled with his own physical self. Too long had his first means of defense been his body and the barrier it presented between him and the onslaught of the outside world. He'd been a fool: he had always fought against the urge to use force for protection, retribution, and outright war. But the demon inside him that Jacob had recognized, the one that fed on his rage and self-hate, was the one who thirsted to fight his battles with flying fists. Not him. Not the mind and heart and sensibility that was Rory. And it was the demon who was now shackled by the handcuffs. *It* was the one unable to act now that its power was laid low.

Rory was the one with the brain and the mouth, and together those were as good a weapon as any. He lifted his downcast eyes to meet Zenobia's victorious ones. "Tell them the truth, Zen."

The shadow of her smile disappeared. Bedassie joined the throng of gawking guests in staring at her. The officers who surrounded Rory halted their arguments about whether they should beat him here or wait a while and beat him at the station, and stared, too. The unexpected calm in his voice stilled all movement until Bedassie left Zenobia's side and came to stand over him, nose wrinkling at some imaginary stench. "Who you think you talking to?"

Rory looked past the man, locking Zenobia in his direct gaze. "You so busy telling stories, Zen. Why not tell them the one about what really happened? Why not tell them what you wanted us to do tonight?"

Before he could see the blurred movement, the black heel of Bedassie's shoe smashed into his nose bridge. Cymbals crashing in his ears. Zenobia shrilling, "You lie!"

Red pain washed over him. His blood tasted of metal and salt, and the mud from Bedassie's shoe. "Tell your husband how you turn his photo, his daughters' photo, down on the desk, so they don't have to see you undo my belt . . ." All eyes dropped to his waist, where the offending belt had not been closed since her struggle with it in the office. The resulting hush was louder than the babble that preceded it. A swift movement of his head avoided the predictable second kick from Bedassie.

"Tell them," he went on, amazed by the strength and steadiness and deep timbre of his own voice. He shut his eyes briefly, thinking of Jacob. If the demon that lived in his body was the manipulator of his physical self, then surely Jacob, with his quiet wisdom and insight, could guide his speech. "Tell him how you order things you don't need, just to get me to deliver them. How every time I come here, you send a message for me to come to your office, because you have an order you have to give me yourself."

Zenobia's little pharmacist clapped her hand over her mouth to silence a squeak.

"Teddy, he's lying..." Zenobia pleaded. Her husband looked from her to Rory, his skin still mottled with anger, but didn't lift his foot to strike again.

"Explain what it is you don't get from him that makes you want to take from me instead. Why he leaves you hungry. Feeling fat and old, and needing young men to tell you, and show you, you're not."

Victory wiped away, her face crumpled anew. Stinging under the goggle-eyed gaze of her guests, she let the tears flow again, genuine ones this time, narrow trickles following the path of the black, sticky fake ones she had squeezed out before.

Time telescoped again. Rory was aware of the brunt of Bedassie's attention turning away from him to Zenobia: his barked, incredulous questions, her pleading cries and protestations of innocence. Her whimpers as she was ushered weeping back to her office by her taut-faced husband. Party-goers, electrified by the scandal, returning to the back room, aching to be out of their hostess' earshot so they could tear her character to pieces while they finished off her food and drink. As the gaping crowd pulled back, Rory felt the air in him expanding, like that within a diver rising too fast to the surface.

The reluctant policemen let him go, sucking their teeth in annoyance at their time being wasted. The disappointed security guard, who still had not put his gun away, glared at him as he struggled to get the blood flowing again through his cramped limbs, fire in his wrists as the cuffs eased their bite. And Rory walked from the building—walked, not ran, as he wanted to do with everything inside him—walked with his back straight and his head up. His head wouldn't bow to anyone anymore.

When his car did not start he remained calm, coaxing the engine awake, refusing to give in to his customary frustration. The car wouldn't be a tyrant much longer. He headed east along the highway, just past the lighthouse, made an illegal U-turn at the next intersection, bald tires skidding on the wet road. He faced the city again, approaching the lighthouse from the coastal side this time but not passing it. Instead, the sharp swerve and the forceful, final lurch of the accelerator were enough to propel the dying vehicle off the road, up over the sidewalk, and onto the bank where the water's edge ended and the Sea Lots mudflats began.

There it halted, sighing out its last metallic breath, teetering at the edge of the water. Rory thrust open the door and stepped out, still calm, even anticipatory, tossing the now-useless keys onto the seat before putting his back to the rear bumper and shoving hard, pushing up with his legs and arms, until the wreck shifted. If the act required any special effort, he didn't notice. The car eased into the water like a boat down the slipway at its christening.

Hands on his hips, Rory stood on the bank, watching the water rise, first to the tops of the tires, then to the base of the windows. With detached curiosity, he watched the car sink, taking with it the clunking uncertainties and frustrations of his boyhood.

When he realized it would sink no further into the thick, black ooze but would instead sit half covered, like the skeletons of the abandoned boats that dotted the Gulf, he turned his back and stepped away. The taste in his mouth was cleaner than it had been in a long time.

He took the highway, sticking to the streetlights for guidance. Arima and home were several miles away, at least two hours at a steady clip, but the time would help him think about what he would do with this brand-new space he found inside himself now that the clutter and despair had been cleared. A baptism from the sky washed away the last vestiges of blood from his face, taking with it the grime of self-loathing and the ache of futility, reminding him that he was, in truth, a new creation.

Saul

His son would be home soon; it wasn't like he had anything to do with his nights. If he was going to do this, he'd better do it fast. Saul couldn't find a screwdriver anywhere—for all he knew, he'd probably sold the tool kit one drunken weekend—so he settled for a short, sharp fish knife, using the flat side to take the screw off the little metal band that connected the small cylinder of gas to the stove. He debated whether to leave on the three or four feet of rubber hose and the regulator, since the hose was getting crumbly anyway and wouldn't last much longer, but decided that the whole package might be worth a dollar or two more. That was okay by him.

It was late, well past business hours for most places, but he knew a few men who didn't mind keeping late hours, not with the type of business they did, anyway. And he was hurting for a drink. He felt lucky enough to do better than he had on the deal with the weight belt last week: the tank was almost full. Of course, no gas meant no hot food for a while, but he was tired of cooking anyway, and besides, Rory would eventually just get around to buying another one, so no real harm done.

It wasn't that he couldn't lift the heavy metal cylinder; it was just that he didn't feel like it—at least not before he left the house and hit the pavement. Until then, he could just tip it onto its side and drag it backward to the door. Why work harder than you really needed to?

But by the time he made it to the front door, he was winded. Getting older was a bitch. He bent over, feeling his spine creak, propping his hands on his knees, fighting for breath. The harsh rasp in his throat as he struggled was so loud in his ears that he failed to notice the soft click of the latch popping open behind him. When his chest stopped heaving, he yanked on the rim of the cylinder again, but the presence that now filled the room demanded his attention. He lifted his head and twisted toward it . . . and the gas tank dropped from his suddenly nerveless fingers, rolling onto his son's feet in the doorway.

Rory's face was full of trouble-clouds. "What you think you doing?" he asked, too quietly.

Think fast. Come up with a good story. "I was cooking your dinner, and I ran out of gas," was the best he could do.

"It was full when I bought it last week," Rory said. "Try again."

He could have, but there wouldn't be much point. Rory's eyes were like shadows on the moon. When Saul didn't answer, his son spoke once more. "You were taking it to sell."

Saul nudged the cylinder back and forth under his foot, staring down at the floor like a naughty child. Trying to avoid that thing in his son's eyes that he'd never seen before. "Pawn, not sell."

"Same difference," Rory snapped. "My belt—you took that too? And my gloves?"

No sense in answering.

"And the old radio? And the TV?"

The shock in the boy's voice would have made him laugh, if things didn't look so damned grim. Rory had honest-to-God never suspected. What a fool. Saul bared his teeth in an attempt at an appeasing smile. "I didn't mean no harm. I could take you where you could get most of your things back, if you willing to pay the ticket. It's just that you don't give me enough money to live off. I'm a big man. I got things I need to buy, you read me?" That reminded him that this whole mess was actually more Rory's fault than his, and he became more petulant, less guilty. "If you had give me more money, none of this woulda' never had to happen."

"I don't have to give you *anything,*" Rory's voice was no louder, but infinitely more emphatic. "I give you money because I choose to, and what I give you already is more than you deserve. You're strong enough to work, but you choose to live off *me* . . . and you steal from my home?"

Now the little pup was yapping to him about whose house it was? That was a joke. "*My* home," Saul pounded his chest. "I'm the man here. You still a boy. Don't forget that. Don't make me give you a good cut-ass to prove it."

Saul flinched as Rory moved swiftly, but he only knelt, shouldered the gas container with ease where Saul had shifted it with difficulty, and pushed past him to the kitchen, where he dropped it to the floor with a thud. "My home, Pa." Rory never called him "Pa." "This is my house. I pay the bills. I buy the food. You stay here because I let you. Don't ever forget that."

With that stinking lie on his lips, the boy turned his back on him and fiddled at the rear of the stove. No child of his was going to talk like that to him and look away! "Turn to face me, boy," he growled.

Rory picked up the same fish knife Saul had used to get the screw out and started working it back on, without even turning in the direction of his voice.

"You hear me?"

He didn't move. "Don't ever call me 'boy' again."

Damn rude. Wouldn't even look at him while he was sassing him off. Boy needed a lesson, and he was the one to give it to him. His fist drew back, all the way back, and was coming down hard. He didn't care if it got him behind the head, or across the face if he picked this time to turn around. Either way, he was begging for it, and it would teach him to keep a civil tongue in his mouth. But before knuckle could hit bone, a hand shot out, catching his flying fist like it was a ball glancing off a cricket bat. Sensing him unerringly without benefit of sight. His entire fist trapped in a hand so huge it wrapped around his own like it was a little girl's. He pushed against the upraised arm, but Rory, still on his knees, didn't even falter.

Saul felt his bones grinding painfully against each other, the nails of Rory's fingers digging hard into the back of his hand as the skin under them gave way. He could neither free himself nor fulfill the intended blow. The two men stayed locked in struggle for an age, and even when his own strength faltered and his shoulder ached and all he wanted was to take his arm back, Rory wouldn't release him.

Without letting up, Rory got to his feet, the knife still clutched in his other hand. Saul felt pressure behind his own eyes as the knife came into focus. A whine escaped him. Rory followed the direction of his bugged eyes, and looked surprised to discover that he still held the knife. He let the weapon fall to the floor.

Saul smirked, relieved at his reprieve, but contemptuous nonetheless. "After all the old talk, you still a pussy. You really wanna tell me you had a chance to take me and you don't do it? Boy, in all these years, I never teach you not to ever let a weapon go?"

Rory's answer was slow and untroubled. "In all these years, you never taught me shit. And I'm beginning to realize it's not such a bad thing."

And then Saul's hand was free again, pain numbing him from the wrist down, half-moons of broken skin across the back of it, his own pulse throbbing through his palm. He grinned. It hurt like a bitch, but it was still useable. Maybe the little coward bastard didn't want to hang on to the knife, but he had uses for it. His own speed surprised him. Action followed intent so quickly that the knife was in his grasp before the thought was fully formed, and he was swinging at him, straight for the chest and fuck the consequences.

But as the tip pierced flesh, the boy twisted, jerking away. The blade cut into the shirt, slicing cleanly, downward through the nipple—even he cringed deep in the gut at the grotesqueness of that—and Rory reacted with a surprised groan. Saul didn't let go of the knife, but didn't lift it again, either, so shocked was he to see the pain on his son's face. Every beating he had ever given the boy since he was eight or so had been met with stoic silence. The harder he hit him, the less Rory seemed to feel it, or to show that he felt it. Now as petals of red unfurled on his son's shirt, he could see agony on his face. And grief and disappointment. Even Rory looked amazed at having discovered the sensation of pain. He put his hand to his wound, brought it away, and examined the smear in his palm as if it were some strange, wild specimen. When Rory finally looked up, Saul knew he had pushed him too far.

"Out," Rory told him. "Now."

Saul had played his hand and lost. Everything. He knew there was no way to avoid being ousted—only perhaps to delay it a little, if he was lucky. "It's raining," he pleaded.

"Now."

"I'm sick. My asthma . . ." He could indeed feel his lungs tightening up. He needed a smoke to go with the drink he was aching for.

It didn't work. Rory pressed his palm over his heart to staunch the blood flow and said, "You have two minutes to pack as much as you can carry. Then, you go."

Self-pity and fear brought dry, heaving sobs. "I'm an old man. What you want me to do? Where you want me to go?"

Rory shrugged. "Get one of your drinking buddies to take you in. They happy to be your friends when you getting them drunk on my money; they should be happy to be your friends now you need them."

His son watched him as he wadded up the few shirts and pants he owned into bags; then demanded and received the keys to the house and walked behind him to the front door, where he folded his arms and leaned against the door frame. Saul held his bags tightly to himself as he brushed past the thick, dripping hedge and stepped out onto the street, feeling the tiny, hard fruits being crushed under his feet. There was something about sweet-lime that always smelled like home.

Then, just before he hit the corner, he heard his son's voice again.

"Saul."

He spun around, hope swelling, trying not to slip in his worn-out shoes. Trotting clumsily back to the gateway. Rory met him there. Saul tried to read his face. Had he changed his mind?

The boy opened his hand and pressed something small into it. Saul looked down. Two twenties and a ten.

"Take care of yourself," Rory said.

Saul didn't know how to answer.

Odile

Odile was beginning to get worried about Vincent. As the days passed, he grew more and more silent, brooding darkly in their unlit room for most of the day, and lying next to her at night without touching her. When she tried to pull him closer, he complied, not reluctantly, but disinterestedly, letting her draw his limp form against the curve of her body.

She knew she'd hurt him, and that made her feel guilty. She wished she could feel as he did, but wishing didn't make it so. And as good a man as he was, and as much shelter as the Dragon offered her, she knew she was not long for either.

But she wasn't fooling herself: Vincent's fugue was less about her than it was about the Dragon itself. He had taken to patrolling the premises, inspecting the kitchens with a suspiciously detailed eye, staring at the bare barroom walls like a muralist framing his vision. Once or twice she watched in horrified fascination as he stood across the street from the Dragon, rocking himself from side to side as if listening to an inner lullaby, staring up at the facade encrusted with pigeon shit and streaked with the piss of drunks who couldn't make it to the urinal.

When the bar doors opened to let patrons in or out, she could catch glimpses of him out there, and she wanted urgently to leave her post and go out to him—shake him hard and ask him what was wrong with him—but she never did.

Vincent was going through rough and hazardous territory, but he had to traverse it alone, just as she had to traverse hers alone. Voyages of the soul were solitary journeys.

From time to time when the doors opened, she looked up, hoping to see another face, one with shadow black skin and intense eyes that still held an innocence they should have relinquished long ago. She hadn't seen or heard from Rory since the loving they had given each other by the river, and as the days passed she became more and more disconcerted by the longing she felt for him. At their moment of parting at the Dragon's door a week ago, all she could think of was pulling away from the tenuous bond they had reformed through their conversation and the connection of their bodies. Now a yearning to test that bond even further replaced the common-sense determination to forget it had ever happened.

And then, as if by some witch's incantation, her soul had conjured him up out of smoke, a presence filled the doorway, like a silhouette cut out of black paper and held up against the light. Her heart leaped as it shouldn't have. But although the bulk of the shadow told her it was Rory, the bearing of the apparition was all wrong. The athletic figure's grace and supple confidence inside his own skin was marred by a limp which the man at the entrance corrected with the use of a thick staff. Jacob.

He squinted through the darkness, seeking her out, and something about the sharp, frenetic movements of his head filled her with dread. The floor of her belly dropped, and tossing aside her dish towel, she met him halfway.

"Jacob!" She touched him on the arm.

His eyes scared her even more. "Your mother needs you," he said.

"What happened?" Terrible visions arose.

"The baby . . ." Jacob was pulling at her arm, urging her toward the door before he could even explain. "Come."

Lil' Sebastian? She thought simultaneously of a hundred things that could happen to a small child, none of which she would be willing to accept as better than the other. Without stopping to think or to gather her belongings, she followed Jacob as he hurried out of the bar, his haste making him clumsy. Patrick, the big bouncer, left his post at the door, perturbed by her flight, but a few terse words from Jacob made him step back without intervening.

Jacob flagged down a taxi and thrust money at the driver. "Hospital. Fast."

"What happened to him?" she asked as she clambered in beside him, her tight skirt making flexibility difficult.

"He got into one of the cupboards. He drank some ant poison. Your mother was . . ." He clamped his lips shut and frowned out the window, body twitching in agitated rhythm, as if its momentum could spur the car on faster.

Hospitals were ugly places, designed more with death in mind than life. This one had changed little since Odile had last been here, four years ago, brought in bleeding with a child gone from her womb. The emergency room was dank and crowded, with hard wooden benches on both sides of the hall and more people than bench space. Some stood propped up against the walls; others squatted in corners. The sick and injured were among them: children with open wounds, glassy-eyed drunks, old people coughing and pleading for help, or at least comfort, with anyone who would listen.

Odile spotted Myra on a far bench, wedged in between a fat, weeping woman and a teenager whose bluish tinge screamed for air. Her mother was hunched over, fingers covering her face. Odile had never seen her so limp and crushed. She dropped to her knees before her and tried to brush Myra's hands away from her tear-stained face.

"He inside?"

"Yes."

"What'd they say?"

Myra shook her head. "Nothing. They didn't say nothing."

"I'll go," Jacob said. "You wait." And disappeared between the flapping doors.

"Blood and foam from his mouth . . . oh!" Myra wrenched away from Odile's embrace and covered her face again. Odile didn't resist, but put her arms around the shuddering form.

"How'd it happen?" she asked, but what she wanted to say was "How could you let this happen? Weren't you watching him?" Anger laced her panic and compassion with a red tinge. Lil' Sebastian was half hers—not just her brother, but the living ghost of the child she never had. Hers was more of a mother's grief than a sister's, and the resentment that took her unawares more that of a wronged parent than a concerned daughter. Myra could be so careless sometimes. But those were words that could never—*should* never—be said. As with all the pain that had ever looped between her mother and herself, she swallowed it, biting down hard on her tongue to keep it still.

"I only looked away for a minute," Myra said. "I was baking. I turned my back, and then . . . I should have been watching."

Odile thought so, too, even though she knew that the truth with children was that there was no such thing. They flitted from spot to spot faster than you could follow, and all the watching in the world amounted to nothing in the face of chance or destiny. So rather than mouth the blame she felt in her heart, she made her words careful, soothing. "It's not your fault. It just happened. Don't cry."

Myra's hands fell away from her face and her eyes locked with her daughter's. "I let him down. I should have been watching him, just like I should have been watching you all those years. I'm sorry."

"Sorry for what, Ma?" Odile was bewildered. Her mother wasn't the sort to apologize, especially when the exact nature of the fault was unclear.

"For all those times I was thinking about me and not you. For not seeing what you were instead of what I thought I should see. All that time, I told myself you were a little girl with only school and books on your mind. If only I'd looked harder, I'd have seen there were things you needed me to teach you. About men, and how having them didn't make you a woman."

Odile stared, worried. Did Myra know her own when and where, or had she slipped unawares through some crack in time, transported by trauma to Odile's teens? Those offenses, those sins of omission, were so long over. Had Myra's terror and shock over her son stirred up old bygones, like silt from the bottom of a river? The thought of facing old hurt distressed Odile. She floundered, trying to brush it off as pointless. "That's over now. I got past that."

Myra wouldn't be daunted. "But you did it on your own. The hard way. You were carrying a baby, and I didn't know. You went through all that pain, and I couldn't help, because I wasn't paying enough attention to know you needed it."

"That's so long ago, Ma," Odile protested. Tonight was no time for them to worry about the girl she had been and the mess she'd made of her life. They were here for her brother. But hearing her mother put into words the bitterness of her girlhood, just knowing that she understood, so long after the fact, the isolation she'd felt, and the bewildering sensation of drifting unmoored through her teens, was worth more than "I'm sorry."

Odile slumped forward to bury her face in her mother's lap. She felt one hand come to rest at the back of her head, light and soothing. Her own tears made tiny dark marks on the fabric of her mother's dress. "You did what you could," she insisted. She wasn't letting her mother suffer blame alone. Myra had had so little to work with, taking on her responsibilities without complaining. Time had literally meant money, and to give more of one inevitably meant less of the other. For all her lapses, she'd managed to keep her little family—mindless father and distant daughter—fed, dry, and clothed. All without gratitude or encouragement from the very daughter she'd given so much of herself to nourish. What a distant, spiteful, selfish little monster she'd been. "You gave me all you had, even when I didn't want it."

"Not my ear," Myra countered. "Not my help when you needed it."

Odile shook her head. That wasn't true. It was just that she was too full of stubbornness and pride to accept the help her mother had had to give at the time. She wondered if it was too late to start admitting that being alone didn't always mean being strong. "I still need your help," she told her. "It's not too late."

"You'll let me?" Myra sounded incredulous.

"Yes." Her reply was muffled by the folds of Myra's skirt. The flesh underneath was more solid than she remembered, evidence of her mother's settling into her middle years. Odile tilted her chin to look up at her, observing the filling-out of the face and the finest of gray hairs among the black. This new maturity did nothing to diminish Myra's awesome beauty; in fact, it increased her grace by the addition of these details, like an artist going over a finished masterpiece with a final flourish.

But as she stared up into this face, the virulent jealousy of her girlhood was, for the first time, absent. The realization was not as surprising as it could have been. The extent to which she had grown during her year away from Myra's home could be measured by the knowledge that she was a woman in her own right, not her mother's pale and imperfect reflection. Always Myra's daughter, yes, but an entity unto herself as well, separate and complete, but not too self-absorbed to refuse another's wisdom. She sat back on her heels, still at her mother's feet, and would not let go of her hands.

"So talk to me now. This man, is he good for you?" Myra surprised her by asking.

The first face that came to her mind was Rory's, but after a moment's confusion she realized that her mother could only be talking of Vincent; she had no way of knowing what had happened between her and Rory last week. Her mother had never come out openly and asked her about Vincent, and now she didn't know what to say. Good for her? Maybe. Vincent was a good man. But *right* for her? She didn't know anymore. As for Rory, he was just as good a man, but most likely even less right for her: everything she knew about him, and about herself, told her this was true. But part of her yearned to learn more, to find a loophole in her logic that would allow her to make space in her doubts for the possibility that "rightness" could be changed by sheer will. Rightness could be molded to take the shape of her desires, couldn't it?

Myra sensed her hesitation, and her woman's instincts let her read the reasons behind it. "People don't just come into your life for no purpose," she said. "Everybody you meet, you meet because they got something to teach you. And when the lesson is over and it's time to move on, you know."

She thought of the lessons that Vincent had taught her: about finding a single man preferable to many; about having the space to create oneself rather than leaving it up to others—to men—to create it for you. She was grateful to him for those lessons, and for having the patience to let her discover them through him. Would he be hurt if she moved in a different direction? Or had he of his own volition moved forward without her?

Giving voice to Odile's thoughts, Myra rubbed the sheer material of her blouse between her fingers, and said, without a trace of judgement in her voice "And maybe you learned enough from this to move on, too?"

Odile looked down at herself, remembering that in her haste to leave the Dragon she had not stopped to change her clothes but was wearing her tight, revealing uniform. It left her long legs exposed to view. All year, she had gone to great lengths to keep her mother from ever seeing her like this.

Now, she knew that she needn't have worried. Their tenuous new understanding made the old accusations of *jammette* unnecessary. That alone was beyond price. Myra was right: moving on from Vincent would also mean leaving the safety and sameness of the Dragon. Seizing and weathering the liberty that she and Rory had talked about. That required strength—but she knew she had it.

Her mind was playing tricks on her again. For the second time that evening, she became convinced that the sheer power of thought could make Rory appear, swirling from formlessness into form, and stepping out of the shadows. Then the apparition solidified, and illusion was made flesh. Rory was running along the Emergency corridor, fast for a man of his size, darting between harried nurses and cumbersome gurneys, anxiety written on his face.

And the sight of him alone was enough to thrust from her mind all questions of "good" and "right" for her, all logical debate about will and doubt. Because logic ceased to rule her now that her oldest friend, this solid rock she'd walked past all her life, was to be an anchor for her and a lodestone from which she was to draw her strength. Logic couldn't explain her sheer exhilaration at his presence. He brought comfort with him—no, he *was* comfort. And stability and tenacity. Just by being there, and by being him, he let her know that all would be right with her world again.

Rory and Jacob

When Rory saw her there on the bench with her mother, he almost sagged with relief. She was okay. And Myra was okay. He'd made it across town on foot, terrified that something had gone awfully wrong. When he'd turned up at the Dragon, he was told by the fat bouncer—who still looked at him with dislike but had at least been civilized enough to speak to him—that Odile had rushed out to the hospital with a man carrying a stick. His relief died when he remembered that if Myra was okay, and Jacob had been the one to get Odile, then there was only one person who could be in trouble: Myra's baby.

When he got to the two women, he wasn't even winded; there was air enough in his lungs to demand, "The child?"

Myra didn't get up from the bench, but Odile shot to her feet from her position at her mother's knee. He was close enough to see the tracks of tears drying on her face. Panic knotted his stomach for the child he had seen only once but who meant so much to the woman he loved.

Without answering, she held her arms out to him, like a toddler wanting to be lifted by her daddy. She felt light in his arms, although she was not a small woman by any means. He found himself murmuring every soft thing that came to him, whether it made any sense or not. Her lips were soft against his ear. "Poison," she sobbed.

He set her down on her feet, holding her away from him just enough to see her face. "What?"

From behind them, Myra answered for her, voice surprisingly strong. "Sebastian drank poison from under the sink. I should have been watching him. I wasn't."

Odile whipped around, her back now against his belly. "Ma, I told you it wasn't your—"

Myra cut her off with a grunt and turned her face away.

Rory was glad when she let her hand lie in his firm clasp, not trying to take it away. "Tell me what I can do," he said to Myra.

Her eyes were on Odile's fingers, entwined with his. She looked a little taken aback, and he had to resist the urge to let go abruptly. He didn't doubt that Myra knew of the feelings he had always held for her daughter, but having her see them manifest even in this light touch made him feel exposed.

Myra shook her head. "You're doing enough now." Her eyes didn't leave their joined hands.

A space opened up next to Myra and he motioned to Odile to sit. He stood facing the two women, still holding onto Odile. He wanted to do more: hold her closer, comfort her, smooth the lines of worry from between her eyes, lay himself down like a bridge between her and her pain. But he was afraid to move; her silent acceptance of his light touch was so tenuous that he was afraid of crushing this minute trust she had placed in him.

Around them, the hubbub rose and abated as the sick and wounded came, waited, and were ushered in through the wide steel doors. But even the pain and death that loomed could not diminish his contentment at being once again on the peripheries of this tiny family, and being allowed access— if only briefly—within.

The doors swung open for the hundredth time and Rory glanced up disinterestedly, just in time to see Jacob stride in, holding his staff with the elegance of a gentleman with a walking stick. Myra swiftly followed his gaze, turning her wide, anxious eyes to Jacob as he reached her side. He smoothed her messy hair and then cupped her face, kissing her on her forehead. "He's over the worst," he began. "Still serious, but at least . . ."

"Yes?"

"He's out Emergency, up on the wards. He has to share a bed with another little boy. . . ."

Myra was too tired and relieved to complain about over-crowding. "I need to see my son."

"You can, but not for long. And two visitors only."

Myra held both hands out to him. "Come with me."

Jacob and Rory glanced simultaneously at Odile's stricken face. There was something about motherhood which, when it touched a woman—no matter how briefly—left her painfully aware of the suffering of a child, as if her womb constricted at the mere idea. Odile's fear and agony were no less than that of the woman who had given birth to him. Being men didn't prevent them from seeing this. "Not me," Jacob told her. "Take your daughter with you."

Myra looked around, flushing with embarrassment at having turned to her man before her daughter. Odile hung her head slightly, not wanting to show the hurt reflected there. "I don't have to," she murmured.

"No, let's go see our boy."

Rory reluctantly let Odile slip from him. If he let her go, would she ever allow him to hold her again? As their bodies broke contact, he felt pain so sudden that it knocked the wind out of him, like a sucker punch to the gut. She heard the air rush from his mouth and guessed the reason.

"Wait for me," she said.

He didn't have the breath to answer. He watched as Odile let her mother take her by the arm, and the women worked their way through the mayhem to find the right ward. Alone, the men faced each other. The noise around them swelled again as a new wave of emergencies surged in.

"Seems like death and sickness don't take time off for Christmas," Jacob observed.

"No."

"Need air?" Jacob jerked his head toward the exits. Rory didn't need to answer. They walked out together.

Listless ixoras and crotons dotted straggly, weedy patches of green in the hospital garden. Young men in grubby aprons, which seemed to comply more with food sale regulations than with those of hygiene, hawked peanuts and meat pies to worried family members driven from their bedside vigils by hunger. Children careered along the paths, whooping, yelling, throwing flimsy missiles at each other, oblivious to the rapidly gathering dusk.

Rory walked alongside Jacob, watching him out of the corner of his eye, waiting for him to speak, but nevertheless content to enjoy their silence. In the same way that Jacob drew strength from the *bois* that he held, he drew comfort from the solid presence of the old stickfighter.

Jacob eventually spoke. "I got your belt ready. You want to come by and pick it up day after tomorrow?"

"That's Christmas Day," Rory reminded him.

"Oh, right. Slipped me." Jacob's broad smile told Rory that the date hadn't slipped him at all. "You'll have to take lunch with us, then."

Rory stopped short, and Jacob halted next to him. Lunch? On Christmas Day? That was for families. He tried to think of the last time he had a Christmas lunch in company other than his own. That would have been so long ago, when he actually had a family to lunch with. His mother always cooked far too much, and his father tried to stay sober and grumbled about how much all the food was costing him, but it had been a happy time nonetheless.

Myra's kitchen would be different. There would be warm smells, spice in the air, ham with cloves and honey heated up in sizzling fat, pigeon peas, potatoes, people laughing, and carols playing on the radio. And Odile in her Christmas dress, across the table from him. Family time, and he would be in on it. He tried to keep the anxious hope out of his voice. "Would Miss Myra mind?"

"Mind?" Laugh lines crinkled. "She hasn't stopped talking about you since she saw you last week. How good you look. How much you grown. Nothing she likes better than feeding people, especially big strong men with a healthy appetite like yours. You have to come. And bring your father."

The warmth in Rory was immediately extinguished. He was an idiot for thinking that Jacob had extended the invitation to their intimate gathering because he wanted to draw him into the one place Rory hungered to be. To spin around on the heels of such generosity and ask to let Saul into that sacred circle—a man Odile loathed and for whom Jacob had no respect—made the invitation hollow. Good manners on the part of an old country gentleman. Embarrassed, and angry at Jacob for shattering his fantasy with his kindness, he floundered for a way out.

Jacob watched him gravely as he began to stutter out a lie, cutting him off before he could further shame himself, by saying quietly, "It's Christmas, son. Nobody should have to eat alone on Christmas."

Rory felt ashamed and selfish, angry with himself for appearing so unfeeling toward his own father—in the presence of the man who called him "son." "But—"

"I know how you feel. I know what he did to you when you were a boy."

Rory looked away, embarrassed at hearing mentioned aloud the taint that had seeped into his life like rot through wood. Even more embarrassed that Jacob was delicately pretending not to know that the abuse had extended way past childhood.

"I know what happened to you because I used to watch it happen from across the yard. I should have gotten up and come over and stopped it. But I didn't. I was too busy thinking about myself and my leg and my own problems. I could have stopped him, you know."

Rory had no doubt he could have. Jacob's skill with his *bois*, his grace and speed, would have been more than a match for Saul's clumsy brutality. But it had never occurred to him that anyone would have wanted to intervene, even if there had been the chance to. For him, the ugly conflict in which father and son were locked was a private place. Nobody, not even Jacob, had the right to enter. He tried to dismiss the admission with a slight shake of his head.

But Jacob wasn't being cut off from saying what he had to. He filled his lungs. "Rory . . ."

"Don't, Jacob." No "Mister" Jacob this time. Their complicity in this taut conversation made them equals.

Jacob pretended not to hear. "I didn't try to help you. I sat on my bench and watched you get hurt. That makes me less of a man than I want to be."

"You could have stopped it once, or twice, but that wouldn't have been enough. The only person who could stop it in the end was me."

"Not true. I'm a man. You were a child. And maybe if someone—if *I*—had done something earlier, maybe . . ."

Rory knew what he was about to say, sensed it from the pain that crossed Jacob's face, smelled it coming like a storm sweeping down from the hills. "No," he said, trying to head him off. "Not that."

"Maybe what happened to Odile . . ."

"Wouldn't have happened?" He didn't want to believe that. All the well-meaning babble about violence toward children begetting violent children—that was the coward's way out. That made him the victim, and victim wasn't something he was willing to be anymore. He snorted. "So I hit Odile and it's Saul's fault?"

Jacob nodded gravely. "And mine. And Myra's. And everyone who saw it happening and didn't speak."

He couldn't bear the shame of having others take the

blame for something *he* had had done, on his own. He pointed at himself. "I am the cause, Jacob. And the effect. It doesn't go past me."

"And what you plan to do with all this blame? Wear it like a badge?"

"No." He was firm. "I'm not going to wear it. I wore it long enough. But I'm not going to let anyone else wear it for me, either. Not Saul, not you, definitely not anyone else. Okay?" He regretted the harshness in his voice, but Jacob didn't take offense.

"Okay."

Rory tried to blunt the edge of their conversation. When it all came down to it, the invitation to bring Saul to lunch was a moot point. He hadn't seen his father in days. "Besides, my father—" that was a word he didn't like tasting in his mouth. "—Saul, doesn't live with me anymore."

"He left?" Jacob's face told him he knew otherwise.

The truth was too ugly to hide. "I put him out."

Instead of asking the obvious questions: why it had happened, and when, and how, Jacob startled Rory with, "And how you feel?"

Rory blinked. *Feel.* A funny word to use where he and Saul were concerned. Saul tried hard to inure him to feeling, every offense against his person and his spirit layering into a scab so thick that the emotions between father and son were too blunt-edged to be identified as such. Up until his liberation from his self-imposed anesthesia. Now that he was free to sample and taste and feast his eyes upon the astounding array of sensations, thoughts, and feelings laid out before him, he was surprised at the colors and flavors that the word 'father' assaulted him with. They ranged from the bitter black of neglect at the memory of his own child-self, to bile green resentment every time he walked past Saul's vacant room, to the soft purple ache of regret that filled his gut whenever he reminded himself that he was a bad son, because good sons didn't throw their fathers out into the rain.

Unconsciously, his fingers found his left nipple through his shirt, bandage crinkling softly under them. He had seen enough fighting wounds to know that Saul's final assault would leave the nubbin of flesh disfigured, a permanent, hideous souvenir. "I don't know how I feel," he finally admitted. The directness of the question made him aware that there was no direct answer. "When I was a boy . . ." He stopped in anticipation of the images that should have flooded his mind: beatings and loneliness and self-loathing. Days of sitting out in the yard under the tamarind tree, creating in his mind a universe in which he was big enough and strong enough to meet his father blow for blow. Two man-crab couldn't live in one hole, the old folks used to say. He had loved the image of himself in his hard blue shell, scuttling sideways on quick legs, pincers up before him not just in defense but in outright attack, locking huge claws with the older crab and feeling the carapace being crushed under his vicious, vindictive grip. Flesh tearing soft and white at the joints until the vanquished oppressor limped away on the sand. That drama, written, directed and edited in the dark silence of his own mind, had never failed to please him and make up for all the unrighted wrongs he had suffered.

But with those images came others, these more brightly colored. Picking brilliant blue morning glories off the vine that ran along the fence in St. Ann's for his mother. Smuggling bread or corn out for Gracie, who, after she was done eating, would flutter up onto his shoulder and ruffle her feathers affectionately against his cheek. Listening to old Sebastian, Odile's grandfather, in his more lucid moments, talking about the life of the old-time police officer while he took out his silver dress uniform buttons and polished them. Myra laughing with Jillian from next door as they hung out pretty-colored laundry on lines strung out behind the house. And

Odile, with the sun running its fingers through the hair that fell down her back. With the exception of that one dark, ugly moment in the rain by the engorged river, every memory, every thought he had of Odile, found her clothed in sunshine. Surely that alone, that one persistently perfect memory, made his childhood all worth the while?

Saul hadn't succeeded in poisoning everything, as long as Odile and sunshine both glowed equally bright in his boyhood memory. To think that she would still be waiting for him when he and Jacob made their way back into the hospital! He coughed softly.

Jacob hadn't moved, but waited patiently for him to find his voice again. Rory fought between the urge to explain the decision to make Saul leave and the need to keep his dirty linen private. "My father . . . took things. My radio. My clock. The weight belt I asked you to replace."

"Not the addicts after all, eh?" Jacob looked as if his private suspicions had been confirmed. "He sold them?"

"Yes."

"For drink."

"Yes."

The shrug was philosophical, but the eyes piercing. "Then maybe you're better off."

That was the problem. Was he? No more thievery and no more abuse would make his life more livable. But Saul was out there somewhere, moving from friend to friend, and when the patience of each of his drinking *comperes* ran out in turn, his options would run out as well. Saul had fed and clothed him for many years, until the time had come for him to return the favor. He had failed in his duties as a father, but now that the boy had become father to the man, wasn't he shirking the responsibilities that his "fatherhood" brought with it? Duty cut both ways. "Better off," he repeated musingly. "They how come I feel like I failed?"

Jacob stretched out a slow hand, first and middle fingers extended, the other three curled over each other, and Rory watched, fascinated, at the dark skin on the back of it, thick veins writhing like baby snakes, until just two fingertips came to rest lightly on his forehead, between his eyes.

"Son," Jacob lowered his voice, intensifying the intimacy of the bold touch. "My boy, listen. Nobody can't tell you what to do about that, because nobody but you got to live here." He tapped Rory's forehead. "Inside your skin. I can guess what went on between you and him, but I'll never know all of it. I can only tell you one thing."

Rory waited. There was so much strength and wisdom emanating from this man. So much to learn. Everything inside him longed to call him "father" and put his arms up around those shoulders—to be held, just once, as every boy needed to be. But embarrassment and a sense of infidelity—even though that "infidelity" was toward a man who wouldn't care—prevented him from moving a muscle. He shut his eyes against the irony and listened to Jacob as he went on.

"What you do now makes you what you are later. What you plant now you reap later, only bigger and better or worse than it was before. You plant anger, you get a fury tree. And you won't be the only one to have to eat the fruit."

"But I'm afraid if I stay near him any longer, I'm going to be like him. I can't even look at him, because all I can see is myself, older and uglier and alone." Rory still wouldn't open his eyes, focusing on Jacob's low rumbling voice.

"He chose the seeds he wanted to plant a long time ago. You don't have to make the same mistakes. But between men, you can find a way to help him, no matter what happened in the past. Because that's what men do. They get past the pain and do what needs to be done."

"And if I fail?"

Jacob shook his head firmly. "You won't."

The immensity of the task humbled him. Scared him. But finding Saul and stepping in to do what his father no longer could was the only option. Jacob was right—he had to be. He could save his father and still retain his sense of self.

Heredity didn't need to be a contaminant, not if his own spirit was strong enough to resist the enslavement of his own genes. When Jacob explained it, it seemed so obvious, so simple.

He felt his face suffuse with heat and was shocked to feel wetness spill past his lashes. Then, miraculously, Jacob's staff fell between them, and Jacob was pulling him to his thick chest. Rory let himself be drawn against the older man and willed himself to commit to memory every detail of the sensation of being held as he never had been by his father, even as a baby. In that embrace there was liberation, expiation, consolation. When Jacob let him go, Rory laughed, hastening to wipe away the traitorous dampness on his cheeks, but the laugh was more due to a delirious relief than to embarrassment.

Awkwardness had no time to set in, because shouts in the distance made them both spin around to see Myra and Odile running toward them, arms waving madly. Rory's stomach tautened with dread. From this distance there was no telling whether the source of their agitation was distress or gladness. He left Jacob's side and ran to them.

"Sebastian?"

As he came closer, the relief on their faces became his. Jacob was close enough behind him to catch Myra's half-laughing, half-sobbing revelation that her son was past danger, asleep, and breathing on his own.

"He looked so tiny," she marveled. "And still. Like a doll."

Jacob managed to be both soothing and brisk, shepherding his woman toward the main hospital doors. "We'll sit with him. Next to the bed. If he wakes up, we'll be there."

Odile made to follow them, but Jacob stopped abruptly, causing her to crash into him.

"You don't need to stay. It wouldn't serve any purpose, all of us being here."

She frowned and protested. "But he's my brother!"

"I know he is. But you're tired, Odile. Go home and rest. You can see him tomorrow, when he's awake." His eyes met with Rory's over her head. "Rory will take you home."

Then Jacob smiled at him, a knowing smile that men exchanged only between themselves. Rory looked away, abashed, and became even more so when Myra supported Jacob's urging with insistence of her own. Odile said nothing, but didn't protest. He avoided looking at her until Jacob and Myra disappeared together into the building.

Rory and Odile

He was alone with her for the first time since she had let him love her on their rock. He contemplated taking her hand again but didn't. His conviction that she would want him to was not as strong as it had been before she was once again near him in the flesh. Of course, he'd held her earlier, but then she had come to him scared and distraught for her brother. The calm that panic had left in its wake was another matter. He kept his hands at his sides.

"You didn't call me." She was watching him coyly, out of the corners of her eyes. "Or pass by the Dragon. What, you afraid of Patrick and Teeth?"

He laughed. "No. Not afraid of them. And in any case it looks like they let bygones be bygones. They were nice enough to tell me where you were tonight."

"Without hitting you?"

"Without hitting me." He took his teasing like a man. But then he was serious again. "I wanted to call you. I didn't want you think I was the kind of man who wouldn't call, after . . ." He was too abashed to finish.

Her hand flew up before her face to hide the sudden deepening of her coloring. "I know you're not."

"But there were so many things going on . . ."

"Trouble?"

"Not anymore."

"All better now." She sounded so confident for him.

He thought of Zenobia and the fiasco he had been drawn into. That was certainly as over as it would ever be. But as for Saul, well, some things didn't end, only changed direction. "Most of it." He was wrung out after spilling all to Jacob; he didn't want to go through it a second time tonight.

Better to guide her away from the subject. The sky had closed up, shutting off that endless drizzle that had so dampened his soul and threatened to send him mad. Even the ground under his feet was dry. "Nice outside tonight. For a change."

She let him get away with it. "Maybe it won't rain for Christmas after all."

"Good. Christmas is one of those days when it just shouldn't rain. No magic in the rain. Only sadness."

Odile slipped her arm through his, long fingers squeezing gently on his biceps. "You're wrong. Lots of magic comes down on the rain. And on the wind. You can feel it, and hear it. It was there, in the bamboo, rustling the leaves above us. Remember?"

He remembered. Prickles ran down the back of his scalp, and each hair on his back and chest and arms and between his legs uncurled against his skin, like tall grass ruffled by an unexpected breeze. He bit his tongue. There had been magic there, and the residual sparks were still alive and arcing between them. To deny it was blasphemy.

"Where's your car?" Practical Odile.

She was finally willing to ride with him, and now it didn't exist. "It . . . uh . . . died."

"Sorry. We can walk. I don't mind."

The route they had begun would take her directly back to the Dragon, but he steered her away, going west a few blocks toward the main shopping area, before heading south to the Quay, telling himself that a gentleman should always choose a route that was better lit and more traveled, to make the lady feel safe, but secretly glad for the few precious minutes his detour added to the walk. In spite of the hour, Independence Square was still thronging with people: vendors, foodsellers, late shoppers, children, restless teenagers searching for a bar that might let them slip inside for a while. When they were within view of the Dragon, Odile stopped.

"It's so early," she murmured. "Too early to go in."

He glanced surreptitiously at his watch. He disagreed with her idea of "early," but didn't contradict her. He looked down at her uniform. "You don't have to go back to work?"

"Yes." She didn't move.

He waited, watching her eyes as she looked across the street at the Dragon. They were too far from it to hear any music, or to recognize the faces of any of the figures coming in and out. A terrible conflict was going on inside her, a tugging and pulling from one conviction to the next. He wanted to think he understood at least part of it. "Nothing wrong with outgrowing something. You stop growing, you die."

"I know."

"You could finish out the night with them. Or the week, or even the year. Then you can start looking for what you were always meant to do. Whatever it is, it'll still be there waiting for you, because it's yours."

"I don't want to finish out the night."

He was barely brave enough to hope. "What you want to do?"

She turned her eyes on him. He could see the moon in them. "I want to be with you."

The taxi they hopped into took forever to get them home. Rory hated the length of the lines at each traffic light, hated the driver of every other car on the road that made it so congested, hated the three other people they had to share the cramped little car with: their endless chatter; their requests for the taxi driver to go off-route—because it was, after all, Christmas, and they had armloads full of parcels, and he didn't expect them to walk in from the main road laden down like donkeys, did he?—and the fact that they took up space in the suddenly private world that should have been his and Odile's alone.

But after an agony of a wait, they alighted from the car at the top of his street. He touched the small of her back, guiding her along the uneven pavement. He watched her eyes dart from side to side, taking in the guttering streetlights overhead and the gaudy strings of fairy lights, streamers, and Christmas trees that failed to disguise the shabbiness of the houses behind them. If only he lived somewhere pretty and airy and green.

He felt her stiffen and stop short. Her face was stricken, and his heart sank. Was this ugliness too much for her? "Don't worry." He tried to be comforting. "It's not pretty, but it's safe."

Her voice was strangled. "Your father . . ."

He'd forgotten. Damn Saul, making his life pain even when he was no longer there. "He's gone."

She spoke through clenched teeth. "But he'll be back."

He hastened to reassure her. "No, no. Not tonight. He's *gone*. He doesn't live here anymore." He didn't want to tell her that his dismissal might prove only temporary, once he figured out how best he could help steer Saul away from the mouth of hell. "We're alone." Her eyes were still pleading for reassurance, so he added emphatically, "Trust me."

She took his arm again and walked beside him to his house. He tried not to see the ugly, dingy, yellowing flaky paint, the broken windowpanes, and the rickety steps leading to his front door. She stopped in the open gateway. "Oh!"

The hedge that lined the front of his yard was strung with lights, long sparkling loops of them. He had lingered in the store over whether to get the traditional red, white, and green, or something modern, like all gold or all red; but boyish pleasure won out at the prospect of bringing Christmas back home after so many years, so he had given in to the lure of the many colors, and now his hedge glittered with reds and blues and pinks and yellows and greens. Their twinkle was answered by the lights and baubles that weighed down the too-tall tree that now dominated his front porch.

"Real pine," she observed gleefully. "Not plastic."

"Real pine." He remembered her saying she didn't care for Christmas, one way or the other. Right now, she didn't look as crusty and cynical as she liked to pretend. She closed her eyes and tilted her head back, sniffing noisily like a little girl in her mother's kitchen on baking day.

"Sweet-lime in the air," she sighed.

He looked down at her, not even bothering to resist smiling. What a beautiful woman. What a beautiful night. The crisp December air ruffled her short hair. She sipped at the air like a wine taster, holding it in her mouth and then exhaling through pursed fat lips that held him riveted.

It hurt to look at her. He had watched her from a distance every day, greedy and feasting, not caring whether his persistent gaze had annoyed her or that she was adept at putting him in his place when she caught him staring. It was like stargazing: you could look as much as you wanted, because the star you coveted neither knew nor cared that you were there. Now the star that had been the only light in his young life had condescended to bend near enough to the earth for him to touch . . . to possess . . . That brought a pain in his heart and his gut and the base of his spine and his crotch. Blood pounding in his temple.

He hoped he wouldn't fall on her as he leaned forward. His legs might go dead under him without warning, and he was a big man; he'd fall like a tree, flattening her. But he somehow managed to keep his balance as his mouth pressed against hers. *Careful, now. Don't let anxiety and hunger and lust and delirium make you suck her in, inhale her like a vapor into yourself.*

Be calm.

Breathe.

She kissed him back, and the sweet-lime-scented air she had taken in so greedily now filled *his* lungs. The perfume of the tiny white blossoms clung to her mouth and the skin at her throat. Her teeth small and hard, too light against his lower lip. He wished she would press them harder against him, harsh enough to split the skin, so that when all was said and done he would bear a scar on his face that would remind him every day that she had held him that close and warred against his tongue with hers.

His Christmas tree dimmed in the wake of the light that his glittering star trailed behind her as he led her up the stairs and into the house. Her glow softened the ugliness of the bare rooms inside. His bed was barely large enough for him alone, but tonight somehow they would both fit. He wanted to undress her, but she shucked off her uniform as if she were peeling away layers of herself she didn't want to be covered in anymore. Then she was naked.

Back at their old apartments in St. Ann's, he had spent many an agonizing sleepless night struggling to picture her nude, yet terrified to do so. It was as sacrilegious as seeing a female deity unclothed, even if the disrobing took place only in his frenzied teenage imagination. Twice before he had made love to her, and each time the fact that she had allowed him to gaze upon her bare skin had humbled him. This time even this awesome nakedness took second place to the unflinching honesty in her eyes. For the first time, she was allowing herself to be truly unclothed before him, not hiding behind her shuttered look and jealously guarded emotions. He stripped off his own clothes as fast as she had and lowered himself upon her.

The frankness of her own gaze proved to be too much even for her. He felt her arms go up around his neck and her face come to nest against his chest, close to the thin bandages that protected his torn nipple. The bandage rustled against her cheek. "What?"

Now was not the time for explaining. "Nothing. Not now."

"Okay."

She was warm and slick and supple. Open. Waiting for him. He wanted to savor the precious few moments of urgent anticipation, but she was impatient. She reached down and grasped him, throwing her legs up around his hips, forcing down on him with her own until he was enveloped in so much heat that he thought he would be scalded. He lay on his side and pulled her shuddering body against his, too afraid to move lest that set off an explosion in them both.

She murmured something faint against his neck.

"What, love?" he wanted to know.

"Searching and searching," she sighed. The pressure of her breasts against his wounded nipple brought no pain. "All that searching."

He rocked against her gently. "For what?"

"For a center." She tilted her head back so she could hold his eyes. "And now I found it."

Him. Her center. He closed his eyes, reading her face by touch alone. Wanting to hold this scary joy inside for a few moments in case it came spilling out of him in such a gush that he wouldn't be able to control it.

"You didn't find me," he reminded her. His rocking motion increased its tempo, slowly, sweet sensation in every fiber of himself. Wanting it to last, but finding forbearance impossible. "You didn't even need to look, Odile. I was always . . ."

Heat seared his tongue. He tried again. "I was always . . ."

Pleasure so intense it robbed him of breath enough to speak. Fighting against the undertow. One word. One last word. It oozed out of him, half whisper, half gasp.

". . . there."

Odile and Rory

They couldn't stop talking. Or rather, *he* couldn't stop talking, and she couldn't stop listening. Odile sat on Rory's narrow bed with her bare back against the wall and her legs splayed wide enough to allow him to lie between them, head resting against her breasts. He prattled on excitedly about everything that came into his head, seeming to want in a single night to fill her in on everything he had done or thought or desired during the years they had been apart.

She listened gravely to his talk of the boxing ring and about this man named after a shark with whom he boxed. About how afraid he had always been that the ring would swallow him up and he would lose control, and the sport would in a flash become something horrible and brutal and deadly. How he'd wrestled with this demon inside him and won, so he wasn't afraid anymore. He told her a story about some crazy woman in a drugstore who had young boys for lunch.

She listened with her mouth slightly open—not in awe of the tales that he told, but because it let her keep adding the sense of taste to those through which she was already experiencing him. All night he'd drowned her with sensation, his rough-smooth touch intensified by the heat of both their bodies, the uninterrupted whispered endearments, the hot, raw scent of him, and his awesome beauty. The salt of his skin still lingered on her lips, but there was something else there, too: a kind of sweetness.

She let the pink tip of her tongue slip past her teeth. This sweetness she was tasting didn't stop there, not in her mouth. Masking—no, replacing—a flavor she now recognized as counterfeit, like the fake sugar they put in diet fare. This new taste was so sharp, clear, and definite that she wondered how she had never noticed that all she had enjoyed before was not real.

Hunger did that to you, she decided. Just as a hungry man enjoyed the meanest of meals, so, too, did a hungry spirit relish even the bitter fruit of unhappy relationships, desperate copulation, and pairings that shared no common ground. But satiation changed things. It let you look at things differently and somehow brought with it the sixth sense that allowed you to tell the real from the unreal, the sweet from the tart.

Rory's voice rumbled deep in his chest, vibrating through his back against her skin, interrupting her thoughts. "Come to church with me tonight. Come to midnight mass with me."

She was a little perplexed. "What? Tonight?"

He twisted his arm up to show her his watch. "It's one in the morning. Already tomorrow. It's Christmas Eve. And I want to be in church with you later, to see Christmas in."

She frowned. "I don't know. Church . . . it's not my thing."

"You've been before," he reminded her.

"That was a long time ago," she countered. "Not since I was a girl. I'm not sure if I even remember what to do, when to stand, what to sing . . ."

He slipped from the enclosure of her arms and stood up, facing her, feet apart, hands on his hips. So, so beautiful. "It comes back to you. It's one of the things you never forget." His voice grew coaxing. "Come on, Odile. Sweetheart. Come for me. Make it my Christmas present. It's all I want, just for you to be there with me, at midnight. That's where I want us to start over. Together." He cocked his head to one side and waited.

She didn't have to think too long or too hard. His fervor was infectious. "I'll meet you," she promised. "Tonight." She stretched her limbs, pointing her toes, and reached for the ceiling with her hands, enjoying the languor in her bones. He was right. There was no better place to start.

Vincent

'Twas the night before Christmas. That made Vincent grin. The visions that had danced in his head this past week had nothing to do with sugarplums, far from it. They were all of blackness tinged with flickering red. As for no creatures stirring, well, although this was the one night on which the Smiling Dragon shut its doors to the public, quite a few people were still milling about. Miss Ling was in her quarters; with the bar's sound system silent for a change, he could hear the high-pitched strains of her Chinese music being torturously eked out of a scratchy old record player. That stupid goddamn peacock was singing along, and he didn't know which racket was harder on the ears.

In the maze of bedrooms, the prostitutes tittered and fidgeted, getting dressed for some event or other. A few were off to enjoy themselves at Christmas Eve parties: some to be entertained rather than entertain for a change; others to earn a little spare cash that would be exempt from Miss Ling's "rent." Some were spending the night out with their boyfriends. The Catholic girls were headed for church.

Odile was getting dressed for church, too. She was going with a friend, she said. Vincent wondered if it was the same "friend" who had kept her out half the night. He watched her in silence. She looked so beautiful, with her hair freshly shampooed and clinging to her scalp, single pearls in her earlobes. Her face was closed, her emotions hidden from him, foreign to him even as they surged behind her eyes. His fault. He'd shut her out this past week and repulsed her every attempt to coax him into explaining his sudden, brooding silence. Maybe his silence had killed what little they ever had, or maybe it was simply wounded, not dead. But silence had been a necessity. Silence gave you time and space to plan. After tonight, he would have all the time he needed to make up for it. She claimed she didn't want to make any promises to him about their future together, but when she finally saw the logic to his actions, when he was done wiping the slate clean and ready to start over, she would come around.

"Say a prayer for me," he joked weakly. "Light a candle."

She gave him a cautious look. "You need praying for?"

Bad idea. Sounds suspicious. She was smart enough to figure out he was up to something tonight if he was careless enough to let his guard down. He shrugged, got up behind her, and put his arms around her waist. Her skin smelled sweeter than the perfume she was wearing. "We all need praying for. You don't think?"

She didn't struggle out of his grasp. She seemed to be thinking about it. "We do," she agreed finally. "I'll light one for you. And one for me, too."

He bent to kiss the back of her neck, but she was already slipping free and turning around to face him. This time, he could see something in her eyes: a kind of sadness. Panic shunted aside his complacency. What if she was so far away from him now that, when all was done, he couldn't draw her near again? Maybe he could take her into his confidence now, get her to help him see this through. Sharing a secret always brought people closer. He cleared his throat. "You *have* to go out tonight?"

Her brows drew together. "It's . . . Christmas Eve," she answered stupidly. "I thought I'd go to mass." Then, "Why, you want me to stay home?"

He scratched his head. "Noooo . . . ." *Yes.*

"You sick?"

He shook his head vehemently. "No. Not sick. I just . . ." *I just need you to stay and help me through tonight,* he wanted to say. He wondered whether, in the year they had shared, he had ever told her he loved her. And if he did, had she ever responded? Would tonight be too late? He let his breath out in a gust, bent over to scoop her small white handbag off their bed, and passed it to her. He would see it all through alone, but after tonight, he would ensure that whatever needed to be done to make her his again would be done. He'd stake everything he had on that.

Odile took the bag and stared down at it thoughtfully. Then she looked at him. So much sadness in those eyes. Wordlessly, she slipped her arms around him, pressing her body against his. He wanted to hug her back, but he ran the risk of falling apart and begging her not to go. So instead, he glanced at his watch and said, "You'd better go. You'll be late for the carols."

She didn't relinquish her hold on him; in fact, she clung more tightly. Her voice was muffled against his throat. "Vincent . . ."

"Later," he said firmly.

"I . . ."

"When you get back." He didn't resist her kiss; her mouth was soft and open. Then she drew away and walked out the door, head bent.

He stretched himself out on the bed, hands behind his head, listening to the sounds of the building. The girls in the rooms all around left in twos and threes, tittering, bracelets jangling, chatting excitedly about where they were going tonight, and with whom. When he was sure they had all left, he got to his feet, put his shoes on, and made his way downstairs to the kitchen.

He flicked on the lights and surveyed the room. The cooks had washed up all the dishes the night before, and they were stacked in old drying racks on the far counter. The dishwasher would go there, once he bought it. Two hulking old gas stoves took up most of the space along one wall. They were reasonably clean, if you were able to turn a blind eye to the years of caked-on, yellowed grease that had solidified into an irremovable gummy layer that covered the tops, sides, and the wall behind them. They were stacked with ancient woks and empty cast-iron pans, black with age. The fridge wheezed. The freezer pissed water onto the floor.

No more.

He could hear his grandmother's music through the door to her quarters on his left. It sounded like the needle was stuck in a groove, but with the shrill, repetitive music she loved, it was hard to tell. She had probably fallen asleep and left the record player on. That was okay. He would have ample time to start the fire, wake her up, and rescue her.

He went to one of the stoves and pulled the gas line out from the back, working it free from the clamp, just enough to make it look as if it had popped off on its own. As the air filled with the smell, he checked the three new fire extinguishers he had installed just two days ago, arguing to his grandmother that the old ones were useless, and, well, you never knew when you could have an unfortunate accident. He'd thought of using newspapers for kindling—heaps of them, in the center of the kitchen floor or in one of the ovens or something, but if after he put the fire out there were bits of paper left unburned, there would be some explaining to do. So he decided to use only kitchen flammables.

The five-gallon drum of cooking oil was half empty, but there was enough left in there to do the trick. He dragged it to the middle of the floor and kicked it over, watching it pool and slowly flow away from him, toward the wall. Should have known the damn floor was uneven.

A single match lit the burner on the second stove, and then he backed away, leaning against the door that led to his grandmother's rooms, ready to spring into action the moment the fire took hold. He figured he could have *Apo* up and out of there in under a minute and then run back in and use the fire extinguishers, making sure he messed up the kitchen in the process. By that time there would be enough damage done that Grandmama would have no choice but to let him do it over: new stoves, new equipment—all nice and modern. And once she'd given in to that, once he proved to her that he could handle that job, the other rooms would just be a step away.

The force of the blast surprised him. The cloud of gas he had liberated came into contact with the lit burner, belching forth in an orange ball that blew across the room at him, making him bring his hands up instinctively to shield his eyes. The open gas stream burned like a torch as the length of rubber hose snaked onto the floor, leaping like a living thing, setting the puddles of oil alight. Liquid flame oozed toward the wall, and that ugly, ugly wallpaper caught fire. Vincent watched, pleased, as the fire spread across the tops of both stoves. The gummy coating of grease caught surprisingly quickly. He wondered how the cooks managed to work with those stoves alight every day without burning the whole damn place down. He turned his back on the flames and banged on his grandmother's door.

Only the scratchy old record shrilled and shrieked in response. He banged harder, yelling, first in English and then in Cantonese, that she had to get up, and get up now. The stuck record started its tedious sequence, once, and then again.

Vincent looked back at the fire. The wallpaper had been

eaten clean through, and now the wooden wall behind it had begun to singe. The fire-snake on the ground still writhed. *"Apo! Apo!"* He banged on the door with both fists. The door rattled under his blows. He tried the handle, knowing that it was locked. "Grandmama!"

He could feel the heat on the back of his neck, more intense than he had expected. Maybe he could put it out now. But although the stoves were alight, they were far from damaged, and the refrigerator still hummed noisily, unaffected. Putting it out now would defeat the purpose.

It took only two or three swift kicks to send the door caving in, and he was through it. Running to the back, to the place where his *Apo* slept. Tripping over the stupid peacock. He cursed it and shoved it out of the way with his foot. It rose with a flutter of wings, screeching at him, and then scrambled out the entrance. Grandmama's bedroom door was shut but not locked. She was curled up like a small bundle of laundry, heaped in the center of the bed. He touched her lightly, then more urgently. "Up! Up!"

Her tiny eyes were barely visible in the dark room. "What?"

"Fire!"

She blinked, not comprehending.

Without waiting to explain, he scooped her up in his arms and ran with her to the door. The flames were in control now. Too fast. They weren't supposed to move so fast. The fridge and freezer were ablaze, too, and bright blue sparks shot from their wiring. His grandmother wriggled from his arms, fully awake, and taking in the horror. Arms waving agitatedly over her head, she bolted back into her quarters. Vincent raced after her.

"What you doing?"

She ran to the little altar that stood atop her wooden cabinet, and began gathering up the photographs of her husband and her dead children, shoving them into the pockets of her nightgown and clutching to her breast those that couldn't fit.

Vincent yanked her away. "No time for that, *Apo*. I promise you, the fire won't reach inside. Just go. Just leave, run out to the front. Let me handle this, okay?"

She struggled against his grip, reaching for one more photo, but he was stronger than she, and he lifted her into his arms again and ran to the door. The heat stopped him. Thick clouds of black smoke billowed in, blinding them both and making the old lady cough. The fire was moving inward from the stoves to the middle of the room, and farther still. The skin of his face tingled. How did it get so hot so fast?

His grandmother was screaming, panic making her stronger, beating against his chest as her photos fell to the ground and smashed. The only way out was through the door, the heat. Pinning her arms down, he half lifted, half dragged her frail but struggling form through the smashed doorway, feeling the heat of the blaze against his face and arms and the smoke tearing at his lungs. Then they were past the kitchen into the cool, clean air of the bar. He took her to the front door and all but shoved her outside. She was screaming frantically and incoherently at him.

"I'll handle it!" he shouted, but there was more fear than confidence in his voice. He shut the door against her and ran back inside. Time for the extinguishers.

The kitchen was alive with flames. Bright red, orange, and yellow claws reached for him. He protected his face with his arm and stepped in. He knew the closest extinguisher was to the right, but in the thickness of the smoke he couldn't see it. He inched against the wall, feeling his way, willing himself not to run as the beast snarled. The wall was hot under his fingers. Then the extinguisher was there, a hard metal cylinder. He snatched it up, pain tearing from his throat in a howl as the metal seared his hand, but he had it, and it was open and spewing a thick, white stream at the blaze.

The red, bounding beast laughed in his face. Licked at him, taunted him: *Catch me if you can.* His palms stuck to the heated metal, but he kept his finger on the trigger, spraying the room, trying to cut a path through to the second extinguisher. The fire was growing so quickly. This was wrong. The path closed in as if it had never been there, sealing off the way back to the door. He felt the rubber of his sneakers soften. The white gush from between his fingers sputtered and died, and he threw the useless canister away.

Flames in front, behind, and on all sides. Heat. He coughed, lurching around blindly, trying to make out the shape of the doorway in the darkness. How could a fire be dark? The flames reached for the doorway to the bar, greedy for fresh air, turning the hanging beads into teardrops of molten plastic. He walked in their wake, leaping through into cooler space. He could smell his own hair singeing. The beast swept past him, grabbing, tearing, smelling alcohol and longing for a taste. Reaching up and over the counter, grasping at the rows of bottles, not discriminating on brand or type. The counter was a sheet of fire.

Back against the main door, Vincent watched, too fascinated by the spectacle to be concerned for himself. One by one, and then in a chorus, bottles of rum and scotch exploded, spilling their liquid hearts. Blue shining waterfalls. Chinese fireworks. He could hear his grandmother screaming on the other side of the door.

Still feeling no emotion, he watched as the fire danced to music that only it could hear, swaying to the reggae and dub that was as embedded in the walls as the smell of the thousands of men who had drunk and laughed and played there. It pulsed to the throbbing soca beat, rhythms of calypso accompanying it on its way to the stairs. It burst in unannounced on the gambling room at the back, like a police raid, searching wooden tables and chairs for contraband.

Darkness and light, both at the same time. His dream ablaze. The Dragon spitting flame from its nostrils: no longer smiling; enraged now; storming and slashing at him with its tail; scales glittering every imaginable color: shooting sparks from its eyes. Heat making his skin bubble.

He staggered outside, into the gathering crowd. People gaping, excited, pointing. And Grandmama, his *apo*, tears flooding down her cheeks, clawing at him, shrieking in her mother tongue, crying for her peacock.

Odile and Rory

The soft flames of candles flickered on the cathedral walls, brass candlesticks and censers glowing in the soft light. The choir singing in angels' voices. The cathedral was crowded beyond capacity: people stood in the aisles when the pews could seat no more, joining in song with the angels in the balcony. In the spirit of the night, people shared hymnals, making space for others, whereas in circumstances other than this they would be shoving and complaining, marking off their territory.

Odile felt Rory pressed against her, one arm protectively around her. He could barely get his arm up, as he sheepishly explained that he had shrugged on his only suit jacket to discover that it was now too tight for him. He squirmed but wouldn't let her go.

As he focused on the hymnal, singing surprisingly well, notes rumbling up and out of his deep chest, she watched him. The planes of his face. The thick black lashes that curled down as he read the lyrics. So settled. So content. His calm gave her a thrill. There was no word she had ever come across in any book she had ever read that would describe the feeling it gave her to know that this new wholeness and tranquility in him had come about because of her. He had settled into her without question, like a big dog coming in out of the rain and unerringly finding that dry, warm spot it knew was its own.

Although she knew she didn't—would never—deserve such pure and simple adoration, it delighted her. It made her feel proud, of her womanhood and of that small spark he had seen in her, even as a boy, and long before she herself even knew it existed.

He brushed her temple with his mouth, unabashed. Kissing her in church. He was singing softly in her ear, singing those worship songs to *her*, not to the heavens. How he managed to sing and smile at the same time was beyond her.

She wished her mother were here. And Jacob. This new warmth that infused her deserved to be shared, to spread outward and bind her to her family. But they were both still at the hospital, sitting with their boy. Myra bolstered by hopes for Sebastian's recovery and by her man's strength.

The strength that a man could give. How she had held it so much in contempt! How she'd laughed at her mother, thought her weak for allowing herself to be saved. She was wrong. Each had saved the other. There was no shame in that. Just as there was no shame in letting the strong man at her side hold her up when she needed it, luring her out—talking her out—of the torpor she'd let herself be mired in. Using reason where she had felt only guilt and diffidence.

She pressed her lips against his jaw, returning the kiss, lifting one hand to his cheek to bring him closer. Closing her eyes and willing everyone else to disappear, that they would be alone in the huge cathedral, with only the soul-infusing organ music and the orange candle glow. The peals of clarion bells made them both start, and they stared into each other's eyes, surprised, and awakened from their shared reverie. As the bells in the tower overhead rang out the joyous midnight hour, families hugged and kissed. Whispered happy greetings rippled through the crowded hall.

Rory showed all his teeth. "Merry Christmas."

She was too overwhelmed to answer with words, but he understood her response all the same. He took her hand, turned it over, and kissed the back of it.

The doors at the back were thrown open and the procession began: archbishop, bishops, priests, altar boys, all in ceremonial vestments. Candles held aloft. Huge brass censers twirling overhead, infusing the air with sweet scent. Gray fingers of smoke curling up to the ceiling, carrying messages to heaven.

Something about the smoke caught Odile's eye: the way it swirled, like cursive writing. Bearing tidings. Of what? She stiffened. Her heart hurt.

Rory, immediately concerned. "What?"

She shook her head. "Nothing." It was stupid. But her heart was tearing at her ribs like a trapped animal. The incense was acrid at the back of her throat, and the heat of the hundreds of bodies around her was unbearable. Something was so, so wrong.

"Tell me," Rory said. He dropped the hymnal and spun her to face him. "Odile, please."

"I . . . have to . . ." she couldn't breathe. It was sweltering in here. The candlelight danced in her eyes. Mocking tongues, threatening rather than soothing. ". . . go," she managed.

Before she could frame another sentence, Rory had her by the hand and was leading her through the crowd, heading for the nearest exit, murmuring polite excuses to the people who shifted to let them pass, until they were out of God's house, into the cool night. As late as it was, the noise and bustle of Independence Square went on unaffected by the sanctity of the spiritual oasis in its midst.

She realized she was running in the direction of South Quay, with Rory keeping pace, not even bothering to ask questions, just being there next to her. The ugly, tight rows of neglected buildings lay so close to the cathedral's doorstep that she was not even out of breath before she neared it. Her eyes were wide, anxious, and fixed on the sky. Its blackness strewn with Christmas lights that outshone the moon: bright oranges and reds, golds, and blues spurting upward. Hot stars shooting. Awesome.

But wrong. Not Christmas lights. Not fireworks. No children clapped and danced and pointed, or were held up in parents' arms for a better look. There were crowds, yes— gaping, looking up, but not celebrating. People converged on the Dragon, running, some horrified, some excited.

"Fire," Odile gasped. She broke from a trot into a full-out run, but Rory was right beside her, matching her step for step. They shoved through the crowd, elbowing the gapers, panting apologies, until they reached the roadway. There they stopped.

The front door of the Dragon was a yawning hole that looked in on darkness. From the upper floors, flames shot out through the shattered panes of windows that had remained blacked out and unopened for decades. The stench of burning wood and alcohol was awful, the heat intolerable.

Miss Ling was screaming above the noise, and Odile ran to her. Vincent, black with smoke, hair singed, was holding her in his arms, rocking her, but was unable to lessen her screams. He looked up and caught Odile's eyes.

He saw shock, and questions. She saw guilt, and then she knew. Vincent had set the fire. Through anger and frustration, or maybe a need to start over. And it hadn't been on impulse. All those brooding silences. The hours he had spent walking around and around the building. *Oh God.*

"For you," he said, softly enough that only she could hear. "You and me."

She shook her head. She didn't want to hear that. "No."

"We'll build it over. A new Dragon."

She wanted to cover her ears. "Not for me, Vincent. Not this."

Miss Ling's ululating cry precluded any answer. Vincent set her away from him, spoke words that she seemed too distraught to hear, and turned to the building again.

Odile caught his arm. "Where you going?"

"My grandmother's peacock . . ." Then he was across the road and running toward the mouth of the inferno.

She was after him, Rory streaking past her, reaching Vincent first.

"No, please, Vincent . . ." she begged. Shreds of his charred shirt tore away as she tried to grab at him.

"She wants it. I have to."

"Vincent, it's dead by now! Don't!"

"It was there. I saw it. It's not too late." He stepped back, but Rory's arm shot out, twisting his body and pinning him against the scorched wall. The belching smoke blinded them all, bringing tears to their eyes. Vincent bucked against Rory's grip like a marlin on a line, cursing, begging to be let go, twisting his neck to bite at his forearm.

"Calm, brother," Rory said, his warrior's hold more of an embrace than a menace. "It's over."

Vincent slumped, panting, head drooping. Odile's belly twisted at the sight of the ugly red blisters on his face, and she was unable to stop herself from reaching out, touching them. Vincent seemed too distraught to feel pain. His blackened lips moved.

She leaned closer, trying to catch the whisper. And then his leg lifted as he arched his back against Rory, foot flat, connecting with her breast, and she was flying backward, hitting the pavement with a thud that rang in her ears, skidding, rolling toward the drain. Before her vision cleared, Rory had let Vincent go and was at her side, gathering her up, hands moving frantically down her body, searching for injuries.

She struggled to her feet. "I'm not . . ." She pushed his questing hands away. "I'm . . ." She stopped. Vincent was gone, disappeared into the black, hungry mouth behind them. Rory struck his forehead. Tricked. His dark eyes were on hers and then he turned to the building.

"No!" she shouted.

He didn't answer. He glanced from her into the heart of the fire . . . and stepped inside. She tore at him, clinging. Smoke in her throat, eyes closing in their own defense. Over the bar, the fire burned bright blue, alcohol turning it into a light show. "Rory, Rory, Rory . . ."

He tore off his jacket and threw it over her, covering her hair, pulling it close around her face, and shoved her to the door. "Out. I mean it. Let me do this."

"No, please." Her tears were not from the smoke alone. "Don't. If you go, I'll die." She clutched at his arm, feeling the muscle like rock under his sleeve. She was as afraid for him as she was for Vincent. In the midst of the smoke, something moved. "Vincent!"

She could hear his voice over the ghastly noise of the greedy fire. He was calling the peacock by name, his voice shrill and panicked, crazy.

Rory pulled free and took a few steps in the direction of the voice, but then the ceiling erupted, sending chunks of wood and metal into their path, making access to the room impossible. They staggered back, turning away from the brilliance. Clawing and grasping for the way out. And above the shattering of windows, Vincent's shout. "She loved it more than me! Better this way."

Rory's hands on her waist, lifting her out of the bar, delivering her to the safety of the waiting crowd, before he dropped to the ground, rolling out the flames that had snared his shirt. Kind people carrying her to the other side. She struggled and kicked, protesting, but stopped when he joined her again, smoke and dust making his face a mask.

He held her, one arm under her back and the other under her knees, striding away from the inferno, deliberately turning her so that the blaze would be shielded from her vision.

But he couldn't shield her ears. With a noise like God enraged, the Dragon collapsed, folding in on itself. Debris scattered over those of the crowd who dared come too close.

Odile couldn't be sure how long she lay curled in his arms, clinging to him. The unrelenting fire, resisting the efforts of the fire engines that screeched onto the scene, tore at the Dragon's neighbors, racing along South Quay, touching everyone. Building after building sucked the flames into its entrails and passed them on to the next in line. The city block was a dense forest of blackened timber and flickering red.

She tilted her head back and looked up into the cloudless night sky. Not a breath of wind. The moon, pale and clear, not shimmering in a veil of mist as it would have been had a shower been on its way. Nature not caring enough to deliver them. Six months of unceasing rain, and everyone, including her, had prayed for a dry, rainless Christmas. And they got it.

At the end of the street, far from the crowds and excitement, safe from the rushing, clanging fire trucks and the pounding feet of men with hoses, the peacock stood, head cocked to one side, bright eyes blinking and curious, watching on.

In the middle of the chaos, Miss Ling's screams went on unabated.

Rory

Rory let her grieve. It was the hardest thing he had ever done, pulling back just enough to allow Odile to feel her grief for Vincent and work her way through the slow and agonizing cycles of shock, pain, guilt, sorrow, and acceptance on her own, without forcing his way in. To save her from her hurt was all he wanted to do, but although his interference might have meant a faster scabbing of the wound, the depths of it would have gone unhealed.

It was torture, watching her as she waded through her anguish over the next few weeks. Instinct made him want to foist his help upon her a thousand times, and a thousand times, logic stayed him. Patience would win out.

Bright sun, cut into squares by the open windows of his living room, made patterns on the floor like Spanish tiles. Odile's bare feet interrupted the pattern as she crossed it, but the light closed in behind her and the shining squares were once again undisturbed. "Work, on a Saturday?" she wanted to know. He was dressed in a long-sleeved shirt and neatly pressed pants. Working clothes.

He shook his head. He held his wrists out to let her do up the buttons on his cuff, although he had learned a long time ago to open and close them with his teeth. Her simple gesture made him feel special—no point in refusing. "I'm going . . ." He hesitated. Her brown eyes were both curious and knowing, so he went on bravely. "I'm going to see my father. I found out where he's staying, and it's time we . . . talked."

There was no contempt in the look she gave him. "You sure this is the right thing?"

He nodded emphatically. "I'm sure." He waited to see if she would try to dissuade him. She didn't.

"You're a better son than I am a daughter." Her voice caught a little.

He buried his mouth in her hair. It needed cutting, but he was the last person to tell her that. He used to like it long. Maybe if nobody reminded her, she'd forget to get it done, and let it grow again. "That's not true. You and your mother will find your way. Soon. You just need to remember where she's coming from. Our parents, they look for us to be something that, sometimes, we can never be. But we look to them for the same thing. Once we realize that, it gets easier. They accept our faults, and we accept theirs, and then we can move on from that common ground."

She resisted his attempt to let her go, but eventually she stepped back, and when she did, she was smiling. "Every day's a new chance to do that, I guess."

"It is. And today's mine." He kissed her on her forehead, let her walk him to the door.

Saul had been staying much closer than he'd expected, still in Arima, on the northern side of town, with a retired prison officer he often used to play cards with. This was the third friend to have taken him in since he left the house: with Saul, welcomes wore thin quite easily. As soon as Rory walked into the unfenced yard, he spotted him under a large mango tree, squatting on one of the prominent roots that were high enough to make a convenient stool.

"Saul." He crossed the yard and stood at the periphery of the spreading tree.

Saul's head shot up so fast he almost hurt himself. His eyes bugged, and Rory could see the confusion in his eyes. Vision or solid flesh? "Rory?" He squinted uncertainly.

Rory couldn't remember the last time his father had called him by his first name. "Me, Pa," he answered. "How you doing?"

Saul shrugged expressively, indicating the shabby yard with a sweep of one hand. "Well, you see . . ."

Rory shoved aside the twinge of guilt. "You drinking?"

Saul laughed at that. "I ain't got the money to buy a drink, boy. When you living in someone's house, you just got to be grateful they offer you a plate of food and a cup of cocoa-tea when the night come. You don't ask for anything more."

"And how you feel, not drinking?"

Another shrug. "What you want me to tell you?"

Rory persisted. "Because you know, if you didn't drink so much, maybe you could . . ." He bit his lip, unsure of the response, but pressed on resolutely. "Maybe you could get a job. Then you could find your own place, and pay your own way. You wouldn't have to depend on anyone else for cocoa."

Saul's voice was tinged with self-pity. "But I'm old, boy. Who want to hire me? To do what?"

Rory shook his head. That excuse wouldn't wash anymore. Not with him. "You're not too old to work. And if you look, you'll find something. You have to. Because this can't last. Your friend isn't going to feed you every day of your life. And I'm not, either. But I'll help you look. You want to go somewhere to ask for a job, I'll take you. You want new clothes and a shave, you'll get it. But you're the one that has to get the job, and you're the one that has to keep it."

Suspicion replaced self-pity. "Why you doing this? What you coming here to help me for?"

Rory was amazed that he was able to give his father a genuine smile. "Because this is . . . a two-way street. You and me. Time for me to give back. Something real this time, not just handouts."

Sobriety had made Saul pensive. He looked down at his sandals, dusty from the yard. "I never . . ." Breath escaped

him. He tried again. "I never give you much to begin with."
He couldn't meet his son's eyes.

"Doesn't matter. It's my turn now." It was so easy for him
to say. "Monday, we try. New clothes, and a haircut. Yes?"

Saul didn't ponder long. "Okay."

"Okay."

Silence fell. They both wondered what to say next. Saul
was the first to talk. "Monday, you ain't got to work?"

"I could take the day off."

"Careful you don't lose the job *you* got."

He hadn't thought of that, but the idea didn't distress him.
"It's nothing. I won't be there much longer anyway." He
clenched his fists and showed them to his father. "I'm going
to use these now. Someone at the gym, my trainer, told me
there's a promoter looking for boxers. Young ones. Good
ones. For travel: Puerto Rico, Cuba, America. I think I can
do it. I think I could be good." He waited for his father to
laugh at him and remind him he was a coward and a pussy.

Saul stared at his big hands, not taking his eyes off them
even when he let them fall again to his sides. Rory could hear
the wind rustling through the leaves of the mango tree overhead. Saul scratched his stubbly chin, contemplatively. "I
think you could be good, too."

Rory didn't want to answer. He was afraid that anything
he said then would dull the elation that soared within him. A
compliment. From his father. He was sure that had never
happened before. Saul had faith in him: that there was something he could do, and do well. That was as good as a bless-
ing. Deep in the dark corner of his soul—a corner that grew
more constricted with every life-affirming step that he took—
his personal demon groaned. As Jacob had promised, starva-
tion had made it too weak to fight. His opponent was
proving weaker in battle than Rory had ever dreamed. He
laughed.

The look of surprise on Saul's face was almost comical. He
bristled a little. "I say something funny?"

Rory forced the grin from his face. "No, no. Nothing funny. I . . ." He was floundering again. "Thank you."

Saul kept his eyes on his feet.

He had to leave. There would be ample time to talk again. He fished into his pocket, pulled out a few battered bills, and offered them to his father. "This is not for drink. Understood?"

Saul took the money and stared at it. There was longing in his eyes, but he swallowed hard and said, "Understood."

"Pa, I can't do this for you. You do this for yourself. If I come for you on Monday and I find you drunk, the deal's off. You hear?"

Saul nodded and folded the money away. "Monday, then."

"Monday," Rory echoed. He waited a few moments more, but Saul had fallen into a brooding silence, with his chin on his knees, so he retreated, picking footholds carefully among the contorted tree roots, until he was out of the yard and onto the pavement that ran alongside it. He waved good-bye, and his father acknowledged the wave with a dip of his chin.

His feet, his head, his whole body felt extra light, like helium balloons buoyed by the heat of the sun. Maybe Saul would be drunk on Monday. Maybe he wouldn't. He would deal with whatever he found.

He hopped a bus to Port of Spain. The Christmas frenzy was long past, and the streets of the city were back to normal. Shopping would be easy and unhurried. He wanted to buy Odile a present, although he couldn't for the life of him imagine what. He hoped a good idea would strike him once he got there.

But first, St. Ann's, back to the yard where he was born and to the man who hadn't fathered his corporeal self, but who had, by word and example, become father to the man he wanted to become. The one who had taught him how to fight the battles of the spirit with dignity and courage. With weapons like that, a man couldn't lose. He ached to tell him that he'd pondered, prayed, looked into his soul, and discovered he was ready to box. He'd found his center of control, he would say, and knew now he was master of the ring, and not the other way around.

Rory smiled in anticipation: Jacob would be pleased.

EVERY BITTER THING SWEET
Roslyn Carrington

ABOUT THIS GUIDE

The suggested questions are intended to enhance your group's reading of Roslyn Carrington's EVERY BITTER THING SWEET. The title of this book is taken from Proverbs 27:7 which states "To the soul that hungers, every bitter thing is sweet." We hope you have seen the common theme in this work and the author's first book A THIRST FOR RAIN. Rory and Odile are characters that have had to deal with many difficulties throughout the story in addition to dealing with a past filled with great tragedy. This story is a testament to the strength of the human spirit.

DISCUSSION TOPICS FOR
EVERY BITTER THING SWEET

1. Proverbs 27:7 says, "To the soul that hungers, every bitter thing is sweet." How significant is the title (and its attendant theme of hunger and yearning for satisfaction) to the lives of each of the main characters? Are their needs and longings eventually filled from within themselves, by others, or through external forces?

2. When viewing Miss Ling's cruelty in the light of her horrific experiences in China, Odile wonders if knowing what makes people the way they are makes it easier to forgive them. Does understanding what Rory has gone through as a boy make it any easier for her to forgive him? Does it make it easier for him to forgive himself?

3. Will Saul be sober on Monday when Rory comes to get him? Was Rory right in trying to help his father the second time

around? Do you agree that a child's responsibility to a parent is as great as a parent's to a child? What does each of the two men need to do in order to have a wholesome father-son relationship? Is it worth the effort?

4. Odile fears that not much separates her from the girls who work in the bar as prostitutes, and that it is only by the grace of God that she has not found herself in such a despairing position. What do you think keeps a young girl from falling into such a trap? Luck? Self-awareness? Or a host of familial, social, and moral influences?

5. Did Vincent really run back into the burning bar to rescue the peacock? Why didn't he save himself when he had the chance? What alternatives to this drastic act of arson could he have explored? Just how far can one identify self with one's personal achievements in life before the lines become dangerously blurred?

6. What makes Zenobia dally with young boys? Is it just her relationship with her husband, or is it something within herself that hungers to be satisfied? For a woman to falsely cry rape is a heinous act, because it infringes on the credibility of true victims. Why does Zenobia do it? She is selfish and spoiled, but do you think she deserves the unhappiness she suffers? Why does such an intelligent woman choose to stay in a marriage that makes her so miserable, when it is obvious that she has the wherewithal to strike out on her own?

7. As Lil' Sebastian grows, will Odile's need to use him to fill the gap left in her life by the death of her own unborn child become greater or less? Will it further threaten her relationship with Myra? How far can a woman allow another woman to mother her child before she becomes uncomfortable or jealous? Does she make more allowances if that other woman is her daughter? How healthy or unhealthy is Odile's fixation on Lil' Sebastian?

8. Has Odile found real love in Rory, or is she merely settling for a relationship that satisfies her needs at that particular

time, much as she did with Vincent? She has already out-grown both Vincent and her job at the bar. Do you think she will one day outgrow Rory, or is this a love that lasts? What does Odile really want from life?

9. Violence pervades Rory's life. He himself has committed an atrocious act of violence that resulted in the death of an un-born child. How easy has it been for you to view him with compassion? Has he been for you someone you were able to root for and wish well? Have his experiences made it any easier for you to understand or sympathize with real-life men who have committed similar acts of violence?

10. *A Thirst For Rain*, the precursor to *Every Bitter Thing Sweet*, ends with a faint glimmer of hope, yet leaves the reader with the gut sensation that things will never change. Does *Every Bitter Thing Sweet* leave you convinced that the lives of the main characters are so entangled that, struggle as they might, they may never be truly happy and free? Or do you believe that their lives have finally taken a turn for the better?